STRANGE MEDICINE

Jim Stein

Legends Walk Series

Strange Tidings
Strange Omens
Strange Medicine

Digital ISBN: 978-1-7335629-2-8
Print ISBN: 978-1-7335629-3-5

First printing, 2019

Jagged Sky Books
P.O. Box #254
Bradford, Pa 16701

Cover art & design by Kris Norris
Edited by Caroline Miller

Acknowledgements

Thank you to all the people who helped make my Legends Walk series a reality.

Claudia, John, and Joncine for Beta reading and catching so many embarrassing mistakes.

Kris Norris for the wonderful cover art on all three books.

Caroline Miller for editing books 2 & 3.

Melanie Billings and The Wild Rose Press for editing and producing book 1.

All those who have jumped in to leave those early reviews so critical to new authors.

My readers, past and future. It's all pointless without someone to enjoy the stories. Hopefully I've given you a few hours away from the stresses of life.

The Native American nations. I hope this work of fiction sparks an interest in the rich heritage, history, and beliefs of the nation's First Peoples. Several non-profit organizations and online resources are dedicated to preserving important cultural, spiritual, and linguistic aspects of the tribes. That is where you will find the true heroes and legends.

Visit 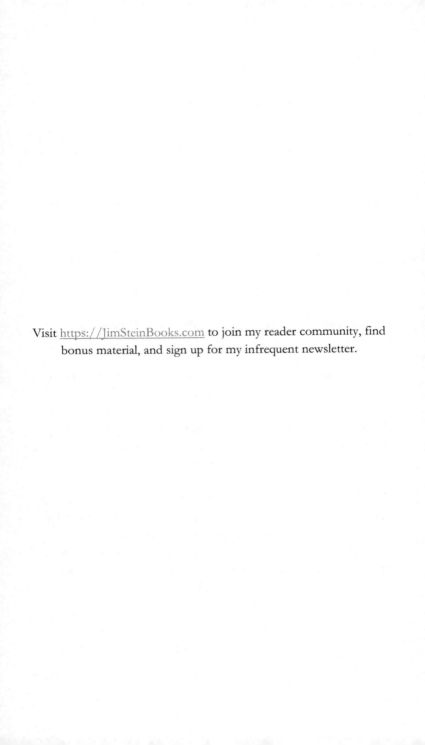https://JimSteinBooks.com to join my reader community, find bonus material, and sign up for my infrequent newsletter.

Prologue

C ORRUPTION AND greed spread across the land. With a heavy heart Sotuknang came to the Spider Woman. "Take those still with songs in their heart to the river and seal them into hollow reeds. You will save them when the waters destroy this world."

- Excerpt from *Legends of the Third World*

(This page intentionally left blank)

1. Boots on Ground

THE HILLSIDE across from the moldering loading dock shifted and shimmered as a living carpet of muddy green flowed down the dune.

"Here they come!" I looked to where my sister and Pete hustled the refugees onto an old school bus.

"Everyone's accounted for." Pete gave me a thumbs up and scowled at the oncoming horde from beneath the mop of straw he called hair. "Ed, we're out of here. Don't get stung. Okay?"

"A little water will turn them around." I waved away his concern, but frowned as I turned back and flipped on my gear.

Powerful bass guitar ripped from the speakers. We didn't necessarily need external music, but it made the job more fun. Keyboard and guitar joined the opening lyrics, bringing back my smile.

Ya wanna race me,

I wanna race you,

Fire 'em up, let 'em roll, there's nothing more to do.

"Now that's music I can work with!" Quinn popped up on the other side of our makeshift enclosure.

Her tilted brown eyes gleamed behind dark curls artistically plastered to high cheekbones. By contrast the heat and sweat turned my wavy black hair into a deranged kraken with wet tentacles attacking my

1

neck and regal nose. Quinn's skin was a fine Asiatic bronze compared to my sunbaked native olive. We made a good team. Cool blue magic curled around her right hand, while her left rested on the valve to the building's fire main.

Of course Quinn could work with one of the A-Chord's biggest hits and her own bass beat. The crossover song focused both Fire and Water elemental spells. I had no affinity for the latter, but water would drive away the horde of green-brown scorpions.

Most of the monstrosities that scurried, slithered, or flew in from the shifting sands were dull brown, dingy green, or black, colors devoid of joy. The dune itself swelled and shifted, propelling the nasties on a wave that devoured the street just behind the departing bus. New Philadelphia was supposed to be a safe haven from the eroding world. Set in the suburbs of its decaying namesake, it had been one since I was a kid. But in recent months our oasis had turned nightmare.

"Let them have it!" I said.

Scorpions didn't like getting wet. Thanks to Quinn's insane mother, she could control water, an ability my half-siblings and I had not inherited from Kokopelli. Unfortunately, we were running the girl ragged, and there were other...things that didn't mind moisture. So far, Earth, Fire, or Spirit elemental magic took care of those not balked by water, but sooner or later something we couldn't handle would make an appearance. Puzzling out where these creatures came from and how to stop them was a full-time job.

Quinn grinned, whipped back her long chestnut hair, and opened the valve. Her power spiraled in my magical Sight, sucking up the gushing water. The stream swirled out, shooting tighter and farther than a simple firehose. The lead bugs shifted and flowed back over themselves to stay out of the stream. But rather than simply soaking the ground in front of them, the water curled up on either side, blocking all directions except a direct retreat.

"Sending them running is just a Band-Aid," Quinn said through gritted teeth. "I wish these little bastards burned."

"You and me both."

My hands itched to let loose with a blast of my own. Not only would the water quench my Fire spell, the damned things were resistant to the strongest element at my command. A concentrated spell would broil the poisonous critters in a second or two, but nowhere near fast enough to deal with the numbers that swarmed out of the desolate sands dividing New Philly. For now, herding them back to wherever they came from was our best solution.

With her spell well underway, I shut down the pumping music and gathered my gear. We needed to haul ass back to headquarters. All too often, people lingered after one of these little encounters and found themselves cut off by shifting sand. At first it seemed only an inconvenience, since few cars had four-wheel drive, but driving wasn't the only problem. Even when the stretch of encroaching desert was whisper thin, we'd lost people—literally lost them. Witnesses would see someone tromping out across the dune, a little blowing sand, and then nothing. Mr. Conti kept records down at the radio station and had coordinated with the far side of town until communications went down.

"Ed?" The uncharacteristic note of panic had me dumping my equipment into the car and sprinting the few yards back to the loading dock. "We've got a new one!"

"Ah crap."

Scorpions roiled over one another to avoid the water, but the mass split apart, leaving ten feet of open sand halfway up the dune. Something swelled beneath the surface. Long brown spikes jutted up, much like the spikey green plants that foreshadowed each wave of desert. But these shifted as they slid toward us. Quinn sent a jet of water straight into its path and the spikes slipped out of sight.

"Water wins again!" she crowed.

Our smiles slipped as the ground erupted in a spray of sand and dirt. Segmented armor shot upward, a dark column supporting a shining brown head topped with the spines of a lionfish. I had no doubt the bone-white tips of each dripped with venom. Black horns or pinchers bracketed either side of a flat head below shiny black eyes. I'd dealt too much with the mythical horned serpent and couldn't say for sure if the ten-foot-tall creature was snake or centipede. Those stubby little protrusions at each seam in the armor could be legs folded flat or simply the joints between scaly plates. A bug might be just as immune to fire as the damned scorpions, but heat would cook a reptile.

"Stop admiring it and do something!"

I snapped my jaw shut, erred on the side of caution, and reached for Earth. Crushing this monstrosity seemed best, and music was the hammer that drove my magic. The heavy beat from Imagine Dragons' "Radioactive" called to the power swirling in my core. Elemental Earth rose on the solemn beat, flowing from my outstretched hands into the shattered hole the creature emerged from. Under the sand, sturdy Pennsylvania rock softened and flowed around the lower section of the snake-insect as it rose high to strike. I clenched my hands, drawing the ring tight and slamming the stone shut to cut the thing in half. But the hide was impossibly strong. A high pitched squeal jabbed ice picks into my ears as the upper half slapped back and forth trying to get free.

"It's a tough one." I dredged up more power, pulling in granite and quartz to keep it from wriggling out of my grasp. Its slick shell repelled the clinging rock. Sharp ridges formed in the thickening tunnel clamped around what now was clearly the chitin of an insect. "Get to the car."

I tied off the spell, anchoring it in bedrock to hold the centipede while I sprinted after Quinn. When the magic was spent or the creature broke free, the residual power would drain safely back into the earth rather than backlash on me. Earth magic in particular took a toll on the caster, and I'd learned the hard way about the pain of an ungrounded spell.

"Go, go, go!" Quinn slammed the passenger door shut as I slipped behind the wheel.

I slapped my ancient Toyota RAV4 into drive, and we shot through the drifts accumulating along the warehouse. Blowing sand darkened the sky and intersection ahead as the frantically whipping centipede shrank in my rearview mirror. Several humps formed behind the trapped creature as more dark heads crested the surface. I concentrated on the bit of blacktop peeking through the wind-driven drifts trying to cut us off.

One last blast had me flipping on the headlights. The tires grabbed, and I floored the accelerator. Just like that we were clear. I took the corner too fast and lost the right mirror on a streetlamp as we bounced off the curb. The swirling maelstrom dropped behind and settled into eerie stillness now that its prey had escaped.

The writhing creature and its companions stood out as dark strands against the sand mounded around the warehouse, a new dune claiming another block. Spiny green fronds already clustered along the rusting rail at the near end of the building.

2. A Great Divide

"FIVE HUNDRED and forty-three." Mr. Conti shook his head. "We're still missing so many."

Quinn and I found the old man hunkered over the massive city map carpeting our conference table at the radio station. Refugee housing was marked in green along the southern border. The freak desert hemmed us in between the river and ruins of Old Philadelphia. One of the bridges was still passable, but little lay on the Jersey side except the opportunity to hunt up an entirely new place to live.

Mr. Conti managed the local news station and had been my boss—I supposed he still was. We came home from the A-Chord's cross-country tour to find the little old Italian dealing with the impossible events transpiring in New Philly. A true believer in magic from the old country, he organized the locals as desert sprang up to cut the city in two—an event that left our small police department and town council floundering on the far side of the divide.

"How many are on the far side?" I asked.

"Sheriff Connolly reported nearly half again what we have here before he disappeared and communications tanked."

Mr. Conti's frown brought out deep lines beneath that perpetual gray stubble. His bulbous nose had been baked dark and his eyebrows white from constant exposure to the sun, another byproduct of whatever magical storm brought the sand. We should have been pushing into winter, but the ever-present sun scorched the town by day, while frigid air swept beneath sparkling stars and crystal-clear skies by night.

"Still no comms?"

"Everything is down." The station manager took the blackout as a personal affront. "All frequencies, phones, even shortwave is out. According to Billy and David, the equipment works perfectly, but something interferes."

"Like it or not, we might have to move after all." Billy ducked to get his six-foot-five frame through the glass security doors and join us in Main Line Studio's lobby-turned-war-room.

In addition to leading the band from his keyboard, Billy was tops with the station gear and telecommunications. If he and David, our shortwave expert, were stumped, no one else was likely to come up with a solution.

A wisp of a man with mousy brown hair neatly trimmed to the demanding specifications of a cereal bowl trailed behind the big black man. David had gone from geeky intern and ham radio hobbyist to communications expert. He and our other intern, Hassan, were as much a part of the team as any of us, except the latter had been lost in a routine rescue just last week. Not dead—we hoped—just gone. *So many gone, but we can't give up.*

"We still have three neighborhoods to pull in," the boss said. "The sand accelerates. I dislike it, but we need to move everyone out by the end of the week."

"There are new monsters to deal with." I hated bringing bad news. "Centipedes the size of an anaconda. A half dozen or so came in with the scorpions down by the old trucking terminal."

"Which is now Sahara central," Quinn added.

The doors swung open again, and the last two band members tromped in. Jinx was thirty with a shaved head and round hipster glasses sitting askew on his narrow nose. Our vocalist and lead guitarist didn't look nearly as stylish as when on tour, especially with his normally neat red beard growing out in all directions, torn jeans, and a rumpled, sweat-stained shirt. Charles, the band's new percussionist, wore a similar outfit, but managed to make it look tailored. His clothes hugged a trim, muscular form and there wasn't a perspiration stain in sight. Beneath a squared-off buzz of black hair, piercing blue eyes raked the room and settled on the big clock over the receptionist's desk.

"We're missing people." Charles addressed Mr. C as he consulted his watch with a precise flick of the wrist.

"The other leads will be here," the boss said, then surprised me. "Edan, I want you to recap our situation after the five o'clock reports. Everyone needs an update on our status and these new creatures you encountered."

"Sure, Mr. C."

Charles gave me an appraising glare that dripped disapproval. The drummer had pushed for us to use the eight am and five pm reporting structure. In the military he'd found them critical for coordination and tasking. I had to admit the meetings kept everyone on the same sheet of music. We kept them short with people standing in a loose circle so all could hear. Charles tended to dominate the gatherings, and his current expression said he wasn't thrilled with me running this one.

Five came and went with people trickling in. I launched the meeting at half past with roll call. We only had two recovery teams, but the meeting space overflowed. Billy represented the band; Meg was our five-foot-four dynamo in charge of operations; and Manny, with his GQ looks and gelled black hair, had elevated himself from being the band's road manager to corporate liaison and general pain in the ass. With Charles trying to run every meeting, Mr. Conti as our overarching supervisor, and all the usual suspects, we packed twenty-plus sweaty bodies into the studio. I called for verbal reports while the stragglers handed Mr. C written notes.

"David still has no communications." Short dark hair slapped Meg's round face as she shook her head. "Food's holding out pretty well, though it's mostly canned. The Easton farm fell to the sands early on and we haven't heard a word from the Amish since the desert cut us off from north New Philly."

Though technically the station's supply clerk, Meg was our backbone of operations. Back before the desert moved in, she'd coordinated more than just advertising, because radio's main job was attempting to stitch together the country's failing infrastructure and logistics.

"Where do we stand on transportation?" I asked. "We'll need people haulers to get this many out on short notice."

"Way ahead of you. Public Works raided the container ships. We pulled a fleet of buses out of storage, replaced all the rotting parts, and are installing oversized fuel tanks. A lot of folks want to use their personal vehicles when we leave. We've got one small fuel truck lined up too, which should keep everyone running for the foreseeable future. I'll have a full list to you in two days."

"Wednesday works." I nodded my approval and turned to Manny, but had to smile at the couple of inches Meg gained as she stood taller, though she still only came up to my shoulder.

"Red Team engagements have picked up." Manny said. "In addition to the evacuations, we're called out daily to handle unwanted guests. Mostly aggressive flora and fauna, but we've had to drive off two-legged things my guys call shamblers."

"People?"

"Unclear." Manny shrugged, a nonchalant gesture that had me grinding my teeth and counting to ten. "Engagements are brief and fierce. My people focus more on staying alive than taking notes."

Red Team was a half-dozen strong with a mixed bag of firepower, a combination of magic and mundane weapons. As Double-M Records' assigned road manager, Manfred Slack had been a thorn in my side—and vice versa—on the A-Chords' concert tour. With his slick black hair, dark eyes, and angular good looks, I'd considered him a thirty-year-old punk with way too much interest in my girlfriend. But Manny'd proven more than capable in a fight and helped us out of a tight spot back in Milwaukee, an act that put him at odds with his superiors. Some faction of the "Company" was tied into the dark forces that plagued me and my friends. I didn't like Manny, wasn't sure why he'd stuck around after the tour, but I trusted the man and his strange abilities.

Trust aside, my temples throbbed at the unwelcome news. "Blue Team?"

"You were there," Quinn said, then seemed to remember her report was for the benefit of the others.

"Market section is clear. We got twenty-seven out by the skin of our teeth before the dune rolled in."

She summarized the operation, including the horde of scorpions and the new creatures we'd dealt with. I shivered at the memory in spite of the broiling office. With a little help from my sister's ever-present library of reference books, we discovered the giant desert centipede has some of the most debilitating and painful bites in the animal kingdom. It was mind-numbing to consider taking venom from the fifteen-foot monster we'd fought. Billy must have seen the sweat popping out on my forehead. He propped the front doors open, and a knife of cool evening air sliced into the room as Quinn finished her account.

"So the sand is definitely accelerating." I read off the reports Mr. Conti handed me as Quinn drew the shrinking boundaries on the map pinned to the wall.

"Three blocks in the last two days." Charles scratched his chin, sounding more reflective than worried.

I nodded into the silence, as several of us realized we might not even have a week.

"Best we can do is be ready. Meg, let's use those private vehicles as a supply train. Distribute food and essentials that don't fit on the buses. Round up some camping gear too and have everything non-perishable ready to go on a few hours' notice." I turned to Manny. "You've got experience with things like these. Will they follow us?"

I suspected Manny was deeper into the supernatural than any of us. He definitely had dealings with the Dark Court through Double-M. I wasn't even certain the man was strictly human. We'd seen all sorts of creatures use illusion or glamour to disguise themselves.

"If I had to guess…" a shadow fell across his handsome face. "I don't think so. They seem protective of the desert area and don't stray from the shifting dunes. If everyone can keep off the sand, we should be safe enough."

Nods from around the room agreed. I was glad to see Manny took the question seriously instead of in his usual flippant way. Though it worried me too. I'd suspected this was another ploy by the dark forces lined up against Kokopelli.

Having the ancient Native American deity as my biological father gave me my regal nose and control of the elements, but it also invited danger. Specifically, Koko's penchant for seeing the human race survive and his efforts to father children like myself who were immune to the ravishes of the C-12 virus did not sit well with the Dark Court. It was a touchy and complex topic, but I'd spent the better part of a year learning to control my inherited magic to fend off evil creatures that had no desire to see mankind "saved."

Even the forces of light weren't fully behind Koko's scheme. None of them had come to our aid when my siblings and I were overrun by nightmare creatures. To top it off, a third faction called the Neutral Council was so wrapped up in their non-interference policy that they'd commanded me not to train the Brights, my half-brothers and half-sisters—Kokopelli's other children—who had come out of the woodwork to enjoy the A-Chords' music. Of course, I'd blown off that commandment.

I kept hoping all parties would realize mankind's survival was a win for everyone. After all, no people to suffer and coerce meant no sustenance for the things that fed on us. Manny himself proved that in spite of Dark Court politics people were capable of thinking for themselves. Yet he insisted these desert creatures weren't sent by the Dark Court, which raised new questions.

"Good advice. Stay off the sand, but don't count on the critters keeping to their side. Blue and Red teams will schedule the last three extractions. Keep everyone else focused on packing essentials for the big road trip. We'll get the vehicle fleet ready and rations stowed. What am I forgetting?"

"Radios," Billy said. "At some point we'll be clear of this freak interference and need to find a landing spot."

"Medicine and first aid kits." Mr. Conti flashed a good-natured grin. "We'll have everything from diabetes to arthritis to manage. In addition to prescription refills, we need antibiotics and supplies to handle injuries. We aren't all youngsters."

11

The C-12 virus left the world with abandoned cities, collapsing infrastructure, and a severe drop in population and birth rates that drove the average age steadily upward. The boss's thought also had me worried about our driving situation, but I trusted Meg to make certain we didn't have anyone behind the wheel who shouldn't be there.

"That's going to mean a raid on Bryn Mawr hospital. Your mom—" Quinn broke off with a little gasp.

My adoptive parents worked on the far side of the sand. Dad's job at the census bureau kept him working late and nursing kept Mom plenty busy. They'd been on the other side of town when the sand cut New Philly in half. I hadn't spoken to my parents since the phones died.

"We've lost enough people trying to cross that drift. Hit the drugstore and clinic for medical supplies on this side of town." The whine of an engine drifted through the open doors. "If anyone comes up with other things we need, let Meg know and we'll build it into the plan."

The obnoxious engine noise drew closer—definitely not a car. The pitch was higher and crazy loud, like the thing had no muffler and was rattling up and down between gears on an engine made of chainsaws.

"Holy crap!" Jinx leaned out the door and waved us over.

We piled outside as a silver and blue all-terrain-vehicle careened toward us. The erratic exhaust note bounced off abandoned buildings along Delaware Avenue as the rider steered his vehicle in a drunken zigzag, skipped up onto the sidewalk, and clipped a streetlamp. We scattered as the ATV skidded to a stop in front of the station.

Thick leathers covered the rider from head to toe, their face hidden beneath a silver helmet matching the filthy quad-runner. The engine cut out, and the rider slumped over the handlebars, fueling a flash of annoyance that someone was drinking and joy riding. Then the torn clothing and silver star on the dented tank registered.

Quinn and I rushed forward, helped get the helmet off, and lowered the man to the sidewalk. The round face had thinned and those soft brown eyes hardened since the last time I'd seen Deputy Cochran. Normally tight-cropped hair hung to his thick eyebrows in greasy strands. The sun had baked his neck a deep red-brown beneath pale features. He licked cracked lips and tried to speak, but only managed a dry croak.

"Water for the deputy!" Quinn shouted.

Meg handed her a bottle so fast it made us both blink. Normally, the man groomed and dressed with military precision that would impress even Charles. It was difficult to recognize him under the scruffy beard and grime, but this was definitely Deputy Vance Cochran. I wiped my hands. Sandy grit came away with the dirt and darker stains

"He's hurt, help me get his gear off."

"I'm okay." Vance gurgled as he gulped down water and tried to push us away.

Meg appeared with a fresh bottle and a first aid kit, making me seriously wonder if she had some sixth sense. I stepped back and let the women work. Even through the heavy gear he'd picked up abrasions, slices, and a few missing chunks that looked suspiciously like bites. A solid ten years older than me, Vance was one of the Sheriff's sharper officers. Though small, the entire police force had been cut off on the far side of town.

"You crossed the sand!"

"Yeah." He poured the last bit of water over his face and started on a third bottle.

"But…" The dented ATV, his torn clothes—it made sense. Except the man looked like he'd just finished a cross country race rather than crossing a mile of dunes. "How long were you out there?"

"Not sure." Finally sated, Vance let the half empty bottle rest on his chest as Quinn bandaged a nasty gash on his right calf. "Left Sunday."

"A whole day out there." Billy sat on the sidewalk next to Vance, which was a nicer gesture than towering over him.

"Seemed longer." Vance screwed up his face and took another sip. "Left on the 4th."

That was a week ago.

3. Teaming up

"WE HAVE to warn them!" Vance levered himself up to a sitting position on my leather couch.

In addition to suffering from exposure, the man hadn't slept in days. Once we peeled him out of his riding gear and got his wounds bound, he fell into a near coma on the drive back to my house. I still had a bunch of Mom's supplies handy and plenty of space.

A night of sleep, more water, and food did wonders to restore his energy. Piper and I stayed with him while Quinn headed in to cover the morning reports. My sister took a seat by the fireplace. Her long red hair framed green eyes that bored into Vance with fanatic intensity. Piper had been obsessed with the occult since birth. Current events stoked her passion higher. Even though she had no magical abilities, her research continued to prove valuable in dealing with supernatural forces.

Piper scribbled in her ever-present notebook as Vance recounted his impossibly long journey across town. Despite hauling spare fuel, he was on his last tank by the time he careened down Delaware Avenue to escape the drifting sand. Sun streamed through the blinds, chasing the lingering chill from the family room as he finished. It was going to be another scorcher out there, but I was more worried about what our guest was saying about the people stuck on the north side of town.

"They can't think this is a natural phenomenon." I'd been jaded by supernatural overload, but no one could believe the creatures coming out of the desert were normal critters.

"The sheriff was good at keeping everyone calm." Vance sat up with a wince and rubbed his right thigh above the bandages. At six-foot, he was just a tad shorter than me and we were about the same build. I'd lent him a pair of shorts and my old Metallica tee-shirt. "Even when communications went down, he wrote it off as sun flares, which sort of made sense given the unseasonable heat.

"Of course none of us could explain the sand, but Sherriff Connolly warned everyone to keep back, especially as it started to grow. We nuked the hell out of those strange plants and the…insects. I mean tankers full of herbicide and pesticide. It helped for a while. But Ed, have you seen what else is out there!"

He throttled down a note of panic, threw back his glass of water, and fell into silent appraisal of the toast and eggs sitting on the side table. Dealing with the unknown was hard enough. Add in creatures no sane person would believe existed and compact the experience into a few short weeks—it was a miracle we hadn't all gone insane.

Vance was tough, but cracks showed through his sanity. Months ago, he'd come to help when Quinn and I had been trapped in a mudslide orchestrated by the dark forces. He'd sifted through the shattered remnants of our attackers, thinking it to be unearthed garden statuary. The deputy was made of sterner—yet more flexible—stuff than the average citizen. I came to a decision, hoping my logic was sound. Time was short, but if this didn't work, it could break instead of help heal him.

"Do you remember the night we got stuck in the mud down by the river?" I continued at his cautious nod. "The footprints and broken stonework?"

"Ed?" Piper's voice quavered, but I held up a hand.

"Even back then?" Vance massaged his temples. "They weren't statues, were they?"

"No." *Did I really want to do this?* "Can I show you something?" In response to his weary nod, I crossed the room and called up the stairs. "Pina, would you come down?"

I'd started off in my colonial two-story alone. The place didn't feel as lonely after my sister moved in and had really shaped up with the addition of Max, the wonderful big black mutt I'd rescued. Max was gone now, too brave and loyal for his own good in a crazy world of magic and monsters. But Quinn still lived with us and so did my best friend from among the magical folk. Pina bounced down the stairs, taking them two at a time and holding the rail to keep it from hitting her head.

The forest sprite stood better than two-and-a-half feet tall, with lustrous blond hair and porcelain skin. Though small, her perfect features and emerald eyes had captivated me, even flaring with anger at my ignorance when I first approached her lord Kokopelli. Now Pina stayed in the blue "bedroom" with the diamond window, a room we humans referred to as the hall closet. But it fit her diminutive size and needs.

I used to think of her as living with us, back before we lost Max. My big, goofy dog loved to sleep over in Pina's tiny bedroom. I'd hear her chatting away with him late into the night. But the nights were quiet now, the house more somber without furry tumbleweeds and drool spatters to contend with. And Pina was gone more than not nowadays, either off to visit Koko or her own people.

"Hi, Edan. Who's our guest?"

Pina radiated exuberance. It was one of her talents, along with illusion and who knew what else. She often projected her calming influence to soothe Koko when he was overtaxed. Vance's eyes flew wide as she entered the room, but her effervescent nature, openness, and possibly a touch of power put the man at ease almost instantly.

"Vance Cochran at your service. Pina, is it?" He smiled despite his ordeal.

"Oh honey, you're all beat up!" Pina took the hand he offered and hopped up on the couch. "Ed, how'd he get hurt?"

"Got lost in the dunes. We're still trying to puzzle out how he spent a week crossing town."

"There're a lot of strange things out there. It's all a blur: giant bugs, walking trees, huge creatures and little…" Vance trailed off and studied Pina.

"You poor baby." The sprite patted his hand, either not noticing or ignoring how the man scrutinized her. "What can we do to help?"

He blinked at Pina for another minute, gave his head a little shake, and looked to Piper and me. "I already feel a hundred percent better. But people need to know what's going on. If others try to cross or those things wander out into the city, there'll be hell to pay. People just aren't prepared. They need to arm themselves."

"We've been organizing and evacuating toward the river, but we're running out of room to maneuver on our side. The sand keeps flowing south, and we're getting ready to leave the city." I saw his back stiffen and raised a hand to forestall any argument about making a stand. "We've got more resources than anyone, but it's a lost cause. You need to understand what we're up against. Piper, bring Ralph up."

We sat in tense silence, while my sister hunted in the basement for our other houseguest. A moment later, she clomped up the steps with Ralph trailing behind and clutching a marshmallow in the talons of his left hand. The quiet room dropped into an icy, brittle stillness.

"You brought one here!" Vance pressed back into the couch as Piper and Ralph stepped farther into the room. "He'll bring the hordes down on us. My god, you don't have the giant ones too, do you?"

The imp's barbed tail lashed as he looked up at Pina. Ralph stood shorter than the sprite. Where Pina was a picture of beauty, Ralph was…less so. His hairless body rippled with oddly placed muscles beneath gray-green skin, and bat ears perched high on his elongated head. Although he could communicate with Pina's people, how much English our imp understood remained a mystery. I was afraid he'd take offense at Vance's attitude, but he simply dusted the marshmallow off against his cutoff jeans and took a bite, which unfortunately drew attention to his formidable fangs.

Vance made a choking sound, seemed about to speak, then clutched at the hand Pina slipped into his. Waves of serenity flowed from the little woman. Vance's frantic breathing slowed, and his face gradually relaxed so there were no longer white rings around his eyes. I gave Pina another minute to work, then explained.

"Ralph is a friend, an imp from the old world. He's here by mistake and we want to get him home. We know what's coming in from the desert, but not why. Our teams are better prepared than anyone to deal with this. We can fight fire with fire, but it isn't worth risking lives over."

As I spoke, I snaked a bit of power into my palm and let a flicker of flame dance to a simple beat. Fire didn't like being summoned with nothing to consume, so I kept the demonstration brief. Chilblains made my fingers itch after the flame winked out. Vance's gaze traveled from my raised hand, to Ralph, and then to Pina. Dots connected behind his eyes, and I was certain the sprite's magic was all that kept him from freaking. But he looked none too happy.

"So how do we let HQ know what's going on? The police need to get things moving on the other side."

"That's a problem," I said. "We're hemmed in against the river. Once we cross, we could send someone around the long way through old Wilmington. Public Works would know if the bridge there is passable."

"Might work, but sand's stacking up fast along the riverfront. When he disappeared, the sheriff had a small team down there trying to figure out if the dunes looped up behind us. It would help if the damned radios worked."

"I've been thinking about that." Piper unwrapped a candy bar and handed it down to Ralph, which was ridiculous. The little guy was more than capable of opening his own treats. "You should send Anna or one of the other Brights over to the north side. It might not be perfect, but firespeak would give us a way to coordinate."

Anna was the first half-sibling I'd met on the road. Her sunny five-foot-three frame hid a mountain of magical potential. In one particularly harrowing situation, she'd flown into a rage and unleashed a devastating Spirit spell that had saved our butts. Since then I'd been working to refine her control, but we couldn't come close to the level of power she'd released by accident.

At sixteen, Anna was among the youngest of Kokopelli's children. We called ourselves Brights in honor of the group's carefree attitudes and outrageously colorful outfits—characteristics that fit Anna perfectly. But as the first of Kokopelli's kids, I tended to fall outside their norm. For me the name was simply a reminder we were the good guys. Anna and a few others had followed the band's tour all the way back to New Philadelphia. She'd kept in touch with her family back in California, more of a wandering free spirit than a runaway.

We'd experimented with a number of new spells among the Brights that were left.. Having Kokopelli as a father gave most a bit of magic and we'd figured out how to use what power each had to best effect. For the Fire element that meant making a lot of smoke for those who couldn't summon flame and sending terse communications across the ethereal plane the element traveled, firespeak. The technique was by no means perfected. We'd only managed a few yes and no exchanges, plus we didn't have any Brights across town. I said as much to Piper.

"What if you use candle halves that were once joined, or wood from the same log—that sort of thing. Fuel from a common source should focus the flames and connect them better."

"Interesting. Fire certainly has a mind of its own. Common fuel just might focus things enough to get whole messages through."

Lack of magic didn't hamper my sister. Her lifetime of occult study and recent delving into true magic let her puzzle out problems with astounding clarity. Piper saw connections I couldn't—either because I was too close to the problem or my limited instruction from Koko and Pina predisposed me to think of spells a certain way.

Sometime during our discussion Ralph jumped up onto the couch. I blinked at our odd audience. The three shared a bowl of cereal Piper had added to the array of food for our guest—dry cereal because my sister had something against milk. Pina picked out the little sweet bits for the imp. In the end, we worked out something that just might work. Vance and I headed downtown to round up the Brights for a practice session—just like old times.

"I didn't want to get Ralph's hopes up back at the house," I said as we pulled out of the drive. "But tell me about the imps you saw in the desert."

"Ed, you know this is Mondo weird right?" Vance didn't quite blanch, but it was clear he no longer had Pina's calming influence. "Magic and monsters from another dimension?"

"Ralph isn't a monster." My voice came out sharper than I meant, and I sucked in a deep breath before continuing. "I didn't know what he was at first, but after a while…well, he's just one of the gang now, a person. He's separated from his own kind. If there are people like him out on the sand, maybe it's a way to get him home. Tell me what they were like."

"Wild and naked is what they were like!" He paused then rushed on at my scowl. "Seriously, Ed. Your…friend back there may be all civilized, but if what I saw were his people, they acted more like a rabid pack than a social group. They carried stone knives and swarmed the things shambling around in there on at least two occasions. Never attacked me, but I was booking along and didn't wait to see what they were up to."

"Are you sure they were imps?"

"Hey, all I can tell you is they looked like carbon copies of your little gray man there, devil tail and all."

I turned down Garnet Street, and we cruised past empty houses. Manny and Quinn hadn't needed to evacuate the area. This neighborhood was deserted and under township maintenance, awaiting the day people might want to occupy the luxury homes—a day that would never come. As we drew closer to downtown and the studio, the homes shrank in size, if not extravagance.

"Watch out!"

I had been about to turn onto Delaware, but a wall of sand forced me to swerve right even as Vance called out his warning—as if I could miss that! But it wasn't the ill-placed dune he'd been worried about. A half dozen brown tumbleweeds thundered down the sandy slope.

"Hang on!" I swung left in the loose sand flowing across the street, intending to gun down a side street, but the damned things actually turned to intercept us like a pack of self-guided bowling balls. They came on the cresting wave of sand as it smashed into a bank, cutting us off.

I jerked the wheel and slammed my poor car into reverse, turning into the skid, slewing away from the creatures, and steering by frantic glances over my shoulder. And they *were* creatures. Through the patchwork of curled branches, boney claws raked at the loose surface to direct each ball's motion. Yellow teeth flashed inside the lacy exterior where a solid entity of some sort managed to glare at us despite rolling at break-neck speed.

Five of the balls tracked low around the turn created by the sand piled against the building. The last took the turn too high, slid off the dune, and slammed into the brickwork with a sickening thud. Bricks and broken bits of what looked like bleeding sticks rained down and lay still.

"There!" Vance pointed at the open alley ahead on our left.

We looped behind a stone building that had once been a quaint church. The sand stretched and flowed in pursuit, impossibly fast. I spun us around and shot out of the far side of the parking lot. The damned tumbles had taken the short route around the building. The closest creature swelled in the rearview, and the rear fender sank under a heavy blow.

The double yellow line shone clear beneath thinning sand as another tag on my bumper had the rear wheels skidding left and right. Woody mandibles gaped wide in the rearview, a two by five inch horror show as the tumble dropped back then put on a burst of speed. I braced for the impact.

It never came. I glanced in the mirror. A spill of sand marking the edge of the dune dropped behind. Three creatures still pursued us coming on full speed, but each winked out as it hit the line where sand gave way to blacktop.

"Where'd they go?" Vance asked.

"Not sure." I shook my head and stopped at an angle so we could see the street behind us. "I get that they can't leave the sand, but those things had momentum. They must have gone…somewhere."

The church and houses were gone too, replaced by a sandy mound that buried the drives to either side of the road in foot-deep drifts as it stretched toward us. Wind swirled gritty clouds across the dune, but even these dust devils disappeared at the blacktop.

"I guess anywhere but here is good." Vance shrugged. "But I see what you mean about the sand accelerating."

We scanned our surroundings. Nothing stirred so I let out the breath straining against my ribs and drove on to the studio.

Accelerating was one thing, but the desert had pursued us with deliberate intelligence.

4. Firespeak

A NNA'S PALMS turned clammy, and she couldn't catch her breath as she swept a stray lock of blond from her eyes. Too many people packed the small room. Ed and Mr. Conti stood at the map marked with ever shrinking safe zones, listening to the team leads finish their reports.

"This leaves us little time," Mr. Conti told the group crowded into the radio station. "Quinn, Blue Team's sector is clear, yes?"

"Everyone's settled into the shelters by the bridge." Quinn nodded and gave Anna a wink.

Anna liked the woman, especially the way she made Ed think things through. He didn't need the help as much anymore, but on the road there'd definitely been a repeating dynamic between the two. Anna shivered. Gaps riddled her memory, but what she retained sent chills up her spine. The worst was supposed to be behind them; coming back to New Philadelphia was supposed to mark a new beginning.

The people scattered around the room each handled something important. Ed's request for her to attend the meeting came as a surprise. She stood back against the wall as the senior Bright manned the maps and added his perspectives to the report from Deputy

23

Cochran. More strange creatures were bad news, but the thought of an intelligence behind the desert made her sick. She clasped her hands to keep them from shaking.

"Manny?" Mr. Conti turned to the band's handsome manager.

"One neighborhood left for Red Team to clear. This new wave of sand makes it difficult. The major roads have been cut, isolating about thirty people. We'll have to go in on foot to get them out and hope the sand holds back long enough. If all goes well, we'll have everyone safe by noon."

Safe? Anna suppressed a bitter laugh. None of this felt safe. If it was safe, they wouldn't be about to flee across to New Jersey. Her hands just wouldn't stop shaking, and she hugged herself tight. She wouldn't trade her experiences with the A-Chords for anything, but this wasn't the carefree life she'd left California to find.

The Brights were wonderful and Ed's training so very helpful, but she wanted to go back to just being happy. And with the phones out, her parents back in Bakersfield would be worried to death. What good was this rogue magic power if she couldn't even let them know she was okay?

An arm snaked around her shoulders, and Anna leaned into Piper's half-hug. She'd spent plenty of time with Ed's sister. The confident redhead always maintained control and acted so grown up. Piper knew gobs more about magic than anyone else and probably knew why Ed had invited her to the evacuation planning session. After the meeting would be a good time to pick Piper's brain.

"Mr. C, we should get the buses loaded and ready to move as soon as Manny's team returns." Ed's shoulders sagged. "Things are too unpredictable. If we caravan down to Wilmington, we can find temporary shelter, make a long-term plan, and get a team back across to check for survivors on the north side of town.

"We've worked out a way to communicate when the radios are down. Even if the main group needs to move on, we can stay in touch and bring the rest to the permanent location."

"Make that happen." Mr. Conti pointed at Meg who bobbed her head. "Plan on setting out at 2 p.m. Crossing the old bridge will not take long, but finding a stopping place and ironing out sleeping and cooking arrangements could be challenging. Make sure everyone knows the schedule."

The meeting droned on. They talked about getting the rest of New Philadelphia's people out before heading for New York or south to Baltimore. If radios and phones worked on the far side of the river, Mr. Conti's contacts would help them find a new home.

The thought of home brought a pang of longing for her soft bed and the scent of almond blossoms drifting through the curtains on dry air. But the Brights were her family on the road. She'd grown close to Ed and Piper during her recovery from the strange ailment Pina had helped her shake. Then there was cute little Ralph and the ever-present warm weight of Max laying across her lap, keeping her calm when the world spun out of control.

Her breath caught, and she swallowed an ache thinking of Ed's beautiful doggie. So many nights he'd calmed her. But Max was gone, leaving a hole in her heart like when she'd left her parents' farm to follow the music. That the music had power—she had power—had come as a shock. Her illness made much of the time in Milwaukee fuzzy, but the Spirit element rising to do her bidding had felt glorious and empowering, even if she'd collapsed from the effort. She hadn't been able to recreate that spell, but Ed worked with her as time allowed, helping focus her talent with the Spirit and Fire elements.

"What's Ed want me to do in Wilmington?" Anna asked Piper after the meeting broke up.

"Fill in as a radio." Piper's lopsided grin made her green eyes sparkle. At five eleven, the woman was better than half a foot taller and towered over Anna as they hunted through the supplies spilling from the back of the big black SUV. Ed's sister could be intimidating, especially when at odds with her brother, but she'd always been kind to Anna. "Ah, here they are!"

Piper pulled a box from the jumble, flipped open the lid, and withdrew a fat candle made of dark yellow wax. The cylinder was scored in the middle. Piper snapped it in two and handed her half. A wide wooden wick sat amid the wood shavings molded into the wax, and the scent of lavender made her smile.

"Candles?"

"Yep, to help with the communication spell you all have been working on." Piper waved at the box of candles. "My theory is that using common fuel when you call Fire will provide a binding to help us get more than just single syllables through. These are made from the same batch of wax with maple wicks and ash chips to aid in communication—again from the same branches. You're one of the strongest Brights. Ed wants you and a few others to test these out so the main group and the ones heading back to New Philly can talk."

"This is all crazy, right?"

"As nutsy as it gets." Piper nodded, but her eyes shone with excitement.

It wasn't her fault. Ed's sister was a self-proclaimed lover of all things occult. The biggest mystery Anna had ever contemplated was why Da's honeybees kept disappearing. It was bad enough that people were dying out, now some evil force came after her friends.

"Why can't they just leave us alone? We're not a threat."

"Good question," Ed said as he crossed from the back door to join them. "The more I see here, the less I think this is the work of the Dark Court. Their prior attacks targeted those of us with the most power. The dark can't stand the thought of Koko's kids repopulating the planet. Heck, even the Neutral Council doesn't want anything to interfere with the 'natural order'—as if the C-12 virus was some god-sent punishment and not manmade birth control gone rampant.

"But this is different. The sand swept in while we were gone. As far as I know there're no other Brights in New Philly. The desert isn't focused on us; it's claiming normal humans minding their own business. Something's definitely changed."

"Maybe they aren't satisfied waiting for us to die out," Piper said.

"All I know is we need to get out of here." Ed looked tired and older. "Much as I hate to abandon our hometown, we just don't have the resources to fight this thing."

He took the other half of the candle from Piper and flowed Fire magic into it. The wood wick crackled to life. Anna took the hint and did the same for her half, using the chorus of the A-Chords' "Live for Tomorrow" to fuel her spell. Fire was still tricky to handle. It wiggled and squirmed, wanting to eat the entire candle. She throttled it down, only letting a trickle through—so much harder than using Spirit.

"Fire is always too eager, but you're managing." Ed's voice held a strange echoing quality, and...

"Your lips didn't move!" Her eyes went wide.

"So you heard that. Good, you try."

"Uh, hello? Testing one, two, three." Anna found it hard to think with Jinx's lyrics running through her head so clung to the instrumental portions, which made it easier to focus on the flame. *"What did you say into a spell like this? She could talk about her problems adjusting in New Philadelphia, how she missed poor Max, or even her desire to..."*

"Okay, a little too much there," Ed thought into her mind. *"That's all coming through loud and clear. Don't let all your thoughts merge with the music, just the ones you want to send out."*

"Oh, sorry." Her face grew warm. What a stupid mistake. Ed must think she was such a child. Her hands flew to her mouth—a totally unreasonable action given they spoke silently. She reviewed her thoughts, looked to Ed, and decided she hadn't broadcasted the last bit.

"Piper, you're a genius," Ed said aloud. "We'll have to practice more, but these work brilliantly!"

5. Dreamspeak

"TOMORROW'S THE DAY." I threw another pebble into my fountain.

My feet dangled above the clear water. Ralph sat to my left clutching Mr. Rabbit and mimed a throw. The dog toy had been Max's favorite, and showed up when our imp grew melancholy. I blinked when a small splash sent ripples out to intersect the ones from my rock. Very little surprised me lately, especially when it came to the imp or my other guests.

"Yep, sad times." Pete sat on the far side of the gushing guitar sculpture. "Wish I could see the farm once more."

My stocky friend had the square jaw, stormy eyes, and straw-colored hair characteristic of his family. Generations of Eastons had grown up on the farm outside of town. Unfortunately, the sand hit hardest out on his homestead. I'd spent a fair amount of time there before the tour, helping level boulders and later dealing with a weird insect infestation.

On the way home from the band's tour we'd heard about the unidentified spikey weeds overtaking their soybean field. But after we lost radio contact, sand had bubbled up and swept the fields under in a matter of days.

"We'll find our folks on the north side." *I hope.*

No reason my parents shouldn't be there, Dad still slaving away at the Census Bureau and Mom at the hospital. Both organizations would be desperate to figure out what was going on. I was less confident about Pete's family. Not just his Mom and Dad, but his sister Melissa and a boatload of cousins worked the farm and had been cut off by the swift encroachment of desert. Pete had been house sitting for me when the desert cut New Philly in half. But the rest of the Eastons were at ground zero.

"Hope so." He ripped a handful of green spikes from the fountain's stone wall and hurled them into the lawn. After I left on our road trip, he managed to keep ahead of the pervasive weeds—the same weeds that had overrun the Easton farm and cropped up just ahead of the drifting sands all over town.

"Wonder why don't we get sand here? It's sort of where it all started."

Pete had helped fix my decrepit fountain—a testament to the upper middle class who built the place. He got the plumbing working, and I'd used it as a training ground for practicing magic—everything from sweeping out the debris with Spirit to reflowing the cracked base with Earth magic. At first I thought the weeds cropping up were evidence of seeds left behind by some long-gone greenhouse, but the tenacious plants kept coming back.

"Your scorched earth policy might have helped." Pete shook his head. "But we tried that out at the farm too. Can you believe we deliberately set more fires? These things barely burn and if they do the smoke chokes like tear-gas. Probably toxic."

"Yeah, took quite a bit of power to wipe 'em out here, and the Fire element usually eats anything. I've seen rocks ignite easier than this stuff!"

I tugged a long fat leaf out from under the slate capping the wall. The pale green spike was thick and heavy like yucca or aloe—definitely a succulent. The high water content would make it naturally fire resistant, but not to the degree I'd seen.

I hurled the plant onto Pete's pile as Ralph tore out the last small shoot on our side. Rather than throw it, he bit the pointy tip off and chewed with his mouth open so we could enjoy watching the plant get pulped into slimy purple gel. With a shrug, Ralph tossed the rest of his leaf on our little pile. The imp would sample almost anything, but always came back to the base of his personal food pyramid, sugar. The purple sap might be sweet, but not imp-sweet.

"If Deputy Vance saw imps out there"—Pete jerked his head in the general direction of our little strip of Sahara—"then Ralph should know what's going on."

"Pina hasn't been able to get anything useful from him. Koko and Pina say he's from the 'Old World,' whatever that means."

"Ralph, what's with the desert, the sand?" Pete mimed what looked like a butterfly getting flattened on hot pavement.

Our imp studied my friend's flying hands, pulled a strip of red licorice from his hidden stash, and chewed on the near-extinct candy. Pete finished and leaned forward as Ralph lowered his licorice and pretended to pick something up from the lip of the fountain. Fangs poked out as the imp's face drew into a ghastly smile. In one smooth motion, he heaved his arm back and flung it forward. Nothing left his hand, but a mighty splash erupted just in front of Pete, drenching him thoroughly. Ralph didn't generally make sounds, but his stuttering hiss sounded suspiciously like laughter.

"Crap, that's cold," Pete managed through a shocked gasp.

Night fell fast along the border of our mock desert. I hustled Pete inside to change before the icy wind sapped away his body heat.

There wasn't much left to do. The cars were already crammed full. Since we weren't taking furniture or appliances, packing for the trip pretty much just came down to clothes, Piper's research, and the few spell components I kept in the basement lab. Of course I had my box of music, both salvaged records and mixes I'd remastered. Meg made room under one of the buses for the equipment needed to set up a temporary station and for my personal gear.

I scoured the house looking for Pina, but the sprite had gone off again. She had to know more than she let on. But I couldn't press her for information about the desert and Ralph if I couldn't find her. We stayed up late double checking our list, closing up the house, and— much to my sister's and Quinn's chagrin—playing video games.

When the house grew quiet, I laid in bed staring at the shadows playing across the ceiling. The thought of leaving my house—my home—kept sleep at bay. We'd sealed the windows and doors as best we could, hoping to keep the sand out as it swallowed our town, but odds were I'd never return.

A half-moon lit the landscape, causing shadows to stretch and surge as branches outside twisted in the wind. The nights were clear and cold, but a solitary cloud floated across the moon, and my ceiling darkened. Music drifted in as my eyes grew heavy. A lonely flute echoed, twisting the gloom into half-suggested figures before smoothing into a gray void.

I fell through the gray to land on solid yet yielding ground. Shadows swirled, indistinct but somehow inviting. The flute grew nearer. I stood and shuffled off to the right. The cold damp sand under my bare feet made me thankful for the breechcloth and leathers I wore.

I walked toward a dim spark in the darkness. The sand grew warm. Unlike prior dreams, the cheery fire with its teepee of ever-lasting logs remained indistinct. A curtain hung over the scene, and it was hard to make out the shadowy forms to either side of the fire ring. The taller figure, a hunched old man dressed in buckskin, lowered the wooden flute he'd been playing. His final notes rolled off into the distance, a coyote yipped, and the fire flared brighter.

"It has been too long, Edan." Kokopelli's voice was muffled, and he sounded grumpy.

"No kidding. In case you haven't noticed, we could use a little help."

The small figure stepped up next to the old spirit. Pina slipped her hand into Koko's, and his scowl eased. Relief and annoyance washed over me as I squinted at the silent pair. Usually, I couldn't get a word in edgewise. Koko liked to use his dream visits to lecture and grill me for information.

Shadows from the fire danced across wooden boots and supple moccasins. The sand under their feet was whiter, purer than the yellow moonlit dune surrounding mine. Once, in a delusional fever, I'd glimpsed Koko's realm and reached through the veil between worlds to enter his adobe halls. I saw those walls behind him now, shimmering and indistinct. I reached out, but couldn't quite touch the barrier separating us.

"This stupid desert is pushing us out of town." I swept my hand to either side, suddenly angry. "How about throwing some of your omnipotent attention our way?"

"I have." The hint of Koko's old smile raised the weathered corners of his mouth. Beady black eyes set above an impressive hook-of-a-nose sparkled momentarily before fatigue again creased the old man's features.

"My lord holds back the desert. It's taking all his power to—"

"Brightness is correct." He cut off whatever more the sprite might say. "I do what I can. The veil between worlds thins. It should not be so. Something reaches out from the other side, pulling at Earth magic, using it to draw together realms that should never meet."

"Earth magic? My magic?" *That can't be right.* "You're the one who showed me how to use the elements!"

"This force was…unforeseen." His eyes went out of focus, making him look old and frail, a thought I sternly set aside. Sometimes it was hard to remember I spoke to a god, and I didn't dare let my guard down. "The source of this disturbance cannot stay hidden forever."

"To hell with forever! My town is about to be swallowed. We've got hundreds of people missing."

"He's trying!" Pina met my frustration with her own. "We'll find whatever dark artifact is at work here. Just don't use any Earth spells in the meantime. Your other magic is fine, especially since you've refined your spells. Do what you need to do to keep your people safe."

"You could have told me sooner." *How long had she been in on this, helping Koko and keeping me in the dark?* Another thought struck me. "You're not coming with us, are you?"

"He needs me here." Pina looked as though she might cry, but simply pointed off to my left. "But I can send help."

A male sprite stepped from the roiling mist. He was short—of course—and had the emerald green eyes of his people beneath a curly mop of dark hair and an infectious grin.

"Dwain?"

"Hey ya, Ed."

Dwain was one of the good guys and a hell of a leader. He'd brought help when we were out of options and stayed to see our last

32

conflict through. A tenacious fighter, he also cared about his troops. I'd seen him triage wounded and get them to safety during the heat of battle. The sprites were more formidable than any of us had expected. I looked out across the sand for other glowing green eyes.

"Just me." Dwain gave me a crooked smile of apology.

"My people gather along our border," Pina said. "The merging realms threaten more than just humans. If it can't be stopped, no place will be safe."

"Safe from what? What is this other realm?"

At a nod from Koko, Pina answered. Interesting how tight they seemed to be again. Pina had been complaining about her lord's erratic behavior all summer. Either Koko had improved or she was trying to help him work through his problems. By the annoyed look on my father's face as he waited for the sprite to explain, I gathered it was the latter.

"It's the world before this one, the third age." Pina spread her hands to encompass our surroundings. "It was a prosperous land, but its people lost respect for the cycles of the sun, moon, and nature. Many grew greedy and cruel, wanting ever more to fill the void in their souls only balance could repair. As corruption spread, the world…died, and people who followed the path of balance were chosen to move on to a new world, the fourth age. The thinning veil means the Old World is no longer sealed away."

"The Old World?" I tasted the words, so similar to how Mr. Conti spoke of old Italy and how Pina herself had spoken once. "You told me Ralph came from the Old World. So this is his homeland coming through?" It made sense given Vance had seen other imps, but the slight hesitation in Pina's story had me wondering. "What do you mean, the Old World *died*?"

"A great flood was sent—"

"Enough!" Koko pushed power into the word, cutting her off. He played a scattering of notes on his flute and the mists retreated, leaving Dwain and me on an island of sand in a sea of vapor. "The problem lies beyond the junction between worlds. You will have to journey there to stop it. Keep away from the sand until then."

"Looks like we're taking a road trip." Dwain gave Pina a sideways glance.

"You both stay safe, while we find the source." Pina's outline wavered.

I looked to Dwain. He gave a shrug and strode off into the mist. The curtain between my island dune and the adobe room grew opaque, fuzzing into gray skies. I found myself alone, the scent of flowers heavy in air turned thick and cloying. An overwhelming urge to act swept over me, but there was nothing to do, nowhere to go.

I awoke stiff and confused. Early morning light flooded through my window. The current crisis had me used to getting up early, but there was something wrong with the red-tinged sunshine.

I scrambled out of bed and threw open the blinds. The fiery yellow ball looked normal as it peeked over the horizon. But the tree line surrounding my neighborhood was gone, replaced by rolling tan hills. I gawked as the desert spilled over the retaining wall separating my neighborhood from the surrounding forests.

"Quinn, Piper, Pete!" I jammed my right leg into my jeans and danced out into the hall on one foot. "Everyone up. We gotta go. Ralph, get Max—" I wasn't thinking clearly. "Get to the cars!"

Piper and I laid on our horns as Pete and Quinn hung out the windows and encouraged the few remaining neighbors with paint-blistering curses. Three cars streamed out ahead of us as a wave of sand and giant insects slid past the empty houses at the back side of the development.

"Fun wake-up." Pete wiped sweat off his forehead as he craned around in the passenger seat to watch my house get swallowed. "There goes the neighborhood, as they say. Hey, what's with him?"

A high-pitched keen like a radio between stations rose from the back. Ralph had climbed into the cargo section, wedged himself on top of our luggage, and plastered his face against the back window.

In my side mirror, my shed floated into the front yard, swept along on the leading wave of sand. Small gray figures scurried over the structure. Two perched on top, riding it like a surfboard. Ralph's wail rose half an octave, and my teeth ached.

"Other imps." My heart went out for the little guy, but there was no way we were going back.

One of the monstrous centipedes slid down the sand over my driveway, spilled into the street, and swerved after us across a dusting of sand. I floored the accelerator as a handful of the imps sprinted after the monster.

"Yeah! Nothing beats good old American horsepower." Pete's grin was strained.

"Not sure where it was built, but I know what you mean. Poor Ralph."

Our imp scrambled around to the side window as I turned, keeping watch as our pursuers dropped behind.

"He'll be fine," Pete said. "Look he's already back to his candy."

Ralph fingered a handful of colorful treats, though he stared out the window and didn't actually eat any.

We weren't the only refugees corralled by the desert tide. A dozen vehicles streamed down Delaware avenue. Pete and I pulled off at Main Line Studios, while the procession continued on to the evacuation site by the old bridge.

"Ed, I knew you'd make it." Mr. Conti looked up from where he helped David load maps and office supplies into boxes. "Meg is double checking, but it looks like everyone's accounted for. Manny's team left early to bring in the last group."

"They better not beat up my ATVs." An older man in grimy blue coveralls popped up from behind the consoles where he was apparently loading his own box of gear. His gray hair stood out in wispy curls against dark skin, but I honestly couldn't tell if he was black or Latino. "I've only got a couple spares and blazing few parts. That damned cop destroyed a fine machine."

Vance picked that moment to stroll through the front doors, but didn't seem offended. "Reggie, if you weren't bitching I'd be worried. Tell me she'll run a few more miles though."

"Yeah." The man grinned, caught himself, and spit. I winced, but the boss didn't seem to mind. "A few more, but the differential and clutch are almost shot. Stop shifting so hard."

"Meg said you might need a hand with labeling." Vance hurried to help the man hoist his box to the table. "Ed, this is Reggie Boyd, mechanic extraordinaire. Retired from the precinct what, three years ago?"

"Five, rookie. You were barely through training. Good to be working again, but our lack of gear is no joke. Trailer's almost bare—a few wheels, chains, and a scattering of maintenance items. They took four machines out this morning. No telling what shape they'll return in—had to give the team a crash course. Not a damned one of them ever owned a manual transmission. What's the world comin' to? I plan to raid the first city we pass, but the kind of parts we need don't age well."

"Sure glad you had enough for this job." I nodded a greeting, turned back to Mr. Conti, and told him how my street had just been overrun.

"Red Team will be in trouble if they aren't back soon." Mr. Conti glared at the one map he had yet to pack. "They're in real danger of being cut off. With our scouts pulled in, all we can do is keep the convoy on hot standby and our fingers crossed."

6. Moving Day

"LAY DOWN cover fire for those kids!" Manny squinted into the driving sand and cursed himself for a fool.

He should have sensed trouble sooner. His time with the humans made him soft. They'd roared down the narrow strip of ground, weaving between houses. Avoiding the sand had been simplicity itself—on the way in. Now, they had a dozen people to corral, and the ground grew loose with sand welling up right beneath them. The lumbering tick rose with the desert to block the path. A pair of four-wheelers roared around it taking pot shots, but the giant bug just soaked up their bullets.

They didn't dare go around. If they strayed into the deeper sands on either side they'd end up lost and wandering—easily picked off by the other creatures trying to flank his team. Though misshapen and fast, the fat-bodied beetles coming at them from the left responded well to conventional weapons. Another striped abdomen exploded in a spray of ichor as the woman wielding an ancient lever-action rifle let loose. Shotgun blasts from Rick, a tall lean black man on the last ATV, were just as effective, but they needed a way out.

His charges weren't infirm, but one old couple could only manage a fast amble. The man gripped his walking stick like a club and wasn't above taking a swing at anything that got too close. Then there were the kids, two honest to goodness toddlers. They reminded Manny of sprites or dwarves, small but nowhere near as formidable.

The girl was a tiny blond thing with a heart-shaped face that oozed feigned innocence—a quality Manny easily picked out. The dark-haired boy didn't bother to hide his demonic nature. The glint in his wide-set brown eyes spoke of a world of mischief. Yet both children heeded their parents and kept close to the middle-aged couple huddling at the center of the rapidly vanishing strip of clear ground.

Rick's shotgun ended the charge of striped beetle-spiders and gave him time to think. These people were counting on Manny's team to get them out. Handguns and rifles did nothing but enrage the tick, which stomped in a circle, scattering sand and a fine spray—

The rifle-wielding woman screamed and fell backward off her ATV. Smoke billowed off the vehicle as it careened into deeper sand. The woman clawed at her heavy jacket, tearing away the smoking garment. Blisters rose on her hands and along her left arm where the tick's acid ate through the riding gear.

Out to his right, the whine of her abandoned vehicle abruptly cut off as a giant black form rose high and slapped down on the ATV. Plastic crunched and metal screeched as the giant centipede slammed down twice more on the hapless vehicle, then turned toward their group.

"Time's up!" Manny yelled. "Be ready to move. Rick, get Deloris up behind you. She needs medical attention ASAP. Take point when the path is clear."

The knife in his hand would do little against the creature. Splintered wood planks showed from beneath the brown carapace, remnants of a shed the monster had toppled as it rose to block their path. Its stomping pounded the tiny building into kindling. *Perfect.*

Manny slipped in close, willing himself to go unnoticed. Stealth was a gift inherited through his mother's side. The eyes of his party slipped away, as did those of the creature. Though it resembled a half-bloated tick—and he didn't like thinking about what kind of host such a massive thing would latch onto—its face lacked the single proboscis. Eyes set wide and back nearly on its shell framed a pair of furry fangs with shining black tips, more like what might be found on a wolf spider.

He reached out with the knife and sent power into the broken wood. He didn't have to hum a tune, sing a rock ballad, or whatever other silliness Ed and his contingent of Brights did to coax forth a bit of elemental magic. The one power his father had given him—the only one he could have given his only son—flowed with a single thought, *burn!*

Arid days prepared the wood, but he didn't expect the whoosh of flames that roared from under the monster. Manny fell back from the stench and sizzling. The thing thrashed like a beached whale as its own acid flared and billowed greasy smoke.

"Get back!" If the tick exploded... "Get those kids moving!"

He turned at a crash. The tick whumped off to the side of the burning shed. It raised itself on flaming legs and slammed down again and again—thumping sideways to deeper sand and into the path of the centipede. Sand spouted up to cover its vibrating back as it shimmied and sank into the ground.

They picked their way through the residual flames and hurried on under covering fire from the vehicle bringing up the rear. No more giants rose to block the path, and it was a relief to finally feel his tires bite into open pavement. Their team driver loaded the civilians onto the waiting bus. Wind and sand swirled in stinging circles as if sensing the escape of prey. They wheeled away as the swelling dune crested and an avalanche smashed through the houses they passed. But the bus proved faster than the desert, and they left the questing sand behind.

They pulled up to the station to find Mr. Conti and Meg running through checklists with Ed and...another toddler? The kid didn't quite reach Ed's waist and had curly dark hair sweeping out in wild directions. Unlike the children on the bus with their prim outfits, this one wore what looked like a sack tied at his waist with rope.

"Red Team's back. Deloris needs medical attention." Manfred pushed through the doors.

"What happened?" Mr. Conti turned with the others.

"Acid burns from a giant bug. No time to explain, where's the nurse?"

"Irene is down at the evacuation site," Ed fumbled in a plastic crate under the nearest desk. "We've got a first aid kit."

"Not enough. Burns all down here and here." He ran an open hand from his neck to wrist indicating the extent of damage. "It was a *big* bug."

"She'll be in shock. Let me take a look; it'll be faster." The little boy's voice was an incongruent tenor.

The small figure stepped from behind the desk and understanding dawned—a sprite.

"Over there with Rick, the skinny black guy." He pointed to the nearest ATV. "Deloris got sprayed with mist from a tick the size of a barn. Ate right through her leathers."

"Can you help her, Dwain?" Ed asked.

"Shouldn't be a problem, but let me see how bad."

The sprite scrambled through the glass doors as Rick lowered the woman to the pavement. Manny wasn't entirely certain they had time for this. He swung back to find the others had returned to their discussion, though Meg cast worried glances out at Deloris.

"She's in good hands," Ed assured her. "Manny, get the rest down to the bridge. We move out at two. They can get cleaned up and find their assigned rides. I assume everyone else came through okay?"

Ed pushed papers across the desk to the other two, hardly phased by the burned woman and perfectly content to let the sprite attend her. He stabbed a finger down to highlight some bit of information, drawing his boss's attention to the rightmost column of a spreadsheet.

The boy had matured. A few short months ago, he would have gone absolutely ape shit over a woman getting hurt. Now he seemed—if not callous, then—content to delegate. But the boy wasn't paying attention.

"One of the all-terrain-vehicles got scorched out from under Deloris, but the team and civilians all made it out. We can't wait until this afternoon."

"Great," Ed gave a casual thumbs up and stacked more pages onto his pile. "Just a few more hours. Reggie Boyd has his trailer lined up with the convoy. Get your ATVs stowed for travel, then—"

"Stop and listen!" Manny slammed both hands flat, wanting to crush the stupid reports into the polished wood. "We're out of time. The desert's expanding."

Meg and Mr. Conti jumped, but Ed stepped close, keeping his voice low.

"We know, but we're sticking to the plan we all agreed to. Listen," his voice dropped to a whisper, "I know you like to run the show, but this is a team effort with a lot of moving parts. Don't go back to being like…that. Just let the wheels turn."

"This isn't about me," Manny hissed. "You're working off old information. There's a—"

"Ed!" Meg pointed out past where the sprite worked.

A brown wall rose above the buildings at the end of the street, a swirling storm front seventy feet tall judging by how it swallowed a five-story office building without slowing.

"Sandstorm!" Mr. Conti almost got it right.

The wall slammed into the tallest building on the street, an old courthouse with a thirty-foot cupola atop its slanting roof. Glass and metal exploded from the structure as the wave of sand tore off the clock tower. This was a solid wall of sand, the dune rising in one last attempt to capture them.

"Move, move, move!" Now Ed got it.

* * *

The wall of sand came on fast as we grabbed boxes and piled out of the studio. I glared at Manny. Why hadn't he just said the fricking dunes had followed them back?

"Let's get her on the bus," I jammed my box of reports and supplies into the road manager's hands and strode toward Dwain.

Deloris' face was slack, which was good considering the agony she'd been in when they arrived. The sprite gave a curt nod, but rather than wait for my help, he scooped the woman up beneath knees and shoulders and carried her to the bus.

"Stay with her." Pete snatched my keys. "Ralph and I will meet you there."

Manny shoved the box back at me and got his riders saddled up while the rest of us piled on the bus. Our driver, an older woman with a steel-gray bun and weather-hardened face didn't need any encouragement. She slammed the doors and drove like a maniac.

As we bumped along, I glanced around at the other passengers, recognizing a few. Sweat and sadness sat heavy on their faces, as well as a stony determination that occasionally gave way to furtive glances at the road behind.

"Mister, where'd my house go?" Black curls bobbed over the seatback that obscured Dwain—no, it was a little boy with a similar mop of hair, standing between his parents.

"Same place as mine went, I guess." The mother gave me a weary smile and coaxed her son back onto the seat.

Now that we were moving, the desert didn't seem as threatening. It still flowed along swallowing the business district, but the horror of it all diminished as we put distance between it and our group.

The mental respite was short lived. Dust rose out to the left and right of the narrow street as we raced toward the waterfront. The sand along our sides wasn't deep, but it was closer—much closer.

"You see it too?" Mr. Conti asked from the seat in front of me.

"We've still got maneuvering room, but Manny's right. We have to move everyone now."

I rummaged in the box for the communication candle. A thought and tight rhythm lit the wooden wick and filled my nose with lavender.

"Anna, get everyone moving across the bridge. This is an emergency. The sands are coming. Get them all out, now!"

The echoing from my words told me they made it through. The ghosting quality flared as Anna lit up.

"Ed? Where do you want us to go?"

"Across the bridge," I thought. *"The desert will come crashing down in maybe fifteen minutes. Just get them moving. We'll gather at the old police station beyond the Jersey tollbooths. We've got the last group on an old school bus and are heading straight for the bridge. We'll meet you on the other side. Don't let anyone drag their feet."*

"I'm on it, Ed. See you on the other side."

I grounded the Fire spell and told Mr. Conti what I'd done. He nodded and turned to speak with the driver. The curls of smoke drifting up from the wick reminded me of how tenuous and insubstantial my life had become. Without my parents, my house, even my home town, I felt adrift. All the work we'd done since returning was for nothing, we'd still lost.

"Achoo!"

The little boy's sneeze pierced my eardrum and blew the smoke stream forward. He had his chin propped on the seatback and gave me a shy grin. I smiled back and tousled his hair. No, it hadn't been for nothing.

7. When Worlds Collide

O UR CRACKLING fire staved off the night chill. Anna and I fed dead branches into the cement fire ring. Quinn and Manny sat opposite us and were engrossed in quiet conversation. Pete refused to sit. Maybe it was a farmer thing. His family was used to going a hundred miles an hour.

"Is it supposed to be this cold in October?" Anna asked.

"No, still fallout from that." I jerked my head across the river.

Cold desert wind whipped out of the darkness to raise ghostly froth on the Delaware River. A constant groan sounded from across the water like the last exhalation of some massive beast as tons of sand settled into the river.

"Sleeping would be hard enough without the constant droning." Anna shivered and pulled her bright pink jacket tighter.

By the time we'd threaded through long abandoned construction sites and crossed the bridge, sand spilled over the bank back on the Pennsylvania side. Hours later it was still coming, steadily burying the waterfront industrial complexes, but also dumping into the slow-moving river.

Getting things organized and refugees distributed to more comfortable buses took an astoundingly long time. With the river as a buffer, camping for the night seemed safe despite the water on the far side roiling like murky cocoa.

"Lucky this station has so many rooms." Quinn leaned back and stretched, and her sweater pulled tight across her front. "Some sort of training complex."

"Won't be this lucky in the future." I fought to keep my eyes on her face.

"Wilmington will have something. And if you were wondering, Deloris is doing much better. She won't have any problem riding tomorrow. Dwain's a miracle worker."

"That's a relief." Damn it, I should have checked on her. "Wilmington's only forty miles downriver, but it's going to be slow going. Mr. Conti says the road hasn't been maintained but the bridge is sound. No way to cross to the north."

"Need to get there before dark and set up a real camp," Manny added. "Those built in toilets are filling up fast. The buses are getting ripe."

"So what's the plan?" Pete swung away from his examination of the dark water, looking as annoyed as I'd ever seen my friend. "How fast can we get back up to the north side of New Philly and who's going?"

His question hit me like a slap. Walks with Max used to give me time to work out problems, but being surrounded by people twenty-four-seven had me buzzing. Instead of quibbling over logistics and toilets, I needed to plan how to rescue our families and the hundreds of others still trapped by the desert.

"Okay." I tried to organize my thoughts. "We have to get this group down to the next bridge and settled for a few days. The north side of New Philly needs to be evacuated. And we have to find a new home."

"Don't forget the people who've disappeared," Quinn walked around the fire and sat on my left.

"We need a good list." Pete cast a glance at the whitecap-strewn water. "Most of my family was at ground zero. If we'd known what was coming after the soybean field turned into a beach... Well, Mom would kill me if I didn't do my best to account for everyone."

I cleared my throat, feeling like Dad weighing in on a prickly topic. If Koko was right, my Earth magic was at the heart of the problem.

With some evil force twisting my spells to bring this "Old World" into existence, it made sense the desert rose out on the farm.

"Pete, we'll find them." *What else could I say?*

My single biggest use of Earth magic had been to remove a boulder squatting right in the middle of the Eastons' new soybean field. I'd spent days chipping away with Earth spells to sink it and flow the minerals out flat. By the end of the week, I'd transformed the obstruction into a fair-sized parking lot. Pete was thrilled to have an area to dry produce and park gear. I'd been proud to have made a lasting contribution to my friend's family, but had instead left them with seeds of destruction.

"You won't find them all in town." Manny broke into the awkward silence in his usual uncaring way. "The deputy proved the sand doesn't lay just in this dimension. If it did, he would have crossed in minutes instead of days."

We pounded out a detailed plan as the evening wore on. Piper joined us and of course took notes. The cold-hardy Jersey mosquitos had only drained perhaps half of our blood by the time everyone nodded in grudging agreement. If the last few months taught me anything it was that compromise never came easy.

We selected the Stubborn Six, a name Anna coined for the half dozen volunteers who would leave the main group at Wilmington and wind their way back to Philly. I knew Pete would insist on going. His entire family stood in harm's way, and he could recognize terrain near the farmstead. Pina offered Dwain's help, so the sprite was a no-brainer.

My biggest point of contention came down to Anna. Though inexperienced, her ability with Spirit and Fire ran strong. She was bent on going back to town with the team, but I wanted her to stay put and relay messages with the two others who could firespeak. Dozens of Brights had followed the A-Chords' tour, but only a handful continued on to New Philly. Plus, there just wasn't room for everyone. Counting Vance's beat-up machine, we only had four ATVs.

The empty buses would get as close to New Philly as they could, and the six would continue on the all-terrain vehicles. Manny insisted he had a talent for telling when drifting sands turned from simply annoying to dangerously disorienting. Someday he and I were going to have a heart-to-heart, and I *would* get some straight answers about the man.

In the end, we settled on yours truly, Pete, Manny, Dwain, Quinn, and Deputy Vance—to coordinate with the police. Quinn stayed behind, and we watched the fire die out together.

"This is so messed up," I said. "Where the hell are we going to put all these people?"

"It'll work out." Quinn slid close and took my hand, which calmed my spiraling thoughts.

"Wilmington's a ghost town, so maybe New York or Baltimore. And there's supposed to be an enclave outside of Harrisburg."

"There ya go. Once we get clear of whatever's screwing up the radios, one of the local governments will take us in."

Her hand warmed mine as I leaned in. It had been a long time since we'd kissed. Our relationship turned cold before the tour began. We'd come through so much and gotten—if not close—friendlier on the road home. Since getting back there just hadn't been time to worry about relationships, yet something changed. For the better I guess because Quinn's full lips touched mine, parted, and my world narrowed to a pinpoint of bliss.

I could have stayed there all night, drinking in the woman who'd snared me. I wanted her, to meld together in our own private concert of exploration. My hands had a mind of their own as did hers. Wonderful, caressing—

Something grated nearby, but I simply nuzzled closer, inhaling Quinn's scent.

cough "Ahem…"

Quinn pulled back with a gasp, leaving a hole in my soul and cool air replacing the heat rising between us. Why—

"I do apologize for intruding." Mr. Conti smiled from across the glowing embers. "Edan, I have a thought."

My wits returned like a snail dragging a brick. When the boss used my full name my mind always jumped to the conclusion it was Koko speaking. "No problem, Mr. C."

"We need a concert, something happy."

"It's getting kind of late." I looked around the dark courtyard between buildings.

"Perhaps tomorrow when we stop?"

"Good medicine," Dwain said from across the fire. "Music will heal your people's souls."

I managed to not jump out of my skin, but had to wonder how long the sprite had been quietly sitting there. Dwain's smile said too long, as he blew out a big, foggy breath that mingled with the rising smoke.

"Exactly!" Mr. C nodded. "A *tarantella* of the old country to heal and unify."

"*Tarantella*?" Quinn leaned forward, forcing me to drop my arm.

"The old ways still hold in southern Italy. Long before Roman, Byzantine, and more modern influences, the people relied on holistic cures. Communities came together with music and dance to bring good fortune, raise spirits, and cure illness. If you've ever watched an old movie with a band of Gypsies, you've probably seen a *tarantella*. The traditional dances vary in style, built around drums, tambourines, and the people's outfits."

"Like in 'Fiddler on the Roof' or 'The Hunchback of Notre Dame,' right?" Piper materialized out of the darkness, drawn in like a moth.

So much for everyone sleeping.

"Exactly! The dresses, the steps"—fond memories pulled up the corners of his mouth—"all focused on the spirit. It brought the people together. When a village resonates with wholeness, its life energies mingle and are shared by all. These people are scared and tired. They need such a thing."

I squinted across the fire, taking in Mr. Conti's somber face, the sad smile lingering in his eyes. *Surely he was no older than sixty—or maybe seventy?* If the latter, he could have spent time in Italy as a boy. Trips overseas became few and far between once the virus took hold. Government officials, the ultra-rich, and corporate moguls monopolized international travel as airlines and shipping fell out of service. Yet he spoke as if from experience—as though he'd been there among the dancers and musicians.

"Medicine as it was meant to be," Dwain concluded. "Same as the First People. Kokopelli would approve."

Humor replaced the sadness in the old man's eyes, shifting moods as fast as the old spirit himself. Pina, Koko, and now Mr. Conti—maybe jumping between emotions was something that came with age.

"Billy will love it." Quinn's grin was infectious. "Not being able to help has been killing him. Worst case we'll go unplugged, but Pioneer's generator is pretty beefy. The RV can power amps and the mixing board."

Quinn and I picked out songs while the others drifted off to bed. Working up a program was fun, even if the magic from earlier was gone. We finished exhausted but content and huddled close with our backs to the glowing embers.

"We're an odd pair," Quinn murmured.

"Guess so." I slid my hand into hers.

We sat in silence, looking out over the water. Though the cool air flowing across the river sent up swirling mist, the sky overhead was clear and dark. It was a new moon, and the stars shone with pure brilliance. Recent events proved there were other realms, but what about other planets? Could there be some green-skinned or hydrogen-based guy out there holding his girlfriend's tentacle and wondering what it would take to get the hydro-gods off his case so he could enjoy life?

Her hand turned soft in mine. Little suction cups pulled with the sound of lapping waves. Her cold tentacle slid across my knuckles. It whipped forward again, pink and glistening as it extended from a black muzzle.

"Max?"

I tried to pull back through the molasses of the dream, but couldn't move. The sensation went from cold to stinging as my stupid dog kept licking. I wanted to tell him to stop, to push him away. Something was wrong with how focused he was—and with his eyes. The blocky black muzzle blurred and pulsed as if behind a veil of energy. It was definitely Max, but his once brown eyes glowed gold with vertical slits for pupils.

"Crap that hurts. Stop it!"

The impossibly long tongue wrapped around my hand. Searing fire shot up my forearm. I instinctively reached for the Spirit element to push him off, not wanting to hurt him—but there was something wrong with the thought. Max was beyond pain, though I couldn't recall why. My feet slipped as he pulled me forward with a mighty yank. Or maybe he pulled himself toward me. It was difficult to tell as we struggled in a silent tug of war with his stupid tongue.

I'd only tried spells in the dream world for practice. Music floated by in tattered wisps, the lyrics and tunes fractured and impossible to grasp, like trying to hum a melody while another blared from the stage. My shoulder was about to pop from its socket. The snout drew closer, grew larger. Max's fur turned green and sulfur overlaid rancid puppy breath that blew hot and scalding. Nothing I did mattered, and I was sick of it.

The thought came as a lifeline with the driving beat of Skillet's "Sick of It." I slid power down my arm, wedging it under the appendage wrapped around my wrist and forearm. Throbbing energy pushed the slimy thing down, forcing it away.

With a wet sucking, my hand came free. I should have fallen back, but didn't. Those golden dinner-plate eyes shone between green snout and upswept horns bracketing a glowing red gem. My breath caught, but somehow I wasn't surprised.

"Uktena?"

Hissing laughter escaped like steam from the dragon's maw. The horned serpent could appear as snake, dragon, or anything in between. The curtain of energy now shimmered behind his haunches and whipping tail. Massive fore-claws gouged furrows in sodden ground covered with pale, springy moss.

"Hu-man." Uktena scraped his tongue across enormous fangs as though trying to clear an unsavory taste. I grinned at the thought of my magic giving the massive spirit a bit of indigestion. "At least you are capable of more than just phantom power here."

I'd caught him spying on Koko's adobe halls when I first practiced my seeking spell. Those sessions simply produced the illusion of magic to improve my focus. An odd sense of pride swelled at the thought I'd just accomplished more. We stood in a copse of oddly straight trees that looked like a cross between palms and evergreens. The bare diamond-cut trunks spread into a feathery green canopy beneath a distinctly purple sky.

"This isn't Koko's domain." *It wasn't even the desert on the edge of his lands.*

"Phhtt…" The expulsion of disgust was accompanied by hot breath and spittle. "You are in *my* realm, son of Kokopelli. The domain of hunters and prey, where I am master and all others shudder in fe—"

Wheeee…Wheew

The piercing whistle brought him up short. A small figure examined the trunk of the nearest tree as if judging it for a climb.

"This place is hard to find. You really should put in a few signs." Dwain gave us a brilliant smile and strutted over. "I nearly didn't make it."

I'd grown used to the sprite's homespun tunic, pants, and wooden boots. Now he sported a tapered green vest and trousers complete with black utility belt, fingerless web gloves, and high-topped commando boots. All he needed was a pair of aviator sunglasses to be right at home on the cover of Mercenary Weekly.

"What the heck are you doing here?" *What am I?*

"Obviously, the old trickster sent him." The dragon settled down onto his haunches and leveled a glare that implied I was responsible for Koko's actions.

"Hey, I barely talk to the guy anymore," I said.

"Nope, Pina sent me."

Dwain circled Uktena with the same interest he'd given the tree. An evil little grin twinkled in his green eyes and pulled up the right side of his mouth. The crescent scar along the arc of his smooth cheek crinkled. Given the sprite's mastery of healing, he must have deliberately left the mark as a badge from the battle his people undertook on my behalf—or he simply thought it made him look rugged. The green snout swiveled, eyes locking on the small man.

"It's your party, so what gives?" I asked to distract Uktena. If Dwain decided to go for a climb, I'd be picking what was left of him from between those gleaming teeth.

"That little female is insufferable," Uktena grumbled, but the words held no venom—more of a grudging admiration as he stomped around to face me, forcing Dwain to dance out of the way. I snaked an arm out and pulled the sprite back before he got any more bright ideas. "There is no help for it. Your world is out of balance."

"Let me guess. The Goddess of Peaceful Death forbids me to interfere."

Nothing rubbed me the wrong way like being told not to do something, especially in the case of powerful beings who refused to take action themselves or police their own. Uktena might be the exception. He'd helped us out on the road, but it didn't give him the right to keep pushing my buttons. Though what I could do to dissuade a multi-ton reptile remained unclear.

"Goddess Tia no longer holds sway over my actions. I parted ways with the Neutral Council, but they and others are watching. Some problems are unique to your world; this current issue is not. It grows, infecting all realms."

He flicked a talon at the shimmering curtain of energy. The rolling landscape beyond the trees was hidden in shifting fog, but the sky lightened from deep purple to azure blue. As if in response to the horned serpent's gesture the trees faded to two-dimensional things overlaid with towering cliff walls of natural and stacked stone.

A flicker of orange shone through the fog, drawing nearer though it remained anchored to the ground. Sand spread from around what resolved into a teepee of cheerily burning logs. A hunched figure peered at us from across the flames. Emerald eyes shone from his right about waist high.

"Edan?" Pina's voice was muffled as if from a great distance.

"These intrusions are intolerable." Uktena sounded tired.

The flames flared, Koko stood straighter, and I imagined heat pouring through the shimmering boundary separating us.

"The problem worsens, and its source remains difficult to locate. But we will find it." Koko nodded off to our right, which I found odd until I realized he looked past Uktena.

I glanced over my shoulder. "For crying out loud."

A slender, elegant woman with hair drawn up in a severe bun matching her cold beauty stood behind us—behind yet another veil of power, in a world of somber hues and waist-high stones arranged to form tidy avenues stretching into the gloom.

"No use crying, human," Tia said.

"No, I didn't mean…oh, forget it." The goddess wouldn't understand our expressions. "What's going on?"

"The third world is tightly coupled to all our realms. After the chosen people rose into your fourth world, the third was washed clean and sealed away. That land remains connected to the fabric of our universe. Now, not just the doors, but the very walls of existence are opening, drawing all our lands into confluence."

"Like a kind of reverse big bang." I waved away my comment at her confused and oh-so-imperious scowl. "Everything's getting drawn together into one domain."

"In a manner of speaking." Koko drifted away, his fire burning lower. "Overlaps are random and fleeting, but will happen more frequently until the borders of our lands fuse. The process will release significant energy."

I hadn't learned much about physics, but history classes covered the discovery of nuclear bombs, which was the vision his words brought to mind. "You're talking about an atomic blast. Total annihilation."

"You are fundamentally correct, Edan. We will work to contain it, but such power is devastating."

Koko and Pina slid off to my left, drifting by like a ship passing through a fog bank. Chilling cold quickly replaced the imagined warmth of his fire. Dwain bowed to Pina as they sailed away. Uktena and Tia glared at each other for a full minute, then her realm too fell away, leaving us under the purple sky.

"What were the chances of that?" I didn't expect an answer, but Uktena missed my sarcasm.

"It happens more and more lately, though having two at once is new. This is why you must act soon."

"Oh, don't worry. I'm heading back to find my parents and get everyone out. In the meantime, why don't you get off your titanic butt and fix this haywire magic?" My hot words were a mistake and unfair. Uktena had saved our bacon in a big way and gotten pretty beat up in the process. I sighed as his eyes narrowed. "No offense, but you're huge, powerful, and surely better able to put things right than a guy who's practiced magic for less than a year. For that matter, Koko or Tia are better equipped to fix this."

"I would welcome a battle, but this enemy cannot be met with fang and claw. Kokopelli does what he can to hold the worlds apart, but it is a losing struggle. This third world is fused to our realms. We have no leverage to fully stop what occurs because all converges on your lands. Think of it as pushing against something you stand upon. You may hold yourself at arm's length, but cannot ultimately stop the movement under your own feet."

"But if he finds the source, the thing that's corrupting Earth magic, what then?"

Those golden orbs blinked, making me feel tiny and weak. He didn't do it on purpose. The dragon form could paralyze with fear. If Uktena meant to, I'd be sniveling and wetting myself. Still, his intensity raised the hair on my neck, and my ears thrummed with his silence. Whatever secret he refused to divulge cut deep across the supernatural society. Maybe it was simply the remnants of his strictures from working for the Neutral Council, but I guessed his reluctance to expound held deeper implications.

"That's where we come in, isn't it?" Dwain's voice squeaked from overhead.

I hadn't seen him climb the tree, but the sprite hung by his knees like a chimp. His upside-down grin looked like a frown as he bounced and the branch swayed, sending down a cascade of white fluff.

"At least, that's what Pina told me," Dwain continued, oblivious to my and the dragon's glares as we batted away the drifting seeds. "We enter through your world—or through the desert spilling out into it— find the magic ring or whatever is causing all the trouble, and turn it off. Zippity-do-dah-done!"

His frown faded into a smile then flipped back when he let go with his legs and hung by his hands over the twenty-foot drop. At least he'd finally noticed my scowl.

"Substantially correct." Uktena surprised me by agreeing. "Although, he has left out several important steps, and complications will undoubtedly arise. But you are here because I sensed something in Milwaukee that should not have been there."

"Most of the things we encountered should not have been there." The band's first tour had been one hell of a ride.

"True, but the vibrations I felt were different, belonging neither to your allies nor your enemies. Though distracted, my serpent form registered a certain signature that flared at the destruction of the gateway."

Distracted didn't begin to cover it. Uktena had his butt handed to him. His natural form—a serpent the size of a small fleet of sports cars parked end to end—was more attuned to hunting. Though formidable by any standards, the dragon had better offensive weapons.

"And you're just now telling me this?"

We hadn't spoken much after the conflict, but if there were other forces afoot he should have made time.

"I could not put a claw on what I felt. The significance escaped me until recently, when I encountered those vibrations again—here."

"What exactly do you mean by 'here'?"

Somehow I didn't think he meant in this dreamscape or his own realm. Uktena had a history of stalking me; it was sort of his thing. The serpent had even linked to my dog with a magical bond when my hiding spell took me off his predatory radar.

"Your city of New Philadelphia resonates with the same power."

Dammit!

"Does that mean Old Milwaukee is turning into a desert too?"

It made sense. The Earth elemental there had been one of the most powerful beings I'd met, and Koko thought something was turning Earth magic into a weapon to destroy the veil between worlds. Plus, the Brights and I had also released a few choice spells.

Fast as thought the landscape shifted. Dwain and I blinked at a beachfront. High dunes cascaded into choppy water as wind dervishes whipped around a white tent rising from the tall mounds. A platform sat atop the spar extending from the tent—no, the material was ridged, metallic or a white polymer.

"That's the Music and Arts Center!" I gaped as Uktena stepped up behind us.

"Yes."

The sand shifted and flowed in an avalanche cascading from the top of the hundred-foot mound covering the majestic building modeled after a ship with white sails. The desert spilled across the streets to flood the ruined section of the city with a ten-foot tide of living sand.

I'd worried the creatures that escaped us would cause problems, but this was far worse. Lamppost tops poked from the sand covering the parking lot where we'd spent so much time, where I'd unleashed an Earth spell beyond my control. *I did this.*

"This isn't your fault." Dwain studied my face, with hands on hips. "Your magic is being corrupted and used to power this, but it's not your doing. Pina says to never forget that."

"The vibrations preceding the sands are subtle and easier to detect in serpent form."

"Why are you showing us this?" I asked.

"You needed to know." The dragon shrugged his massive shoulders, a very human gesture.

"That more than just my hometown is in danger?" I kicked at the cursed sand, but somehow failed to connect. *Was this just a dream vision?* "And you still won't lift a claw to help."

"I have explained we are bound from helping."

"You've told me, but not explained." A herd of shaggy two-legged creatures carrying spears shuffled around the corner of the sail and headed for the ruined sector. "I thought you were a being of action. I respected that."

I gasped as water rushed beneath me and the city dwindled in the distance. A moment later, we again stood on spongy moss. I fought to keep my dinner down and scowled at Dwain's amused smile. The little folk were used to popping around. I'd seen Pina do her in-two-places-at-once trick without so much as getting dizzy. Mere humans—or half-humans—weren't equipped to deal with the lurching changes, especially without warning.

Uktena pawed the ground, tearing up great strips of earth. I waited in silence as he struggled with something. The odd trees swayed, blurred, and disappeared into the grainy fog that was Tokpela, the nothingness before creation. It was the substance my hiding spell drew upon and what existed between the various supernatural realms. I often passed through Tokpela when entering and leaving true dreams.

"I am constrained from aiding you directly." At first I thought he was shrinking, but it was the perspective of distance as I withdrew from Uktena's lands. "We may not enter the third world, but…" More scraping as mist rose to swallow him. "Perhaps another can."

A dark form crouched on all fours beside the dragon, looking small by comparison. *Dwain?* No, the sprite drifted off to my left, doing the backstroke through thickening fog. He gave a sort of half-salute and disappeared with a grin. I tried to copy him and paddle back toward the dragon, but the swirling vapor had no substance and my hands slipped through without resistance.

Uktena cocked his head at my antics. A pair of golden eyes, smaller yet just as intense as the dragon's own shone through the fog near his feet. A moment later, all was mist except for two pairs of eyes regarding me, until they too winked out and I fell through nothingness into slumber.

8. The Band Plays on

H AIR TICKLED my nose. I tried to swat it away, then blew, not wanting to open my eyes. Just a few more minutes would be wonderful. The annoying sensation and a sharp pain in my neck forced me to wake. Dull morning sun filtered through a forest of dark strands. When I batted them away they moaned and shifted, which put me off balance.

"Crap!"

I hit the hard-packed dirt backside first and tried to blink my eyes into focus. Quinn moaned again and sat up on the bench we'd shared. Her nylon jacket rustled as she slapped at a dark spot under her shoulder.

"You drooled all over me!"

"Sorry. It got cold." I wiped my mouth, which tasted of things long dead, and spoke off to the side. "You don't make the greatest pillow."

The way she looked around as I rubbed my neck made me glad we hadn't had pillows. She would have hit me with one if it was handy. Instead, Quinn straightened her clothes, stretched, and poked at the dead coals with a stick. All the while her slippery pink jacket slithered and hissed.

"That's insanely annoying. Maybe you should go back to leather."

A frown creased her face as she stood with hands on hips—yet the sound persisted. Beyond Quinn mist still swirled up from the river, but the water had grown yellow-brown overnight. The waves formed oddly regular ripples, seemingly frozen in place under the fog.

"That's not water." Quinn pointed out past the bank.

"What?" I scoffed, then frowned as I squinted through mist the color of blowing—"Sand! Holy crap, the river's filling up."

The hiss I thought had been her jacket came from the river as tons of sand inched toward us. My mind caught up to my eyes with a disorienting lurch. Downstream was an unbroken ribbon of desert winding between Jersey and Pennsylvania.

"We're lucky." Quinn reached out with her power. "The water's cutting a path beneath. Otherwise we would have woken to a flood. Give me a minute."

A handful of people emerged from buildings and vehicles to gawk at the scene. I waved Pete over as he stumbled to button his jeans.

"Nope. Nothing I can do. There's just too much volume." Quinn dropped her outstretched hand.

"Get everyone moving and find Mr. Conti," I said as Pete joined us. "It isn't safe here."

"How's this possible?" Pete asked, his eyes wide.

"The problem's bigger than we thought." My statement earned quizzical looks. "I had a few dream visitors last night. I'll explain on the drive. For now, we need to head down to Wilmington while there's time to cross."

"I'm not sure that's still a good idea." Quinn eyed the sand as it continued to pile up beyond the bridge. "Maybe we can head north and cross above Old Philadelphia? Sort of get on top of the sand."

"Public works says the other two bridges are out." Pete shook his head. "Even if we sneak across up at Bristol, bringing buses down through the ruins won't work. There's no way those streets are passable and circling the city would take days.

We didn't have that kind of time. Clear water glimmered under the rising sun way downstream where the rusting tanks of an old oil field squatted on the far shore.

"We'll just have to outrun it, hit the Delaware Memorial Bridge, and hope we have time to get everyone back across. Quinn, give the rest of the Stubborn Six a heads up." Speaking of the team, there was one in particular I needed to talk to. "I'm going to find Dwain."

Finding a sprite is easier said than done. By the time the caravan was loaded and ready to go, I still hadn't spotted Dwain, but I was sure he'd catch up. There was no time to wait because sand already spilled over low spots along the bank where reeds rose in a phalanx through the shoreline muck. Mr. Conti walked up to my window before boarding his bus, looking more somber than usual.

"We're ready."

* * *

"He wants me to be a stupid radio?" Anna's huff of indignation fogged the glass and made it difficult for Piper to see her opening as the convoy pulled out.

"To be fair, radio was my term." Piper flipped on the defroster and eased the big black SUV onto I-295 southbound behind a shining silver and red bus. Another big engine roared behind them, and the band's RV lumbered into line.

The teen in the passenger seat folded her arms and glared out the window. Bold geometric patterns covered a pink top that should have clashed with the starbursts adorning her pale-blue capris, but Anna pulled it off. The Brights loved loud ensembles. Piper smiled. It was part of what made them unique. Of course, she couldn't get enough of their stories about using the magic they'd all inherited from Kokopelli, but she also genuinely enjoyed their company. Aside from the bright clothing, they were simply good people.

She reached over and poked Anna under the ribs. When the girl turned away, Piper poked again. The corner of Anna's mouth quirked up, though she tried to hide her face. Piper tickled her fingers back and forth until laughter finally exploded from her passenger.

"All right. Stop." Anna slapped her hand and sucked in a big breath. "You win. I'm not really mad, but relaying messages seems pretty lame, like put the little girl out of harm's way lame."

"My brother can be old fashioned. You got pretty beat up on the road, and he doesn't want to see you put in that position again." Anna's face darkened, so Piper rushed on. "It isn't in a 'she can't take it' sort of way. If I know Ed, it's more of a 'she's already had her fair share of trouble' way. He'll want to spread the bad shit around."

"Except when it comes to him. He's always in the thick of things."

"True enough." Piper wasn't sure where this was heading, but talk was better than brooding silence. "And you definitely can hold your own. You kicked ass during the fighting."

"Well…I was pissed as hell."

"And wasn't going to take it anymore."

"Honestly, I don't know where that came from." A pretty tinge of red crept into Anna's cheeks. "Ed tried to get me to recreate the spell, but I can't whip my Spirit energy up to that kind of frenzy again. He hasn't had much time to work with me."

Oh my god. Did this little thing have a crush on her baby brother? No, that didn't feel right. This was just about the magic. Piper knew how it felt to be powerless. Her own ordeal had driven her efforts to understand magic she couldn't wield.

"Listen, I'll talk to him and try to get you on the A-team. Not to be confused with the A-Chords because, girl, I've heard you sing and…well, we just can't go there."

"Really?" Anna was all sunshine and smiles again. It suited her. "You're the best! *You're the best, I don't jest, yet I have something to confess.*" She sang the last in a lilting soprano-tenor-dying-chicken, crossing notes with wild abandon as she fought to suppress a giggle.

"Stop it! My ears are bleeding."

"*Be a tease, don't you please, they will know you as Louise.*" Anna snorted and rocked in her seat.

"For the love of God, no more. My kidney and left eye have ruptured."

Piper turned up the volume controls on her dash, and the A-chords album blared out on a wicked bass beat. Anna matched her grin and lit into the new lyrics like a tiger tearing into raw meat. Of course she knew the song. All the Brights had the band's music down cold.

Well two could play at that game. Piper lent her own—not insignificant, and certainly not in pitch—voice to the cacophony. The pair ditched their problems and tooled down the road amid laughing, singing, and rattling windows.

* * *

I floored the accelerator and raced back toward the convoy along a clear stretch of route 322. The city workers had been right, Philadelphia's south-most bridge was in no condition to bear traffic, but the side trips gave us a chance to check on the sand. Sluggish water flowed around the broken footers of the old Commodore Barry Bridge. The encroaching sand was nowhere to be seen upriver, but sparkling ribbons in the murky brown waters foreshadowed its coming.

"Four hours to get halfway, but the road ahead is clear," Pete said as I turned back onto 295. "Ought to make camp by two."

"But how fast will the river fill up?" Quinn leaned in between the front seats.

"It's only come a couple of miles," I said. "We'll have two or three days. That's going to make getting up into town and back challenging, especially if we can't get the buses in close."

"Maybe it won't even reach that far south." Pete's raised eyebrows said he didn't really believe it.

"We'll have to station our three firespeakers at intervals to keep abreast of the sand. Anna's our strongest, but I have the others talking well enough to give warning."

"What about help from the horned serpent?" Pete asked.

I'd filled them both in on how Uktena hijacked my dream. Unlike true dreams with Koko, the images of the serpent's domain weren't burned into my mind. I recalled his offer of help, but not the specifics.

"Well, he better cough up something soon if we're going to stop this damned desert. At a minimum, some sunscreen for your sensitive skin." Quinn ran a finger over my cheek, which made it hard to concentrate on navigating the cracked road. "You don't have my natural immunity or even Pete's farmer's tan for protection."

"Hey! My skin's a perfect golden brown."

"Not from the neck down and knees up," Quinn's grin faded as our shining procession came into view. "Are you going to tell the others what you saw in Milwaukee?"

"I guess." *But I'd rather have answers first.* "If we get communications back, Mr. C might be able to help them deal with the critters coming off the sand. We'll give the Brights a heads up too, but I don't want to cause a panic in the general population. Even though we're out of the closet—so to speak—the others won't fully understand."

"Phffftt, like *we* do?" Pete had that right.

We passed the last half of the trip in virtual silence, each of us wrapped in our own thoughts. Spindly pines stood dense to either side of the highway, stretching out across what had once been fields of tomatoes and beans. Broken houses sat within trees as did the occasional rotting strip mall, but for the most part it was simply pine barrens. Something about the naturally sandy soil attracted the sickly-looking evergreens, and I wondered how they would fare in the alien sands encroaching on our world.

We continued past the bridge to Wilmington, keeping to the Jersey side in search of a decent place for a temporary camp. Broken highways formed a tangle of pavement leading to the bridge, and we stopped at a vast expanse of concrete standing apart from the surrounding wilderness.

"Must have been a major shipping exchange." Pete whistled as he walked along raised docks backing to a long warehouse.

"No sleeping quarters, but Meg packed an entire bus with tents, cots, and bedding." I checked my watch. Three o'clock.

The buses pulled beneath rusting canopies to escape the blazing sun, and our camp took shape amidst organized chaos and Meg's direction. The band set up along the loading docks. In spite of our time crunch and the problems I'd seen in my dream—or perhaps because of them—Mr. Conti remained determined to treat our refugees to a healing concert. Jinx backed Pioneer down close to the improvised stage and ran cables from the motorhome to a sparse array of amps and speakers.

After the show, we'd send our firespeak scouts upriver, then start our trip back up to Philadelphia in the morning. Sitting tight for the night chafed, but getting everything set up was critical. We needed several buses to handle the evacuation, and once we left, the others were stuck.

"Do we really have time for this?" Pete eyed the band.

"Of course we do." Dwain strode up and jumped into the discussion.

"Nice of you to join us." I couldn't keep the sarcasm out of my voice.

"Had a few errands to run." In addition to his commando outfit, a leather-wrapped handle attached to a wide blade rose over each shoulder.

"Are those machetes?"

"And a few items to pick up." He gave me a wink in place of further explanation. "The music is needed. Your boss gets it. That man's a gem. This will be the best concert ever!"

"Can't drive many speakers, and the acoustics sort of suck," I said.

"Won't matter. You'll see."

By four, everyone was tired, sweaty, and ready for a break. The people fell onto blankets and folding chairs as the A-Chords tuned their instruments. Billy slid out from behind his keyboard and strode to the mic stand.

"Heck of a day. Am I right?" At nods from the audience he continued, "A big thank you for everyone's hard work. To all those hoofing supplies, planning the route, or simply keeping calm, you helped make leaving home a little more bearable. A special shout out to Meg Pullman and Mr. Conti for having us ready to move on a moment's notice. Where are you?" Mr. C gave a little wave, and Meg raised her hand as color rose to her cheeks. "Give them a big round of applause." Clapping erupted from all around, and Meg dropped her hand to cover a self-conscious smile. "We can do better than that. Give it up for your friends, your neighbors, yourself. We've all done one hell of a job!"

The applause turned thunderous. Billy knew how to whip up a crowd. The new order was skewed toward older folks, but age didn't dim the enthusiasm. Blue veined hands slapped just as hard as my own, which were stinging as Charles' drums led the band into the opening number.

Music rose to envelop us. Dwain was right—the acoustics didn't matter. The hard seat didn't matter. In that moment, even the loss of New Philly didn't matter. We'd make a new home. Our friends and neighbors made up New Philly, and by the gods, we'd get the rest of our people out.

"This never gets old." Pina stood just behind Dwain and me, and I grinned as a kind of wholeness settled over me. "Oh, here come the words. Such a perfect selection."

The three of us bobbed to the beat. Jinx's voice sang out with harmony supplied by Billy's deep voice and a lilting prelude from Quinn.

Where do I sit, where do I stand,
I have no confidence in hand,
For my country and my lovers…my sisters and my brothers,
As far as I can see, there's no place for you and me,
Where do I call home?

The song spoke of displacement, of losing yourself in the shuffle. A tingle crept up my spine as the singer found safe haven, a place to plan and prepare. Pina's shoulder jostled mine as she swayed with the music. Dwain did the same on my left, and I found myself joining in.

Waves of stillness rose from the sprites, soothing my worries and calling my Spirit energy, which rose alongside their own. I squinted and could actually see the shining nimbus rising over their heads, arching over the crowd from our spot in the back row. Other shining arcs rose from the far side and even from behind the warehouse.

What the heck? I scanned the crowd. Small figures in simple clothing stood around the perimeter, mixed in with New Philly's displaced citizens. Perhaps two dozen sprites swayed to the beat and pushed shimmering magic into the air to form a dome over the area. The few gaudily-dressed Brights among the audience unconsciously added their own calming power to the working. A thread even rose from Quinn as she plucked out the backbeat and echoed Jinx's words.

Our combined energy pulsed golden and sheer as a soap bubble in my magical Sight, but I knew the shield was strong; I'd seen it before.

"Are we in danger?" I risked interrupting her spell, needing to know what this was about.

"No, silly." Pina flashed me a smile and squeezed my knee. "Just a little something to keep it that way. Now shush and enjoy the song."

Feeding someone else's spell felt strange and unfocused, but I trusted the sprites and let my energy flow into the protective dome. The final chords rang out, drawing one last wisp of power. Anna was down front with Meg and Mr. Conti. Perhaps it was a trick of the light, but her final contribution rose in twin columns, one golden and the other dark and coppery. Thunder echoed as the protection snapped into place.

"How long will it last?" I wanted to be mad at Pina for not being around, but that was impossible given she'd brought her people out to help keep my own safe.

"Long enough." I frowned at her vague words—there was too much at stake. "Oh, don't be like that, Edan. It's difficult to tell, but with your people adding power, I would guess two or three days. Now, enjoy the show."

The audience couldn't see the spell. The magically inclined would have to slip into the Sight to make out the faint dome of protection, but the show did more. The air of desperation and depression eased. People were friendlier, rested easier.

"Holistic healing," Quinn said when I commented on it after the show. "Dwain and Mr. C were right."

"You sound more relaxed too." I slid my hand across her shoulders, noting the lack of tension.

"It's like I poured myself into the music more than usual. I could sleep for a week."

"Sorry to burst your bubble." I gave her an apologetic smile while wishing we could do just that. "We need to send the scouts upriver, test out our communications, and prep the buses. I have Anna, Aarav, and Clara standing by to be firespeakers."

"Yeah, about that." She sucked in a deep breath between clenched teeth. "Piper and I have been talking. Shouldn't we bring Anna with us?"

"Back to New Philly? Nah, she's a strong speaker. She'll stay here to relay." I didn't know what to make of her pinched features and lip biting. "I can relay our status and get reports on the river. Why bring another firespeaker?"

"Backup?" It sounded more like a guess than an answer.

"Believe me, if I go down under a hail of evil critters, we're going to need more than just more comms."

"Well, aren't we the all-important superhero?"

"No…I just mean if things go badly, everyone will need to get the hell out of there, regardless of what's going on back here. Just start—"

"The buses!"

"What?"

"You and Pete said we're unlikely to get them all the way into New Philly." Quinn sounded triumphant. "We'll want to talk to them, maybe have them meet us somewhere different if problems arise."

"Maybe." The four-wheelers would be able to go anywhere, but the buses couldn't handle obstructions, let alone sandy roads. If the survivors had been forced to gather somewhere inconvenient, moving the transportation would be critical. "I guess I could pull Vicki in to handle things here. We still should put two scouts up at the bridges. I'm not crazy about Anna heading back into danger."

"But she'll be with the buses and the guards. Plus you know she kicks ass in a pinch."

"Once." The image of Anna sick in bed still haunted my sleep. "She isn't ready for any heavy lifting."

"None of us are ready." She put a warm hand on the forearm I'd draped over her shoulder. "You certainly weren't. Oh, don't pout."

"I'm not—"

"I might not be able to see you back there, but I know you, Ed Johnson. Enough talk. Let's get things in motion."

Quinn turned in my arms and gave me a lingering kiss to take the sting out of her words. I sighed as she pulled away, resigned to being ordered around by beautiful women. *There are worse problems to have.*

9. Up the River

WE LEFT camp at first light with three charter buses, four ATVs, and a handful of hearty souls. Plus Dwain the sprite and Ralph the imp, neither of which I could technically claim to have souls, though they had as much right to one as the rest of us. Manny and Quinn each got their own ride, and Pete rode with Vance on his beat-up police cruiser. My ride was more crowded, with Dwain behind and Ralph perched on the tank. Hopefully, we wouldn't need the extra gas and spare parts from Reggie Boyd's trailer—getting those had been like pulling teeth.

The bridge was in halfway decent shape as were the roads north. We had to contend with spurious burned out car husks and the occasional crumbling roadway, but nothing the buses couldn't skirt. Cool air blew from the river to our right as we stopped to go over the plan before leaving the highway.

I slid off the seat and rummaged through the trunk for a snack and my candle. Dwain spun around in the passenger saddle and damned near stuck his head in the compartment.

"Mind giving me some space?" I pulled out my half candle and a lighter.

"Just watching." Today he did have on the aviator glasses, but finding a helmet to fit the sprite had been challenging. The bright pink dome sporting flowers and kittens detracted from his para-military ensemble. "You gonna check in?" He clamored at my arm to sniff the candle, wrinkled his nose, and opened his mouth to say more.

"How about checking with Anna? Make sure she's equipped and ready."

"Sure thing."

He hopped down and jogged over to the lead bus. I sighed and lit the candle. Dwain was a good sort, but he talked constantly. It wasn't easy to carry on a conversation over the driving wind and engine roar, but Dwain certainly tried. The momentary silence was a blessing as I sent my magic questing out through the flame.

"Aarav, Clara, Vicki, we're about halfway up I-95. All clear so far. Report."

"All quiet at base camp," Aarav's voice echoed with that haunting firespeak quality, but otherwise came in loud and clear.

"Water's getting murkier by the hour at the 322 bridge." Clara said. *"No solid sand in the channel yet."*

When the third report didn't come in, I reached out again. *"Vicki, are you there?"* Silence. *"Aarav, Clara, can either of you hear Vicki?"*

"Ed, I'm here." In person, Vicki's voice was a rich alto suiting her round, dimpled face. I'd often though she'd make a wonderful singer. It was interesting how a person's firespeak managed to hold those same qualities. Unlike the other two, Vicki's voice was weak and broken by a sort of mental static. *"Had to pull over to get my candle lit. The sand hit hard up by the airport, and I bugged out. These damned back roads have me all turned around."*

Vicki was stationed the farthest upriver at a bend with a wide field of view along the river. To the north she had line of sight with the edge of the old city ruins and to the south nearly to the 322 bridge. I resisted the urge to shoot down to the bridge and see for myself; Clara would report when she had something solid.

"Don't waste any more time talking," I told Vicki. *"Get back down to base."*

"No need to tell me twice. This map is crap, but I have a clear shot along the river and can cut back to 295 farther downstream. Tell Clara to watch…I hear… Good lu—"

Static cut across her words as they grew fainter and cut out. So much for our bulletproof mode of communication. I relayed the report to Clara and Aarav and let them know firespeak might not be reliable near the sand. I blew out the candle and unfolded my laminated map as Dwain and Anna walked over.

"What's the deal boss?" Dwain leaned in to follow my finger as I traced several lines between New Philly's boarders and our camp over in Jersey.

"As the sand moves downriver, we're likely to lose contact with base camp." I slid my index finger to the blue curve above Wilmington. "Anna, I need you to check in with Clara and Aarav every ten minutes. When you lose Clara, we have to assume the sand is about halfway to camp. When Aarav drops off it'll be three quarters. Let them know what's going on and keep a log to help us estimate how much time we have left."

"You can count on me." Determination shone in her eyes, and I silently thanked my sister for interfering, because there was no way I could have handled the task while taking point with the all-terrain vehicles.

"Dwain, huddle everyone up for a quick debrief. I'll be with them after I talk to Vance."

The deputy leaned against his much-abused vehicle, munching on a sandwich. Vance seemed awfully calm given he'd nearly died from exposure on his last outing. But then he'd always been the stoic sort. Pete rode on the deputy's oversized machine and leaned in close as I laid out my map.

"Where did Sheriff Connolly disappear and where are people gathering?"

"We lost him here on a finger of sand only thirty yards wide." He stabbed down just north of the bridge at Chester. "As the desert spread, public works rigged the power plant to run unmanned and the deputies worked out safe zones. We planned to move everyone here and here." Vance pointed out two areas to the north before settling near Mom's work. "But the buses will be needed at the hospital. The general public has cars, but the patients won't be able to drive. Bryn Mawr isn't equipped to handle an evacuation."

"So we head north, get people moving out, and finish at Bryn Mawr." I didn't like the route because those old suburban roads twisted and turned like paved-over cart paths.

"Chances are slim the buses will make it through," Vance said.

"If 476 is clear, we can send them ahead to the hospital while we check the other two sites."

"We need to check the farms too." Storm clouds gathered in Pete's eyes.

"The Eastons wouldn't leave." Vance grimaced. "When the phones quit, we lost contact."

"They'll be deep in the sand." I couldn't jeopardize getting the others out. "Your folks are smart. Let's see if they made it to one of the enclaves before we jump to any conclusions."

Dwain led the others over. The three bus drivers stood together with their assigned guards. All were fully human, and the guards each held a rifle at the ready and a handgun on their hip. Quinn wore her black riding leathers, which blew my mind considering how hot it was likely to get. Anna clutched the log she'd already started. Manny swiveled around atop his four-wheeler, looking bored.

"We're going to head north on the Blue Route," I said. "But we have to stay flexible."

I told them how Sheriff Connolly had disappeared near Chester and about the two groups we'd be contacting. If we couldn't make the main highway, we'd take our chances on back roads. There just weren't a lot of main thoroughfares in the area.

"If things get really bad, we can run west to get back out," said a short barrel-of-a man dressed in a tan jacket and slacks. "I run produce out that way. It'll be longer, but the roads are clear."

Sid, our lead driver, was an old-school teamster, one of the few who regularly traveled beyond the city limits. The other two drivers delivered supplies in town with occasional runs to the waterfront.

"Sounds like a good fallback," I said. "Run the buses up to Bryn Mawr hospital. We'll join you after we finish at the other two sites. Anna and I can communicate. Don't sit on any information or ideas because we could lose touch if the sand gets too close.

"Lastly, no one's a hero. Strange things are coming off the desert. Get out of sight and move on if you encounter something. If you're pressed into a fight, punch a hole and get the heck out of there. Guns will work on some things, magic on others." I flashed a smile of apology at the drivers and guards. "I know accepting this is difficult, but hang in there. We're all on the same team."

Since returning from tour, the people on the south side of town had been treated to a crash course in the supernatural. Only a few saw spell casting first hand, but rumors spread like wildfire—to the point that Mr. Conti insisted on explaining some fundamental truths. I liked to keep my boss up to date on the developing situation. He didn't spill all the beans about Koko and the thinning veil, but I think talking about the elephant in the room went over better with someone from their own generation explaining things. In fact, the older folks had accepted magic easier than the younger crowd.

"Sid, can you draw out those clear routes to the west and directions back down to base camp?"

"You bet." His tweed cap bobbed with his vigorous nod.

"Anna can help make copies. We'll send the refugees out your route rather than risk them running into sand."

Twenty minutes later, we roared up 476 at breakneck speed, which was about thirty miles per hour on the four-wheelers. With a wave, our cluster of small vehicles peeled off at the next exit, while the buses continued on toward the hospital.

Vance led us to the first enclave, which was at an old apartment complex. Although well provisioned, the people looked haunted and tired, as if they'd aged years in the past weeks. Vance spoke to a fellow deputy who the sheriff left in charge. They didn't have big people haulers, but were ready to evacuate. A fleet of cars, trucks, and vans waited in the adjacent lot.

Everyone clamored for news of friends and loved ones. Thanks to Mr. Conti's foresight, we passed around lists of those back at base camp. As people frantically packed the last of their possessions, Anna read Aarav the names from the apartments. We left the roar of engines behind and headed for the next location as cars streamed west.

The second enclave was smaller, perhaps two hundred people holed up in townhomes. Getting them underway proved just as easy. We headed back to I-476 by late afternoon, easily on track to make Bryn Mawr before dark. Unfortunately, none of the Easton clan had made it to either site.

"Sand!" Dwain yelled in my ear to be heard over the hot, dry headwind.

"I see it." I slowed as we approached the onramp.

An inch of sand drifted across the double-yellow running along the overpass—not enough to hamper our machines, but its presence meant trouble. Quinn and I shot down the frontage street to the left. Manny, Vance, and Pete took the right. We rounded the shell of a gas station, passed several stone houses, and pulled into a dead-end cul-de-sac overlooking the highway. Ralph hopped from tank to headlight and back, swinging between the handlebars in agitation.

"Sweet mother of God!" Quinn gasped.

We stood atop a retaining wall two stories above the roadway. Or at least that's what should have been far below us. Instead we looked at a river of sand. The intersection where we'd started stood off to our right. Guardrails poked out across the blowing sand on the overpass. Which meant...

"The highway must be fifteen feet under."

"We won't be driving down there." Dwain pointed straight out. "Or over there."

The far retaining wall dipped lower than our current perch and the desert spilled out to swamp the buildings and trees beyond. Low rooftops poked out like a village caught in flash floods, and familiar spikes of green gathered in clumps around taller structures.

A grating hiss drew my attention down where a short drop would put us onto the scorching sand. The grainy surface flowed like water—and it rose! The five-foot drop looked significantly shorter and a rooftop across from us sank out of sight.

"Back to the others!" I gunned my engine as a column of black armor erupted just below us.

The centipede shot skyward and towered over us. I wrenched my handlebars and nearly lost Dwain as the ATV kicked sideways. The creature slammed down, catching Quinn's rear tire. Rubber ripped under the short spiny legs, spraying bits of tire and chitin.

Quinn gunned the engine. Her ATV surged forward, flipped onto its side, and crashed into a bank of windows along the nearest building. Glass spilled out as the vehicle ground to a halt, its good rear tire spinning uselessly.

"Quinn!"

The insect scrabbled forward in spite of the broken legs dripping green ichor as sand crested the top of the wall in tan wavelets. Quinn pushed to her feet, but her leg buckled. Rather than reach for a spell, I raced forward, slammed on the brakes, and hauled her onto the seat between Dwain and me.

Screeching rose from close behind, followed by a cry as the sprite leapt off. Dwain drew both his weapons in midair, and the gleaming black blades cut deeply into the right side of the centipede's head.

The term machete didn't do the blades justice. Each had a wide triangular cross-section tapering to a sharp edge. Made of wood rather than metal, three evenly spaced knots made them look like sharpened logs with leather-wrapped handles. Rather than slicing, the beefy weapons smashed and cut, leaving two gaping wounds despite the creature's armor. But it wasn't dead by a long shot.

"Get your little ass back on the seat," Quinn managed to sound pissed and scared at the same time.

"Yes, ma'am!" Dwain jumped on with a grin.

We shot down the road. The thrashing bug couldn't leave the sand and retreated. But the desert was on the move. Quinn pressed against my back, breathing heavy.

"You okay?"

"Fine," she snapped. "Left leg's just stiff, and it's a little crowded to stretch."

"One of us can ride with Manny." I shot a significant glance at our sprite.

"Nah, this is plenty big." Dwain leaned out into the wind like a dog from a car window as he clung to Quinn.

"Hey, watch the hands!"

They jockeyed for position on the short ride back to the others, and I had to push Ralph out beyond the handlebars to keep him from joining the fray. Manny and Vance encountered the same problem in the opposite direction, though had managed to not lose one of their rides.

"Looks like back streets then," Vance declared.

The ever-present groan of flowing sand spurred us to move. Time slipped away with every turn as we skirted westward on a zigzag pattern to keep away from the spreading dunes. With dusk approaching we'd have little time to evacuate the hospital. I couldn't imagine loading up patients in the middle of the night. Somebody or something important would get left behind.

The twisting route and constant grating had my head throbbing. We made too many turns to accurately judge how fast the desert moved. I needed to know if Anna still had contact with the other scouts.

"*Ed, it's bad.*" I imagined I could hear her voice as the pressure on the back of my head grew more insistent.

Stupid.

"Hold up," I called to Manny.

He gave me an exasperated look, glanced back to ensure we weren't about to be swept under, and slowed. I pulled over and lit my candle with a flick of magic.

"*Sorry, Anna, I'm here.*"

"*Thank, God.*" Her firespeak cut in and out like Vicky's had, so I didn't feel quite so dense for missing her attempt to communicate. "*We couldn't wait. Sand slammed in like a tidal wave from the east. If it hadn't been for the elevated train tracks it would have swept over the hospital before we knew what hit.*"

"*We're about two miles away. What's your status?*" If desert had closed in ahead of us, we'd have to cross the dunes after all.

"*Everyone's on the buses. Sid has us up on 202 ahead of the sand. Ed, don't go to the hospital, you'll be trapped. I'm sorry.*" Her voice echoed with anguish.

"*Not your fault. The desert messes with firespeak. Can you still raise the others?*"

"*I lost Clara half an hour ago. Aarav is on line, but it's sputtering.*"

As was she. I tried a quick mental call to the other Bright, but it was no use.

"Vance, how fast can you get us back down to the bridge? The hospital's a bust. It sounds like the sand is arching around up ahead. Buses are already headed west."

"Shit, the desert's on three sides." Quinn's hair slapped my neck as she shook her head.

"We can split off onto Rt. 3. It's about a five mile run to pick up 202 south."

I gave a curt nod then pushed my next thought out to Anna. "*Keep moving. We're on our way, but will probably come in behind you.*"

"*Hurry.*"

Our route out looped north, and we heard the sand up ahead as we turned into the setting sun. The air was full of blowing grit now, coating our faces and plastered to the sheen of sweat we all wore—well, except Dwain and Ralph, who both seemed immune to the heat.

Travel grew difficult as trees and shrubs cropped up in the middle of the road. The four-wheelers could handle it, but we slowed to keep from outrunning our headlights as darkness fell. So far out from New Philly's infrastructure there were no streetlights. Vance led and suddenly slewed his machine left. Even traveling in a loose formation, I almost side swiped him.

"What the hell?" Then I saw the mounds covering the road ahead.

I turned and followed as Vance skirted the sand that had somehow gotten ahead of us. Manny followed close on our heels. The damned desert forced us south into the forest. The narrow paths might once have been roads. Dwain probably felt right at home. We pushed hard, and my world became racing engines and groaning sands following too close.

"More ahead," Quinn yelled in my ear.

She clutched tight as we arced left onto an even smaller trail and climbed uphill. I couldn't swear we were still on pavement. Our tires bounced off rocks and roots as the sand continued to force us left. In short order we'd come full circle and spiraled inward until we hit a low stone wall and entered the ruins of some old courtyard.

"We're screwed." Manny shut off his engine and spiked his helmet.

The helmet glanced off a thin rectangular stone jutting from the ground like an abandoned book and rolled up against another. The sand closed in from all sides, rushing faster now, a flood ready to swamp us. We weren't prepared to get lost in whatever dimension the dunes led to, but there wasn't much choice.

"Hear that?" Quinn asked. "It stopped."

All grew preternaturally still. The smell of hot sand couldn't quite edge out the damp moss covering our little corral's stacked stone wall. The desert had stopped several yards beyond the wall. Rivulets of sand trickled down the leading edge only to disappear where desert met forest floor. We walked the perimeter and found the same on all sides.

"It's a trap," Vance said.

"I don't think so." Quinn studied the ground within the enclosure. "There's power here. Not elemental, so I can't see it. This feels similar to some of the castings I saw as a kid. Human magic, but the power feels…I don't know, like the desire of many merged into one spell to make this place timeless and untouchable."

"Vance, where are we?" I looked where we'd entered. Rust spikes poked from the mortar between stones where there would have been a wood gate. Four stone rectangles poked up at odd angles from the leaf litter and laurel, but other bulges suggested there were more that were either smaller or had fallen flat. I brushed the vines back from the tallest stone, a wide tablet two feet long and almost as wide. The surface was etched with weathered grooves, writing erased by time. "It's a cemetery."

"There're stories of a graveyard lost deep in the state park," Vance said as he crouched to look. "The Riddle or maybe Russell cemetery. What are the chances we'd just wander into it?"

"Pretty good," Quinn answered. "This is a protected place. We were probably drawn here."

I opened my Sight, but there was nothing to see. Quinn was right; this certainly wasn't elemental magic. But there was a certain feel—as if that unseen force refused to budge, refused to allow its charges to be lost beneath the sands of another world. This was a tranquil place, yet it was a place of Earth that would not yield.

"Old magic," Dwain whispered.

"Ralph, have some respect." My imp lined gummy treats up along the edge of a short block marking one of the ancient graves. As he often did at bedtime, Ralph had Mr. Rabbit out—this time, sitting on the other side of the stone in a kind of sugary tea party.

"It's okay, they don't mind." Quinn smiled, apparently sensing more than me.

"What now?" Manny looked none too pleased, and I couldn't say I blamed him.

"This makes the decision easy." Pete pointed off to the southeast. "We'll be riding on the sand no matter what. Our farm isn't far from here. I vote we check it out."

I opened my mouth to argue, but he had a good point. I hadn't been thrilled with the idea of going out to the Easton homestead because of the stretch of desert we'd have to cross—a concern that was moot at this point.

"I'm game." Quinn gave a thumbs up and grim nod.

"Whatever." Manny shook his head as if he couldn't believe the mess we'd gotten him into. "Just don't expect it to be easy."

"Easy?" Vance's calm and collected act went missing in action. "It'll be a nightmare. Downtown I couldn't find landmarks I've known my whole life. Out here—how are we supposed to even get going in the right direction?"

"Sun rises in the east," Pete said in the stubborn voice he used on balking cows. "This time of year, more toward the southeast. We keep it on our left in early morning. I know the land for miles around our farm. We can do this."

"Dwain?" I wanted to give the sprite an opportunity to weigh in because I got the feeling his people were seldom consulted by the more powerful spirits.

"We have enough talent to keep ourselves from going in circles." He paused with a handful of grass halfway to the satchel on his hip, stared at Manny, and shrugged. "These herbs are better than my garden back home."

"It's settled then." I scanned our ragged group as the gloom thickened. Three sets of headlights speared the night in crisp beams that blurred into cones of brown beyond the desert border. Even the swirling dust didn't enter our enchanted oasis. "I'll take first watch."

If I'd taken the second or third watch, someone could have jolted me out of my nightmare—though I couldn't recall ever waking up in the middle of a true dream. I stretched out on the ground by my ATV after waking Manny, jerked as I plunged into sleep, and then found myself standing under those odd trees and again facing the horned serpent.

"How much is Koko paying you? I'll double it." I reached for my wallet, but found I had no pockets.

"You are harder to understand than your mute canine. What need have I for payment?" Steam jetted from his nostrils, and those too-bright eyes narrowed.

"No offense. It's just an expression."

Even in dreamspeak I knew better than to make this ancient creature angry. Muscles already coiled along those tree-trunk forelegs, and the back under his wings was arched like an angry cat's. For a serpent-based legendary being, Uktena sure spent a lot of time out of his snake form. Pina said he tended to hunt as the serpent, but battle as the dragon.

"Waste of words. I have not called you here, but felt it proper to greet you since my realm is to be used for the meetings."

"The Neutral Council again?"

"No." The dragon shook his head, gracing me with a cascade of watery saliva. "Though they are involved. Neither the dark nor the light approved of using council territory, but all have been satisfied with these lands. None may hunt, but all may speak."

Something in the beast's manner piqued my interest. Could the long-standing feud between factions be settling into detente? If so, the Brights might finally be safe.

"Is getting together normal for the courts?"

"It happens on rare occasions when significant events impact all parties. The present danger qualifies, so these gatherings are not unexpected. Many will come, little will be accomplished."

"Your faith is sorely lacking." The haggard voice was a familiar croak.

Koko shambled in from our right. His desert clearing floated as if on a lake of mist just beyond a rippling curtain. All around us, other islands—for lack of a better term—floated in and hovered at various levels like docked airships.

"Did Pina come?" I missed my friend and felt unreasonably vulnerable without her or Dwain by my side.

"No, Edan." Koko gave me a tired smile, the lines of his weathered face creasing deep.

He looked about to say more, but a sonorous gong demanded silence. I blinked, surprised to find people crowded the sparse forest, facing a raised dais upon which were seated three figures. Tia, with her regal dress and dark coifed hair was easy to pick out in the center chair—well perhaps throne would be more accurate. To her left was a woman swathed in dark clothes, with a wide beautiful face and a predatory smile that had me inching closer to Koko and Uktena. The last person—in his casual slacks and button-down shirt—looked distinctly out of place. He was a tall, powerfully built man with curly red hair and a bushy beard hanging over his open collar.

We stood at the back of the crowd, but through some trick could easily see and hear the stage. Although many of the people *looked* human—which of course meant little—tails, hooves, and the occasional set of wings graced other spectators. Arrayed like a loose army opposite their leaders, the crowd formed three living cones of light, dark, and neutral beings. The GQ Viking on stage gave Koko a friendly wave.

"Kokopelli, come forth and give an update."

The staff appeared in my father's right hand as he stepped forward. The carvings along its length glowed, imbuing the old spirit with power and washing away his fatigue. He leapt onto the platform.

"We have slowed the situation, but our intervention will not last." Behind Koko, Tia made a face like she'd swallowed a lemon dipped in hornets. "I again implore all parties to aid in holding back the veil before more worlds are lost."

"We need a permanent solution," The Queen of the Dark Court said, earning gruff cheers from her constituents. "I'll not throw away more power."

"We are close to understanding how to fix this." Koko looked to the Light Court crowd before shooting me a sideways glance. "But time must be stretched to enable that solution."

A man dressed in black sidled up behind the dark queen and engaged her in whispered conversation. There was something familiar about the way he held himself, though I could only see his neatly combed hair glinting under the muted light. When the two broke apart, I caught a glimpse of his square lean face. *Manny?*

"Aid might be forthcoming if certain…concessions can be made." She swept up from her seat to tower over Kokopelli who seemed indifferent to the woman's theatrics. "First, tribute will be paid by any realms touching our own; second, all current disputes against my court will be dismissed; and I think one final item is in order—the impure offspring will be turned over to us."

That last one brought Koko's head up like a whip, and his staff flared. Any hope she might not be talking about the Brights—about me—vanished. The glade erupted into shouts of protest and roars of approval.

"We should have seen that coming," Uktena said over the uproar. "The dark have never been ones to let things go."

"Should I be…worried?"

"No violence may occur during a session, and this will not be a short discussion."

"You call this a meeting?"

Individual voices were lost in the free-for-all shouting match. I breathed a sigh of relief as the bedlam finally subsided, but quickly realized the scene was not growing quiet. I was pulling away. Uktena's land dropped below me, and I drifted out between the island realms.

As Tokpela closed in to drag me back to slumber, the two outermost islands pitched, bucked, and slammed into each other. They disappeared in a flash of green, leaving a dense patch of mists to swirl and dissipate. Then—for me—all was grainy fog, oblivion, and dreams of my family.

"Wait, no!" I woke with a start and looked around the cemetery to see if I'd shouted out loud.

My back ached. I stood and twisted out a series of satisfying cracks to ease the stiffness. Manny stuffed items back into the trunk of his vehicle. He wore jeans and a red shirt under his leather jacket, a totally different outfit than the one worn by the dark queen's advisor. My street clothes changed in the dream realms, but he would have been on watch during the gathering in Uktena's realm, so couldn't have dream walked.

This was one of the few times I'd come out of a true dream doubting what I saw. Being confused by Koko's evasiveness was normal, but my recollection of events always remained preternaturally clear.

"You went without me," Dwain said as we gathered our meager belongings, and I doled out breakfast—protein bars for us and bars of sugar formed into toaster pastries for Ralph. "I felt you slip away, but couldn't follow. Hit a sort of barrier. It felt like a keep out sign."

"Some big powwow to discuss the situation and ask for help keeping the worlds apart."

Dwain frowned and his face darkened. "Was Pina there?"

"No. Koko showed up alone."

"Any of us at all?"

"Forest sprites?" I'd seen all shapes and sizes in attendance, but no little people with their distinctive green eyes. "I don't think so."

"And I'm sure no desert or water sprites either." Dwain bolted down the last of his bar and crossed his arms with a huff. "Typical!"

"If you two ladies are done gossiping, Pete wants to get moving," Manny called as he swung a leg over his seat.

"How was watch last night?" I asked.

"Quiet as the grave."

Though his response dripped sarcasm, there was no indication he'd abandoned his post or fallen asleep. Manny was just being...Manny. Quinn hopped up behind the road manager as Vance edged his and Pete's four wheeler toward the entrance.

I'd need to let Quinn and Pete know about my dream. But Piper would recognize the main players, and I found myself eager to get her take on things. *First things first.* I saddled up with Dwain on the passenger seat and Ralph perched between the handlebars.

"Everyone ready?" Pete asked before slapping Vance on the shoulder.

Our machines crunched out over gravel and grass that gave way to a steep sandy slope. I glanced back at our stoic little oasis, wondering if we'd get a chance to come back and explore whatever power kept the desert at bay.

Jim Stein

10. Down on the Farm

"ABOUT A half mile down this ravine, then back over the next ridge and we should catch sight of the outbuildings," Pete said as we huddled behind the ATVs and waited for the line of fist-sized scorpions to march by.

We'd run across several nasties throughout the long day. These seemed less inclined to attack than the ones along the expanding border, though we'd had a bad run in with a centipede early on. Vance shot it, and we'd ended up roaring away from ten feet of angry insect with a hole in its head.

After that, we'd adopted the strategy of not antagonizing the desert denizens since we no longer had the luxury of simply stepping off the sand to safety. In return, the insects pretty much ignored us. Fortunately we hadn't run across any shamblers or imp herds. Something told me the former would not pass us by quietly, and I wasn't ready to discover how Ralph would react to others of his kind—or vice versa.

"That's what you said two hours ago." Manny frowned at the steep incline ahead, and I had to admit my own confidence ebbed low.

"Yeah, well a few frickin' trees would help," Pete shot back.

Except for occasional clumps of the octopus weeds, all signs of vegetation and forest had been erased. At one point, Quinn helped me

84

dig until we hit bare dirt three feet down—no grass, leaves, or any sign we traveled over what had been forest or farmland.

"Let's get a move on it, daylight's fading." I waved at the retreating column. When not attacking, the scorpions ran in single file like a line of lobsters across the sea floor.

We'd started out with the sun off our left shoulder, but now it settled toward the horizon directly ahead. I worried we'd overshot the farm, but if so we should have hit the edge of town by now.

Pete looked determined as we turned uphill and chugged out of the ravine. He nodded to himself as we approached the summit, then sagged in his seat when an endless vista of sand greeted us. With a heavy sigh, he tapped Vance on the shoulder and pointed to the right. The deputy inched his vehicle along the ridge, sending cascades of sand down either side of the dune. The sweet musty scent of baking sand held a hint of wet stone, a sure sign cold air would rush in the moment the sun set. I turned to follow, but my handlebars jerked back to the left. *What the*—

"Ralph, let go." I glared at the imp straddling my tank.

Ralph had his knees locked tight and heaved again on my left handgrip, forcing us out of line. I braked rather than roll down the slope.

"What gives?" Quinn called from behind Manny.

I tried to complete the circle and get back on the ridge at the end of our little procession, but when I turned back uphill Ralph yanked on the right handgrip. He'd fearlessly ridden to battle on the shoulders of my massive dog, but I'd underestimated the little guy's strength. I tried to pry his hands off, but it was damned difficult.

"Ralph won't let me drive that way. He must sense something."

"Path's clear." Manny shielded his eyes and gave Pete a sneer. "Sand, sand, and more sand."

"The only ridge this long and tall runs along the west side of the grazing pastures. If we follow it, we'll eventually hit the lake and can turn east onto the lower pastures."

"For all we know the damned desert changes topography," Manny shot back. "If it swallows hundred-foot trees, what good is following a ridgeline?"

"Hey there, Ralphy. What's the matter?" Quinn crept over, her hand extended to our agitated imp.

Ralph stood with a foot on each fender and slapped the tank with his knees like a jockey urging my ATV onward—which definitely was not happening since I'd switched off the engine. Quinn patted his back. He sank down onto his butt and gazed out at the adjacent dune.

"Nothing bad out there," Vance walked to the edge before climbing back on his ATV. "We need to get going. It's already cooling off."

"I don't think he's worried about danger." Quinn turned the handlebars all the way left. When she let go, Ralph reached up and pulled them back. "How about this?" She turned the bars right, and once again the imp deliberately brought them back to center.

"Ralph, can you find the farm, the place you came through?" As soon as the words left my mouth, Ralph was up on his feet playing jockey.

I started the engine and looked around the wagging imp butt at my fuel gauge. Hopefully half a tank would get us somewhere safe before dark.

"Let Ed take lead." Quinn hurried back to Manny's machine. "Ralph has a bead on the farm."

Pete looked like he might argue, but waved us forward. I pulled out and headed downhill. Halfway up the opposite slope, Ralph tugged on my right sleeve until I veered off at a thirty degree angle. I drove on, following our imp's random course corrections and getting slapped with his cordlike tail whenever he hunkered down to urge more speed from his steed.

"These turns are random," I complained as we veered off to parallel the ridge of yet another dune. "You better not be playing a game."

"I don't think he is." Dwain's head poked out from under my right bicep. "More than just sand shifts out here. I can't track the changes, but the landscape is fluid. Either he can adjust for it or doesn't notice."

"Farm ho!" Pete yelled as we turned uphill and topped the rise.

Wood fence posts stuck out of the sand ahead. Two parallel lines ran into the distance like runway markers with each subsequent post sticking further out of the sand. The fence ran straight and ended in the gathering gloom in front of Pete's home.

The old farmhouse was just as I remembered, with white board siding and a wide porch circling the front. An older stone section sprouted from the left and tapered off into a barn, while rectangular additions bumped out under a complex roofline to our right.

"Nice job." I rubbed Ralph's head making his bat ears flop and slipped him the candy bar I'd been saving for dinner.

"It's all boarded up," Manny said.

We parked on the crushed stone drive. Much like the cemetery, a no-sand-zone ringed the house and main barn. The knee-high brown grass hadn't been cut in a very long time. Beyond the structures, the dunes roiled and shifted as if searching for a way in. Pete and I clumped up the stairs.

"Looks like some windows blew out and they shuttered the rest," Pete knocked on the heavy wood door. "Ma? Pa?"

Baskets nailed to the doorframe held desiccated wildflowers. In spite of the scorching days, the delicate petals retained a blush of color above burnt brown stems. Pete's second knock echoed within. Something shifted inside, a slow drag-thump that drew closer. I stepped back to get some maneuvering room. A final thump shook the door, the knob turned, and Pete's sister rushed out to wrap her brother in a bear hug.

"You found us!" Melissa's sandy-blond hair, height, and square face mirrored her brother's, although in a much more feminine way.

"Good to see you too, Sis." Pete returned the fierce hug before holding her out at arm's length. "Everyone okay?"

"They're in the barn working on the pumps. Most of the wells dried up, but Pa cross-plumbed the system to keep some flowing. Ma and I are pulling dinner together." Melissa bowed her head. "We lost a few, including Norm. Anyone trying to find a way out just sort of disappears."

Every farmhand was a relative. The Eastons weren't a big clan, but their sturdy farmer genes made them resistant to the C-12 virus without the involvement of an ancient Native American deity. The last time I'd seen Cousin Norm, I'd treated him pretty badly thanks to the magic playing havoc with my emotions.

Melissa's rumpled overalls, wild hair, and weary expression screamed that things on the farm were no picnic. Wood slats were duct-taped to either side of her lower right leg. A dirty-white plaster cast covered her foot but left the toes exposed—the source of the thumping.

"What happened to your leg?" I asked.

"Crashed my ATV thanks to a tumbleweed with an attitude."

Melissa turned and wrapped me in a hug. A lean muscular woman in a flowered dress materialized in the darkened foyer and cleared her throat. Mrs. Easton smiled as I hastily released her daughter. My face grew hot when I caught Quinn's smirk.

"Come in before the sun sets." Pete's mom was all business, even as she studied Dwain. Ralph pulled his disappearing act and was nowhere in sight. "Bring in any food you have too. The things in the night are hungry. I'll set extra places at the table."

By the time we brought in our gear and pulled the vehicles into the barn, Mrs. Easton had dinner laid out. The kitchen was organized chaos as men and women dished up plates of food. Half of them headed back to the barn, and we wedged ourselves around the ancient dining table on stools and crates.

"What's happening in town?" Mr. Easton asked after everyone got settled. Like all of the family, he was sturdy Nordic stock, an older image of Pete with gray lightening his once-blond hair.

We took turns telling how the desert overtook town and our eventual evacuation. Crestfallen expressions met our description of recent events, but resolute nods greeted the news that we'd managed to get most everyone out of town.

"Bugs and monsters got some, and it's unclear how many are lost in the desert," I said with a grimace for their own casualties. "It took Deputy Vance here a week to cross town. Something is distorting things out there."

"I agree," Mr. Easton said. "Everyone gets disoriented. Trees, landmarks, and even buildings are simply gone, but it's more than just that. We've ridden out in a straight line far enough to be absolutely positive to hit the freeway, but all we find is more desert. And there are always plenty of creatures."

"Are they what got Norm and the others?" Pete asked, his mouth a thin line.

Pete's dad shook his head and scanned the room as if looking for words. When he finally spoke, his deep voice was heavy and slow.

"Not all of them. The critters were nastier early on. They ate or attacked everything. Cows and pigs never stood a chance. The chickens faired best, funny seeing those roosters back down giant scorpions."

He paused, seeming unwilling to continue. I glanced at the fried chicken leg on my plate and felt a stab of guilt.

"Norm and Bethany rode out early on, before we knew the sand was screwing with us. It was a routine supply run in the pickup. Four-wheel drive handled the sand fine. We loaded them up with crops and actually waved them out the gate. Stupid…we didn't know." He took a moment, shook himself, and continued. "After that, we only ventured out in groups. Damned radios don't work, so everyone stayed in line of sight. But rifles only work on some of the monsters. It's relatively safe back here at the house, but the sand's creeping closer by the day."

We talked into the night. Obviously, we'd all go out together, but the farm only had three ATVs and the sand had grown too deep for the trucks. Manny pulled Dwain off to the side and came back reasonably confident the two of them could keep us heading west until we cleared the desert. I still wasn't certain what the road manager's deal was and said as much to Dwain later after we'd bedded down in a corner.

"He sees things in a way you can't," Dwain replied. "Says he feels the sand bunching up before it changes our path. I don't get any warning, but can tell when it shifts. Between us, I think we can outmaneuver it."

"Still leaves the transportation issue." Pete crawled on his elbows to our corner of the parlor, trailing a blanket like a cape-wearing alligator. "No way can we stuff twenty people on six four-wheelers—three really, since ours are already full. Bertha, our old tractor, has big spade wheels that can handle anything, but it's a one-seater. With the right parts, we could rig the trucks with tracks and skids—turn them into giant snowmobiles."

"Don't suppose you have that kind of stuff lying around?"

"Nope, but I'll grab a couple of the guys and see what I can dig up in the morning."

Pete was a wizard with mechanical systems, but I suspected manufacturing parts from thin air was beyond even his skills. The longer we waited, the farther the desert would spread. Mr. Conti might have to move base camp before we found our way out, which would make linking back up difficult.

The braided rug sure beat hard ground, yet I still slept fitfully. Rather than true dreams, talking serpents, arguing spirits, and glowing gold eyes chased me through vanilla nightmares that had me running in molasses.

I awoke sweaty and tired. Pete and Quinn were nowhere to be found. The rest of us helped ourselves to delicious fresh-baked muffins and breads. Mrs. Easton must have been up before dawn. The wonderful aroma filling the house pulled tension from the air. I was bolting down a blueberry-filled scone when the back door slammed open. Quinn hurried in looking grimy and tired.

"Didn't you sleep?" I asked.

"A little." She ducked her head and grabbed a thick slice of buttered bread. "Pete's mom needed help hauling in flour, so I gave her a hand then made the rounds to talk to the morning watch. Ed, they've been dealing with a lot of crazy shit here.

"Not just the insects and tumblers. Groups of shamblers come through almost every night. Big, hairy things on two legs that groan and shuffle past. They haven't bothered the farm yet, but out on some of their excursions…"

"What?" I asked when she trailed off and shoved bread into her mouth.

"Two men were lost to them." She swallowed hard. "Went down shooting. The shamblers opened their arms, pulled their fur wide, and swallowed the men. I don't know. Maybe they were just wearing fur coats. But it freaked the Eastons out, and their people were gone."

"We'll have to keep clear of those."

"There's more." Quinn bit her lower lip and grabbed my arm. "You have to see this to believe it."

She dragged me though the back door, across the porch, and out behind the stone barn. The dry grass gave way to a flat stretch of sand. Something shimmered in the distance, a column of green light surrounding what looked like a tornado paused in mid spin.

I looked back at the house to get my bearings. A line extending from the porch out past the backside of the barn would have led up to the new soybean field. The lack of outbuildings made it difficult to judge distance, but I'd spent a lot of time over that way.

"That's where I flattened the boulder for Pete."

"Bet you had to use the Earth element," Quinn said.

"Yeah, a lot of it."

The boulder had been massive and pushed me to my limit several days running. The sheer mass of the rock prevented me from simply melting it away. That was back before the band's tour, before I knew a force twisted and used Earth magic to destroy the veil between worlds.

"I can feel the wrongness from here," she said. "Like the moment you walk into the wrong store or mistakenly climb into a car you thought was yours. I bet you could walk right through that thing into the third world Koko told you about."

"Maybe, but we've got other things to worry about, like getting the Eastons and ourselves back to base camp. We just don't have time to make multiple runs on the ATVs."

I stared out at the glowing column, and a cold hand clenched my heart. I'd done that—without knowing, without meaning to. Gods, if my spell had simply ripped through the veil, Pete and I would have been swallowed on the spot. The frozen funnel definitely extended beyond the flattened boulder. I squinted across the blowing sand. Was it wider than a minute ago?

"That thing's making my skin crawl. Let's find Pete and figure a way out of here."

We scoured the house then headed for the barn. Melissa and a handful of the others worked on a huge metal cart while Mr. Easton managed a team sealing cracks in the stone foundation and layering plastic over the plank walls.

"What're they doing?" I asked.

"Making us sand-proof." Melissa wiped the hair out of her eyes, pulled a tire leaning against the wall upright, and rolled it to a scraggly long-faced man at the rear axle. "Keeps everyone busy, but I don't fancy being trapped under a sea of sand any more than I like the idea of it flooding in."

"So what's this contraption?" Quinn banged the wagon's tailgate, which sat a good four feet off the ground. Heads turned at the resounding echo and someone inside the vee-shaped interior cursed.

"Big-ass harvester wagon. Pete and I figure it's big enough to hold the whole crew once we get the axles freed up and new rubber on her. We'll have her ready in another couple of hours. Won't win any beauty contests, but who cares as long as we can ride her out?"

"Yeah, but—" I broke off and walked the length of the massive cart. It perched high over two axles, with the upper lip ten feet overhead. Sloped metal sides formed a vee-shaped keel along the thirty-foot length. There was no doubt the thing could haul a boatload of people. Leaning against the slanted sides and the lack of suspension would make it uncomfortable as hell, but that wasn't what had me puzzled. "There's no engine. It's just a big wagon on wheels."

"Big brother's working his own project." She pointed her wrench at the towering wooden doors at the back of the barn. "With a little luck—"

An explosive growl drowned out her words, sounding like a jet airplane with a bad cough. Dust and bits of chaff rained down from the rafters high overhead. I dusted the falling gunk out of my hair as three explosions sounded in rapid succession—after which the engine roar settled down to a more regular cadence.

A man and woman hurried over and slid the doors open. Spare parts, engine pieces, and dissected mechanical components lined the walls of the shop area beyond. A grating clunk lowered the engine's pitch, and a behemoth of a tractor chugged through the doorway with Pete proudly perched high in the glass-enclosed driver's seat.

The dingy grey battleship-of-a-tractor coughed and spit its way into the barn proper. Two front tires nestled close together with barely a hand's-breadth between, while the rear sat wide apart and rose high over my head. The rubber was old and cracked with treads like stubby paddles.

"Meet Big Bertha!" Pete shouted.

Making the wagon ready and getting the tractor to run smoother took the bulk of the morning, but by noon the farmers had formed a bucket brigade to pass supplies from the house to the jury-rigged vehicle.

"How fast can she go?" I eyed the high sides of the harvester as Pete used a hand pump to top off the fuel tank.

"On a flat straightaway, probably close to twenty, but towing will slow us down and turns will be dicey. Stay down around fifteen miles per hour if you don't want us all to have bleeding kidneys."

"Should be fifteen miles to the bridge, triple that once we hit the roadways." I squinted at the sun blazing in its too-blue sky. *So not a normal Philly fall.* "We're talking at least three to four hours—assuming we get off the sand quick."

Our odd procession pulled out just past noon. A guard with binoculars and long rifle clung to the ribs at each corner of the trailer. Melissa's team had spot welded benches inside, so the others could sit.

ATVs zipped ahead and behind the tractor like jet fighter escorts. Long holsters jutted up to the left of the driver on each of the three farm vehicles. The Eastons certainly didn't lack for firepower.

"Slow going," Quinn slipped a hand to my thigh and squeezed as she pressed against my back.

"I hope they know what they're doing up there."

We'd been on the move less than an hour, but turns were frequent, and only the sun off my left shoulder told me we still headed generally westward. A constant stream of discussion drifted back from Manny and Dwain, usually punctuated by a curse from the former before another course adjustment.

With Dwain and Manny leading, I got Quinn back. Ralph perched between the handlebars, looking excited and jittery, so I figured he'd just pounded a bunch of sugar. The imp had simply popped into existence there between my arms and damned near gave me a heart attack. He wasn't visible to the farmers, but glances from Pete and Dwain told me our own folks could see the little guy.

"Incoming, two o'clock!" The front right guard's yell was followed by a call from the left.

"And ten o'clock!"

Manny saw the dark shapes vectoring toward us and looped back before I could relay the warning. There wasn't time to simply outrun them. We'd rehearsed our defensive maneuver after leaving the farm, but there wasn't much to it. Manny, Vance, and I rode back to take up positions on either side of the tractor. The Eastons formed a ring beyond us with guns drawn, and rifles from inside the wagon were trained on the shamblers.

Each group was small, resolving into four or five individuals, but they came on fast. Mr. Easton's ATV was in front of mine. He fired a warning shot over the group coming in from the left. The crack of his rifle actually brought all the shamblers up short. They turned to face one another as if in discussion. They were taller than I expected—every bit of seven feet—shaggy as Melissa had described, and wore no clothing.

Their light brown pelts darker than the pervasive sand hung about each like Spanish moss. Long arms bore hooked claws like a sloth's. My hope that they'd learned respect for guns vanished as they turned toward us.

Rather than charge, those hooked hands raised high, talons clacking together. The clicking rose, reminding me of an applauding audience. Mr. Easton gave me a questioning look just as the ground behind the shamblers exploded and tumbleweeds burst out onto the surface. They raced toward us, trails of dust rising behind each.

A shot rang out from above my head, followed by another. Woody chunks flew from the lead creature, but it didn't even slow. They ignored the ATVs and crashed into the wagon before veering away. The harvester rocked with impacts from both sides. The nearest ball of branches circled wide, giving me a view of flashing teeth and red eyes as it looped back for another hit. Guns blazed but had little effect.

These rolling dervishes might be dense, but they were still made of wood—and wood burned. The band's "Bring the Fire" began with explosions from Billy's synthesizer and bombs dropping off Quinn's bass. I fed the music Fire magic and launched a dart of flame into an inbound tumbleweed.

The streak of flame disappeared into the spinning sticks, and the creature slammed into the wagon's front tire with a resounding boom. I cursed and rubbed my numb fingers as it sped away. My second shot flared out as a fist-sized ball and hit the next one at ground level. It burst into flames and veered wide. Ice crystals formed around me as I coaxed the magic to feed from the sunbaked sand and fired off two more.

The burning weeds tumbled themselves apart, and whatever was in the core flashed into greasy yellow flames as if made of gasoline. I grinned as what should have been the last careened wildly and exploded. But another roared in from my right, and a second from straight ahead. Manny stepped in front of the vehicles. A tongue of liquid flame swept out from the knife in his hand, damned near vaporizing the weeds as they dove at the cart. Still they came.

With each exploded attacker, another gout of sand erupted behind the shamblers as they called up a replacement. I didn't know about Manny, but I was rapidly running out of resources, despite using my surroundings to fuel the spell—the magic could only stretch so far.

"It's the shamblers," I called to Mr. Easton. "Concentrate your fire there."

The sporadic gunshots changed to steady sustained fire as the farmers hammered at the stationary sloth creatures. A half dozen high-powered rifles concentrated on the nearest shambler. The creature staggered as it absorbed the punishment and the weed it controlled shot off into the desert as if running for the hills.

The Eastons walked their way through our attackers as Manny and I continued to destroy tumblers. The clacking of those raised claws intensified, a chattering of bones below the deafening gunfire. Sand exploded up around both groups, and I braced myself for a new round of attacks. Dust and sand swirled higher, wind roaring in two tight circles. The guns fell silent simply because the men and women could no longer sight on their targets.

As suddenly as it started, the swirling wind ceased, the sand dropped to the ground, and the shamblers were gone.

"That's what I'm talking about!" Pete hung out of his small driver's compartment brandishing his rifle.

I should have realized my friend wouldn't be content just driving. Shouts and cheers rose from the others.

"Everyone sound off," Mr. Easton boomed.

It took a minute to account for everyone. Manny looked as tired as I felt. Using so much fire had drained me, but the blazing sun did wonders in keeping the deep chills and hypothermia at bay.

I turned to ask Manny what form of magic he'd used, because it certainly wasn't elemental. But the sheer joy of surviving slipped away with my grin. The attack had badly dented the wagon and worse. Ragged rubber strips hung from wheels that wanted to head off in different directions.

"Okay, enough celebrating," Pete walked the perimeter of the harvester with his dad, inspecting the damage. "Guards keep watch, and the rest of you clean up this mess."

"Yeah, but Pete…" I was no engineer, but could tell we weren't going anywhere.

"Cheer up." Pete gave me a wicked grin—of all things—and yanked a cord on the back of the wagon. His dad did the same on the far side, and the entire back end clanged to the ground forming a ramp.

Not only had I missed the fact our tow had a tailgate, the Eastons stowed *way* more in there than I had thought. A parade of tires, tools, and portable torches spilled out with the men and women not on watch. Ten minutes later, I could hardly hear myself think as the shredded tires were cut away, axles bent straight, and repairs made to linkages underneath our ride.

"Good thing they didn't mess up my tractor tires." Pete swigged from his water skin and patted Big Bertha's rear tire. "They're old and decrepit, but solid rubber. No way to cart spares along."

"I can't believe you brought as much as you did."

"If there's one thing we farmers know how to do besides grow things, it's fix stuff. This lot wouldn't be caught dead without the means to repair just about anything that could get broke." Pete jerked a thumb at his family, slung the water skin over his shoulder, and got all serious on me. "Get us off the sand soon. This little shindig just sucked up all our spare tires. We can always patch a flat, but no more wholesale replacements." His voice dropped to a whisper, and he eyed Manny and Dwain. "Do they know what they're doing?"

"I hope so," I said and headed over to find out.

11. Rearview Mirror

T HANKS TO the Eastons' ingenuity, the attack only cost us an hour, but the sun was clearly on the decline by the time we rolled on. Manny said the perturbations in the path forward came more frequently, which was evident by our numerous course corrections. Sometimes we'd only turn a fraction. Other times we'd come close to backtracking for no apparent reason.

And of course, there was the ever-present sand. Unbroken vistas in every direction, heedless and uncaring of our convoluted path, our starts and stops, our turns and ultimate confusion. The baking sands would wait. Hours passed with no further hint of shamblers or any creatures at all. We rode alone through the dry sea, stopping occasionally to stretch, eat, and drink.

"Damn it, nothing!" Quinn swept up the feather she'd dropped.

Rather than zipping off toward base camp, it had simply fallen to her feet. My own seeking hadn't done any better. Apparently, whatever blocked the radios and firespeak also messed with seeking spells.

"At this rate we won't make it out before dark."

The others were already climbing into the wagon or onto their rides. But it didn't matter, we had nowhere to go. Manny and Dwain insisted they were adjusting as best they could, but both had clearly lost confidence.

"We couldn't even find our way back to the farm at this point," she said. "I'm so turned around that I'm dizzy."

"Ralph could point the way again." I mounted the four-wheeler and scooted forward so Quinn could swing her leg over.

At the sound of his name, Ralph flashed teeth through lips coated in white powder, the remnants of three sugary cakes he'd eaten while watching our magic fail. A thought struck me as Manny pulled out.

"Ralph, where's base camp?" I kicked us into gear to follow the procession, but kept one eye on the small figure straddling my tank.

Ralph bobbed his head and pointed at me—no, he pointed back along our track, opposite the setting sun.

"That can't be right," Quinn said over my shoulder.

"No it can't."

Manny took us through two more turns over the next ten minutes. Ralph continued to point behind us, never varying by more than a few degrees. We'd made some extreme turns throughout the day, but always came back so the sun was properly oriented relative to our westward trek. Making a one-eighty turn would put the sun at our backs and have us heading back to…

"Ralph, show me the farm like you did yesterday."

The little guy dropped his arm, flashed his mildly horrifying grin, and stood to point over my head.

Laughter exploded in my ear along with a spray of spit. "Should've seen that coming," Quinn said as she got herself under control.

"I sort of did." I wiped at my ear, decided to share, and smeared my wet fingers across her cheek, earning my abused eardrum a shriek.

"Sure you did. Poor guy can only find the farm. That's where Melissa caught him isn't it? All he knows is the way home, and that's exactly where we don't want to go."

We crested a hill, spitting sand behind us and looking out across another vast expanse of dry wasteland. The sun tinged the distant dunes fiery gold with nubs of shadows just starting to stretch toward us.

"Think about it. What would you do if you needed to go north but your defective compass only points south?"

"Sounds like opposite day!" Quinn punched me in the side—I think harder than she meant—and I doubled over, nearly clunking heads with

Ralph. "Sorry. We need to rein in Manny and figure out how to do this."

"Apology accepted." Her hand felt warm and enticing as it slipped up under my shirt and those long fingers worked along my sore ribs.

Manny glared daggers when I zoomed around front and cut him off. Yelling between vehicles wasn't going to cut it. Pete and his dad joined us once we got the procession stopped. The others grabbed snacks and water while we worked out the details. I ended up having to ride in circles to demonstrate Ralph's unerring ability to point back to the farmhouse. Dwain and Manny studied the imp and compared notes before concluding it just might work.

We had a few false starts, mainly because Ralph wanted to point around me, which made it difficult to tell when I needed to come left or right. With Quinn's help, we finally trained him to just point with his finger instead of throwing his arm out. He brimmed with excitement and had to be constantly reminded to calm down and just point.

Of course Ralph's jittery disposition could also be due to the mega-sized chocolate bar he ate just before we set off again. I'd often wondered where our imp stored his treats and the stone knife that appeared on demand. Now I had to question where his snacks came from—I hadn't had that kind of candy and the Eastons didn't do the whole sweets thing.

Sometimes the changes in direction were subtle, other times not so much. Once I got the hang of turning away from where his finger slewed, we were able to keep our speed up. The technique was similar and just as disorienting as driving by looking in the rearview mirror. There was nothing to hit out here, but I could still flip us or the wagon over if I didn't pay attention. When Ralph pointed at my left shoulder, I'd come right until his finger was again aimed at my sternum. If he strayed right, I came left. It became a game, and both of us grinned when the other had to make an adjustment.

We made good time—or at least moved quickly. Progress was hard to judge in the open expanse. I kept fooling myself into thinking less sand swirled around us and we were about to scoot out from under the baking sun. But that was due more to the sun racing toward the horizon.

"What's up ahead?" Quinn asked as Ralph had me turn left.

I spent more time staring down than looking where I was going. I glanced up and caught sight of a dark line shimmering on the horizon. Just a smear, but as we rode on it stretched before us like storm clouds cresting the distant dunes.

"Weather maybe." I put on more speed because Ralph was giving me the jockey signal, which meant no turns for a while. "It'll be cold, but we can huddle in the harvester overnight. A storm is bad news."

It was a long way off, even at our current speed. Without warning, my navigator signaled wide, sending me on a dangerously sharp turn to the right. I looked back, worried the tractor couldn't negotiate the tight maneuver. Pete did some fancy driving, downshifting so that his tires sank deep, and managed to turn the big rig on a dime as he called out for everyone to hang on tight. The right wagon wheels lifted off the ground a few inches as it pivoted and landed with a jarring whump.

"They're buildings!" Quinn slapped my shoulder and pointed ahead.

With the last maneuver, the distant line I'd mistaken for clouds had jumped close. Squared-off apartment buildings towered over smaller structures forming the suburban skyline. The edges blurred and shifted as if on the far side of a thin waterfall. Distances could be deceptive, but what had been hours away moments before now couldn't be more than a mile or two ahead.

Shadows stretched across the ground reaching straight toward us, which seemed odd given the sun sat thirty degrees to our left. True shadows would slant off to the right, and these grew faster than reasonable given the slowly setting sun.

"Something's on the ground ahead." I couldn't spare more time to examine the phenomenon because Ralph fired off course changes like he was conducting an orchestra.

We zigzagged right and left, until the imp again gave me the jockey signal. The buildings stood sharp and clear ahead, as did the swarm of brown-green scorpions boiling across the sand to intercept us. Magic surged behind me as Quinn readied a spell, but it dropped away almost instantly.

"There's no water out here!"

Gunfire cracked from behind. The Eastons might be crack shots, but there was no way they could possibly pick off so many foot-long attackers. The little bastards would swarm over us faster than my fire could cook them.

"Maybe we can hold them off with Spirit, build a mini hurricane like Anna did with the ghouls." Even as I said it, I knew it wouldn't be enough.

We didn't have the power between us that the young Bright had marshaled as she lashed out against her captors. Any winds we summoned would peter out long before we crossed the hundred yards of pinchers and stinger. I might be able to sweep them aside using Earth, but the paw tattoo on my shoulder flared painfully, warning me away from the thought. I'd acquired the mark as a result of my first major healing, and it did its best to keep me from making dangerous mistakes. Unleashing a blast of the very magic being used to invade our world was not a good idea.

Ralph urged me forward with his finger aimed directly at my chest and bouncing on his oddly jointed legs as he stood in the saddle. I couldn't just plow on. The little monsters would be hard pressed to get at Pete and his folks, but climbing the four-wheelers would only take seconds once we stopped...*if we stopped*.

"Ed?" Quinn sounded panicked as I mashed down the throttle and we jerked forward.

"Bug stomping time," I called over my shoulder. "If we don't stop, they can't get us, right?"

"Fuck yeah!" She planted a kiss on my cheek and laughed. "Go get 'em, tiger."

Quinn waved frantically, encouraging the others to put the pedal to the metal, then clung tight as we plowed into the leading edge of the swarm. Our tires slipped on those hapless bugs, churning the first few dozen to bits. The ride grew bumpy as if we drove a rock-strewn creek bed. Dark ichor and shell fragments splashed up to coat our floor boards and legs. The scorpions shifted up ahead, piling three and four deep. It was like driving into mud. We slowed as the tires churned the wave into mush.

Pain lanced through my right calf. I slapped away a fat scorpion, but others clung to the underside of the frame and worked their way up around the wheel well. The first to reach the front springs and scuttle up toward Ralph ended up skewered on the stone knife that appeared in the imp's free hand. The second and third crumpled and flew back into the mass below as Quinn's darts of Spirit energy picked them off. But we ran axle deep, and soon there would be too many to handle.

I let off the accelerator, threw out my left arm, and called up Fire. The scorpions might not burn well, but they didn't like the heat. The spell bought us a little breathing room as the swarm thinned back down to a manageable level, but I didn't dare stop. Buildings loomed just a hundred yards ahead. Between my throbbing leg and the bitter cold spreading up my arm as the Fire took its toll, I knew the spell would be short lived.

"Signal Pete to take lead," I told Quinn. "Straight ahead. We'll follow them out."

"Are you okay?" Her hands felt hot on my shoulders.

"Just do it!"

She waved the big tractor forward. Those massive wheels couldn't care less about a few thousand bugs.

"Straight ahead!" Quinn shouted. "Head for that apartment building. Make a path."

Pete gave a thumbs-up as the tractor's engine roared like a t-rex and smoke billowed from his stacks. Farm equipment was designed to move down planted rows without destroying the crops, but the bugs weren't lined up to avoid the tires and Pete slewed right and left as he drove, crushing a wide path for the ATVs. The music in my head sputtered out and the fire followed. Pain seared up my leg toward my groin, and my world narrowed to following the wagon.

The jarring ride smoothed out, but my wheels slipped left and right in the gory paste. I leaned heavy on the handlebars, crowding poor Ralph to the point he climbed over to sit between me and Quinn. The sea of broken claws and smashed shells thinned, and I blinked down at a yellow line flickering beneath the ATV. The sucking grind of Pete's tires turned to a hollow slapping. Sometime later he pulled to a stop, and I managed to swerve before plowing into the harvester.

"What?" The air grew oppressive. Didn't we have to get to the farmhouse?

Hands pulled me from the saddle, and I found myself looking up into a beautiful face that seemed familiar. The angel smiled, then frowned. Then a stinging slap rocked my head to the side.

"Get a grip, Ed." Quinn looked angry. "I know you're cold, but focus some more Fire magic on yourself. You've been poisoned—here and here."

There was numb pressure on my calf and knee where she touched. The last thing I wanted to do right now was magic—especially a Fire spell. A nap sounded so much better. My teeth chattered, which seemed at odds with the burning heat searing up my leg and spreading into my gut. But Quinn had that "don't you dare argue with me" set to her jaw.

"And do it fast. The sand's still coming."

"Yes, dear." I managed a grin, then reached for music and Fire.

I'd healed myself of poison before, and it hurt—a lot. Clearing out the scorpion venom was no exception. Fire burned and cleansed, forcing the last of the poison to my right knee, which managed not to explode before I sagged in relief and exhaustion. Satisfied I had things under control, Quinn took the driver's seat and wrapped my arms around her waist.

The town flashed by in spotty patches—empty stores and houses, then a jarring road through forest. More than once, I jerked awake and found I'd left a drool stain on Quinn's back. Healing took a lot out of a guy. The thought made me giggle, but that took too much effort. I sagged forward to rest my head on the wet spot.

"Wake up, slim." Quinn called over her shoulder. "We're turning onto the highway. Time to check in."

"Sure thing." I blinked, feeling a little more alive.

The tractor pulled up along the berm, and the ATVs clustered in close for one final rest stop before we headed south toward the river bridge. I got down and stumbled on leaden feet, but there'd be time for sleep once we were safe.

Lighting the candle took *way* too much effort, as did my call to Anna and the others. Pete had a map open and jabbed his index finger down on our current location. If the sand hadn't reached the bridge, we had a clear line of sight to base camp.

"*Aarav, this is Ed. Can you hear me?*"

The connection echoed in my now throbbing head—definitely too much magic.

"*Anna…anyone?*"

"Crap, I don't think they're in range." I held up a hand to forestall Quinn's response.

"*Ed, I've got you.*" Aarav's firespeak was strong, so maybe the desert hadn't progressed as far south as we feared. "*Anna's here at basecamp with the buses and told us you went back in. Mr. Conti wants your status.*" He paused as if listening to something outside our conversation. "*And he says to get your butt back.*"

"*We have the Eastons and are heading for the bridge. Tell Mr. C my butt is on the way.*" I had to smile at the thought of our kindly old boss using that term. "*Watch for a big tractor and half a dozen ATVs. It's slow going, so another hour.*" I looked to the map, and Pete gave a noncommittal shrug. "*Maybe ninety minutes.*"

"*Should be okay.*" Aarav said. "*The sand stopped dead a couple miles upstream. It's been holding there for hours, but don't waste any time. You hear?*"

"*Loud and clear.*"

12. The Source of the Problem

T HE BUSES got back a day ahead of us, but celebrations continued at basecamp as people searched for friends and family and happy reunions ensued. We checked in with Mr. C before I was afforded that luxury, but Anna finally walked me down the line of buses to the band's RV where Meg poured over stacks of paper.

She handed me the annotated list of newcomers without preamble and returned to scribbling notes in the margins of her printouts. I scanned the pages and found "Johnson, Phillip" and "Johnson, Simone."

"B3 and NF?" I asked pointing at the notes scrawled next to my parents' names.

"Bus three is one of the big gray ones we'll be using. Numbers are in the windshield." Her glare at being interrupted softened. "NF is not found. Or more accurately not yet accounted for."

"But Mom was at the hospital. She should have come in with the rest."

Meg gave me a helpless shrug before turning back to her reports. An arm slipped around my own, and Anna led me away. My feet felt like lead, and drawing in breath hurt.

"Let's talk to your dad." The girl pulled me past happy knots of people.

Bus three was surrounded by gray-blue dome tents. The driver lounged across the front seats of her rig, watching an old ball game on the coach's big screen and eating a hot dog.

"Excuse us," Anna said from the top of the stairs. "We're looking for Mr. Johnson?"

The woman's frizzy gray hair matched the bus's exterior. She sat up and pointed her foil-wrapped dog out the left front window. "Right down there. Tents all look the same, but his has the folding table out front. So happy we get our own bean counter from the bureau."

I didn't have the energy to get mad, but shook my head at her derisive snort. Anna had more class.

"Thanks." The girl's smile changed the old woman's demeanor better than anything I would have said.

"Take care, sweetheart." She shrugged, and her sneer softened into an actual smile as she settled back to watch her game.

We circled the bus. The green folding table was easy to spot, as were the stacks of reports neatly filed in boxes underneath.

"Hello?" Anna rapped on the table in lieu of a door.

Muttering and the zing of an arm dragging across nylon came from within before the tent flaps parted. Dad's salt and pepper hair emerged at chest level, followed by his lanky frame. Light spilled out into the darkening gloom as he stood with hands in the middle of his back and stretched.

"Edan!" Dad rushed forward and swept me into a hug.

"Hi, Dad." I patted his shoulder and disengaged from the awkward embrace. "This is Anna Banks."

"Sure, Mom and I met this delightful young lady out at Bryn Mawr yesterday." He shook her hand and gave a bow.

The ache sitting deep in my chest released. *Mom's okay.* The stupid NF tag was an admin foul up. Not surprising given the number of people Meg dealt with and the general chaos. But we needed to be vigilant for little mistakes that carried such an emotional punch.

"We got most of the Eastons out too. Pete's farm is an oasis, but everything else pretty much disappeared. Getting out was a hell of a ride. When we get this show on the road, maybe you and Mom can ride with us—" Dad's frown made me pause. "Or do you have the truck stashed somewhere? That'd be cool too; we can see whose car has more muscle."

Apparently, it was the wrong thing to say too. My dad wasn't a prude by any stretch of the imagination. I'd caught him revving his old blue pickup just to hear it roar. But his face settled into the neutral, disapproving look I'd met as a kid sneaking back from scavenger runs into the city ruins.

"Ed." Dad look away and cleared his throat with a rolling little cough. "Mom didn't come out with us."

"But you met at the hospital." I looked from Anna to Dad.

"We did, but Mom stayed behind."

"Why the hell would she do that?"

None of this made sense. If Mom and Dad had been at hospital evacuation site, they both would have hopped a bus. Knowing my folks, it would have been the last bus, at the last possible moment, but neither was a martyr likely to stay behind just for the hell of it. *They* weren't the ones who'd flirted with depression and suicide.

"You have to understand." Dad laid a hand on my arm, but I pulled away. "Not everyone could leave. A handful of patients were too fragile or dependent on equipment to be moved." His blue eyes glistened, threatening to spill over—yet he smiled. "You know Mom. She wasn't about to leave them. She stayed behind with a doctor and two other volunteers."

The world spun, and I found myself sitting on the ground, one hand on a cool metal table leg.

"We have to go back." As the words left my mouth I tasted the lie.

We'd ridden back through pure desert. No signs of the suburbs remained, no trees, no buildings—not until we'd moved far to the west, well past where Bryn Mawr would have stood. That entire section of town was simply gone. There was nowhere to go back *to*.

Night stole into camp among the buzzing throng. I moved through the motions of helping Quinn set up tents. We'd be pairing up: she and Anna, Manny and Vance, and then me and Pete sharing a tent.

"You okay?" Pete asked later, as we sat in subdued silence. Crickets and frogs chirped from the edges of our expanding little community, but it was getting late enough that most people had crawled into their tents or cars.

"Don't know." I shrugged and studied the grass sprouting between my feet. "What do I do?"

My voice sounded hollow, my words useless. There *was* nothing to do. The desert swallowed her—swallowed the whole damned city—leaving a sandy hole where Mom had been. It wasn't even like the buildings were simply buried and waiting to be exhumed. I'd proven that when Quinn and I dug down to solid ground. Everything was just gone, no logical explanation; this was magic.

"Maybe Koko or the serpent know where stuff goes when it's caught in this thinning veil?"

"I don't think it goes anywhere." I pictured the islands colliding during that impossible gathering. "The realms in my true dream flashed and vanished, like matter touching anti-matter—gone."

"We've seen portals before." Quinn scooted over with Anna in tow. "You can't just assume everyone's dead."

I didn't have strength to argue the point. This was no portal. In spite of the healing spell, my leg ached horribly. I rubbed my knee under the shorts I'd changed into.

"What's this?" I asked as Anna pushed a small box into my hand.

"Some new music, I think." She gave a shy smile and swept a stray lock of blond hair from her face. "From the gift shop at the hospital. We did a sweep for supplies, and I grabbed a souvenir. I like the cover art. Getting it for you just seemed…right."

A battling dragon and knight were barely visible under decades of grime and scratches. How she managed to spot the disk on the shelves was a mystery.

"Thanks. I'll give it a listen before bed."

We talked about the coming move. Mr. Conti decided continuing down to Baltimore gave us the best chance of establishing a semi-permanent residence. He hoped to radio his connections once we got away from the sand. The exodus would start as soon as Meg's team finished their accounting.

I headed to bed wearing earbuds and listening to Anna's compilation album. The tracks were full of hidden gems. A couple graced my childhood collection, but most were new and fresh, with a consistent undertone of quiet, enabling power. Though most of the songs didn't feel right for elemental spells, they made the horrible day a bit more bearable. Even my leg stopped aching by the time I drifted off.

I rolled out of bed feeling refreshed. Oddly, Pete wasn't on his side of the tent. I threw back the flap and squinted into sunshine reflecting off the tall dunes. The tent dissolved as I stepped out, into another dream. Smoke drifted on the dry air, and the fringe of my buckskin vest flared out as I spun to confront the old man sitting cross-legged at the fire.

"Welcome, Edan." Koko mustered a bit of his old joviality, though his eyes drooped with fatigue. "The source of disruption is an ancient medicine shield, a magical artifact lost in the floods of the third world."

Being direct was out of character for the old spirit. He stroked the walking staff lying across his lap. Its symbols flared under his palms, but the effect quickly faded. It was great they'd found the problem, but my mind was elsewhere.

"My Mom disappeared in the desert—several people did. Where'd they go?"

He started, surely thinking I'd meant Ankti, my biological mother and the Hopi woman he had loved so long ago. Then he seemed to understand and sucked in a deep breath, considering the question.

"Colliding realms are unpredictable. Your lands may slip into the third world or simply…cease."

"But they might be alive?" I grabbed the lifeline. "I can get them out."

"If you do not find the shield and stop the process, there will be nowhere to bring them back to. Do this thing first, then worry about your missing people."

"Is this shield out in the desert?" I could look for Mom at the same time.

"Not in the way you mean. The shield is ancient and powerful, crafted from sacred materials in an age when people needed guidance and healing." Fond remembrance gleamed in his eyes. "The people lived in balance. The shield served them well, keeping the lands, waters, and people healthy and productive.

"But as it always does, greed found its way into the good-hearted. Some used the shield and other artifacts for unintended purposes. War shields and lesser medicine shields drew off power, power used to destroy instead of heal." A tear slipped down his left cheek. You would have thought someone—

"*You* made that shield!" I was certain of it.

He nodded ever so slightly. "It had to be abandoned when Sotuknang ordered the third world destroyed, but yet somehow it remains. Now, the worlds merge, and the shield calls in pain and despair for having been twisted so far from its intended purpose. You must travel here." He stood and traced a map in the sand with the tip of his staff. The drawing sprang to life, showing a river winding along the base of a sheer cliff with peaks lost in snow and clouds. "I know little else of the landscape, but have constructed this to help guide you."

Koko gripped his staff, twisted it in two, and held out the upper two feet. The length of wood was warm and prickled with power. As I took it, the carvings on the reminder of his staff dimmed. The old man grunted, and his shoulders dipped as if he'd just caught a heavy sack.

"Everything out in New Philly is desert. There's no mountain."

"None of us know what waits in the third world. The staff head will be your guide after you cross."

"Cross how?"

Instead of answering, Koko drew a spiral in the sand. A wave of his shortened staff stretched the symbol vertically. It glowed sickly green as it swirled and slowed to a stop. The cyclone of energy stood frozen in place, a three-dimensional snapshot of the glowing tornado behind Pete's farm.

If the staff only worked on the other side, I needed to take Ralph at least as far as the farm. I'd been friends with Pete and Quinn too long to fool myself into thinking they wouldn't insist on coming along too.

"Will my magic work in there?"

"Yes, but the effects may be unreliable." He plopped back down into his cross-legged pose, breathing heavy and coaxing power from his staff. "I can speak no more. Be careful, my son."

The staff flared, washing away the map of river and rocks, but leaving the frozen portal to shine green light across the sand—as if I needed a reminder of the chore he'd set for me. Glowing eyes glinted atop a dark muzzle from within the still vortex. I should have felt fear at that otherworldly scrutiny. But if there was to be any chance for my world, for Mom, this was something I needed to do—wanted to do. I'd get back to the farm, find the shield, and what? Destroy it?

"Wait!" Gray fog swirled around my feet, threatening to pull me out of the true dream. "How do I shut it down? You know, stop the shield?"

He gave me one of those enigmatic looks as if the answer should be obvious, then cast his gaze on the fire and disappeared. I opened my mouth, but the gray enveloped me and I fell into a cocoon of nothingness.

This time, I awoke to Pete's snoring, a sure sign I was back in the real world. I kicked his foot to disrupt his next attempt to start a chainsaw. Farmers were supposed to be up at the crack of dawn. Light spilled across the encampment, and people already gathered for Mr. C's big meeting.

"You're looking especially grim today," Quinn said by way of greeting as I staggered out of the tent and nearly tripped over Dwain and Ralph. "What's with the stick?"

The imp and sprite were just outside engaged in slow-motion combat, like tia chi, except they faced each other and connected with soft slaps at hand, wrist, knee, and foot in a parry-and-block dance.

Pina's people were skilled in hand to hand combat. Ralph already moved like lightning in a fight. I cringed at the thought of combining his speed with the sprite's prowess. But it was good to see him taking up a hobby instead of just moping around with Max's old toy rabbit.

"A little gift from father Koko." I stepped around the pair and handed over the club that had been the top of Koko's staff.

"There's power here." Quinn studied the simple carvings of deer, snakes, and what looked like a wolf or coyote, then shivered and handed it back. "It doesn't like me."

"Yeah, right." My smile slipped at her grim expression. "It's supposed to lead me to some ancient medicine shield that's causing the world overlap problem."

I explained what Koko told me and how the vortex behind Pete's farm was in fact the portal into this elusive third world.

"We better take plenty of water," Pete said when I fell silent.

'Wait a minute—"

"And food," Dwain added. "Plus marshmallows for Ralph. He's running low."

"Now, hold on—"

"What's going on here?" Manny asked as he and Vance strode up to join us.

"An expedition into the third world." Quinn went on to summarize my story.

"Hmm, true medicine shields are rare nowadays." Manny scratched his chin and dimples dotted each cheek as he screwed up his face in concentration. "Even with your mini-staff as a guide, this could be dangerous. Magic can attract unwanted attention so we better bring conventional firearms. Vance and Pete, what can you pull together?"

Pete and Quinn coming along was inevitable. I supposed the same went for Dwain and Ralph, but Manny and Vance wanting to tag along was a bit much. Getting a word in proved difficult as the group discussed what we'd need. Piper even joined us and whipped out her notebook to start a list of supplies.

"Can't believe we're back up to six people," I said as Quinn and I headed for the meeting.

"Seven, counting Ralph. Stop grumbling. Everyone wants to help, and you get extra firepower in case things go wrong."

"True." I swung a leg over the rusting guardrail near Pioneer. Mr. C wanted his team leads up front. "I just don't want anyone getting hurt. Plus we're already doubled up on the damned ATVs."

"You don't think the cop and farm boy can hold their own?" Quinn raised an incredulous eyebrow. "They can't sling spells or handle swarms, but anything big is going to make a nice fat target."

I exhaled through my teeth and nodded. Red Team only had Manny's magic to fall back on, and by all reports they seldom had need of it. Pete and his trusty pump-action shotgun had gotten me out of a few jams, especially when he loaded up with rock salt—the darker critters really hated that. We hadn't tried the salt trick on creatures from the third world, but if they were as corrupt as Koko claimed, the mineral should disrupt their magic just fine.

"Settle down everyone!" Billy's voice boomed from the band's speakers.

With a thousand people spread across the old terminal, amplification was a necessity. Faces turned to the tall man as a hush fell and the boss stepped up. Billy nodded, shaggy beard splaying across his chest, and stepped back from the microphone stand.

A ripple of laughter swept through the crowd. Mr. Conti's pursed lips set his whiskers on end as he glared at Billy, reached high over his head, and collapsed the stand down to a reasonable height. Billy looked mortified, but relaxed when Mr. C winked. The boss knew the power of comedic relief.

"That's better." He stopped the mic just below his chin and swept out an arm. "These are sad times, but I am so very proud of how you have all pulled together. We've lost, and grieved, and persevered. Now, my friends, it is time we found a new home."

Nodding heads were accompanied by grumbling and a few cat calls. Not everyone was pleased about leaving, but what choice did they have? It was either move on, or stay and disappear.

"I know how you feel. Our homes are here, our traditions live here, and our hearts ache. Cheese steaks, soft pretzels, and raviolis are our food. We pride ourselves on hard work, family, and dare I ask if a few mummers still dance on New Year's Day?" That earned chuckles, and an old man with pants hiked up to his armpits by garish suspenders strutted in a circle while other old timers in folding chairs slapped their knees. "These things we do—things we make—come with us. Our heritage is in us and will rise in another New Philadelphia."

"Where?" a woman with wild gray hair called from the front.

"First stop is Baltimore."

Mr. Conti assured them we would use every means possible to locate a place meeting our needs. We'd talk to other towns, but also speak directly with truckers and maintenance crews to ensure the location was accessible and well maintained.

No one was happy. Most just wanted life to go back to normal. The undercurrent of concern wasn't just due to being dislocated; there was palpable fear of the unknown and the supernatural force driving us out. Yet, there were smiles and laughter as a portable mic passed through the crowd and people asked questions or made recommendations. They turned away from the absurdity to focus on the task at hand, more than happy to wall off things that couldn't be explained.

In the end, the plan didn't change. A few suggestions to detour around bad roads and juggle vehicle assignments proved useful. But such a large group did not make an effective committee. The migration would continue in the morning as planned. We'd have a truly impressive string of vehicles. Our convoluted route to Baltimore was less than a hundred miles. Not that I was heading that way.

Since Pioneer already powered the A-Chords' speaker stacks, they closed the meeting with an impromptu show. Nobody wanted to slog back to their tents and worry about tomorrow. Chairs and blankets materialized as an air of comradery settled over those that stayed. Billy kept the volume down. I usually considered talking during a performance rude, but the low buzz of conversation meant people were pulling together.

"Are you leaving when the first group heads out?" Piper asked when the band took a break.

"I think that's best. Ralph can steer us to the farm, but who knows how many twists and turns there'll be along the way. We won't be lucky enough to score another sheltered cemetery if nightfall catches us on the dunes."

"I've been thinking about that place. You felt power there, but nothing elemental?"

"Definitely not elemental. There weren't any distinct flows with sharp edges. The place was saturated with quiet energy." I shrugged away the effort to describe it in more detail.

"I bet the Easton farm had the same feel."

"No, their farmhouse was bustling—totally different." *But was it?* People had been climbing all over Pete's place, sealing the structures, repairing the tractor, and gathering supplies. I thought back to the quiet times when Pete and I sprawled on the floor to sleep. It *had* felt secure and inviting despite being surrounded by desert and critters from another dimension. "Well, maybe it did feel similar. What are you thinking?"

"Ancestral energy." Piper beamed, her enthusiasm for the occult shining through. "I bet that's what both places have. Generations walking the same path, reinforcing traditions and customs—even when it comes to burying their dead—adds power bit by bit.

"Over time, the thresholds and perimeter of such places become hardened, immune to entry by evil. It's the same with sacred ground, all that ceremony and reverence translates to power, and when it's the same family, the same bloodline—poof, instant sanctuary!"

"I just hope it lasts when nobody's home," I said as Charles tapped out a beat and counted the band into the next number. "If the farm disappeared after we left, it might mess up Ralph's navigation."

Our friendly kung-fu-learning imp sat on my shoulder nibbling a marshmallow. Meg had sent me down to the stores bus to outfit our party. Whoever had the marshmallow fetish must have thought we'd be singing songs and cooking over a campfire for years to come. Grabbing a few bags of the fluffy treats didn't even make a dent.

"How's Dad doing?" I asked, breaking my own rule about not talking over the band.

He'd put on a good front about Mom staying behind, but his sad eyes and the little cough whenever the topic arose told me the truth.

"He's a trooper, but it's hard." Piper sagged against me and idly ruffled Ralph's ears. "Do you think we'll find her in there?"

"*We* will certainly try," I said to highlight the fact my sister would not be on this mission, no matter how much she insisted. "You keep Dad and the others safe. They need experienced eyes, someone who won't let their brain dismiss what they see. You can spot issues with the world veil and Dark Court players better than anyone."

She seemed on the verge of arguing, let out a big breath, and handed Ralph another treat. We both smiled as the imp lapped at the marshmallow with his skinny, forked tongue—a sure sign he was full.

But the little guy never passed up a treat. Soon enough, Ralph lost his self-control and a moment later frowned at his empty hand.

The other hand was on his taut, round stomach, which gurgled as something close to a moan escaped him. Ralph didn't get full often, but when he did it usually resulted in a stomach ache. Piper swept him into her lap as he hugged his middle and thrashed. The theatrics would only last a minute thanks to his hyper-fast metabolism. Anna, Manny, and Pete were among the few who turned to watch.

Although the imp came and went with impunity among the townspeople, it was clear he only let himself be seen by certain individuals—be they Bright, human, or other. Manny was one of those others. And so was Dwain, who skipped over to check on his small friend. Everyone could see Dwain, but—much like Pina—his magic aura put people at ease and simply kept them from wondering about his size and origins.

"You know he can't resist." Dwain shot us both a reproachful look.

"Ralph has access to candy twenty-four-seven thanks to his magic pockets," I said. "We just gave him the marshmallows you asked for."

Dwain shook his head as he knelt to examine the imp. "Just give him the whole bag next time. If it's more than he can hold, he'll squirrel them away. Out of sight is out of mind. If you hand him one at a time, he'll eat until he bursts."

What Dwain said made sense. Ralph never left sweets just lying around. Early on, I'd decided he had a secret bottomless storage method. Although candy appeared from his magic stash more often than not, the few times he'd gotten sick could well have been when I'd metered out his treats—ironically to keep him from gorging.

"I should have figured that out earlier."

Ralph's thrashing slowed. He sat up looking much improved and eyed the two bags of marshmallows peeking out from behind Piper. I grabbed both and, after a moment's hesitation, ripped the plastic bags open and dumped two pounds of spongy sugar into my sisters lap, filling the space between her crossed legs.

"Hey! A little warning would be nice!" Piper glared at me. "I don't need ants deciding I'm their new dining room."

"Sorry."

I gave a shrug of apology and bent to re-bag the marshmallows. They were gone. Ralph leaned against her knee with arms crossed over his chest. Fang tips poked from the corners of his self-satisfied grin. The little guy certainly hadn't eaten all that in the blink of an eye.

"You sure called that one, Dwain." I stuffed the empty bags in my pocket and joined the spatter of applause as the current song ended on a keyboard flourish.

"We're going to take a short break," Billy announced. His voice came through the speakers with scratchy feedback that made everyone wince. He tapped the mic—standard troubleshooting procedure—producing staccato explosions from the speakers. "Sorry, a short lunch break and we'll play one more set this—"

The feedback grated like nails on a chalkboard and drowned out his words. Billy quickly unplugged the mic and speakers. Impossibly, the noise continued, like being inside a tin can full of marbles or—

"Sand!" The cry came from the back of the audience nearest camp.

13. The More the Merrier

T HE SAND came on fast, sluicing down the creek running
through base camp. Most of the cars were on the far side, but
the parking lot around Pioneer held a dozen vehicles including our little
pack of ATVs.

"If it's coming up the streams, the river's not far behind," Dwain
said.

Mr. Conti stood onstage in frantic discussion with the band. He
called something out, but there was no way to hear him over the
panicked crowd. Billy stepped up and sucked in a huge lungful of air.

"Everyone to your vehicles. Move out now!" His bellow cut
through the bedlam. "Let's be orderly. Lend a hand to those who need
it."

The simple act of providing direction calmed much of the panic.
People hustled across the intersection over the stream. Engines roared
to life throughout camp as the word spread. Thanks to Meg's and Mr.
Conti's organization, we were ready to go on a moment's notice. And it
looked like that moment was upon us. Manny and Vance headed for
the ATVs.

"Dwain, set Ralph up. Quinn and I will join you. We need to get to
the Pennsylvania side before sand undermines the bridge." I turned to

Piper. "Take care of Dad. We'll firespeak if we can, but that's been a crap shoot. If I don't—" I didn't know how to finish the thought.

"You'll be back, little brother." She gave me a fierce hug. "Just don't take unnecessary chances."

Pioneer's big diesel fired up, effectively ending any further discussion. Piper broke away and headed for the RV, while Quinn jogged over and we went to meet the rest of our small expedition.

By mutual agreement, we sat astride our idling rides watching cars and buses head south. Dust clouds billowed up obscuring much of the scene. Pioneer lined up behind the cars crossing the stream. The wide, shallow waterway ran brown with clots of sand. Three cars crossed the intersection and merged into the fleeing traffic, but the next one in line slammed on its brakes. Brake lights cascaded all the way back to Pioneer as the procession came to an abrupt halt.

Thunder rumbled over the thrum of engines. Rather than rolling off into the distance, the roar grew louder. Off to our left, where the stream bank curved around a point covered in tightly-packed pines, brown clouds roiled low. Beneath them raced a twenty-foot-high wall of sand.

White backup lights sprang to life on the RV and cars at the end of the line. I thought for sure they'd crash into each other, but miraculously everyone reversed in unison and gained enough separation for each to start a three point turn. Honking and pointing drew the other drivers' attention to the threat, and the remaining cars slammed into reverse—all except the red sports car that had been about to cross. The dark-haired driver looked to his passenger, then back out at the speeding wall of sand. He gunned the engine and surged forward, but his rear wheels slipped in sand blowing across the road. He fishtailed toward the intersection, refusing to yield.

Halfway across, the wave slammed into the small bridge. Cement guardrails exploded in a spray of sand. Fragments of concrete shattered the left side windows a split second before the tidal wave smashed through the crossing and the car vanished. The dune slid on to our right, obscuring the fleeing refugees.

"Manny and Vance, get these cars in line with Pioneer. We have to get out of here." I scanned the grim faces of our little group.

We needed to cross the Delaware Memorial before we got cut off. The band and cars could escape down the Pennsylvania side. It wasn't a direct route, but at this point the objective was to get away from the desert. They could worry about hooking up with the others later.

Camp was just over a mile from the river. Rusted metal girders loomed ahead, supporting the graceful arc of suspension wires that held the bridge surface. Rust and moss dripped from the cables, and many of the vertical wires had snapped and lay curled on the roadway or dangled over the side.

"We'll have to split off once we cross," I said over my shoulder. "Keep your eyes peeled for a good spot to pull over. There ought to be enough room just past the old toll booths."

Quinn nodded just as our front right tire dipped into a nice deep pothole. Her head cracked into mine with a painful crunch, making me wish we'd strapped on helmets. I focused on the rutted bridge, picking a path through potholes and strewn rubble to give the street vehicles a fighting chance.

"Water's cloudy," Quinn studied the river as openings in the guardrails flashed past. "I think it's—"

The roadway lurched left. I knew without looking that the wall of sand had just smashed into the bridge's foundation. The roar of tons of sand echoed through clouds of dust rising like smoke to either side. The roadway bucked and swayed, and I imagined dunes piling high around its supports.

A glimpse downstream showed the river's surface changing from rippling white caps, to brown sludge, to flowing sand sprouting tufts of spikey green plants.

I took the leftmost lane through the ruined toll booths, slowed, and scanned the roadway for an exit heading south. The street signs were little help. Most of the massive green placards had rotted or blown away. Aluminum posts arched overhead like the dull gray ribs of some massive dinosaur. I stood on the floorboards to look down the road curving off the far right lane.

"Aw crap!"

"We're trapped," Quinn said, echoing my own thoughts.

Eight lanes merged down to four with spurs curving off to right and left. Each exit lane extended perhaps thirty yards before disappearing into a rising dune. Sand glimmered beyond the elevated surface on both sides. Even the main roadway vanished a hundred yards ahead where it turned to unbroken desert stretching off into the distance. We stopped. We had to.

Billy and the band piled out of their RV, and more than a dozen people spilled from the cars that followed. Pete's sister Melissa and her friend Brent hopped out of a pickup. Brent waved at Ralph—of all people. When I'd first met the buff blue-eyed redhead I'd unfairly judged him a stuck-up frat boy with a weak stomach. But he'd proven me wrong, helped us come to terms with Ralph, and adjusted remarkably well to the supernatural strangeness we'd thrust upon the poor guy. The fact he could see Ralph meant that even our imp had accepted him.

"You tried to ditch me," Melissa clomped up and punched Pete in the arm.

"Little sisters are like boomerangs coated with superglue." Pete dodged her second swing, then turned to me. "So, fearless leader, what now?"

"Level up our skills and horde weapons." It was a stupid kneejerk answer from our video gaming days. A mix of smiles and scowls flickered through my small audience, yet they still hung on my every word. *Since when was I in charge?* "Well, the cars with four-wheel drive might do okay on the sand, but…" I waved at the hulking outline of the band's ride, at a loss for words.

Familiar faces graced our group. Anna must have been backstage during the show, and Maggie Parker's curly gray-blond hair was easy to spot because I'd stopped at her bakery for a jelly doughnut every chance I got. I couldn't put a name to several others. *So much for a small expedition.*

"We could go back," Brent offered. "Maybe catch one of the rural roads between the river and camp."

All heads turned to the rippling sand beach that had been the Delaware River. Rising dust enveloped the stanchions and suspension cables halfway across.

"Don't think that's an option," Pete said.

Manny climbed back over the guardrail off to my right and joined the group. I hadn't seen him leave and couldn't believe he'd risked walking out onto the sand without backup.

"We're cut off all right." He jerked a thumb at a rusting skeleton rising above the roadway. "I climbed that old billboard. It's desert as far as I could see."

"Damn it, we need Bertha," Pete said.

"Unfortunately, she's back at base camp. Any other ideas?" I worried we didn't have enough daylight to make the farm.

A hunched figure in the back, an old man with face averted, reminded me of Koko. It would be just like the old trickster to slip into our group, but the profile was wrong. Although his hat was pulled low, the protruding nose was bulbous rather than beak-like and scruffy whiskers covered craggy skin from cheeks to chin. He pulled his cap lower and tried to hide behind Reggie, the retired police mechanic.

"Mr. Conti, any ideas?" My question forced a wry grin from my boss, who simply shook his head and waved for us to continue brainstorming.

"A spray of water could harden the top layers," Quinn said. "Maybe enough to support cars, but I'm guessing Pioneer is a lost cause."

"It's risky, but I could bring up some calcium and other compounds to further strengthen the surface and make a sort of poor man's concrete." I'd used the trick to reinforce weak spots in the crumbling sidewalls of my fountain. If Quinn could dredge up enough water, we might just be in business—assuming using Earth magic here where the worlds already overlapped didn't cause monumental problems. But first I needed to address the strange looks being directed my way. "You've all seen or at least heard it's true. Some of us can perform magic. Honest to goodness spells to help."

Manny swung away either in disgust at the blatant statement or in some dark-court snit over me using the term "goodness." But people already knew, even if they didn't admit it. Sometimes it was easier to ignore the obvious, to simply not talk about the elephant in the room. But we were out of options and didn't have that luxury.

A murmur ran through the group. I braced for backlash but none came. Anna beamed, while Billy smirked. Even Jinx looked nonplussed, so I figured Billy and he had been talking. On the other hand, Charles' eye held a nasty glimmer as though he'd outed some secret, which of course was ridiculous.

"Hold on a minute." Reggie stepped forward and poked me in the chest with a long boney finger, hard enough that I'd probably have a bruise. "You all are making this too goddamn hard!"

Vance snickered at the old man's ire, which earned him a glare. But I'd seen this interplay between the two back at the station. The game was similar to good-cop bad-cop, only this was more like young-whippersnapper-cop cranky-old-mechanic.

"How so?" I asked.

"Look back there." He puffed out his chest and pointed at our assembly of mismatched vehicles. "That blue POS truck has a four-wheel-drive off-road package, them three sedans are electronic all-wheel imports, and my Jeep could climb the Appalachians. And of course *my* ATVs will eat up the dunes.

"We just let some air outta their tires, put 'em in low gear, and keep the momentum—that's important, gotta keep moving or these city cars *will* bog down. Then we'll be digging our way to China tryin' to get moving again."

"Makes sense," Pete said. "When the fields are mud, we bleed air from the tires too. Spreads out the footprint so more rubber contacts the ground."

"Exactly!" Reggie beamed. "No need to wizard us across, just use common sense and we'll be fine. I've hauled world-class racers out of worse places than this without special gear. Keeping the speed up is critical, but not too fast. And if your tires start slipping, for God's sake don't gun it."

Our resident expert gave the drivers a fifteen minute crash course on everything from dealing with slopes to braking and keeping momentum so they didn't dig into the soft terrain. Mr. Conti held a whispered discussion with Brent, handed the man his keys, and came over.

"Someone younger can drive my car," he said by way of preamble. "I was taught to drive in the old country with a…let's just say no-holds-barred approach."

I raised an eyebrow as concern settled over his features, bringing an uncharacteristic sternness.

"Brent's a solid man, good choice."

"That is not what worries me. Edan, we cannot all go where you go."

That put an awfully fine point on a problem that worried me too. Presumably this new stretch of desert linked up with the vast expanse surrounding the Easton's farm. By the look of things, cutting the others loose to head south wasn't in the cards. Driving across the desert would attract unwanted attention that those without magic were ill equipped to handle.

"I'm hoping we can leave you and the rest at Pete's farm. Piper thinks the desert stays off it due to some ancestral strengthening of the surrounding thresholds. I honestly don't know what will be left after we deal with the problem on the other side. Hopefully the third world will just close up and things here will go back to normal."

"Your sister's quite the thinker. Generational energy explains a lot." He scratched at his stubble in thought, looking for all the world like Piper puzzling over her mystic theories. "It would be interesting to see if the Amish farm also survived. Meg didn't have any of them on her rosters."

"The Millers? They're farther out than the Eastons. I sure hope they managed. Will you check on them? You know…if I'm not able."

Mr. Conti slapped me on the back and slid his hand up to squeeze my shoulder. "We'll check on them together when this is over."

"Thanks," I said around a lump in my throat.

Fitting everyone into five cars was a struggle, but we managed. Ralph, Quinn, and I took point so the imp could steer us through the shifting desert. Following his directions was much easier with him pointing ahead instead of behind us. Reggie's Jeep led the "clown cars"—as Manny called them—to set the proper pace. Manny and Vance brought up the rear, while Pete and Dwain ranged to either side watching for trouble.

Trouble didn't keep us waiting long. We'd only been riding for twenty minutes when two dark groups flickered in the distance. I figured we'd run into the bugs that tried to block our exit. Scorpions wouldn't cause the cars any trouble and with a little care the ATVs could plow through. Details were hard to make out from a distance, but these stood tall and moved slower—something new.

Preparing for the encounter was difficult while constantly turning in response to Ralph's fickle finger. One minute we'd accelerate straight toward a group and the next we'd be angling away.

Unlike shamblers, the first group moved with a stiff-legged gait, swinging arms and legs as if they were too heavy to lift properly. And they probably were because the closer we drew the more it looked like the massive creatures were made of stone—tan granite flecked with black. The grainy surface didn't extend to hands and face. The meaty fists stuck on the end of each stone arm were baked black by the desert sun and all too human looking except for their massive size and thick yellow nails.

Dark vertical folds creased the skin to either side of blunt noses, making their faces look wooden. The barrel stone of each torso merged into similarly dark skin along the upper chest. Each stood better than seven feet and was easily half that wide.

I steered us away from the stone horde, but slowed as Ralph urged us toward the second group, which consisted of true shamblers. Long fur hung from each as though they wore threadbare parkas. Their hobbled gait looked painful, but ate up ground.

I considered ignoring the imp and steering clear. Ralph would reorient on the farm, but we ran along a steep ridgeline. Reggie warned us about the roll-over threat. Plus, making the farm before dark remained imperative. Fire leapt to my fingers along with the driving beat from Fall Out Boy's "Light 'Em Up."

Fire wouldn't slow the stone giants, but the greasy shamblers were another story. Flames encased my fingers as we drove onward. I threw a spear of flame at the lead shambler. It turned with a fierce screech, exposing pointed teeth set in a round mouth under a porcine nose. Manny and Vance rode up on my left, a rooster tail of sand spitting high off their rear wheels. The manager pointed his knife over the handlebars, sending out his own lance of fire.

The shamblers slowed, but refused to move out of the way even though three of them burned. Ralph bobbed and coaxed me onward. Manny and I poured on more fire, forcing them back. Just as they were about to break up, a figure rose in the midst of the group.

Cloaked in black and taller than the shamblers by half, the newcomer raised its arms high, and a shield of sand rose to meet our flames. The cloaked figure flicked a boney hand, and a ribbon of sand coiled like a serpent in our path. Ralph snarled and brandished his knife. Fast as lightning the serpent struck, not at me, but at the front tire. It jammed between wheel and fender forming a solid wedge of sand, and I launched over the handlebars.

Ralph flew wide, but Quinn yelped and bounced off my back as air whooshed from my lungs. The fire element winked out as did Manny's lance when his own ATV spun off to the left.

In a moment the lead shambler was on me. It spread its arms wide. Loose skin connecting arms to torso flared out to block my view. Hooks lined the folds of skin like some crazed fisherman selling illicit goods from beneath his trench coat—except these bit into my shoulders as those long arms wrapped around me. Three round mouths ringed with serrated teeth opened in its chest. The thing reeked of burnt rubber and rotten meat.

A rifle cracked loud, and the fur over one mouth exploded with dark ichor. Two more reports sent the thing stumbling back. Pete and Vance unloaded their long rifles into the group. The spectral figure at its center again raised its arms and swirling sand obscured their targets.

I felt the magic as an oily parody of the Earth element. The power felt corrupt and defiled, and anger rose within me. I was sick of sand, dealing with it, crossing it, and now having it used against me. This demon deserved a taste of pure untainted Earth. My left shoulder burned, but this time I ignored my nagging tattoo's warning.

Crashing drums, guitar, and bass brought my vision to life with Metallica's "Enter Sandman." I hadn't touched Earth in too long. The power flowed thick like honey and smashed into the ground. The impact sent sand and shamblers flying.

The demon staggered, but brought its greasy shields to bear, deflecting the worst of my attack. I spun a column of sand into a spear that ripped through the oily magic and pierced the thing's chest. Startled hazel eyes met mine and then the demon dissolved, leaving a sandy pile beneath its ragged cloak.

I sagged, feeling as if a hole had been torn through my own chest, and struggled to ground the spell. An insulating layer kept the power from rushing into the earth. Instead, it swept into a void opening beneath the sand. The ground shuddered and sank, threatening to swallow our entire party.

More shots rang out. Without the demon's protection, the shamblers fell back. My ATV had flipped twice and sat upright. The engine coughed and sputtered to life with smoky backfires, and I had to bend the fenders off the tires. Ralph vaulted onto the tank and Quinn climbed up behind me.

"Get moving!" Manny yelled. "Bullets and fire aren't going to faze the Nargun rock trolls."

Ralph jabbed his stone knife off to the right, and I kicked us into gear, risking a glance back to ensure the cars followed. They did, climbing the sides of the expanding depression. I sighed in relief as the last car plowed over the lip of the sinkhole. Although the shamblers had scattered, the phalanx of stone creatures broke into a lumbering run. The imp whipped his arm left and right, sending us through an invisible gauntlet. When I again was able to look back, our pursuers had vanished.

An hour later, one of the cars lost traction and we were forced to stop. The white cross-over revved despite Reggie's warnings, and the gnarly old driver looked pissed. I almost laughed at his passengers' startled faces as the car sank to its axles. What wasn't fun was the prospect of digging the car free. We pulled into a loose defensive circle. I rolled my neck, trying to relieve the burning ache.

"You hunch over the handlebars." Quinn ran her hands across my shoulders, pulled me up straight, and kneaded with her thumbs. It felt wonderful. "You'd be in the hospital if you tried an iron-butt run."

"Are cross-country motorcycle rides still a thing?"

"Nothing official, but how do you think I got out here from New Mexico? Try to ride loose in the saddle. Your body will thank you for it." Her magic fingers dug deep once more, and she patted my back. "Time to put those guns and broad shoulders to use."

The ache was back with a vengeance, and I dripped sweat by the time we freed Mr. Leadfoot. The loss of traction wasn't all the driver's fault. Everyone's tires heated up as the day wore on, and higher pressure meant less grip. Reggie bled another five pounds of air out of every tire before we drove on into our own lengthening shadows.

The scorpions came with the setting sun, a dark stain under the next dune. Rather than waste time discussing the problem, we simply plowed on. Our steady pace crunched through the vermin, and this time I had the presence of mind to throw out a bit of Spirit energy to keep the critters from kicking up onto my frame.

"Fence posts!" Quinn cried as we topped the dune.

Shadows slanted away from posts sticking out of the sand like a surreal ladder marching off into the distance—each successive rung a bit longer than the last, each post a little higher out of the sand. Far down at the end of the fence squatted a white house and stone barn. I gunned the throttle, which lifted the front wheels for a split second. Quinn yelped and grabbed tight.

"Sorry." I eased up, but a goofy grin stretched my face despite the blush of embarrassment. *We made it.*

14. Crossing Over

T HE EASTON farm still stood strong—sort of. A strange white mesh covered much of the old clapboard siding as well as the barn doors. We approach cautiously, and I fingered the silky material.

"Any ideas?" I asked when a white sheet pulled away with my hand.

"Mold?" Piper sounded unsure.

I slapped the sticky stuff against my pant leg and studied the front porch. The material coated the walls and the porch ceiling, seeming to extend from a denser funnel near the upper right corner. Vance shined a flashlight across the corner where a small frog statue sat atop the support. Something glinted from within the funnel.

Piper stood on tiptoe to get a closer look, but neither she nor I was tall enough. Billy strode over and wedged between us. His head nearly touched the low ceiling. The stuff inside glinted again, shifted, and a furry form shot out.

"Crap!" Billy threw his arms up and fell back.

A gray blur shot along the wood railing and intercepted the thing just before it hit Billy. The pair thudded against the front window. Ralph snarled and hissed as if yelling into the face of the shiny black thing he'd tackled. But the giant spider couldn't hear the imp's rebuke, thanks to the knife buried in its head.

"Damned thing's as big as Ralph!" Piper said.

"Funnel web spiders, but massive." Pete pointed to more funnels extending from above the shutters.

We cleared the porch and swept the entire exterior before daring to enter. Ralph really hated these things. He took out two more while we worked our way around. Manny and I fried another half dozen by the time the light failed.

"Heads up tonight everyone," I warned as we entered. "Stay in pairs. We'll sweep the house and set a watch."

Our search inside turned up nothing worse than a few mice and normal little house spiders. Even the dusty walk-up attic held no surprises. Quinn and I checked that out, which was when I realized flaming a giant spider in an old wood house might not be the best idea.

"All rooms are clear." Piper designated the kitchen table as command central. "I think the thresholds are still holding. Those spiders might just have gotten bold because of the lack of activity." She flipped through her book, scribbled a note, and chewed on her pencil. "Ed, is the clearing around the house as wide as the other day?"

"Yeah, it's about the same." I thought about the fence as we'd ridden out with Big Bertha. *Hadn't there been a handful of posts fully exposed along the drive?* "Or maybe thirty feet narrower."

Mr. Conti and Piper set up the watch schedule. No one slated to go through the portal in the morning pulled duty. I'd like to say we all got a good night's sleep, but nerves and excitement kept most of us up half the night. Dwain might have been the exception. Although he shared Pina's childlike wonder and reveled in exploring the farmhouse treasures, the sprite curled up around eleven. When sleep finally came my way, it was a fitful, elusive thing that left me sore and drained.

"Anna's your only way to contact us," Piper said for the tenth time as we readied the ATVs. "Keep testing her link as you pass through the portal."

"I will, Sis. And you watch that shrinking perimeter. Pete figures there's about two weeks' worth of food and water. You'll have to make a call if the sand reaches the house. Don't worry about us, just push south until you're clear of the desert."

"Assuming we can even cross over." Pete stared out across the sand. "Why's the vortex flashing like that?"

We had stability problems, not just with the sand slowly closing in on the house—we'd lost another twenty feet overnight—but with the portal itself. The frozen green tornado dimmed and pulsed to an erratic beat, sputtering as though losing power.

"Trust me, we'll get through." No sense being negative. "Koko would have sent a sleepy-time telegram last night if there was going to be a problem."

"I guess." Pete looked unconvinced. "Hey, Piper, there's bug spray in the barn. Might help keep the eight-legged nightmares at bay."

"Yep, give me a can and I'll go Annie Oakley on them." Piper fired off imaginary shots with thumbs and forefingers.

"No joke. We've got high-test concentrate in yellow jugs along the back wall. Directions are on the sprayers. We took down thousands of those locusts last year. Of course there were billions of them so…" Pete trailed off and cleared his throat. "Have whoever douses the foundation wear a mask or they'll be twitching for a week."

My sister looked like she might say more, wrapped me in a hug, and headed for the barn. She'd argued half-heartedly about going with us, but even Piper could get too much of a good thing.

"Do you really think we'll be able to firespeak?" Anna asked when Piper was out of earshot.

"I doubt it. We lost that ability when the sand got between our lookouts. I'm going to be busy as we approach the portal, and who knows what waits on the other side." I pulled out my speaking candle and lashed it between the handlebars. "Keep talking as we head out, say every five minutes. I'll shoot back a quick mental nod if I hear you."

"What if I lose you?"

"Maybe check in every hour or so. Like I said, I don't think we'll be able to talk, but you never know. The portal is acting pretty strange, maybe something's changing."

All too soon, our rides were ready and everyone mounted up. Mr. Conti came to see us off. I admired my old boss's calm demeanor in the face of crisis. Even now, he looked more interested than worried.

"Thanks for all your support Mr. C." I shook the hand he extended. "Not just for me, the whole town owes you big time."

"We each do what we can. Be watchful on the other side, Edan. Little is known of the worlds that came before. Your sprite may be your best resource." Dwain waved from the back of Pete's ATV, shamelessly listening in. "But also trust yourself. You've grown into a fine man with good instincts. Few could have handled our evacuation so well."

"That was mostly you and Meg. I just helped people-wrangle."

"Don't sell yourself short. You brought order to the madness and showed the town we have a chance against the desert. You can't see it, but your very presence fortified and energized people who may have otherwise been driven mad by the notion of magic and monsters." He placed a hand on my chest. "Trust in your abilities."

Others said their goodbyes, and everyone gathered to watch us ride out. The portal flashed and flickered, daring us to approach. Chugging across the two hundred yards took forever, and the frozen funnel cloud rose higher as the minutes passed.

"Ed, can you still hear me?" Anna's firespeak had a muffled quality now that we were halfway across the stretch of sand.

"Weaker than last time." I reached over Ralph and slipped a hand onto the candle, but the link didn't strengthen.

"Same on this end. Your voice is kind of fuzzy." Even that sounded weaker than her prior statement.

"Keep talking, but I think the link is fading."

She launched into a poem. By the third line, I recognized the lyrics came from the A-Chords' latest hit. With each verse her voice grew notably weaker until it was a whisper against my mind.

"Anna?"

Nothing.

"We just lost contact with the farm," I told Quinn.

"Better than you thought though. Now the real fun starts."

Our three ATVs stopped thirty feet shy of the towering emerald column. Even up close it resembled a frozen tornado, but big chucks of debris were suspended in the dirty swirls within. Most had arms and legs.

"Are those what I think they are?" Quinn leaned in close to whisper the words.

The creatures we'd encountered out on the sand were trapped within the funnel cloud like insects in amber. Of course, many of them *were* bugs. Scorpions, centipedes, and other insects we hadn't had the misfortune to meet hung suspended along with the odd shambler and troll—or Nargun, as Manny called the aboriginal monsters. Others I didn't recognize were scattered into the distance above.

"They're watching," Pete said.

The closest shambler glared down, studying us, as did the pair of Nargun hanging upside down above it. It was impossible to tell what the bugs might be focused on, but the intense feeling of being watched had the hair on the back of my neck standing. One pair of golden eyes in particular bored into me. The creature's body was lost in the haze within, but those intense eyes glowed just above the sand.

"Do we just ride in?" Pete asked.

"Manny?" I looked to the road manager. "Ever seen anything like this in the Dark Court?"

"Portals? Sure." He looked the vortex up and down, extended a hand palm out, and shook his head. "Doesn't feel special. I doubt it's really a tornado. Containing that force would take a lot of physical energy. This resonates like any other portal—despite the constant dimming."

"Yeah, I don't sense anything special either." Except all those watching eyes.

I didn't feel any magic at all—certainly nothing elemental. The only other portal I'd encountered had been guarded by an Earth spirit and registered much differently on my magical senses. This construct looked pretty much the same when I stared right at it as it did when I let my eyes go unfocused and tried a true-seeing. The insects and bugs dissolved from sight, leaving only those creatures with power suspended in the glowing vortex along with that pair of golden eyes at ground level.

"Nothing here either," Quinn said.

"I say onward!" Dwain stood behind Pete, brandishing one of his machetes and looking like a knight ready to joust.

The sprite's weapon reminded me of Koko's artifact. I yanked the staff head from the holster on my belt. The carvings along its length remained dark no matter how hard I concentrated and cursed under my breath. It simply looked like an attractive piece of folk art.

"Let's go with Dwain's plan." I shifted the staff to my left hand, figuring I could handle it while driving. "Slow and abreast. All eyes on those creatures. If they drop on us—wait!" I'd forgotten all about my hiding spell.

Initially, that spell had given me trouble, but over the last few months I'd perfected the Spirit shield to the point I could extend it to others. The spell drew on Tokpela, the nothingness before creation, to cloak me from prying eyes and magical detection. Though not foolproof, it had gotten me out of a few tight spots.

I drew from the music that had powered my morning ritual for months and worked my way through the group. Rather than trying to cast a massive single shield, I placed a quick obscuring layer over each individual, tying the mini-spells off to the glowing point of the aura just below the sternum. The spell would draw a small bit of energy from each person's heart chakra, which I had learned the hard way was the safest anchor point.

"You may feel a little tired, but you'll get used to it. I'll cancel these spells if things are safe on the far side. Even if I don't, they'll fade and be gone by tomorrow unless I refresh them."

Already the eyes of our jelly jar full of suspended watchers slipped away. I skipped over Dwain and Ralph, figuring each had their own protections. When I got to Manny I hesitated and the music faltered. I wasn't an expert at reading auras, but his shone pink as fresh salmon, which seemed an odd color. And instead of six clear chakra, his scattered into a dozen lesser nodes of light. I didn't have a clue where to tie off the spell.

"Don't burst a blood vessel, slick." Manny gave me a wry smile. "I'll whip up something on my own."

I turned the half-formed spell on myself and added the two extra layers I usually used. The Tokpela billowed out in nested bubbles, shimmered in my Sight, and settled into an invisible cloak that conformed to my movement. By the time my last spell snapped into place, a blank spot sat astride Manny's ATV. I could still see him, but he was undetectable to my magical senses.

"Looks like we're ready." I strode back to my ATV.

Quinn leaned on the handlebars and grinned, having apparently decided to drive. Ralph perched on the luggage rack extending over the headlights, looking like the masthead of an ancient Viking vessel. I shrugged and climbed on the back. Wielding the staff and magic would be easier with my hands free.

The watchers scanned the desert, ignoring—or not noticing—our approach. All eyes looked outward, except those golden, glowing orbs set in a dark muzzle. Those still tracked our group, burned into us—into me—despite my spell. Few creatures could pierce a veil of Tokpela, and I didn't relish meeting one.

My skin itched as we crossed the border between worlds. Everything went dim, and the muted green light flashed overhead as if we stood in a lightning storm. But it was lightning in a bottle, trapped by the swirling circular boundary. There was motion inside. Not the torrent of activity you might expect within a tornado, but misty particles drifted from the sand in a steady upward flow.

"Everyone okay?" My voice came out flat.

"Good over here," Pete said as he flipped on his headlights. Quinn and Manny followed suit. "Is this fog?"

"Must be." My breath billowed out smooth and smoky to set the particles into a tailspin.

"Nothing's moving up there." Manny scanned the eerie jumble of forms lining the endless tunnel above.

An indistinct black muzzle formed around that glowing set of eyes at ground level and swung to track our slow creep forward. Just as quickly the outline dissolved, the eyes disappeared, and the prickling scrutiny winked out. The temperature dropped and our tires crunched onto a ring of icy sand growing from the center of the vortex.

Tattered sheets of fog spun past and rose in a dense inverted tornado within the vortex. The light flickered faster, and my stomach dropped. Quinn snatched at the handlebars. I clutched her waist with my free hand, but couldn't tell up from down and squeezed my eyes shut to stop a wave of nausea.

Dazzling white lit the inside of my eyelids. I opened my eyes and blinked at sugar-white sand. Sweat popped out on my forehead, but instantly evaporated.

"We're through," Manny said.

"Ed, your staff!"

I looked to where Pete pointed. Sure enough, the end of the staff Koko gave me pulsed with pale blue light before going dark. I held it up, willing the artifact to take me to the medicine shield. Nothing dramatic happened, but every twenty seconds the tip brightened and faded.

Gleaming sand spilled out in all directions around the vortex. Dirty gray clouds drifted in isolated patches high overhead, occasionally obscuring a sun that looked too large and squat, like a sunset back home squashed by atmospheric effects at the horizon.

We'd assumed the land beyond the portal would be nothing but desert because that was what came through on our side. But the spill of sand petered out and the ground turned to hard cracked clay a few hundred yards ahead.

"Looks like a dry lake bed." I pointed with the staff, and it flashed notably faster. I swung it in a slow arc, and the pulse rate increased when pointed off to our left at about ten o'clock. "Looks like we need to go that way."

The landscape continued to change as we crunched over the broken ground. At first, only the hardiest of weeds broke through the bits of shell and rock embedded in the gray-brown clay. But soon enough shrubs and grasses studded the path ahead. No glowing eyes watched among the branches, but we kept our guard up in case some of them turned out to be killer tumbleweeds.

Unlike Ralph's directions through the desert, the staff set a straight path. Compared to bobbing and weaving through unseen turns, following the pulsing rod was downright boring. We passed the petrified remains of ancient trees—only a few at first, but then with more frequency. Ralph sat uncharacteristically still, looking subdued as he scanned the horizon.

"Trees ahead," Quinn said. "An actual forest."

15. Powerful Memories

A NNA KICKED another desiccated spider corpse and watched it roll off the porch. It left a little trail in the sand before stopping next to the others she'd swept out this morning.

"Sand's closer," Charles said from behind her.

The drummer was tall, trim, and athletic. His presence should have made her feel safer, but something about the man put her off. An odd feeling for a dedicated groupie, but he hadn't been with the A-Chords when she fell in love with them. Randy had, but that silly, lovable guy was gone. She turned and studied the close-cropped black hair and piercing blue eyes that looked through her. So stern and serious compared to Randy's adorably vacant expression.

"Right up to the foundation now." Anna mentally shook herself. No one could replace Randy, and it wasn't fair to hold that against Charles. "The pesticide helps keep the spiders back."

"But for how long?" He held up a hand to indicate he didn't expect an answer. "The other things are getting too bold. Those snipers on the roof aren't going to keep them at bay for much longer."

"They won't have to. Ed will make things right. I just know it."

Charles looked like he wanted to argue, but huffed out a breath and shrugged. Anna gave the drummer a tentative smile and stepped back into the house.

As Kokopelli's first child, Ed was strong in all three elements. And he had Quinn. She was scary and caring, a big sister you didn't want to get mad. Anna's training with Ed seemed the perfect opportunity to hone her power and become more kick-ass like Quinn. Unfortunately, those sessions were always rushed. Her control of Spirit energy improved, but came nowhere close to the terrifying force she'd once summoned in the heat of battle. As for firespeaking, Ed still didn't answer her hourly calls. Now, she swept up dead bugs—*so* not kick-ass.

Ed *would* fix things. Otherwise, all was lost according to Piper, and that girl knew a lot. If Anna couldn't be mighty like Quinn, she'd settle for smart like Ed's sister.

"Is there anything in the barn to push back the sand?" Brent asked the group hunched over the kitchen table and studying Piper's notes. "You know, like a snowplow."

"We might be able to rig up a bucket on the front-end loader, but most of the heavy equipment is gone with the outbuildings." Melissa swept back messy hair to reveal tired eyes.

"That would not work," Mr. Conti said. "Physical force won't hold back these sands. The ancestral energy of this house keeps the desert at bay, not the stone foundation or wooden walls. If this were just another building in the fields it would have been swept away with the others."

"With the Eastons gone, that protective energy ebbs." Piper pushed out a graph featuring a fat red line that crashed to zero as it crossed a climbing dotted line. "I plotted the sand's movement and depth near the house and barn. The slope prior to our arrival is just a guess based on what Ed and Pete remembered."

"It's already at zero. There's nowhere else to go," Anna said under her breath.

"Nowhere, except up the stairs and into the house." Piper grimaced.

"The energy could be replenished." Mr. Conti rubbed his stubbly chin, squishing his face through a series of caricatures that would have been funny under other circumstances.

"Sure, if we bring back the Eastons." Piper held up a forefinger and turned to Melissa. "We do have *one*. The power of a threshold comes from its residents' sense of home and safety. Those feelings are ingrained and strengthened by the everyday actions and routines that make a house a home. Layer on generations of those traditions and the power builds, charging the dwelling with the power to deny entrance to the unwanted."

"We're the residents now," Anna said. "Shouldn't that be enough to recharge this force?"

"The house is welcoming and cozy, but I wouldn't say I feel at home. That's what it would take to rebuild the energy, we'd all need to—" Piper paused and leaned in toward Pete's sister. "What sort of things did your family do here every day, what made this your home?"

"Chores I suppose." Melissa nodded at the counters and smiled. "Every day started with Mom cooking. Bread and muffins went in early, long before breakfast. Then there'd be coffee for anyone riding out to check fences." She laughed. "When we were little, Pete and I used to fight over feeding the chickens and pigs. I hated dealing with slop, but we weren't allowed to tend horses and cows until we were older. Then there were family dinners, complaining about the weather, gathering around the fire for cocoa on dark winter nights."

"Wait, we all need to hear this." Piper skipped over to the kitchen and rummaged through the lower cabinets. "Maybe we can make hot chocolate."

* * *

"That's Uncle Bill washing the cows." Melissa pointed at the screen where a man covered in mud struggled to push between juvenile brown cows. "Swiss Browns are like dogs. They loved the attention of getting cleaned up for the fair. Uncle Bill hates being licked and nuzzled and got himself dumped in the mud trying to back away." The home video cut over to show the back of the farmhouse. A woman wearing a flowered dress pinned shirts out on the clothesline. "Ma won't use our dryer. She says the fresh air makes everything smell like springtime. Da gets so embarrassed when houseguests look out back and see his underwear." Melissa's laugh drew chuckles from the group sprawled around the living room. "But Ma always said, 'If you stay at the house, you get treated like family.'"

They'd been listening to stories for an hour. Melissa played to the audience, but Anna could tell she loved talking about her extended family—and especially her folks. They'd already walked the fences with Cousin Norm after that beaver dam flood, ridden to market to help set up the stand, and spent a scary night in the basement under tornado warnings while Aunt Jenny went into labor.

The small crowd hung on her words. Good-natured jibes were aimed at various cousins, uncles, and aunts along the way. Only complimentary comments for Ma and Pa Easton, you didn't bash the heads of the house, even in jest.

Snacks flowed from the kitchen as people took turns passing out crackers, cheese, and other treats from the Eastons' stockpile. Baking up bread was out of the question, but fresh chocolate chip cookies and cocoa from a pot on the stove filled the house with soothing aromas.

"This young lady certainly can spin a yarn." Mr. Conti's eyes shone with delight from Anna's right.

Piper sat to her left with Billy squeezed up against the sofa's arm. Leaving Bakersfield had been hard, but being surrounded by such good people kept Anna from missing home. Even when the dark forces had her in thrall, some small part of her clung to the knowledge that friends were nearby.

"I love her," Anna said as Melissa launched into another tale. "All of you too. No matter what happens."

"We love you too." Piper gave her hand a squeeze. "And I'm coming to love this darned ranch. Between the stories and a belly full of goodness, I'm feeling sleepy and safe. Like this really is home."

"Is it enough?" Anna felt on the verge of tears, either happy tears for the closeness or angry, frustrated tears over their predicament.

"I hope so." Piper flipped through the notebook in her lap. "We should reinforce all the door and window thresholds. A line of salt will help, but it's easily broken."

"We have an old-country trick for that." Mr. Conti shifted around and pulled a big silver roll of duct tape from behind his back. "I found this in the kitchen drawer and said to myself, 'Joel, this will come in handy.' My *nonna* would tape down salt and herbs to ward off evil. Grandmother also kept her windows full of little mementoes, saying they kept curses from slipping in."

"Brilliant! And the little tchotchke idea isn't half bad. Articles hold memories and any handled by the family will definitely add power." Piper's face lit with enthusiasm as she interrupted a barn raising story. "Hey Melissa, what do you have in the way of old photos and knickknacks? It's time to tell this desert to leave us the hell alone!"

Melissa directed the scavenger hunt for family treasures to bolster the entrances. Everyone scrambled through the house and attic collecting photos and memorabilia—anything and everything that might hold sentimental value and be small enough to nail up, tape down, or sit in a window.

Pete's sister barked out assessments as each piece came down, and Piper helped Mr. Conti position the most poignant family heirlooms for best effect. Billy and Jinx laid down heavy lines of salt across each entrance and locked them in place with the duct tape. The house was organized bedlam, and Anna loved it.

"Aw, come on, this will fit," Reggie complained when Melissa waved his offering away.

The scrawny old man had wrestled a stuffed deer head with antlers as wide as he was tall down from the attic. Anna hurried to help him move it to the back parlor, but he seemed intent on taking it to the front door.

"It's too big," Melissa complained. "We'd need an engine hoist to hang that monster. That's why it stayed in the attic all these years. Ma refused to have it downstairs no matter how much Norm whined about his trophy buck. Just sit it by the back door."

She scowled impressively, extended an imperious arm, and pointed out of the room. After a moment's hesitation, Reggie pulled his end toward the back. The oak drop-leaf table by the back door ended up being a good spot, and they positioned the sweeping antlers to align with the settee so as not to block the doorway.

Anna peeked outside. The wrap-around porch narrowed to a three-foot-wide walkway. The rear of the house sat low to the ground with only three steps going down to the backyard. None of them were visible because sand stretched out level with the decking. She shivered at the thought of waking to find they'd been buried alive.

"Buck ain't helping, is it?" Reggie rapped the deer head a few times and jiggled its antlers as though he expected it to turn on.

"Not yet." She sighed as sand crept across the first few inches of deck.

"Best go find more stuff. I saw a doozy up in the rafters that might do the trick."

The old man spun on his heel, darted back to the main room, and sprinted upstairs. Outside, the shadowy silhouette of the house stretched east toward the vortex. The funnel flickered and flashed, painting the dunes a sickly green that made the eerie phenomenon seem closer. It looked bigger too, more like a column because the base had widened to nearly the diameter of its top section. Anna dropped the blinds and went to find Piper.

"We're running out of space." Brent wiped sweat from his face as he turned from Piper, climbed back on the stepladder, and wedged a long wooden spoon between the pictures and other small items tacked above the front door.

The door looked like it had been used for target practice by a militant arts and crafts co-op. The odds and ends tacked to its gleaming wood extended onto the plaster walls—militant artists with poor aim. The windows were similarly festooned and the sills jammed with everything from dolls to old dog collars.

"That's enough," Piper said. "Come on down."

"It's not helping out back." Anna slipped over next to Ed's sister. "And the vortex looks wider."

"Well, we've done all we can." Even as Piper spoke, Melissa waved away the next round of offerings. "Let's see what's going on out front first."

She and Piper joined Mr. Conti, Billy, and Brent at the front window. The reflection made it hard to see the porch in the gathering darkness. Melissa turned off the ceiling light, then hit the switch beside the door to bathe the porch in a soft yellow glow.

"Already over the top step." Billy's deep voice gave her the shivers.

So did the waves of sand creeping across the gray floor boards. Small surges crested the top step, flowing like water. Each wave brought the leading edge a few inches closer.

"What do we do when it hits the door?" Anna asked.

"Things become tricky then." Mr. Conti closed his eyes in thought. "We can stay put and trust in the thresholds. If sand gets in, we know our protection has failed."

"But we don't want to be buried either," Piper said. "We can't sit tight while the desert swallows us."

"We must be ready to travel." The old man opened sad eyes.

"Guys?" Billy pressed his face against the top of the window. "It's too close now. I've lost sight of the front edge."

As the tallest, he had the best angle, which meant the sand was inches from the door. The room grew quiet. The table emptied and people gathered at the windows. Time stretched into the silence of held breath and pounding hearts.

Skittering came through the walls as if mice ran behind the baseboards. Anna imagined wave after wave of sand building up over the doorstop and climbing toward the window sills. Any moment granules would swirl into sight along the glass, the desert rising to swallow them. Her pulse pounded in her ears. *We have to get to the cars!*

"There!" Billy yelled into the silence and everyone jumped. "I think...yes! The sand's receding."

A moment later, a ragged sliver of gray wood showed through the sand. The stretch of decking grew wider as the desert recoiled from the power surrounding the farmhouse. More and more boards were exposed, and counter ripples flowed outward to cancel the surges that had brought the sand over the steps. The movement ceased when the porch was clear, leaving the house an island oasis.

Anna's breath escaped on a sigh of relief, but she jumped as the house shook under the blow of some invisible force. People scattered away from the windows and dove for cover as another thump from overhead shook the room, then another, and another. Melissa strode to the hearth, grabbed her shotgun, and looked from door to ceiling— unsure where the threat would emerge. The floor lurched as something huge crashed down the staircase. Melissa and two others swung around with guns raised.

"Looky what I found!" Skinny arms and legs tangled around a massive slab of wood with a curved prow. The plank bucked and jerked

144

as the person underneath fought their way into a half-crouch while still holding on for dear life. "If this here toboggan ain't got powerful memories, I'll eat my socks."

"Are you insane?" Charles screamed the question as he bore down on poor Reggie.

The old mechanic stared in confusion at the angry faces and Melissa's shotgun, which she lowered with a growl. The drummer looked ready to grab the man by the collar, but stopped short and settled for more yelling.

"We don't need any more damned memories. The sand's retreating." Charles' breath came heavy, as if not throttling the other man took physical effort.

"Okay, okay." Reggie shifted beneath his load and the edge of the massive sled whacked the railing with the sound of a gunshot. "No need to be snippy. I'll just take it back to the attic."

"No!" several voices yelled at once, bringing nervous laughs to the tense room.

"Just put it with the buck." Melissa shook her head and limped over to stow her gun.

Immediate crisis averted, Anna pulled Piper to the back door to see the vortex. An early moon glinted off the rolling dunes. The green flashes made her queasy, and Piper simply ground her teeth at the swollen column of energy. Anna raised an eyebrow as spotlights played over the backyard.

"We'll have two people on watch upstairs, so if you hear walking around up there don't panic. I think Melissa has enough people who know firearms, but let her know if you're a decent shot."

"Never learned." She traced the path illuminated by the glow from their window. The back porch was clear out to the railing where the wood merged seamlessly with desert floor extending away from the house. "Steps are still buried."

"Better them than us."

16. Welcoming Committee

"LORD?" Pina pushed down her anxiety, though her voice still quavered. "Is there no way I can help?"

Kokopelli didn't respond. The old spirit hunched in front of the fire, sitting cross-legged and clutching his staff with white knuckles. The staff blazed bright, the fire roared, and the air vibrated with power. His obsidian eyes reflected the flickering light as he stared, unseeing. Strain lined his face, making the skin look thin and brittle. She imagined the power consuming him, stripping away the fragile outer shell.

Pina laid a hand on his forehead and flowed soothing power into his fevered brow. Her breast ached with the effort. She reached past the pain, dredged up deep reserves, and willed more of her essence into soothing her lord—only dully aware she'd dropped to her knees.

Tears leaked from the corner of both eyes, rolled down her cheeks, and met at her chin. Calming was the only power she could offer to ease his burdens. Her energy flowed away, disappearing into the all-consuming strife of Kokopelli's battle to hold the world veil in place.

The precise teepee of logs had fed the flames of the god's power for all eternity, never wavering, never being consumed. She tried to draw courage from its steadfast resolve, but the fire swam in her vision as—impossibly—the wood charred. *Just a bit more.*

"Enough!" The strength in her lord's voice eased her clutching fear. "You give too much of yourself, Brightness."

Pina slumped. He caught her and lowered her to the sandy floor. She looked up into Kokopelli's ancient face—smiling not at his words, but because his mask of tension had eased. Fatigue still pulled hard at those noble features, and the sadness in his eyes made her heart ache— a dull, distant thing hidden among the all-consuming pain. Oddly, there was concern too as his dark eyes darted about, examining her from head to toe.

"You're better." She managed a weak giggle at the thought of him being worried about her. "Is it over?"

"Your gifts are too generous. I will be better for a time. But the fight is far from over, Brightness."

His flute appeared in his hands. Pina smiled as a scattering of crystal-pure notes drifted across her like butterflies on a summer day. She remembered all the good in the world, happier days when they strolled his adobe halls and she showed him the delights of her forests.

The song wrapped her in loving arms, easing much of the discomfort. She turned her head toward the fire. Angry red cracks glowed along the length of each blackened log as a vision materialized in the rising smoke. The vortex—that swirling mass of energy ripping its way out of the sealed third world and into Ed's—flashed sickly green lightning across the desert behind Pete's farm. The column of energy swelled fat and obscene like a snake greedily swallowing a too-large meal. But instead of choking on it, the vortex grew, spreading across the sands. It swelled wider and wider until the edges threatened the barn and house.

Worry clutched Pina's chest but could not take hold under the echoing music settling over her. She giggled again at the irony of her strained and overworked lord helping a lowly sprite. She should tell him to stop, to conserve his power, but the warm cocoon held her fast, and dark sleep rose to blot out the worry.

* * *

The sound of shattering china rose behind us as we made our way toward the tree line. With one arm tight around Quinn's waist and the other hand holding the pulsing staff, I risked a glance back. The leading wall of the vortex chased us, smashing the dry clay bed. No, that wasn't quite right.

"The portal's expanding!"

Quinn turned her head, cursed, and hit the throttle. Our acceleration caught the other two ATVs by surprise, but they were quick to follow. Our dash didn't last long because the last rise before the forest hid a deep ravine. Our three vehicles pulled up short. The crashing advance of the vortex also halted. I doubt it had anything to do with our route being blocked—just a happy coincidence.

The blue-green wall and its ghastly suspended minions rose like a frozen tsunami teetering on the verge of cresting. Still a hundred yards away, it now stretched a good half mile to either side. The next five minutes were full of nervous glances back at the vortex while we ranged right and left looking for a path. Dwain spotted the shallow grade first, and we had to plow over a tangle of underbrush to get on the winding trail. But the wash proved plenty wide, and we soon rolled out onto the ravine floor amid clouds of dust.

Farther on, the steep walls eased into rolling hills. We shut off the engines and studied the hard-packed roadway running down the far side, through the gully, and back up toward the vortex. The path looked to have been used recently because it lacked the grasses and scrub brush that covered the ravine floor.

"Looks like we found our way out." Manny reached for his starter, but froze as crunching rolled down from overhead.

"Coming from the forest," Quinn pointed at the hill where the road disappeared.

The sound grew louder and closer, the scraping cadence of many feet.

I jumped off the ATV and motioned our small group back. We rolled our rides back down the gully and did our best to hide them behind a line of thorny shrubs. Ralph rode on the handlebars doing his tiny jockey impersonation and clearly not understanding why he was going backward.

"Keep low," I muttered as dark silhouettes crested the rise.

We crouched behind our sparse cover, with little hope our big machines would go unnoticed. For that matter, they must have heard our engines. I reached for Spirit and a thread of music, thinking we could escape under cover of a mini-sandstorm if things went south.

The first ranks to top the rise were shamblers, a good dozen of them. I shivered at the memory of those hungry mouths bearing down on me. A contingent of Nargun followed close behind, partially obscuring one of the tall boney creatures that controlled sand. My confidence took a nosedive. I'd caught the last sand demon unawares while brimming with rage and might not get lucky again.

Smaller creatures scuttled and rolled around the loose formations. Scorpions spread to either side of the roadway like a billowing cloak, ignoring the tumblers rolling roughshod over their armored backs. At the rear, humps of sand and dirt paced the main group and left mole tracks in the softer earth alongside the road, a sure sign centipedes— and who knew what else—traveled along underground.

"They're passing us by," Quinn whispered.

"There's no way they didn't see us." Manny scowled and scratched his chin.

"Maybe that hiding spell?" Pete ventured.

"Probably helped, but we weren't invisible." I should be happy they hadn't turned on us, but it was disconcerting.

"Chalk it up to luck and move on." Quinn waved at the empty road.

Just to be safe, we pushed our vehicles forward, but they were too heavy to manhandle uphill. Before starting them, Pete and I scurried up the rise to our left to ensure the enemy hadn't stopped close enough to hear the engines. The settling dust tickled my throat, and I swallowed a coughing fit along with the foul stench that clung to the hard-packed ground like a sickness.

"Smells like chicken shit baking in the sun." Pete pitched his voice low and wrinkled his nose.

"Thought that'd be right up your alley."

"Trust me, nobody gets used to *that* odor."

We dropped to all fours at the top, which had my eyes and nose streaming. The passing group shimmered in the distance as if a mirage approached the vortex. I wiped at my eyes, but my stench-induced tears weren't what made the scene waver.

"They're going through," Pete said. "Sis is gonna have her hands full."

We hurried back to the others.

"The bad guys are out of earshot all right. They went through the portal," I said as Pete climbed woodenly onto his ATV with his head hung low. "Who knows where they'll come out? I bet even Milwaukee is battling those things."

Anywhere Earth magic had breached could be fair game. Still, I tried to warn Anna using firespeak as we rolled up the hill and into the tree line—no luck.

We crunched along on the primitive road, which shrank to a path as trees rose to either side. The staff pulsed strong, encouraging us forward, so going around wasn't an option. Even in low gear our engines rang out loud through the quiet forest.

"No birds or insects," Quinn said over her shoulder.

"It's more than that," Pete said when the path widened enough for him to pull up alongside.

Rather than the towering hardwoods or pines of our old grove woods back home, these trees looked juvenile—at least in size. I could easily circle the thickest with the fingers of both hands. The sea of trunks off to either side rose straight as arrows and only started to branch at head height. Fungus or lichen clung to the pale bark in patches. The narrow leaves—similar to sumac or walnut—splayed wide and curled as though they'd been bereft of sun and water.

"Well, it smells wrong. Not quite like something's died, but close." I rubbed my nose.

Pennsylvania woods had an earthy, wet scent and a certain stillness that always had me thinking primordial forest—even when civilization was just a stone's throw away. The stillness here was unnerving, the air devoid of moisture. The sharp pungent odor resembled rotting cheese more than healthy leaf mold. In fact, rather than leaf litter, blotchy fungus gathered around each trunk—hungrily awaiting leaves the trees refused to release.

"Everything looks sick, like the trees and bushes are diseased. And there's too much fungus for such a dry climate. This place hasn't seen water in a while."

"If you boys are done reliving your scouting days, there's a clearing up ahead. It might be time to figure out what the hell we're doing." Quinn swung wide and shut off the engine as we entered the open area.

The ground was rent and torn by the passage of many feet. Few individual tracks survived, but the small horde we'd passed and perhaps others had come this way. Most had come straight down the path ahead, but others wound through the surrounding woods.

Low stony hillocks squatted among the trees. I counted five, but more could have been hidden in the dappled light filtering through the canopy overhead. A dark opening took up most of the face of the nearest hill.

"Looks like a cave over there." I squinted and caught the edge of a similar opening on another mound.

"Those don't look natural." Pete backed toward his ATV and waved for the rest of us to do the same. "Let's get a move on it. We can discuss plans la—"

Loud chirping cut him off. It was the first bird we'd heard since arriving. The sound came again from along our back trail. A third call answered from close ahead—too close. This last was more of a chittering near ground level—maybe not birds at all. The trees exploded with chirping, seeming to come from all around.

Manny and Ralph drew their knives. The manager's flared with fire, which seemed a good choice. I drew on the magic, bringing my hands together with the beat of Pop Evil's "Go Higher," or it might have been called "Footsteps"—I never quite figured that out. Either way, the tune was well suited, and Fire pulsed between my palms in response. Quinn already straddled the four-wheeler, but turned to face out from our small circle. Spirit energy flowed across her fingertips, probably because there wasn't enough moisture to feed a Water spell.

The bushes twenty paces ahead rustled, and the chittering grew to a crescendo. A blur rushed through the underbrush, just an outline as if I tried to focus on a piece of glass coming at us.

I fired short bursts of flame, tracking the half-seen thing. Bush after bush burst into flame. The third one just in front of us erupted in fire and an earsplitting squeal as something thrashed within. Quinn flung her arm forward and the energy she released smashed the burning bush and its occupant backward.

A dark form writhed on the ground and beat at itself with claw-like hands. The head to toe body armor saved it from the heat, but portions of the tightly wrapped material had burned away. Perhaps five feet tall, the creature had dark skin and a bulbous, hairless head with big shining eyes. It scurried on its back, arms and legs pumping to get away now that it had been revealed.

"Away, demon!" Manny yelled from my right.

His knife no longer flared, but he swung the nasty blade in a wide arc and sliced across the chest of another attacker trying to pull him from the ATV. Two more of the creatures grabbed him from behind. Shuffling feet pulled my attention back in time to see Quinn blast a pair of the humanoid attackers into the underbrush, but they both flipped to their stomachs, scurried on all fours, and came at us again. I shot a hasty gout of flame that ignited a patch of fungus in front of them and readied another burst when Quinn cried out.

"What *is* that?" She clutched her temples, and her Spirit energy cut out.

A wave of power crashed into me, and I teetered on the edge of falling. The blow wasn't physical. Heedless of the hands I'd clamped over my ears, sound ripped through my hiding spell and tore the Pop Evil tune from my mind.

I reached for the vibrating chords, trying to reset my spell, but found nothing. It was if I'd suddenly forgotten the song completely. No, that wasn't right. Notes did swirl in my mind. A simple tune plucked on an unfamiliar instrument blocked out the song I needed.

"Go Higher…Go Higher." I tried to sing the title, but it left my mouth as a musical blob devoid of pitch.

Quinn spat a curse, pulled a short black stick from her back pocket and pushed the button to release eighteen inches of coiled spring. We'd found the compact batons handy in a fight, but our attackers carried much longer weapons like bo staffs with a nasty hook on one end and a weighty bulb on the other.

They scurried in from all directions, at least six of the narrow-waisted creatures bearing down on us. My head felt clearer so I reached for Spirit, intent on crafting a protective whirlwind to sweep them back. The element rose readily, and I chose Skillet's "Invincible" to carry the spell. But the beat crumbled away, replaced by the strange stringed instrument and its chaotic tune.

I clutched at songs by Seether, Shinedown, and even Metallica. I couldn't have forgotten the music. Yet each attempt fizzled out before I'd grasped a single note, blocked by the foreign music looping in my head. The forest closed in, and I couldn't get enough air.

Rough hands with fingers ending in segmented pads pulled me off the ATV. Pete and Vance were already on the ground; they'd never even gotten off a shot. My vision narrowed to a tunnel as I focused on the creature dragging Quinn's limp body and again reached for a spell. The tunnel shrank to a pinpoint of light, and I slid into oblivion accompanied by the cascade of plucky notes and primitive drums.

17. No Picnic

I FELL through gray that seemed like Tokpela, but the damp cold was out of place.

"Quinn?" The all-encompassing fog muted my call. "Pete?"

Nothing.

I walked toward where the mists lightened ahead. The smell of smoke and sage hung heavy in the air. Flames flickered from a fire ring, pushing back the fog and revealing two figures. The first was small as a child and covered in a decorative blanket. Long blond hair spilled across the beaded pouch serving as a pillow.

"Pina!"

She didn't move, and the larger person slumped by the fire didn't turn. The hunched back and feathered headpiece were hard to miss. At first I thought Koko also slept, but as I moved to the right his face came into view. He stared blearily into the smoky fire as if transfixed. Sweat ran down a face etched with concentration and...pain.

I reached out, but the fog coalesced, growing thicker the harder I pressed. Resistance mounted as I tried to push forward. I managed three steps, but could go no closer. Dark shadows encroached on the sandy clearing. The fire cast jumping shadows against the one adobe wall, making the scene look like a play with scenery painted on cardboard.

The old spirit's brows drew tight. He lifted his flute with shaking hands and blew a dozen notes. The melody quickly fell into disarray. His head drooped, and the god toppled.

"No!" I clawed at the fog, a futile gesture.

He fell hard, and I winced at the sharp crack of his head hitting the ring of stones. Instead of blood, light leaked from the gash on his left temple. The flute was gone—replaced by his staff. The carvings and designs pulsed with subdued energy. He thrust it at the fire, wood and flesh inside the flame.

Green swirled and swelled within the flames, buffeting the staff as Koko's arm shook. This was the vortex viewed as a kind of magical hologram. From his prone position Koko tried to push the mass back, to banish it into the fire. Sullen red sparks dripped from where his staff touched. What started at Pete's farm as a slender tornado had turned fat and distended. Molten material dripped, and a crescent-shaped section of the staff disappeared as the vortex ground away the god's symbol of power.

The ground lurched, sending me to my knees. I whipped my head around at another crash. The tall palm-like trees of Uktena's domain canted over Koko's clearing. Beyond the fire and adobe wall, stark mountains rose against a purple sky that shifted to blue as the mountains turned to forest.

Uktena in his mighty serpent form slithered down toward the prone Kokopelli while a group of people walked out from below the land that had been mountains, then forest, and was currently a frozen tundra. A gangly figure followed the handful of people. He was tall and skeletal under his vest and breechcloth. I did a double take as he drew near— not just thin, the man was a walking skeleton with ghastly tatters of muscle and skin dangling from yellow bones. He miss stepped, made an awkward grab for the sack he carried, and basically bumbled his way down to the fire.

"Watch out!" I called. "Pina, Koko, get up!"

But they still couldn't hear me. Koko's staff was half gone, and he hugged the nearest stone for support. The serpent slid around the adobe wall and flicked a tongue out, testing the air and grazing Pina's hair. I trusted Uktena wouldn't take advantage of my unconscious friend and weakened father. But the skeleton was a total unknown.

I watched helplessly as his people spilled onto the sand. Each dressed differently, from what looked like simple homespun to full ceremonial regalia. Details grew indistinct as the fog thickened and closed over the scene. Koko finally noticed the newcomers and threw his free hand up to ward off the skeleton and whatever grisly offering the bag he pushed at my father contained.

The resistance holding me back disappeared. I stumbled forward only to be enveloped by true Tokpela. I rushed though the gray, calling for Koko, but found only swirling mist.

* * *

"Ed?" Quinn's voice and the constant jarring drew me back. "There you are."

She hovered over me as sickly trees whipped by in the background. I lay on canvas that jarred and vibrated. The only reason I didn't roll off was a wide webbed belt securing me to the incline. The ATV engines whined and we put on another burst of speed.

"For crying out loud, slow down! We aren't athletes." Sweat coated Quinn's face, plastering wild strands of hair to her forehead.

I craned around in my improvised stretcher to see who drove. The back of a shiny bulbous head bounced at the front of the stretcher. Spindly arms with thick sparse hair and oddly jointed elbows dangled down to where hands with long finger pads wrapped around the poles supporting my canvas conveyance. The creature ran effortlessly, dragging me and following the three ATVs that roared ahead. My fog addled mind had assumed Quinn rode, but now I picked out the thudding of her feet as she jogged alongside my stretcher.

"What's going on?" I managed in spite of my teeth being rattled out of my skull.

"Been on the move for an hour." She grimaced and sucked in a breath. "Mostly slow and steady, but something's changed. Damned bugs have been sprinting for a couple miles now."

156

"Forget me. Make a break for it." I fumbled at the belt but couldn't find a buckle.

"Too many of them. We'd need the ATVs."

"Well, who's"—I whipped my head around and would have fallen out of my proverbial chair if I hadn't been strapped in— "They can drive?"

Impossible, yet an attacker straddled each of our rides, weaving and maneuvering through the underbrush like cross-country experts. There was no sign of the path, which left those on foot dodging fungus, trees, and bushes in an attempt to keep up. Pete jogged off to my left on the far side of another sling carrying an unconscious Manny. He and I weren't the only casualties. Two of our attackers traveled in slings among a cluster of their brethren. The brush behind us shook and shimmered as at least a dozen more of the creatures followed, though I couldn't catch more than a glimmer of an outline. The things were damned good at camouflage.

"I know." Quinn stumbled to a stop with hands on her thighs as our progression lurched to a halt. "Barren forest, primitive tribe, and road warrior skills. Makes no sense."

She wiped her face, and the rest of our group shuffled over. Pete seemed more winded than Vance, which surprised me because I knew his family worked him from dawn to dusk. But maybe there wasn't much running on the farm. Dwain skipped over like he'd been out for a stroll instead of a forced march, and Ralph—the imp climbed down from the handlebars of our ATV, pulled a hunk of candy from his hidden stash, and sauntered over wearing a devilish grin that would look suspiciously like a menacing snarl to the uninitiated.

"Consortin' with the enemy to get a ride." Pete gave the imp a glare between ragged breaths. "Treason I say."

Ralph blinked back and tore off another bite with fangs ill-suited for sweets.

"He didn't even fight when the bugs attacked," Quinn whispered.

"Why do you keep calling them bugs?" I tried to get a look past the wall of people gathered around my litter. "Will someone please cut me loose?"

The way everyone patted their pockets was comical, but I found myself doing the same—damned peer pressure. My baton and knife were gone, as was the section of Koko's staff. Thoughts of making a run for it vanished. Without the staff we were up a creek without a paddle.

Ralph pushed over to my side, slid out his stone knife, and severed the restraining belt. I stood shakily and ruffled the little guy's non-existent hair in gratitude. We'd only known the imp a few months, but he'd always been there in a pinch. And since Max had deemed him worthy of riding my dog into battle...well, that said it all. I pushed away from the makeshift stretcher and the memory of that fatal day as a lump formed in my throat. *Stupid dog still gets to me.*

We'd stopped in another clearing surrounded by the strange mounds—entrances to some underground lair. Our vehicles sat close to the nearest tunnel and beyond a loose line of our captors. We stood in roughly the center of a circle of fifty. There hadn't been that many earlier.

Each stood about five feet with a big oval head. Dark shimmering patches like wet window screen on each temple took the place of ears. Their round eyes sat out from the skull like black marbles rather than being recessed in sockets. The nose was non-existent, but each long face tapered into a tiny oval mouth. They'd effortlessly dragged the stretchers, so were certainly strong in spite of their gangly legs and arms and impossibly narrow waist. They did look rather wasp-like if you thought of the shiny brown skin stretched over muscle and sinew as an exoskeleton.

A moan interrupted my thoughts. Manny thrashed on his own litter off to our left. Dwain led Ralph over, the imp cut off the road manager's restraints, and they joined us.

"You okay?" Pete asked Manny, then continued at the man's weary shrug. "If we get to the ATVs, we can outrun them."

"Did anyone see where they put our weapons?" I asked. "If we leave without the staff, the whole mission's a bust."

"I think they took them in there." Quinn pointed to the entrance by our vehicles. "Along with our supplies, first aid kits, everything."

The ATVs' trunks stood open, and the side bags had been removed. Only the spare gas cans remained strapped to our machines. Without weapons, we needed magic to even the odds. These things weren't indestructible. Manny proved that when he slashed at his initial attackers. It hadn't taken much. The flesh wounds he'd inflicted shouldn't have stopped a committed attacker, but the two he'd backed down lay sprawled by the entrance as though they'd been mortally wounded.

"Is your knife special—like poisoned or something?" I asked, jutting my chin toward the injured creatures.

"Just a keen edge made of bronze when I'm not channeling power."

Of course it wasn't steel. Cold iron and its many variants hurt those of the Dark Court. The fact that his black blade avoided the common material served as poignant reminder of his history. But I didn't have time to rehash the manager's intentions and allegiances. He'd swung over to our side and that was good enough for now. The thinning world veil threatened all the realms, so it seemed appropriate someone from the dark lend a hand.

"Maybe these wasps are susceptible to bronze like steel hurts those nasty buggers…" Pete trailed off with a glance at Manny. My friend had been up to his neck in our prior problems and knew as much about the unsavory side of the supernatural world as I did—including when to not ruffle feathers. "Well, the bronze might hurt them."

"I doubt it." Manny looked about to say more, but didn't—one of his many annoying habits.

"Either way, we need to get through these wasps without getting stung, retrieve the staff, and make a run for it." I ticked each item off on my fingers.

"Ants?" Dwain's question caught me off guard, but he stared down at Ralph who for once wasn't stuffing his mouth with sweets. "Of course!" The sprite turned to the rest of us. "Ralph says these are Ant People. That's why he wouldn't fight them."

"Whatever." Quinn huddled in close and kept her voice low despite the fact our captors ignored us. "Once we're through the ring, we take out the two to either side of the door, get our stuff, and we're gone."

"You don't understand." Manny looked from Dwain to Ralph. "If these are *the* Ant People, they helped your first people escape this world when it was to be destroyed."

"Well, they're certainly not in the mood to help us now," I said. "Can you summon fire without your knife?"

Manny looked at me in disgust. Even Dwain seemed annoyed. Although these creatures clearly weren't insects, I could see they indeed resembled giant ants. But we didn't have time for history lessons. If that cave hooked up with tunnels, we might already be too late to retrieve the staff.

"I told you the knife wasn't important." With a sneer, he held his hand palm up, but dropped it a moment later in disgust. "Something blocks my power."

"On to plan B. I'll get us through to the entrance and drop the guards. Vance and Dwain can help me find the staff while you three get the ATVs fired up." I looked to Quinn. "Can you hold them off with Spirit until we come back?"

At her curt nod, I called on Fire. Quinn's Spirit energy surged as I grappled for an appropriate song to tie into my spell. Fire was wild and chaotic, often wanting to lash out on its own. The music had to be powerful, yet not too constraining. I'd lost control of the flames once and didn't want to go through that again. Something from Three Days Grace would work.

"Ed, wait!" Quinn called out just as I reached for the opening synthesizer chords of "Chalk Outline" and shaped the spell.

She looked frantic, but no monsters bore down on us. I had to complete the spell before asking what was wrong. Fire flared, touched music, and—the song vanished, replaced by plucky notes incapable of merging with any element.

I scrambled to grasp the Three Days Grace tune, but it sank away beneath the inane string of notes that rose to loop through my head. Fire lashed, hot and angry—replacing my body heat with cold dread. Out of control and with no music to guide it, I was in real trouble. Looking inward, I grabbed the flames and shoved them down, deep— not a proper grounding, but I managed to wrestle the element back to its resting state.

My teeth chattered uncontrollably while those alien notes ran through my mind, over and over, never relenting. A new ant-creature emerged from the cave. Shorter than the others, it wore an elaborate headpiece and had plates of armor strapped to one shoulder and forearm. Pouches and flasks dangled from a belt riding low on the narrow waist. The masked face turned to me, the music flared, and darkness swept me away.

* * *

I again looked through gray mists onto my father's fire ring. *I gotta stop blacking out.* The vortex swirled out of control, eclipsing the teepee of logs and spreading into the clearing proper. Koko sat cross-legged in the sand off to my left still looking like crap. But at least the old man was awake and aware. He held his ruined staff before him, and the intact symbols below the melted end glowed with power. Pina sat by his side, watching closely.

Others crowded the oasis that was Kokopelli's domain. Uktena was by far the largest. The serpent faced the flames and vortex. His head swayed high above Koko, and those yard-wide coils disappeared into the darkness beyond. The red jewel between his massive horns glowed painfully bright. Power flowed from Uktena, Koko, and the score of others ringing the fire. The energy pushed against the vortex, trying to force it back, to keep it from expanding.

I sensed that without their constraining energy flows, the swirling mass would explode outward to consume the clearing. That so many entities could merge their powers effectively was a miracle. Each flow had a different flavor to it. Koko's smacked of echoing flutes, while Uktena's oozed the primal energy and raw confidence of the hunt. The other streams varied greatly, but one of the strongest held a cool imperious energy vibrating with a smugness I recognized.

I traced that cold power back to its source, a tall elegant woman on the far side of the clearing. Tia, the Goddess of Peaceful Death, held forth a manicured alabaster hand as if daring the rip in the veil to approach. So, the Neutral Council had joined the effort in spite of their proclaimed indifference.

Her dark eyes drifted in my direction, as if to acknowledge my revelation before turning back to concentrate on the task at hand. It must have been a trick of my imagination because despite my shouts and waves no one else noticed me, not even my own father.

With the Light Court and Neutral Council joined in battle to hold the worlds apart, Koko no longer bore the burden alone. More than just those standing before me aided him. Energy flowed from beyond the clearing, spiraling out from many of the distinct landscapes rising along the skyline—sort of like pocketed domains crowding close against Koko's own. The realms of man and gods alike were forced together as the vortex gained strength and the world veil weakened.

An incredible amount of power opposed the vortex—yet it wasn't enough. The sickly green maelstrom bulged and contorted, the suppressing energy coming in from my right faltered, and a grating rumble shook the ground. A skyline of majestic towers and sweeping castle parapets canted sideways into an adjacent mountain region covered in blue ice and snow. Everyone in the clearing staggered and forced more power into their spells as the sound grew in a deafening crescendo.

A blinding blue flash like a spot welder eclipsed the colliding landscapes, and the ground stilled. Even here in a dream, I blinked water from my eyes, trying to clear magenta afterimages. My eardrums throbbed at the sudden silence. When my vision cleared, there was a gap on the horizon. Both the castle and mountain realms were gone.

18. Abide the Dark

"**Y**OU SONS of bitches!" Manny's scream brought me awake with a jerk.

He charged the circle of Ant People, fire blazing in each hand, eyes wild. No one else had moved so I couldn't have been out long. He smashed into a pair of the bug-like creatures. These beings were incredibly strong, but Manny swept them aside with brute strength and fire that left our captors staggering back and batting at their burning clothes.

"You killed them all!" His hands blazed white hot as he reached for the elaborately dressed leader.

I had a vague notion of trying to prevent what unfolded, of keeping him from starting an all-out war we couldn't win. But whatever had set Manny off opened an opportunity. We surged forward, following our unstoppable companion as he bore down on the creature standing between me and my staff.

The leader raised his left hand and leveled the narrowest of those oddly padded fingers at the enraged man bearing down on him. The gesture was casual, as if pointing out an interesting bird, but the fire raging in Manny's hands winked out.

Manny stumbled to a stop, staring at his hands in confusion, and the rest of us damned near plowed him over. Before we knew what was happening, a hooked staff circled each of our necks. The leader shook his head, turned, and walked into the entrance.

From then on, our treatment was none too gentle. We were pressed into the entrance behind their leader, forced to keep up a grueling pace through the tunnels thanks to the ants pulling us along by our necks. When the dirt walls and dripping roots widened to stone, we walked three abreast with an ant to each side and two hooks to keep us from making a run for it.

The push and pull had my neck aching. We'd all be bruised from chin to shoulder, but Manny had it worst. He screamed and fought every inch of the way at first—either due to the madness that had overtaken him or from the touch of what must have been cold iron on his skin. We'd all be bruised, but Manny's skin blistered and burned. Not long into the trek, he collapsed in spite of our captors trying to keep him walking. They trussed him into another litter and we kept moving.

It was a long, uncomfortable walk. After a time, we funneled back into a narrow stretch only to pop back out on the surface. The trees had thinned, replaced by rock outcroppings and hard-packed dirt.

Rather than offering the opportunity to escape, we emerged in the midst of another legion of monsters marching—I presumed—toward the vortex. It looked like the groups would ignore each other, but a troop of trolls vectored out to block our path, forcing the Ant shaman into a discussion with one of the sand-wielding demons. The creature pointed back at where we huddled among the ants. The demon grew agitated when the rumble of engines ripped the air and our four-wheelers careened toward us—each under the expert guidance of an ant.

"They're using up all our gas," Pete muttered.

That this tribal society could even operate machinery was impressive, as was the shaman's calm demeanor in the face of rising tension in the troops blocking our path. I couldn't make out the discussion—even if we were close enough it seemed unlikely these strange beings would speak in English—but the demon clearly made demands concerning us. Our captors were just as clearly unwilling to comply.

The tense confrontation ended anticlimactically when the demon puffed out its chest, spun around, and motioned his troops onward. The trolls looked at one another in confusion, but after some prodding from a large brute who looked to be in charge, the stone goliaths shuffled away to resume their trek—as did we.

"What the fuck." Quinn's voice washed back as a harsh whisper.

Our travel arrangement didn't allow for easy conversation, but I sucked in a breath at what she'd spotted. Boulders rose to either side of the path as we climbed in elevation. Far ahead, the irregular stone blended into smooth, flat walls with broken windows. A majestic building rose at the far end of the city street. Its rectangular base of stone and concrete supported a five-story-high clock tower topped with a slender cone.

Long ago there would have been a statue at the pinnacle of its crumbling roofline because that's what all the historic photographs showed whenever you looked up Old Philadelphia's city hall. The ancient structure certainly hadn't been there a moment ago, and neither had the corridor of building fronts lining the street. The latter merged with the rocky terrain in a Frankenstein blend of alien landscape and ruined city.

With my attention diverted, I stumbled. The hooks tightened into a choking hold, hoisting me up by the neck and preventing me from falling flat on my face. I got my feet under me and glared at my handlers. In that short expanse of time, the path ahead reverted to rocks and scrub brush; the buildings were gone.

The next mirage appeared ten minutes later off to our left. A low line of storefronts nestled under an overhang flickered as if illuminated by faulty fluorescent lights. The buildings were in better repair than the town hall had been, which made sense. Most of the shops were abandoned, but picking out Marge's store was easy because I regularly stopped by her bakery. As with the downtown scene, one moment a half-block of New Philadelphia encroached on the arid landscape and the next…nothing.

It wasn't in my head. Quinn definitely had spotted that first one, and all heads turned as we marched by the latest vision. The desert and vortex had claimed those areas back home. If our worlds were physically merging, this might be a foreshadowing of things to come—pieces of our reality dropping into this one. Teasing out the thought made my head hurt. Forcing solid matter together didn't seem like a good idea. Or maybe rocks and trees from here would phase back into Philly to balance things out. All we could do was keep our eyes open and try not to get caught up in any future confluence.

The canyon walls grew steeper. At the narrowest point, the shaman called a halt by raising one of those flat, oven-mitt hands. Our hooks were removed, and I rubbed my neck. But our newfound freedom was short-lived. A guard pulled my hands down and worked his pad-like fingers around my wrists, forming white mesh shackles. The ridges on those pads felt rubbery where they touched my skin. The new restraints thickened as he worked and drew my wrists together tight with the same material that had secured Manny and me to our litters.

The others received similar treatment. My second guard moved among us, building a tether so we were all linked by our shiny new shackles. I didn't sense any magic so figured they made the material like spiders spun web. Manny slept on, but was secured with more webbing across knees and chest. His outburst and the fact he remained unconscious worried me. The shaman had to be keeping him under on purpose.

Though humiliating, this new arrangement made walking easier. Even the pace proved more reasonable as we climbed rocky terrain to a vista overlooking a wide valley. A road wound down toward a shimmering blue ribbon. The river ran slow and shallow along the length of the valley, curving around more hillocks and mounds reminiscent of the tunnel entrances we'd used. But as we wound our way down, the structures resolved into modest dwellings.

The construction reminded me of Koko's adobe halls, except these were reddish-brown and curved instead of rectangular. Even the base of the red cliffs rising beyond the water was riddled with openings, and people moved between them along narrow paths. My mounting excitement that this might be the shield's resting place from Koko's holographic map died as I realized the cliffs weren't grand enough. Plus, neatly cultivated fields bridged the gap between cliffs and the river's bend.

Our odd procession worked down among glares and muttered curses. Hideous forms squatted in front of the huts along the trail. Discounting the shaman, distinguishing individuals among our escorts was virtually impossible. We weren't treated well, but neither were we harassed by the straight-laced contingent. By contrast, waves of malice rolled off those we passed.

This hunched and misshapen race bore more resemblance to the demons and trolls—or maybe gargoyles. Thicker of body with no two identical, they presented a Picasso rendering of swollen faces and grotesque features. Missing eyes, thick scars, and dangling limbs attested to their aggressive nature. Our flanking guards provided a buffer, and the masses lurking along the road seemed content to glare and leave our fate in the hands of the Ant People.

After winding to the river, we clomped over a wooden bridge. Fields of beans lay to either side as we marched toward the buildings lining the cliff's base. It seemed unlikely the mixed denizens would have time for farming. The shaman and his soldiers would be off fighting or scouting most of the time, and the "people" lining the streets looked to be more of the raw-meat variety. I caught Pete studying the fields and shared my skepticism.

"Might be other farm hands." He shuffled up close, but our guards didn't seem to mind. "Either way, they're crap farmers."

"Why do you say that?" The carefully tilled and planted fields looked well laid out, and with the river so near they certainly had ample water.

"It's all blighted. See those spots on the stems and how the beans curl? I don't know why it hasn't reached the leaves yet, but give it time. I doubt they'll get one harvest out of this."

We were led down to a hard-packed dirt circle surrounding a fire pit. Our ATVs arrived before us and were parked in a neat row off to the left. The red wall towered over us, rising perhaps a hundred feet. In addition to ground entrances, doorways opened in staggered levels a third of the way up the cliff. The craftsmanship struck such a resemblance to the original stone that it was difficult to tell if the dwellings had been built out from the rock face or tunneled into it—perhaps both.

I expected we'd be the center of attention, but only two guards stayed with us while the shaman and the rest carted the injured Ants forward. They lowered both to the ground on either side of an over-sized doorway that opened onto the circle. Someone—or something—moved inside. The shaman stepped up between the stretchers to meet...the shaman.

An identical Ant leader strode out of the shadows and exchanged a few whispered words. The lack of hard consonants and rolling vowels told me they didn't speak English. They wore identical armor, and I searched for some physical difference, irrationally worried they might shift about leaving me uncertain which one was "our" shaman.

"Our dude's a lefty," Quinn said with a flip of her head. "Check it out, all his gear is on the left arm and even the feathers of his headdress angle off to that side. The macho guy has everything strapped on his right."

How she knew they were male was beyond me, but Quinn was correct. With the Ants facing each other, I hadn't caught that their ceremonial regalia sat on the same side and therefore was worn on different arms. In typical Quinn fashion, she'd also nailed the newcomer's attitude. The pair might look like carbon copies, but our shaman acted like a self-confident, reasonable individual, while the new one swaggered and postured, clearly going for intimidation. *Asshole.*

Lefty waved his people forward, and two of our guards carrying a linen sack dumped its contents in front of the pair. Weapons, rations, and my staff spilled out.

"We need that." I gaped at the staff.

"Not exactly in a position to stroll up and grab it," Pete said. "What are they doing to those guys?"

"Buying us time. Ralph!" I called to the imp in a hissed whisper.

Ralph still lounged between the handlebars of our ATV as if our capture was just part of the plan. At my call, he hopped down and strolled toward me while the shamans chanted over the injured guards. Each pulled various items from his belt and waved them over their respective charge in a kind of ceremonial show. Foreign words flowed in a constant sing-song stream as the ritual stretched on. The others stood back, giving them room to work and leaving our pile of supplies unguarded.

"Enough with the eating!" I couldn't help snapping at the little guy as a strip of licorice appeared in his balled fist. "See my staff over there?"

I pointed to where our supplies had been dumped. Ralph frowned at his candy, stuffed it in his mouth, and turned to study the foot of carved wood jutting from the pile. He chuffed out excited little breaths and bobbed his head in what I'd come to realize was a nod.

"Get it for me."

"And the knife," Quinn added. "So we can cut ourselves free."

"And the knife, but be careful—you know, sneak over like when you borrow Piper's toothbrush."

Again the bouncing nod. I grinned at Quinn's wrinkled nose and scanned the circle for our follow-on move. Keys still dangled from each ATV. We'd have to race along the river and get out of the valley downstream to avoid all the creatures that had nothing better to do than line the road we'd come in on. I shot a glance at the road manager, still comatose and strapped to his stretcher.

"Can you two wrestle Manny onto the back of Vance's ride?"

Pete and the deputy gave a curt nod. The Shamans' ritual wailed on, enthralling everyone—including our two token guards. *This could really work.* Once out of the valley, the staff would point us in the right direction and we'd leave the ants in the dust. After Ralph came back with—

"What are you waiting for?" Ralph hadn't budged. "Get going, boy. Bring back the staff and knife." He bobbed and turned toward the pile of gear—and still didn't move.

I gave him a little nudge forward. The imp could be fearsomely strong in a fight, but it seemed impossible someone under two feet tall could suddenly become so heavy. I pushed a little harder urging him forward. He blinked up at me like I was some kind of idiot, plopped down onto his butt, and turned his attention back to the show—a long flat strip of pink-striped taffy clutched in his little gray fist.

"*Where* does he get that stuff?"

Ralph bit off the end and chewed with his mouth open, ignoring Pete's question and effectively squashing my grand escape plan. A good five minutes later, the shamans wound down, put away the assorted tools of their trade, and laid hands on their charges in a more clinical examination.

"Did you sense any magic?" I asked Quinn.

"Zilch."

"Me neither. If any of the elements were involved, I should have at least felt it—even with this stupid song stuck in my head."

The inane music had been whisper-quiet, so I tried to ease an old Ozzie song up from the vaults. My magic roiled just below the surface—ready and willing—but as soon as I brushed it, the damned earworm exploded to full "volume." I hastily abandoned my attempt, and the tune settled down to a dull background loop, which was so much better than blacking out again.

"They lack healing magic." Dwain wriggled into the center of our huddle, looking way too fresh for having been dragged over half the third world. "Those rituals are familiar and should work."

"But nothing's happening," Quinn said.

Which wasn't exactly true, now that I took another look. Both shamans still prayed over their charge, but the patients had curled in on themselves in agony. Although they'd each been cut, the ceremony and exaggerated postures seemed a bit much. The guard who got sliced across the front was hurt worst, but the shallow four-inch cut wasn't exactly life threatening. Neither were the gashes along the other guard's left forearm, and yet everyone acted as if the two were on death's doorstep.

"Enough of this!" Dwain pulled himself up to his full height, slid his hands out of the restraints, and pushed past us to march over to the doorway.

"He could have simply walked away all along?" Vance spoke up for the first time.

I felt his frustration. But then again, where could the sprite go? For now, his destination was all too clear. Dwain marched right up to the litters, ignoring both leaders as he bent to examine one of the injured. A guard moved to pull him away, but our shaman held up a paddled hand to stop him.

"I hope Dwain knows what he's doing," Quinn said.

"Pina calls him an expert healer," I said. "But neither is badly hurt, so this has to be a scam. I'm worried what the big bad shaman will do when Dwain calls their bluff."

Pain shot through my wrists as our bonds jerked tight and dragged us to the left.

"Hey!" we both protested.

Our assigned guard yanked the tether again, and we fell silent. Our wardens moved closer, having realized Dwain slipped his leash. Now, there was no way we'd sneak away without a fight.

Dwain pushed his first patient flat, but the ant groaned and curled back like a spring to protect his sliced chest. I felt the sprite's magic rise. Where Pina's tasted of green grass and flowers, Dwain's was ocean air and sunshine—clean and pure. He stroked the ant's bulbous head, running both hands down over its shoulders and sides.

Acting or not, the pain drained from the creature's face and it relaxed back onto the litter. Magic eased over the wound, cleansing and sealing. Red pulsed in my Sight, but disappeared under his soothing touch—a sure sign infection or poison had indeed settled into the superficial wound. Could Manny have lied about his blade?

Dwain stood as his patient relaxed into sleep, and a collective gasp rose from the guards. Even the shamans looked impressed and fell into animated discussion as Dwain treated their second casualty.

Word spread during Dwain's ministrations. A small crowd of the creatures we'd passed on the road stood outside the circle, and more shambled and stumbled over the bridge, heading our way.

The day we'd met, Dwain struck me as irresponsible. He'd been quite the trickster and totally without remorse when goofing on his friends. Later, I'd seen him as a leader, a force of inspiration to his people in the face of insurmountable odds. Here, he demonstrated compassion, and my chest swelled with pride, which was ridiculous because it wasn't like he was my kid or anything—yet there it was. The sprite had done the Ant People and us a great service. He showed them we were not a threat to be feared.

"I bet we'll be treated differently now." I turned my best let's-be-friends smile on the approaching shamans and their flanking guard.

It took no time at all for my prediction to prove true.

* * *

"You just had to go and jinx it!" Pete kicked up clouds of dust as he stormed to the back of the room—our cell.

The shamans watched as the guard slammed the door shut with an all-too-final clang, but only the new leader gave a self-satisfied smirk in response to Pete's outburst. Our original shaman looked sad and tired, as if he'd lost an argument about how best to honor us—I wish.

"We've done nothing to deserve this!" I grabbed the bars out of reflex and gave them a good shake. *Definitely locked.* "We aren't criminals." Shaman better-than-the-rest spit out a little disgusted laugh and turned to leave. "You're not fooling anyone. I know you understand us. Hell, we saved your men."

Good Shaman started at my words as his counterpart spun on me. "*You*—" the word dripped with scorn—"saved no one. That was the little spirit's doing."

I bit back a self-satisfied laugh at having gotten him to speak, and damned if it wasn't in English—or maybe their magic just let us hear it that way. Quinn, Pete, and Vance pressed close to listen. Dwain had been taken elsewhere, probably to be put on a pedestal and adored. Ralph had gone missing in action. When the guards herded us to the far end of the cliff and our...accommodations, the imp simply vanished. The Ant People didn't notice or care, which left me wondering if they were even aware of our small friend. If not, that gave us an advantage, although how to capitalize on his freedom was a head scratcher.

"What about him?" I jerked a thumb at Manny, still unconscious and strapped to the stretcher laying along the wall.

"That one is dangerous." The shaman's voice was shrill as a cracked wooden flute.

"You haven't begun to see dangerous."

His continued smug attitude had me seeing red. I leaned hard against the bars I still gripped. The sheer gall of attacking and then imprisoning innocent passers-by, especially when the stakes for our world were so high and after Dwain helped them…

"Ed?" The warning note in Quinn's voice had me blinking to clear my vision.

Black veins snaked from beneath my hands, the metal responding to the Earth magic called up by my emotion. I hadn't cast a spell. The power snuck under the rising crescendo of the tune blocking my music. The shaman stepped back, eyes wide, pulled a pouch from his belt, and sent a reinforcing wave of will to bolster the earworm. I staggered as my element warred with the counter-spell. Rather than black out, I shunted the Earth power into the bare dirt and forced my hands to unclench. The lines of corrosion faded, and the bars returned to normal.

"You see how they repay us, Muki-Dawa?" the more aggressive of the two asked. "With disrespect and treachery."

"Peace, Maasi-Muuyaw. The boy is clearly over-wrought. How would you behave in his place?"

"I would never find myself in such a position." Maasi-Muuyaw threw up his hands in disgust. "Your people found them. Treat them as you like. You always do."

He spun on his heel and stomped off, taking half the guards with him. The shaman that captured us regarded me for a long moment. He grasped a rough-hewn figurine hanging from his belt and made a deft series of symbols in the air with the fingers of his other hand.

"Your friend will wake soon. Give your word that he and yours will bring no harm to my people." He too reminded me of flute song, but his high-pitched words lilted pure as a concert piccolo.

"We won't harm you. That was never our intent." I stopped short of revealing our reasons for entering their world. "Just let us be on our way, and we won't trouble you at all."

I scowled at the bars, having no clue what we'd done to offend his people in the first place—aside from defend ourselves. Had we strayed into sacred lands, or disturbed some woodland preserve?

"My brother thinks me too soft-hearted." He cast a glance at the retreating leader. "But Muuyaw's concerns are not entirely unfounded. You bring machines from another time—another world. We cannot know your true intent. You will be treated well, but must stay here for now.

"Speak with that one, soothe him." Dawa pointed his mitten-hand at Manny, who rocked beneath his restraints as if fighting back to consciousness. "He is out of balance, even for one of his kind. We will see what tomorrow brings."

"We don't have time to waste." How could I convince this guy to let us go?

"You wish to enlighten us as to your purpose in our lands?"

He cocked his head and made a clicking noise through flat plates that passed for teeth. A crease at each corner swept up from non-existent lips to where cheekbones would be if his face wasn't so round. The overall impression was indeed of an ant scissoring its mandibles. When my silence stretched, he gave a very human shrug and shuffled away with his guard in tow.

The whole situation felt very good-cop bad-cop, and I had to wonder if we were being played for fools. If Muuyaw had his way, we'd never be released. Dawa seemed more reasonable, but there was no guarantee he'd let us get on with our mission any time soon.

Neither came across as truly evil. Oh, Muuyaw was filled with disdain and a superiority complex, but not the gleeful malevolence those of the dark cultivated. I'd promised not to hurt their people, but breaking free was on the top of my to-do list.

"Let me up!" Manny's demand snapped me out of my thoughts.

"Ed, a little help here." Quinn struggled to keep the road manager from flipping face-down into the dirt as he thrashed against his restraints.

I rushed over and steadied the stretcher, but had nothing to cut him free.

"They're gone. All of them. It's all gone." White showed around his wild eyes.

"Take it easy and tell us what's wrong. We've gotta find a way to cut you free."

I ended up using a jagged rock to saw at his bonds while Quinn told him what had occurred while he was out. Her voice calmed his thrashing, but Manny vibrated like an over-taut guitar string. As soon as the last strap parted, he leapt to his feet and rushed the bars.

He spent his fury on the metal, trying to tear the bars free amidst a steady stream of curses. In the few months we'd known him, Manny had never thrown fits of rage—arrogance and condescension yes, but always controlled. He eventually ran out of steam, sank to the floor, and covered his face with both hands.

"Everything is gone." Desolation teetered between his ragged breaths.

"What's gone?" I crouched down by the door.

"Our majestic mountains, the rivers and lakes, the people. My world is gone—annihilated in the blink of an eye."

"They're messing with your head. I can't escape this song blocking my magic. The Ant People must have done something similar to you. It's a spell to block magic." It was the only thing I could think of.

"No." Manny shook his head, which looked to take supreme effort. "Their spell quells the flow of power, wrapping it in cotton. What I saw in my mind was different. The castle crashing into the blue mountains of another world. The terror as thousands of my people realized the end was at hand. The flash of light as both worlds erupted into pure energy." He grabbed my shirt in both hands and looked me in the eyes. "Ed, I felt them die."

I'd seen mountains and castles collide in my dream as the forces of light fought to contain the vortex. Two of the pocket worlds collided and were gone in the blink of an eye. Manny must have seen the recognition in my eyes because he sagged back, his head slamming the bars with a sharp crack.

If my dream had been real, if two worlds had been vaporized… I didn't know what to say. I'd long suspected Manny came from one of the dark lands where beings still plotted to stop Koko and capture his children. But even they didn't deserve to be wiped from history without warning.

19. Wasting Time

A NNA WOKE before sunrise to the crack of a rifle. She stumbled over the groggy forms strewn across the living room floor, nearly skewered herself on the stuffed deer head by the back door, and peered through the curtains. The moon had set, but the sand around the farm flashed green in time to the vortex. Two spotlights darted across the ground in stark white ovals. Dark shapes scuttled along the dunes, probably more scorpions or spiders. But larger silhouettes rose in front of the glowing green gateway—a lot of them.

"Piper, Melissa, you need to see this!"

The women were already halfway through the doorway. Pete's sister held her shotgun in one hand with comfortable ease, a mirror image of Piper and her notebook.

"What ya got?" Melissa asked as another shot rang out from the second floor.

"Looks like a small army." She tried to count individuals but gave up after twenty because they swayed and mingled, making the task impossible. "Guys upstairs are taking pot shots, but nothing's going down. Will the threshold keep them out?"

"Good question." Piper's pen flew across the paper. "There's more than one type of creature out there. Those skinny ones move like the shamblers Pete described. I don't recognize the others. That squad of hulking brutes over to the west are huge, but if the threshold keeps the sands at bay, it ought to offer some protection."

"My god, that thing's close." Melissa pointed up at the vortex that now stretched across most of the landscape.

Anna found it hard to tear her eyes off the incoming hordes. The gaunt feral faces of the ghouls in Milwaukee flashed though her memory. She shivered and pushed the past down deep where it couldn't hurt her. Beyond the monsters, the leading edge of the frozen tornado stood only a stone's throw from the back wall of the barn.

"The process is accelerating." Piper flipped through some sketches she'd made of the vortex since their arrival. "We don't want to be in the house when it gets swallowed."

"We can load the vehicles using the inside barn entrance without exposing anyone to those creatures." Melissa jerked her chin at a group of confused shamblers, which had stopped short a hundred feet from the porch.

"Get everyone ready to evacuate." Piper squinted into the pale light of approaching dawn. "Let's hope they stay around back."

Anna closed her eyes and stoked her Spirit reserves with a simple opening from the A-Chords' title track. The magic rose like a loyal dog, warm and reassuring. She wouldn't be taken by surprise again.

"What about the desert?" Anna asked. "Ed couldn't hold a direction without Ralph's help."

"Best we can do is head west and hope to get clear before we run out of gas." Piper shrugged. "The threshold is holding. Things will work out."

The window to their left shattered, spraying glass across the floor as a fist sized rock rolled to a stop on the braided carpet. Thuds on the roof and against the siding told them more projectiles were inbound. Something heavy crashed upstairs, followed by muted curses and gunfire.

* * *

A heavy weight pinned my left arm and pulled me from dreamless sleep. Perhaps Koko and the others were succeeding in their efforts to contain the vortex and reestablish the world veil. I held to that hope. If the Light Court and Neutral Council got the job done, our abysmal progress might not matter.

After Manny had calmed down and fell into fitful slumber, the rest of us stretched out using blankets we found tucked away in a corner cupboard. Although our prison wasn't furnished, the small conveniences of the blankets, a basin of running water, and a private alcove for personal business made our treatment seem less harsh.

If I'd been inclined to curl up with any of the others it would have been Quinn, but she'd opted to stay near Manny in case he flew into another rage. A burning ache blossomed in my numb arm. I squinted through the dim light, happy she'd decided to come back over. But the small form shifted with an impressive snort that definitely wasn't my girlfriend's.

"Wake up." I prodded the lump, and it rolled over in a clear attempt to ignore me. "I saw your eyes open, Dwain. Where have you been?"

"Where haven't I been?" The sprite sat up with a wry grin. "These folks dragged me all over the bloody place. I had to sneak in here just to get some peace and quiet."

"What's going on?" Quinn asked as she scooted over to investigate.

"Dwain was just about to tell me how he got in here without causing a fuss."

"No, I was sleeping." He looked pointedly at the blue-striped blanket, but I refused to let him off the hook. "Fine! I came in for a nap. These guys are working me to death. You're lucky to have such cozy digs."

"You're helping them?" Pete sounded incredulous.

Everyone was up at this point and gathered around. Manny hung at the back, scowling and leaning against the wall with his chin tucked on his chest. He had the look of someone who'd lost interest in his surroundings, which was better than flying off on another tirade.

"Sure." Dwain propped himself up against the wall with his legs out straight and clonked his boots together. "They need healing—not just the two guards Manny hurt. There are scads more with recent injuries. Even the most minor cuts get infected."

178

"If the Ants have been fighting, they ought to put their own healers to work," I said.

"Nah, these are more like accidents: twisted ankles, scrapes and cuts, those sorts of things. And I haven't seen any healers. Their leaders are smart, but not one of them has an ounce of common sense when it comes to treating wounds."

"Not everyone has healing powers," I said.

"Forget about magic, though you're right there's none that heals. The thought of cleaning a cut or splinting a broken bone are foreign concepts. To be honest, I pretty much drained my energy and was falling back on the old standbys. They've got a few of the common herbs too, but again no clue what to do with them. I tried explaining things, but it's like talking to rocks. They nod politely, then do something stupid like trying to walk off a broken leg."

Complaining knocked the last vestiges of sleep from Dwain's emerald eyes, but the sprite really did look exhausted. The Ant People must have their healers off doing other work, like maybe supporting the troops funneling into our world. But that didn't make sense. From the exchange we'd seen on the road, they were no friends to those invading forces. Regardless, we had more important things to worry about.

"Can you get us out of here?" I waved Vance over to the entrance, and he shook his head after a quick check of the door.

"So...they don't have healing magic, but they've got plenty of power." Dwain gave me an apologetic look. "I'm sort of a trusted agent, but you're not going anywhere until they say so."

An icy chill ran up my spine, and unseen eyes settled on me. Dwain jerked upright, narrowed his own eyes, and looked from me to the door. His face scrunched up in thought, and he raised a skinny forefinger as if to ask a question. A gray blur shot between us. Dwain's breath whooshed out as if someone'd stepped on his stomach.

The cell door rattled. Ralph materialized with each hand wrapped around a bar and shaking the door for all he was worth. The scrutiny intensified, feeling almost familiar—needing something from me, willing me to—

The presence winked out, and Ralph went ballistic. The imp tore around the room, throwing blankets into the air as he shot past, slamming the cupboard doors open, and generally ransacking the place in a panicked search. Everyone gaped and backed to the wall as he repeated his circuit again and again.

Ralph didn't so much run out of energy as give up in disgust. I jumped as an uncharacteristic snarl tore from his throat. Then the little guy's face crumpled. He gathered a brown blanket into a tight hug, eyes drooping and yellow fang-tips poking from the corners of his frown. Ralph pulled a marshmallow from his hidden stash, raised it to his mouth, but dropped his arm as if it was too heavy.

"Not eating again," Quinn whispered. "And where'd that come from?"

She pointed at the small blanket cradled against his bare chest. All our bedding bore bright, simple designs. The brown bit of cloth was smaller too. Ralph shifted onto his side, and a strip of the furry material spilled to the floor. In the crook of his elbow a pink felt tongue showed beneath beady eyes set in a furry face. Mr. Rabbit gazed calmly back at us.

"Those damned magic pockets again." I tucked one of our blankets around the now snoring imp and Max's old toy. "As long as it makes him happy."

"I could seriously use pockets like that, but we need to get out of here before the rest of us go nuts." Pete glanced at Manny, but instead of taking offense the manager pushed off the wall.

"We're useless with these counter-spells hobbling our power," Manny said. "We need to get to the ATVs and put some distance between us and those two psycho-ant-priests. Their magic will fade with distance. Once it's weak enough, I can break through and ward us against another attack."

"We need the staff or we'll never find the stupid shield," I said. "If Dwain can't help, we'll have to figure out how to escape on our own, take advantage of the next changing of the guard or something."

"There's a big gathering by the bridge today," Dwain offered, then clamped his mouth shut.

"Out with it, munchkin," Manny said, but Dwain shook his head.

"Did they say it was a secret?" Quinn used a different tactic as she nodded with a feminine empathy the rest of us could never manage. "If so, then you're right not to tell."

"Well, no." Dwain's face scrunched up in thought. "They didn't say not to tell. In fact, everybody's talking about it. Most of the village is going to be there to see the twins."

"The shamans are brothers?"

"Yep, just like the twin gods. That's part of why they get to lead. They're going to try calling on the polar gods to save the crops." Now that he was talking, information spilled out of the sprite. "Winter's coming, and there isn't enough food. Things have been growing worse all season—I think since the portal opened. Dawa is the one pushing for the ceremony. Muuyaw sees it as a waste of time because they'll be moving soon."

"I *knew* the crops were failing!" Pete punched his left palm with his right fist. "Where's Mr. Contrary think everyone's going? The forest wasn't exactly brimming with health either."

"Muuyaw wants to lead them out into the fourth world." Dwain had the decency to blush, making the scar across his left cheek stand out as a stark white slash.

"Of course, into our world." Things were starting to make a little sense. "But the vortex is turning everything into desert. They'll be going from the frying pan into the fire."

"I've overheard a lot of debate about that," Dwain said. "The growing desert is an unexpected side effect. Maybe things will return to normal after everyone's across and the portal closes. The Ant People aren't in charge of the portal, or even responsible for it. That's something their twin gods came up with, but the Ant folk aren't complaining too hard. It might be their only way to survive."

"Not at our expense they won't." Quinn stomped in a tight circle. "Even if Earth doesn't become a wasteland, the world is fragile enough. There's no way people will be able to cope with all these creatures, which—by the way—seem awfully bent on taking out everyone they run across. Not to mention this whole other issue of instability across the realms. People *live* in those other planes and they're being snuffed out as we speak."

"The shield is the key." I ticked off what we needed to do on the fingers of my left hand. "We get out of here, get the staff, and find the shield. Once I have my magic back, we can burn the damned thing and this all stops dead in its tracks."

"We've got company," Vance announced from the doorway.

Muuyaw wouldn't deign to speak with us, and the approaching Ant's expression was one of calm endurance rather than a haughty sneer. I figured stepping into the conversation might help build trust.

"Good morning, Shaman Dawa." I tipped my imaginary hat and was rewarded with a wry grin.

"Dawa will do. I am neither shaman nor priest, simply a servant of my people."

"Fair enough. I'm Ed, and these are my friends." I named everyone except the sleeping imp and finished with our suddenly-sheepish sprite. "Of course you already know Dwain."

"Yes, the sprite's been a great help. I'd wondered where he'd gone off to."

"Says it's restful in here. I can't say I like your hospitality, but I get the feeling your brother would rather see us in chains."

"We are"–he looked uncomfortable and struggled finding the right word—"different. But Muuyaw's precautions are not entirely without merit." Dawa's gaze swept over the locked door separating us. "What brings you to our lands?"

"Things are pretty messed up where we come from." I shook my head while formulating a half-truth. "Desert swept over the city and monsters chased us through a swirling green portal. We're just trying to find our way back."

"Come now," he chided. "We are not ignorant savages. It seems unlikely you are here by accident, especially bearing an artifact from antiquity."

Dawa pulled a familiar object from one of the larger pouches on his belt. The length of Koko's guiding staff gleamed in the rising sun, just inches away. So close, but it might as well be on the other side of the planet—unless.

"If you give that back, we'll be on our way." I held out my hand, but let it drop at the hard glint in his eye. "Look, we don't mean you any harm. Your people attacked us."

"We cannot allow you to proceed." Dawa looked around our little prison with sad eyes as he dangled the staff just out of reach. "You travel toward the sacred mountain to shut down the portal and trap us in this dying world. Say it isn't true, and I will consider releasing you."

"We have no desire to lock you in this world." Hell, we hadn't even known there were people here.

"And the portal?"

"It's destroying *our* world!" The glimmer of hope that he'd let us go winked out. "You're invading a wasteland. If you think growing things is hard here, try it in shifting sand. That portal is dangerous and unstable."

"Invading." Dawa spoke to himself, tasting the word I had used—weighing it. "The desolation on both sides of the portal will dissipate. We must move on to survive, just as your ancestors did eons ago. We…I would prefer a peaceable migration."

He bowed his head with a sigh. Seams ran down either side of the smooth crown, reinforcing his insectile appearance.

"So stop it." I couldn't keep the venom out of my voice. "Call back those monsters and let's work something out."

"We don't have the authority to negotiate something like that." Quinn's cautious tone pulled my eyes to her frowning face.

"If not us, then who?" I whispered.

"No matter," Dawa said. "My brother and I serve the twin gods. Muuyaw's god, Pöqanghoya of the northern pole, has set the method. I am but a humble servant of Palöngawhoya of the south."

So his brother and the god of the North were the ones sending shock troops into our world. I thought of the other Ant leader's dismissive and oh-so-superior attitude. If he didn't have a hidden agenda in his back pocket, I'd eat my shoe.

"Muuyaw doesn't strike me as anyone's humble servant."

"We are each cast in the image of our creator." He gripped my staff tighter and slipped it back into his pouch. "As are you. Food will be brought to ease your hunger."

"There'll be war."

People would freak out when the hordes came crashing down on civilization. Even if the sands did recede, humans weren't forgiving.

Dawa spun and marched off, leaving me to stare at his rigid back and contemplate the pouch slapping his spindly thigh. Getting my staff just got a lot harder. Even if we did manage to sneak out during the coming ceremony, how on Earth were we supposed to steal Koko's artifact back if the leader wore it like a handbag?

Our two guards turned mournful eyes my way, the first I recalled them looking at me instead of through me. If I didn't know better, I'd say they felt sorry. I spun around to glare at the room, with arms folded across my chest. Cold metal bars pressed into my back. Out of spite, I dug my heels in and pushed, but the door didn't budge.

"One thing at a time," Quinn said, reading my mood. "First we break out and get to the ATVs. Maybe we can send Ralph in to sneak off with the staff. We'll get Dwain to explain how important it is. Sprites have a way with the little guy."

"So how do we unlock the door?"

"These guys aren't good jailers," Vance said. "They only give the handle a jiggle to make sure it's locked, and the mechanism isn't even a dead bolt. I can shove a wad of cloth into the strike plate the next time they open it, so the latch won't fully seat. It's an old trick that won't work on newer locks, but this thing isn't fancy."

"We'll need a distraction." Pete held his stomach and moaned. "I can fake being sick. You know, cause a real ruckus so they come in and take their eyes off the door."

"As good a plan as any." I shrugged and sank to my butt as everyone turned out their pockets, and Vance looked for something to work the door latch open.

The ATVs were parked in an alcove off to the left of our cell. Dwain swore the keys were still in the ignition, so as long as they had fuel we were golden. Ralph snored on with Mr. Rabbit in a death grip. Hopefully the little guy would be calmer after his nap, and we could see if he understood the concept of pick-pocketing. He'd managed to converse with sprites in the past, so I was counting on Dwain's help in asking him to steal back the staff.

Our developing plan wasn't fool-proof. Hell, it leaked like a sieve and pretty much stunk, but what else could we do? Prickling above my collar had me scratching in earnest before realizing it wasn't a physical sensation. My ears grew hot, but I forced myself to suck in a calming breath.

A year of slinging magic had heightened my perception. The damned guards were watching me, eyes brimming with pity for the foolish human who ended up on the wrong side of their boss. I was sure of it and spun around to glare back, but one of the Ants had left— presumably to get the promised meal. The other gazed off toward the crowd gathering along the fields for the ceremony.

No one so much as cast a glance in our direction as more of the monstrous inhabitants shuffled in to join the crowd, but the sensation of being watched clung like a wet shirt as unseen eyes settled on the back of my head. I resisted the urge to move away from the door. If one of the twisted creatures skulked in the shadows, my back would block their view of our planning. If Koko or one of his cronies watched…well, there wasn't much I could do about that. But it would be decent of them to lend a hand.

20. Glimpse the Dragon

T ROLLS PUSHED forward in a wave with the rear-most monsters prodding those in the front closer to the house. Anna held her breath as the shots from overhead ricocheted off their rocky hide. On her left, Melissa waited with shotgun pushed though the screen.

"Those poor bastards in the front row are disintegrating." Piper's pen flew across the page.

Rifle fire still rained down from the second floor windows, but didn't account for all the chunks of stone sluffing off the lead creatures in sparkling showers. Rage twisted the faces of those pushing from behind, but the ones in front dug in their heels and howled, a sonorous roar like wounded lions.

"They're sacrificing their own." Melissa leveled her gun as the line pressed to within fifty feet.

"Absorbing the protective energy," Piper said. "Look, the shamblers are right on their heels."

Anna reached for her magic and sent a whirlwind out with a sweep of her arm just as Melissa fired. The blast nearly knocked the A-Chords' song out of her head, but Anna held to the bass line—Quinn's part— and pushed her spell past the dying front line. Desperation lent her strength as the shotgun rang out again, but the spell was a mere fraction of what she'd managed in Milwaukee.

Her whirlwind tore at the trolls, blinding a few with sand, but the creatures were simply too massive. Three attackers staggered off in the wrong direction only to come up against the now steadily sparking protective barrier.

The attack faltered. The driving line lost traction as the mass of trolls came up hard against the ancestral barrier twenty feet from the house. The air grew thick with thrumming pressure that squeezed until Anna's teeth ached. She screamed and flew backward as the sparking front line exploded in blue-gold energy. After images made her eyes stream, but the terrible pressure winked out—along with the protective barrier.

Trolls, shamblers, and gaunt creatures on spindly insect legs picked themselves up as the women clawed over broken glass and the tumbled remains of memorabilia that had lined the now windowless sun porch.

"Here they come!" Melissa pushed a box of shells into Anna's hands. "Five at a time when I run out. Piper, grab the double-barrel from over the fireplace, but brace yourself or you'll be back on your ass."

Pete's sister fired, picked a new target, and fired again. Anna's head rang with each blast, to the point she was certain no music would come. The ache deep in her core meant she probably couldn't manage another spell anyway. She focused on counting shots as Melissa pumped off round after round.

Stuttering gunfire sounded overhead as the men rejoined the defense. Anna fumbled getting the next five cartridges to the other woman. Melissa was an old hand with the weapon and calmly reloaded before sighting on the nearest troll. The brute tried to tug its leg free of the splintered back steps that gave way as it tried to climb onto the deck. The blast took it full in the chest, dropping the monster in a spray of rocky debris. Melissa whooped and gave Anna a high-five.

"Less celebrating, more shooting, ladies." Piper hoisted the massive double-barrel to her shoulder. "They aren't staying down!"

Although slowed by their defense, the trolls trudged forward. Even the one Melissa shot point-blank pushed to its feet, despite the gaping hole in its chest that bled a sandy gray slurry. Piper gave it both barrels. A post supporting the roof burst into a cone of splinters, but part of the blast caught the troll's shoulder and spun it around. Anna winced as Piper rocked back. It would be a miracle if the recoil hadn't dislocated her shoulder, but Anna scrambled to put two new shells in her open hand.

Three trolls tore at the floorboards, wading through the decking as if in a waist deep swamp. The floor buckled as they approached the door they couldn't possibly fit through. Boots pounded down the steps in the main room.

Six men streamed in to flank the shotgun-wielding women. It was odd to see the band with guns instead of instruments. Mr. Conti called directions to the others, moving them away from the firefight. Deafening didn't begin to describe the roar from those weapons. Yet it wasn't enough. Shamblers and the spindly creatures flowed up behind the trolls. Scrabbling on the outside walls and then in the rooms above told her the latter were in the house.

They abandoned the sun room and fell back into the main house. The exterior wall collapsed, sending rubble across the broken toboggan and trampled deer. The trolls stood with backs to the rising sun and green vortex, the last sight she'd ever see. Or would these monsters take her prisoners, force her back into captivity... *never again!* The promise had her feet moving.

"Anna, no!" Brent tried to pull her back.

His grip was weak, his hands as shadows in the face of the power welling up from within. *Never again.* The room darkened, narrowed to a tunnel ending at the horrible creatures. Calloused hands reached; fetid breath panted hot. And Quinn's bass thrummed in her soul as "Lightspeed" rose on staccato drums. A departure for the A-Chords, the alternative beat spoke to her and pulled every bit of power to the surface. Her Spirit energy rode the lyrics, stoking the storm within.

Rising to the setting sun,
Continuing to move beyond,
Sing our praises now and then,
Forget not that we were once human,
Riding at lightspeed.

Anna held nothing back...*never again!*

Raw power tore from her, threatening to rip away her soul. Spirit drove away at impossible speed; thunderous claps followed the spell as displaced air rushed in to fill the void. The front line of enemies sheered in half, startled eyes darting in confused horror as the life faded from them. A score of trolls and shamblers simply ceased to be in that instant of raw intensity.

The world swam. Her companions materialized around her, only to spin away as she dropped to the floor. Lips moved, but no sound came. Piper and Melissa dragged her by the arms to the dining room.

The men formed a defensive ring around the doorway as hulking shapes moved into the ruined sun room. She hadn't gotten them all. Gunfire filtered through her muffled world like popcorn just getting started, but it wouldn't help. Even with all their efforts, all her power, they'd lost.

Screams ripped through the muted popping. The men stood with guns dangling in loose grips. Dark shadows and tangible dread fell over the room of attackers. Fear thrummed along the walls. Anna looked to Melissa's gun, but couldn't move, couldn't think through the unreasoning terror gripping her throat.

More screams, and the room beyond was suddenly only half full. A wall of green flashed into view, pausing long enough for golden cat eyes the size of headlights to blaze from the darkened room. Great horns swept up from the reptilian forehead.

Only the front end of the dragon fit inside the house as it flattened trolls and shamblers. The last time she'd seen the horned serpent he was a massive snake. In dragon form, Uktena brought his full power to bear, crushing, skewering, and chomping the hapless attackers.

"Look out!" Billy was the first to snap out of the dragon-fear Uktena projected.

He swung to intercept movement on the stairs, slamming the butt of his rifle into the head of the first sinuous insect to flow down behind them. For all his power, Uktena's sheer size prevented him from moving further into the house to help. Billy and Brent clubbed back the horrors, but others crawled down along the sloped ceiling. Hooked forelegs clicked across the crown molding, and both men dove away to let the others open fire. Unlike the trolls and shamblers, bullets made short work of the skulking nightmares.

"Where'd the horned serpent go?" Anna levered herself up and managed a smile of thanks as Piper steadied her.

"Back outside," Piper said. "Sounds like a full-scale battle out there."

Melissa scooped up her shotgun and joined the others. Although the house was clear of attackers, shouts, roars, and other less easily categorized sounds shook the broken house. Billy and Melissa had everyone pile furniture along the missing wall.

Gunfire rang out as they fired over the makeshift barricade. The sizzle and crack of magic joined the sound of battle. Bursts of energy and flame blossomed against the green expanse of vortex. If the enemy's magic overwhelmed Uktena, the rest of them would be sitting ducks.

Anna wished Ed was here. He was always so calm and collected in a fight. Her nerves were frayed to breaking and Piper—for all her comforting words—didn't look much better.

"We better see if they need more ammo," Anna said.

"You okay to walk?" Piper's concern was touching, but walking was the least of her worries.

"If I don't move, I'll probably drop into a stupor. But no magic for a while."

A massive explosion drove dust and plaster from the ceiling. They stepped around the mess and froze as three sharp raps sounded from the entryway. Piper closed her hand around a broken chair leg and hoisted it like a club. Three more precise reports echoed from the entry.

"Monsters wouldn't knock. Would they?" Anna asked.

Piper shrugged, and they crept to the heavy front door to peer through the sidelight. A neatly dressed man with close-cropped hair scowled down at his watch, raised his arm, and tapped out three more knocks.

"When did Charles leave?" Anna opened the door as she spoke, revealing the A-chords' drummer flanked by Manny's assistant Rhonda and a bent old man reminding her of Mr. Conti, though he wore a fur coat and rounded black hat with feathers sticking from its silk band.

"The cavalry has arrived." Charles gestured the other two in with a haughty flourish.

"Weren't you helping upstairs?" Piper leveled her question at the drummer.

"I *was*." Charles gave a casual little shrug at odds with his rigid demeanor. "But someone had to welcome the reinforcements."

"So good to meet you." The old man shuffled forward and grasped Anna's right hand in both of his. "You are the image of your mother, especially your hair."

"You know my mom?"

Warmth radiated from his calloused fingers, sending a pleasant tingling up her arm and easing the aching hole from which she'd pulled too much power. He must be confusing her with someone else because Mom wore her raven-black hair short—very different from Anna's long blond curls.

"Vanessa was always a delight. You certainly must have her lovely voice as well."

Impossible! Vanessa Forbes was her birth mother, a fact Mom and Dad proudly explained to anyone who asked where Anna got her singing voice. The woman was a bit of a legend up in Oregon and was one of the few child-bearing women who felt no compulsion to be tied down with family. That she'd been given up for adoption had never bothered Anna; she was a free spirit herself. The sparkle in the old man's eye, his hawk nose, and the way he smiled encouragingly as the wheels in her head ground away…

"You're him…Kokopelli!" The warmth of his hands—the power flowing from them—had her gasping and wanting to pull away, but she stood frozen by that beady gaze.

"You may call me Koko." He beamed, dropped her hand, and stepped back. "Edan seems to have made the nickname stick, and I find it rather fitting. You of course know Rhonda and Charles."

He raised his palms to encompass the tall black woman and the A-Chords' drummer. Anna hadn't spoken to Manny's assistant in months. Neat, professional Rhonda had forgone her typical business attire for a tight black body-suit that hugged her lean figure. Her cheeks looked more angular and her eyes more slanted than Anna remembered. She strode over to the kitchen table with catlike grace and peered out at the defenders.

"So much noise and so little benefit," she said to Koko. "Give them another task. You've brought ample help."

"They have more right than we to fight for their land," Koko said with a tilt of his head. "Unless your own forces are ready to contribute?"

"We have our own problems." She waved away the old god's suggestion.

Old god. Anna knew it to be true from Ed's stories. Yet it was hard to accept she stood here with an ancient spirit, with the Native American god of dance, healing, and fertility. Heat rose to her face with that last thought. Not that she planned on testing it out any time soon, but she and the other Brights were able to bear children, which wasn't a very lady-like thought to dwell on, especially in the presence of the others and…her father. She pushed the thought away to focus on the here and now.

"Uktena helped clear the house, then headed toward the vortex." At least, she thought that was the direction he'd gone. "Is he a warrior for the Light now?"

"That great lummox?" Rhonda scoffed, but bit back any further words when Koko glared.

The old man—god—might look frail, but the look he leveled at the woman could peel paint and held a threat of barely contained power. For all her brashness, Anna liked Rhonda. She'd never gotten involved in the cross-country feud that always got Ed and Max assigned to crappy rooms. Rhonda might be outspoken and opinionated, but you always knew where you stood with her. Fast as thought, Koko's smile returned.

"We have help from those aligned with the Light, the Neutral Council, and a few stragglers like Uktena who owe allegiance to neither." He pointed to the far side of the room.

Anna crossed to the one window that had miraculously survived. A sea of creatures moved across the sand stretching from house to swollen vortex, which now was easily seen even from the side yard.

Trolls and shamblers pulled into a tight knot to repel what could only be Koko's companions. Beings large and small swarmed over the trolls trying to get past their swinging clubs and meaty fists. Magic sparkled and took down two, but the battle was a sea of confusion with many fronts. A herd of gangly, furry-legged creatures separated a shambler from the group and rammed it with horned heads. It stumbled back to the vortex, fell into the green energy, and was swept up to disappear within.

A trio of tall beings dressed in dark rags appeared behind the goat-people. They each formed a tan ball between their bony hands and tossed it overhead. Arrows of sand speared down, dropping the goats before they could mount a defense.

Mammoth creatures waded through the smaller ones. Uktena appeared around the edge of the farmhouse, locked in battle with a monstrous armadillo crossed with giant boar. The fight was short-lived as the dragon clamped his jaws on the back of the monster's neck and twisted its head out at a sharp angle.

Dozens of skirmishes raged under the scorching sun. A wave of scorpions—or perhaps they were the giant spiders—flowed from the vortex and disappeared around the back of the house. A flash of crimson light painted the sand, and several of the bugs flew back into view—or at least pieces of them did.

"I *think* we're winning," Piper said cautiously. "But to be honest, the bad guys look more organized."

Like Uktena, most of their force fought alone or in small groups. If there was a coherent effort underway, it was lost on Anna. Adding to the confusion were grey-robed figures who strolled through the melee, metering out punishment or skirting the fighting as they saw fit.

"My contemporaries don't—how would you humans put it?" Koko grasped the air as if physically reaching for words. "Don't play well together. This level of physical opposition was not expected. Once we have control, the real work starts."

"What work is that?" Anna asked.

"The veil between worlds is failing. Even with the Neutral Council's gray-robes help, we've been unable to constrain the growing vortex."

"When Ed and Quinn destroy that shield on the other side, this all goes back to normal. Right?" Anna needed to hear good news.

"The pipsqueak's running out of time," Rhonda said in her flippant, direct way, which suddenly didn't seem at all endearing. "If they don't get the job done soon, things go kablooey." The explosion she made with her hands helpfully illustrated her meaning.

"Why are you even here?" Piper rounded on the woman. "Last we knew you were heading out with the others to Baltimore."

"The Company had urgent business requiring my attention," she said in a dangerous purr.

"Sure, the 'company.'"

Ed and his sister figured the band's promotor, Double-M Records, had something more in mind than advocating live rock shows. They'd been at the center of all the nastiness on tour. Although Manny turned out to be okay, some disagreement clearly festered between Rhonda and Piper.

"Ladies, please. The veil teeters on the cusp of failing completely. Working from my realm we've been holding it together, which in turn holds this world apart from the third world. But the process is accelerating. We have come here, where our magic can directly oppose the vortex's growth.

"We will buy young Edan a few more days. But if the veil fails before they find the shield, the gateway will expand to encompass all the Earth. Once that happens, no force in the cosmos can reverse it. Chaos will be visited upon your world and all of our realms. This must not come to pass."

"That's putting it mildly," Charles said as he traded a guarded look with Rhonda.

Koko ignored the comment and turned to Anna. She blinked. The old Indian now wore leather regalia consisting of a white breechcloth, jerkin, and laced boots. His fedora from a moment ago transformed into a simple leather band with a line of beads and three feathers standing proudly over the knot of sandy copper hair pulled tight at the crown of his head.

"Your people's help is welcome," he said with a wave to the porch barricade. "Not all of us are immune to human weapons. Please let your friends know we have arrived and urge them to choose their targets with care."

"Sure thing." Anna pulled Piper toward the others. "Can you *believe* this?"

"That's what I love about magic." Piper spoke in a dreamy whisper. "Everything is connected. Everything's for a reason."

"I don't think we've shot at any good guys," Melissa said after they outlined the situation. "Our main focus is keeping things out of the house. We sent two rifles upstairs to watch the sides, but all the action's out back, mostly shamblers and insects. Everything else is busy with skirmishes by the vortex."

"Does anyone else find it odd that Charles and Rhonda are walking around with Koko?" Brent asked. "I mean, Ed's the only one the old guy spends any time with, unless you count Pina."

"Rhonda's certainly being bossy," Piper said. "There's something going on between her and Charles. They keep making eyes at each other, but haven't exchanged a dozen words before."

"War makes strange bedfellows?" He didn't sound convinced.

"Forget them. Where *is* Pina?" Anna missed the sprite. Of all her friends, Pina had risked the most to help Anna.

"Tell you what"– Piper pushed Melissa and Brent back toward the defenders—"let everyone know the deal. The gray-robes and Uktena are easy to pick out, but put anything that fights the shamblers, trolls, and the like on our do-not-shoot list. Anna, let's go get the rest of the story."

Anna followed as Piper stormed back in to the living room, certain she was going to give Koko hell. But before she could open her mouth, the front door burst open to admit a frantic man dressed in black.

The newcomer was lean and handsome with wavy dark hair and stormy gray eyes. He bore a startling resemblance to Manny, except she'd never seen the mixed look of terror and anger on the road manager.

He pushed past Koko and fell to his knees in front of Rhonda. The woman—so brash and confident a moment before—turned fearful eyes on the man.

"The home realm has...fallen!" He sagged as if the statement took the last of his energy.

"Explain!" Rhonda's cocoa skin turned ashen and her lips pressed into a tight line.

"Energy spikes from the failing veil have the realms in chaos. Power from the vortex sent our world on a collision path with another. Both lands obliterated each other. Shadowhame is no more!"

"Our other realms?"

"Unaffected, for now. Court members who were not on the home world have declared war. Your presence is required. I arrived just ahead of our warriors."

A massive explosion shook the house as if to emphasize his words. They rushed to the windows. A new force joined the battle. Though as diverse as Koko's legion, these moved in unison. Dark and twisted shapes marched from a massive crater, sweeping the field with weapons and magic. They were none too careful about targeting. What looked like a tree elf and a vaguely reptilian biped scurried away from the sand demon they fought to keep from getting blasted.

In short order, the battle that had slowly been drawing to a conclusion ceased. The last of the invaders were pushed back through the vortex and guards took up position around the swirling energy.

"I must leave you now." Koko had his wooden flute clasped in his right hand and his carved staff in the left. "You should make ready to depart in case we fail."

"Why?" Anna asked. "You said the vortex would encompass the world. There will be nowhere to go."

Koko gave her a sad smile. "It's something to do."

Ed's father—her father and father to all the Brights—turned and strode out the front door with Rhonda close on his heels. Without constant gunfire, the room grew deathly quiet. Piper's hand slipped into Anna's with reassuring warmth. Could they really be that close to the end of all they knew and loved?

"Ed will make things right, won't he?" Anna gazed out the broken rear wall to where trails of energy streamed from the hands of many casters to splash against the pulsing green wall.

"Little brother is nothing if not headstrong," Piper said. "He'll get it done."

After all they'd been through her simple words took the edge off the worry. Ed had overcome obstacles the rest of them hadn't even known existed. Not only was he powerful in elemental magic, he was kind. Sure, he got confused sometimes—didn't they all? But in the end he would do what was right. Plus, Ed inspired the people around him. Quinn and the others would be there to back him up.

"Sure he will." Charles had stayed behind and looked none too pleased.

"He's got lots of help and a piece of Koko's staff to guide them." Anna nodded with conviction.

"Think this through. Let's say they find the cursed shield, mange to destroy it, and everything returns to 'normal.'" He put air quotes around the last word. "He's being duped. They're just using him to make their own worlds safe."

"You're being a douche," Piper said. "That portal needs to be shut down for all our sakes."

"And how long do you figure that will take, once the shield is destroyed?"

"Once the shield is gone, there'll be nothing to sustain it. That's the nexus of all the changes." Piper launched into professor mode. "The desert expanded over the course of several months, but it needed to feed off Earth magic while gaining momentum. Things should reverse much quicker. Nobody knows if the sand itself will vanish back to where it came from. If it has to naturally dissipate, we're probably talking years for it all to be absorbed into the soil. But the climate should revert as soon as the portal collapses."

"So your boy in there drives miles across an alien world to trash the artifact holding open the only way home. Doesn't sound like a good plan to me."

"Ed will be trapped!" Anna saw it now. "Piper, we have to do something."

"Let's not jump to conclusions. Koko wouldn't send them in if there wasn't a way back. Maybe I'm wrong. It might take time for the energy to dissipate, time they can use to get back out." She shot Charles a glare. "I'll chase down Koko and ask. Stay with Melissa and the others. If it does take a while for the desert to disappear, we might need to be packed and ready after all."

Anna bit her lip as the other woman grabbed the big shotgun and headed out. She really ought to help, but Piper had a look in her eye that said she needed to do this alone. With the invaders pushed back, it ought to be safe out there—or as safe as it could be with Dark forces mingling with Light.

It was surreal to think the Dark Court had come to help—or what was left of them had. She didn't trust any of them, not even Rhonda now that it was clear the woman was part of that world. Piper should be safe enough. She'd never been the direct target of their attentions—unlike Anna, Quinn, and Ed.

"He's not going to tell the truth. Check your legends. Kokopelli is called the trickster for good reason."

The drummer needed to go help the others and give her time to think, but he seemed perfectly happy to stay and torment her.

"Ed trusts him and so do I. Is 'Trust no one' something from your military background?"

"No." He reigned in an explosive laugh. "That would be the teaser for an old science fiction show. My motto is do it yourself because no one will do it for you."

"Sucks to be you." Seeds of doubt made her queasy and rude.

"All I'm saying is to give it some thought."

21. Doppelganger

"NO WONDER Ralph's stuffing his pockets. This tastes like bittersweet honey." Pete licked his fingers and handed another sticky brown cube to the imp.

"I can't believe they bought your act." Pete had been hamming it up so badly I'd expected our captors to laugh.

Instead, the guards had rushed in when Pete went into his wailing and thrashing fit. His performance had them worried. One ran to fetch the heap of sweet treats to round out our meager meal of stone-ground bread, veggies, and soft cheese.

"Dwain's right, they know squat about medicine." Pete shrugged as he counted the messy sweets. "How could anyone think I was simply hungry? Dry heaving and praying for death? That was some top-notch acting, and these heathens throw food at me."

"Ancient cultures used honey as a cure-all," I said.

The fact they trotted out a good two pounds of the stuff for a prisoner spoke to a hidden generosity, especially with the crops failing and winter coming. Or maybe it was perishable, and they just couldn't take it along on the invasion of our world.

"No, it's just a treat." Dwain studied a cube, shook his head, and made a sour face as Pete popped another into his mouth. "I've heard them talking about how it's the one thing growing well. These forest fungi get aged in urine to draw out the toxins and bring the sweet sugars to the surface."

Pete gagged and spat. The cube he'd been chewing arced to the sandy floor amid sputtered curses. He pushed the pile out to arm's length while continuing to spit and hack. Ralph took that as a sign to help himself, and the pile dwindled as those tiny gray hands blurred into action.

"They're trying to poison me!" Pete scrubbed his tongue with a thick slice of bread.

"It's getting dark. Can we focus?" I asked.

The door was rigged to open. During Pete's flailing, Vance jammed his wad of cloth into the lock's receiver along the door jamb. So we could back the bolt out once the ceremony began.

"I don't know if your imp is going to have room for that short staff of yours," Dwain said, motioning to the wet stain where the pile of sweets had been.

"Let's just assume his magic pockets are bottomless. I'm more worried about him understanding what to do."

"He's got it." The sprite ticked off Ralph's role on stubby fingers. "Go find Dawa, make sure he has your staff, and bring it back to the zoomy cars." Dwain rushed on when I raised an eyebrow. "That's how he thinks of the all-terrain vehicles. Ralph wants to drive one someday."

"Good." I nodded and Ralph mimicked the gesture with a goofy fang-filled grin. "Let's give the ceremony twenty minutes to get rolling. It'll be a little darker by then."

Thanks to Dwain we knew the Ants planned on a long litany of prayers and offerings to their twin gods. Hopefully, they would be so absorbed in their rituals that we could slip away unnoticed. The early moon was bright enough to keep us from running into a gully, so we'd push the vehicles around the river bend before firing them up.

The hard part would be quietly taking out our guards. Bashing them over the head felt pretty barbaric, especially given they'd tried to help Pete. But we couldn't risk them sounding the alarm.

"What if we head in the wrong direction?" Quinn asked. "You haven't used the staff since that first day in the forest. If we have to backtrack through the village, they'll be waiting for us."

"It really doesn't matter." Manny shrugged. "The only flat road out of here runs upstream. If we have to circle back, we'll do it on the other side of this ridge."

"We can always do a quick staff check when Ralph brings it back," I added to head off another argument.

"I wouldn't risk it until we are well away." Manny hadn't agreed with a single idea all day, but he might be right. "These beings possess potent magic. If they sense the staff's power, our plan is toast. Let's find our stuff and get the hell out of here. Then you can pick a direction."

Time crawled by as more and more creatures shambled down from the village. By sunset, the road between fields was clogged for a stretch of perhaps two hundred yards. Even more packed into the section of crops cleared for the dais. Two thousand twisted creatures and Ants prepared to call on a pair of deities at war with Earth. And if there were more Ant colonies, this could just be the tip of the iceberg.

"Time to go," Quinn whispered

I was shocked to see the too-blue moon already sat low on the horizon as Vance worked on the lock. The guards stood together at the cliff face nearest the river. They hadn't exactly abandoned their post, but clearly picked the spot closest to the ceremony, perhaps hoping to catch a few words of the opening dedications.

Voices did drift up from the field that now glowed under a sea of torches, but only Superman would be able to pick out words from this distance. Although the guards had made getting the door open less risky, we had a lot of ground to cover without one of them noticing.

"Got it." Vance eased the door open.

"Head for our rides. If our stuff is still lying around, get as much onboard as possible, but gas is the priority." I waved Manny and Vance into the shadows and turned to Dwain and Ralph. "It's go time, little buddy."

The sprite huddled with Ralph, and the next thing I knew the imp was gone. Dwain gave a thumbs up and followed the others. Pete, Quinn, and I moved as quietly as we could toward our guards. I scanned the ground and picked up a heavy flat stone. Pete grabbed a similar weapon.

My self-congratulations spiked into anxiety when the feeling of being watched returned. Not only that, the guards were gone. Both had been leaning against a short wall sheltering the entrance to a first-floor dwelling. If they'd seen us approaching and waited in ambush, our rocks would be useless against those nasty hooked staffs.

I pointed two fingers at my eyes and waved Quinn out to our right with my best commando impersonation. Pete and I hefted our puny weapons, worked our way to the end of the wall, and waited.

Quinn darted between carts parked in the open circle until she reached the stone well rising at its center. She moved stealthily, but was all too visible under the rising moon. The angle gave her a better view. She'd either wave us forward or act as a decoy so we could jump the guards.

Quinn tilted her head for a long moment, scratched her temple, and stood. The rough surface of the rock sat cold in my sweaty hand. Pete and I exchanged a nod, both ready to strike when the Ants went for Quinn. But she waved and motioned for us to circle the wall. *What the hell?*

Pete shrugged and cocked his right arm back, ready to bring his fist-sized rock down on someone's head. They waited on the other side—I could feel it. We crept around the stonework. Sand drifted to the ground as my left hand skimmed along the rudimentary mortar. The acrid smell of burning pitch wafted on the wind as we rounded the corner.

Shadows clung to the alcove beyond the wall—no guards, no hooks coming for my throat. The inky blackness shifted against the rock as clouds drifted over the moon. Something watched from within the darkness.

The shadows stretched and billowed as if alive. Dark wisps swirled from the ragged edges to disappear on moonlit stonework like licks of overly eager flame dancing skyward from a raging fire. Close-set golden eyes opened near the ground at the center of the shadow, shattering the illusion that the entire shadow was some monumental beast.

Clear sky unveiled the moon and the shadow dispersed to reveal a shaggy four-legged animal the size of a small pony. The wolf—or maybe it was a dog—studied us from a narrow recess. Our two guards lay prone at its feet.

Its golden eyes blazed like headlights. The animal stepped over its kill, and a growl rose in its throat. Unless I brought my rock down just right when the thing lunged, I'd be dinner. The growl rose in pitch, changed to a simpering whine, and a big dog stepped fully into the light. *Impossible!*

The boxy black muzzle dropped open, revealing gleaming teeth and a lolling red tongue. The head dipped on his broad shoulders, and the breath I hadn't realized I held whooshed from me. My stone thudded into the sand, just missing my right foot.

I shook my head and blinked back tears as the giant dog took a tentative step toward me. I wanted to believe it was really him. But I'd watched my dog get crushed by a creature of the dark, spoken words over his grave, and yet...

"Is that Max?" Pete sounded incredulous.

This had to be an illusion, a trick to keep me off guard. Yet I knew that goofy grin and battering ram of a tail with its cautious have-I-done-something-wrong half-wag. The only things different were his eyes. Once soft brown, they now shone with gold flecks and vertical pupils, as if he'd acquired snake eyes.

"Why are you two just standing there?" Quinn came up behind us, and I heard her breath catch. "No way!"

I drew in a ragged breath not trusting myself to speak and took a step forward. Max leapt at me, hitting me on the shoulders with his front paws. My spike of fear melted away under the onslaught of wet tongue, cold nose, and fetid doggie breath. I wrapped both arms around his barrel chest, buried my face in thick fur, and laughed. Or maybe I cried because my face was wet when I finally pulled away. I didn't care. My dog had returned!

"I missed you, you big doofus," I whispered.

"Careful," Quinn warned. "He took out the guards. We don't know what's going on here."

"Hey, they're not dead." Pete bent to examine the Ants. "Just knocked out. Their collars are wet, but how would he...I mean did he get a strangle hold and choke one out while the other waited for his turn? Doesn't make sense."

"Sense or not, we've got to get moving." Quinn waved to our cell. "Help me drag these two back. We can tie them with strips of blanket."

By the time we had the guards secured, I'd grown used to having my furry companion back by my side. My hand had a mind of its own and wouldn't stop scratching his bony head and fingering those soft, floppy ears. The golden eyes threw me. When he stepped into shadow, I swear they actually lit the ground like headlights. I'd seen eyes like that before, but couldn't recall where.

Max followed along as we headed for the ATVs, just like in the old days, except he didn't stop and sniff every five steps. A glow from the entrance told us Manny and Vance had found the flashlights. In fact, as we entered the garage-sized room it became clear they'd recovered the bulk of our gear.

"Food and firearms are missing," Vance said.

"What the hell's that?" Manny asked, which took me by surprise until I saw Max had stuck his head though the doorway.

He didn't exactly growl at Manny's tone, but it wasn't a pleasant come-pet-me sound either.

"You must remember my dog, Max. You and Rhonda complained about him enough on tour."

"I remember burying your dog. This can't be good."

"He took out the guards." Pete mimed strangling himself, and then falling into fitful slumber. We'd created a thespian monster.

"Any sign of Ralph and my staff?"

"He must still be waiting for his chance." Dwain gripped Max by his floppy jowls and turned my dog's head right and left before staring into his eyes. "This is big-boy magic. Somebody broke the rules."

I'd have to find and thank that somebody if we ever got out of here. Having that big goofy presence in the room was like getting a piece of myself back. The day he died, a ragged chunk ripped from my soul. The wound scabbed over, but never truly healed. I vowed to never let him get hurt again fighting my battles.

Dwain clearly recognized the magic, but stayed tight-lipped about its origins. Pina had been awfully busy lately. As queen of the sprites, she just might be able to tap into the kind of power it would take to bring Max back. Dwain adored Pina—probably was in love with her—so if the spell was against the rules, it made sense he wouldn't rat her out. Still, I owed her a huge debt for returning my boy.

A roar sounded from the fields below. I thought it was a cheer, but the voices rose into an angry buzz punctuated by occasional shouts.

"Here comes Ralph," Quinn said from the doorway as another flurry of shouts drifted in.

"Now we're cooking," I said. "Does he have the staff?"

"Um...in a manner of speaking." Her cautious tone had me hurrying over.

Ralph limped across the open ground, his pace deliberate but labored. At first I thought he'd been hurt, but he staggered forward with each step as though dragging something heavy.

"That's weird," Quinn said. "I swore he had—oh there!"

A slender person wearing ceremonial robes flashed into sight behind the imp, but vanished just as quickly. The imp struggled the last few yards, pulled himself across the threshold, and held out what I thought was my staff. But what I took from him was a simple length of wood wrapped with cord trailing back to—we all jumped. Dawa stood glaring down the cord binding his wrists.

"Well, that shoots the plan to hell." Manny glared at the imp, who had collapsed on the floor.

I held tight to the strange, silvery cord. It had to be magic to have let the tiny imp drag the Ant leader away from his ceremony. Dawa held his tongue as he took in the loaded vehicles and gear. There was no hiding the fact we were making a break for it.

"Dwain, I thought you told him to bring the staff."

The sprite reluctantly stepped out from behind Vance, nodded, and winced at Dawa's frown of disappointment. Instead of answering, Dwain pointed to the long pouch at Dawa's belt. Quinn strode over, opened it, and retrieved the tool Koko had given me.

"Hell of a way to bring this over." She stared daggers at Ralph, but shook her head when he nodded and grinned as if accepting praise. "Now what?"

The shouts outside drew closer.

"They know we're here." Pete nodded at the ATVs. "Run for it?"

"Your machines will not work." Dawa's statement got our attention.

"But *you* can make them work." Manny clutched a spring loaded club similar to my own and closed in on the Ant leader.

"Only with my brother's help. It will take us both to undo the block."

Feet shuffled outside, too loudly to be more than a few yards off. I made a snap decision and untied Dawa. The mysterious cord read my intent, and the restraint slipped away without me having to figure out the knot. I wrapped the line into a loop and handed it down to Ralph, who made it disappear.

"That little one is intriguing." Dawa rubbed his wrists and eyed our imp. "His kind rarely travel alone, and I've never felt their power first hand. How have you managed to train him?"

It wasn't really stalling because a contingent of Ant guards already shuffled into the room with hooks poised. I shrugged and reached down to rub Ralph's head. The little guy's face had fallen when the room began to fill up, and he needed to know we weren't mad.

"We haven't trained him. He's just a friend who got caught up in the early stages of your invasion."

"A long-overdue plan that is about to come to fruition." Muuyaw strode into the room, and the guards deftly parted to make a path. "Well, brother, are you ready to concede the prisoners are dangerous? Their guards have been driven into hibernation and may not recover."

"You work magic in spite of my blocks? Interesting." Dawa cast a curious glance at each of us, as if puzzling out who had circumvented his nullifying spell.

"I suppose it's back to our cell?" I refrained from pointing out my dog had taken down their finest, no matter how satisfying it would be to get under Muuyaw's skin.

I looked around the room and frowned. Max was gone.

"First, we will talk," Dawa said. "Join me in conference so we may select a path forward."

Strange Medicine

22. Guiding Light

"**D**ON'T DO THIS." Piper pulled a sparkly green top out of Anna's bag, undermining her preparations.

"You can't find Koko, and Charles says nobody knows how long the portal will stay open."

"Going in there won't help. How will you even find them?"

"Someone needs to make sure Ed returns to the vortex before destroying the shield. That way they can all step through before the portal closes." Anna snatched her string bag off the table to keep Piper from undoing the few remaining items she'd packed for the trip.

Piper threw up her hands. "Pina, talk some sense into her."

Anna and Piper stood on opposite sides of the kitchen table while the others busily loaded the vehicles under Reggie's demanding eye. Pina showing up had been a surprise. Anna hadn't seen the sprite since the end of the A-Chords' tour. The small woman sat on a bent-wood chair at the head of the narrow table. The way she swung her legs should have been endearing—like a child sitting in an adult's chair—except weariness etched Pina's porcelain skin. Fatigue also dulled her natural effervescence and enthusiasm, which told Anna more about the state of things outside than any reports from Charles or Piper. Time was running out.

"Anna might be right." Pina's statement clearly took Piper by surprise. "With the amount of magic our forces are pouring directly into the portal, it could collapse faster than anyone suspected. Ed should have been warned, but everything has just been so crazy. Koko told Dwain to be careful, but that might have gotten lost in translation. He's a cute little bugger, but not the most responsible."

Pina got a dreamy look in her eyes and a crooked half-smile lifted the corners of her mouth. Being overly tired could do that to a person, have them flipping between weary and giddy. Anna herself was excited and terrified about stepping through the portal. She'd seen way too many invaders pushed back through, which had her worried about popping out in the middle of all the monsters.

"That's a pretty big oversight," Piper said. "And she'd need wheels to catch them in time."

"Oh, no! Dwain could be miles ahead by now." Pina hurried on at Piper's raised eyebrow. "I mean Ed, and the others. Wait, you can firespeak once you're on the other side."

"You're sweet on Dwain." Piper gave the sprite a wicked grin.

"I just want them all safe." A warm red glow rose on Pina's cheeks.

"I saw how he fawned over you in Milwaukee with all those get-well gifts. You were loving it." Piper was relentless, and it was contagious.

"Remember that giant banana tree?" Anna said. "He looked like a walking plant-monster carrying the thing. And you kept it too. Ed bitched about how those big leaves blocked the rearview mirror."

"I don't know what—" Pina's gaze darted from her to Piper. "Fine! He's cute, and funny, and...I guess I do like him a little. He keeps bringing me gifts, but I'd rather just spend time with him. Not that there's much of that nowadays."

"Aw, honey." Piper flipped from wicked tease to concerned sister in a flash. "He'll be fine. When this is over, you two have all the time in the world. Some men need a clonk over the head. Stop waiting around and ask *him* out."

"Can I do that?" Pina's emerald eyes went round.

"Sure, we'll help you plan it out, but first let's get everyone back safely. You're definitely onto something; firespeak might work fine on the far side and solves the transportation problem."

"Success-oriented plans are doomed to fail." The condescending male voice intruded on their girls-only bonding, but Charles was either oblivious or just didn't care. "Go in fully prepared to deal with whatever you may find. That means transportation, defensive capability, and an agile team."

"This isn't a commando raid," Piper snapped.

"Peace." He held up both hands in surrender. "I'm here to offer help, not start a fight. Reggie got an ancient three wheeler running. It's the dinosaur of ATVs, but can get two people in and back fast. That way if talking by magic fails, you'll have a way to catch them."

"I'm not exactly comfortable driving something like that," Anna said.

"No need. I'm here to offer my services as driver and tracker. I realize you don't want to think about there being trouble, but I'm also handy in a fight."

The idea of going alone into the vortex was scary. Having Charles along would be a comfort, even if Piper still looked like she wanted to punch the guy. They argued about the arrangements for a good fifteen minutes, but in the end there wasn't much to discuss.

All four headed out to inspect the ride. It was smaller than Anna expected, like an oversized faded red tricycle with knobby tires. Charles kicked it to life, sending billows of smoke into the barn's rafters. The thing was so loud she doubted they'd be able to talk.

It would be nice if Piper or Pina came along, but the vehicle just wasn't big enough for three, plus Pina had to get back to help Koko. The sprite excused herself after Anna knelt for a reassuring hug.

"I'll let the defenders know what's going on so they don't bother you. You've got this," Pina whispered in her ear. "Bring them home."

Piper had wholly different advice.

"If you're in there overnight, keep your eye on him," she jerked a thumb at Charles who was gathering tools from the workbench. "Men are trouble."

"Please!" Anna felt her cheeks warm. "He's like thirty."

"Oh, honey. That doesn't matter."

Before she knew it, Anna found herself on the back of the noisy, smoky three-wheeler. Either Charles wasn't a good driver or their ride was inherently unstable. The machine canted wildly with every turn. As they cruised over the gently rolling dunes she had to cling to his waist or risk being thrown.

In spite of a blazing midday sun, the air cooled as they approached the vortex. The wall of green towered high and the brilliant sunshine changed to a muddy green-brown, like the oddly filtered light before a storm.

They passed dozens of...people all focused on the swirling vortex. Some wore the gray robes of the Neutral Council, others the black armor-like garb of the Dark Court. The rest would be part of the Light Court and wore everything from simple tunics to elaborate dresses. Eyes tracked them as they passed, before turning back to the bombardment of the vortex. Between the crimson bolts, golden energy balls, and crackling of power—all part of the magical onslaught attempting to stop the portal's expansion—Anna felt as though she rode to battle.

"Hold on tight and keep your head down," Charles yelled over the roaring engine. "We're going in under their spells."

The green wall took up her entire field of vision like they were racing toward the leading edge of a hurricane. When they first arrived, the vortex had been a frozen tornado. Now there was movement inside, debris zipping past at high speed from left to right and swirling up to disappear overhead. This was going to be a wild ride.

* * *

"Conference my ass! This is a trial." Quinn kicked the table leg. "The only thing missing is the hangman's noose over the door."

I wanted to argue, but she'd pretty much nailed it. We'd been led deep beneath the cliff-side dwellings to the massive round hall. Our crude wooden tables stood well below the elevated platform where the twin leaders sat flanked by their entourage. For some reason the underground setting made the skinny creatures look even more insectile. Domed heads leaned toward each other to discuss our last exchange.

Convincing them to let us go looked like a losing proposition. While Dawa and the three councilors to his left were willing to concede we posed no threat once escorted from their lands, his brother's cronies just kept circling back to how we'd snuck in and wounded innocent Ants. Of course, they consistently failed to mention we were attacked first.

The observers ringing the hall were every bit as unnerving as the tribunal. Only the most monstrous of creatures from the village came to bear witness, or maybe they were waiting to dispense punishment. Demonic faces watched our every move. They stood three deep, those in back often clamoring for a better view. There'd be no escaping this chamber because even the entryway was jammed with the nightmarish watchers.

"What the hell are they?" Pete asked when he saw me searching for a way out.

Good question. No two were the same. Many bore horny protrusions on head or shoulders, but they were stunted growths that stuck out at odd angles. Distended jaws, twisted faces, and thick bodies dominated the assemblage. Grotesque, squatting brutes surrounded us, a disparate gathering of shock troops, suited to smashing opponents into paste with arms and hands that often thickened into brutal clubs.

"Monsters." Though not a variety we'd encountered in the desert.

"Nah, they're just Ant People." Dwain shrugged at my skeptical sneer. "I told you they don't do medicine. That's what happens when they get sick or hurt. Their bodies try to fight the infections in really strange ways. The ones I've been helping were recently hurt. The older the wound or illness, the less I can do for them. Something inside them just keeps working and layers scar tissue, skin, even bone to seal off the problem."

"You can't be serious," Pete scoffed. "No way they're even the same species."

"Crap," I studied the nearest of the deformed demons, really looked at them. "Look close. There's sort of a person inside the person. Discard the broken horns and jutting chin. The long faces beneath are kind of ant-like."

Even the clubbed hands had vestigial pads folded at what looked like a painful angle across the balled fists. There was no way to see the slender forms beneath those barrel chests and tree-trunk legs, which had me doubting again. All of these creatures couldn't have sustained the same injury to torso and below. I said as much to Dwain.

"Once an Ant gets hurt, their bodies never stop." The sprite wrung his hands. "Instead of making repairs their systems just keep laying down more protective tissue. It's never enough. The infection spreads, causing more mutated growth." He waved a hand at the ring of watchers. "These people could have started down this path with a broken arm, a splinter, or even a simple cold."

"Weird," Pete said. "I can't say the results are pleasant to look at, but at least they have some way to deal with problems."

"Will you three shut up and pay attention?" Quinn looked pissed "I think we're about to be sentenced."

Dawa and Muuyaw stood and held up their hands for silence.

"You're missing my point," Dwain said as the murmuring crowd fell silent. "Their bodies *never* stop. Soon, these people won't be able to support their own weight and will smother under the buildup of flesh. It's a terrible way to die."

In hindsight the grunts and threatening growls from the gathered assemblage as we'd been marched in transformed into labored breathing and desperate attempts to clear throats clogged with malignant growths. Even now—with no one speaking—the rattle and hiss of straining airways merged into a low roar like a failing air conditioner.

These people needed help. The medicines back home might hold a cure, but would be unavailable if the world veil collapsed and sent the cities of Earth into oblivion. Even if the vortex did no more than transform a few square miles into desert, humans would never accept or aid the invading forces. A truce might eventually be brokered, but it would be too late. I stood in a room full of dead people, unless—

"Before we render our decision, do you have anything else to say?" Dawa ignored the scowl and huff of indignation from his brother.

"Your people are dying." I knew it was true by the shocked gasps and startled expressions. Even Dawa looked outraged.

"They don't like to talk about it," Dwain said under his breath in a nervous singsong.

"You are not—" Muuyaw began.

"Yeah, not supposed to state the obvious." And it was so very obvious now that I knew what to look for. "But face the facts. The whole point of this session is to figure out if we pose a danger, right? Well, folks, you have bigger problems than us. Maybe those of you up on the podium aren't worried, but you can bet the crowd down here is." Pete must have been rubbing off on me because I couldn't help strolling away from our assigned table—right into the midst of the front row of startled, misshapen Ants. "These poor bastards want to know how long they have. They want to know what you're going to do to help them and their sick family members. My mom's a nurse. I've seen my share of injured and sick in our hospital. I can tell you the thing on each and every one of their minds, the question they ask their doctors and themselves every day. When will I be better? When will the pain stop?

"My people aren't going to welcome you with open arms if you come to them on the tail of an attack. Heck, right now it looks like if your attempt to destroy the world veil succeeds, there won't be any of my people left in the fourth world to share their medicine and knowledge. Maybe you'll figure it out for yourselves…someday. But while you fumble about to rediscover medicine, the people standing in this room, their friends, and their families will grow weak and die—as will others."

"What is your point, human?"

Muuyaw stepped down from his pedestal and would have grabbed me, except I kept threading through the crowd, never giving him a clear line of attack. I smiled at his frustration and circled around to speak directly to Dawa.

"My point is that we can help. You've already worked Dwain half to death. Let us go bargain on your behalf for medical supplies and experts. My mom works in a building filled with professionals who make people well again."

"Except the hospital went missing," Pete muttered under his breath.

"So it's another trick." Unfortunately, Muuyaw had excellent hearing. "There is no hoss-pittle!"

"Not in New Philly because *your* stupid desert wiped the town away." I couldn't help getting fired up. Mom was among the missing, and I prayed destroying the magic artifact would restore not just our climate, but the lost buildings and people. "There are plenty of other medical facilities where we come from, hundreds of doctors and nurses who take care of the sick and injured. I know we can work something out."

The funny thing was that I really did want to help these people I had deemed monsters just an hour ago. What I'd taken for aggression and viciousness were in truth just the inner battle of individuals coping with constant pain. No one should have to live that way.

Although Muuyaw was certainly a dick, the Ants as a people didn't have much to do with the invasion of Earth. Sure they wanted to move to a land where the soil wasn't poisoned, but the real culprits were these twin gods of theirs. In fact, Muuyaw was the only one who agreed with going in guns blazing.

Dawa was reasonable enough to admit there might be another solution. If I could convince him his people had a chance, that we could help if our world was spared, then maybe we could work out some sort of agreement. Either way, we needed to get moving toward the shield. It was a catch-22 situation. I had to turn off the doomsday device to save my bargaining chip, but I needed the portal open long enough to move supplies and medicine through if I was going to help the Ants. One day at a time, as my therapist used to say. We'd have to figure it out as we went.

23. A Dying Land

T HE AIR grew thinner the higher we went. Our engine coughed and sputtered, seeming to shy away from the final climb to the plateau overlooking the river.

"Engine isn't getting enough oxygen," Quinn said over her shoulder as she gunned the ATV out of its funk. "I'm feeling a little lightheaded myself. You sure this is the right way?"

I swung the staff in a wide arc. The blue glow intensified when I held it about ten degrees to the left of our current path, but I'd rather we followed the tight road than drive off into thin air. The slope on that side was wickedly steep.

"Yep, looks like the top is just ahead. We can take a break and see how everyone's faring."

I glanced over my shoulder to check on the other three vehicles. Vance and Pete's ATV followed about ten yards behind. Then came the strange carriage drawn by two giant fleas. Dawa, Muuyaw, and their advisor rode the open buckboard. Manny and Dwain brought up the rear. Even from this distance, I could tell the road manager was still pissed.

After much argument, the Ant leaders agreed to let us be on our way in exchange for a promise of medical help. Muuyaw of course opposed the idea, but Dawa argued they had nothing to lose and could pursue the bridge to the fourth world—our world—as soon as it was fully open. The room of angry citizens helped. Something in my little tirade struck a chord, and they weren't about to let Muuyaw throw away a chance for a cure.

Of course there were strings. Even Dawa wasn't naive enough to just let us ride off into the sunset. The Ants coming along ensured we wouldn't do something rash, like closing the portal before coughing up medicine and a way to save their people. We got my staff and a few weapons back, but not our guns. When I told Dawa I needed magic to set our course, he even turned off the damned music looping through my head.

Quinn and Manny weren't as fortunate. Even I didn't buy the argument that my girlfriend needed her powers to help me wield the staff, and no amount of coaxing was going to get Manny's restriction lifted. They'd seen his tendency to shoot first and ask questions later. Since his magic didn't rely on music, he didn't have an insufferable earworm. But his perpetual scowl spoke of something damned uncomfortable shackling his power.

I'd do what I could to honor our bargain, but our real enemy was time. The vortex approached critical mass and already played havoc with the other realms. Retrieving the shield, traipsing back to the portal, and negotiating medical assistance from back home would take days, maybe weeks—time we might not have.

"Holy fuck!" Quinn said as the road leveled off.

At the top of the rise, the view opened on a wide expanse of fields like nothing I'd seen before. The land was strewn with boulders, looking like something out of an old Mars probe documentary, but the silent rocks flashed a thousand colors under the cobalt-blue skies. Mineral deposits sparkled and jutted from every surface, reflecting the morning sun. Rainbow flashes assaulted us as the other ATVs rolled up with a collective gasp.

Though impressive, it wasn't the jeweled plateau that had everyone yammering at once. A city skyline rose on the horizon beyond the rocks. Even from a distance, the jagged buildings and broken windows spoke of massive neglect, and the old wire suspension bridge rising off to their right looked all too familiar.

"That's the Ben Franklin Bridge," Pete said. "I can tell by those stone towers."

"What's it mean?" Quinn asked.

I had a sinking feeling it meant our world was disappearing into the third world. All of old Philadelphia didn't stretch out before us. The skyline broke off about halfway across the horizon, giving way to another field of shining boulders.

"It means nothing. Pieces of your world come and go." Muuyaw dismissed Quinn's concern, then looked to me. "Which way, human?"

"Nothing? That's my home town!"

Well, technically it was an abandoned section of Old Philadelphia, but people were missing in New Philly too. I hoped everything would go back to normal if I destroyed the shield, but what if they didn't—or what if burning the shield turned out to be a bad idea? If sections of home came through, we might be able to rescue the people.

If I'd learned anything during the wild ride that had become my life, it was Koko didn't always have the answers—or if he did, he wasn't necessarily going to share them. I believed the shield was the crux of our problem, but the old trickster usually held back key bits of information. Coming to understand the plight of the Ant People had me churning on how best to proceed once we reached our objective.

"That way." I tapped Quinn on the shoulder and pointed to the low line of factory buildings squatting to the left of the bridge. "The city will be a maze and difficult to get through, but there's always a chance we'll find supplies, maybe medicine."

"We must be quick," Dawa said. "The joining of the worlds draws close."

Weaving through the rainbow rocks was a surreal trip. Insects darted among the boulders, rising in glittering clouds that winked out as fast as they got airborne. The ground in the Ants' domain had been a sandy mix, but here our tires ground through rich loam full of decaying leaves.

"Where are the trees?" I asked.

Talking was easier now that the vehicles could ride abreast, but the jerking movement of the flea-steeds had the Ants alternatively surging ahead and dropping behind.

"Not leaves." Pete scooped up a wad of debris that kicked up onto his floorboard and split his attention between driving and studying the clump. "These are wings. Some sort of insect swarm died off and—oh crap!"

He flung the dirt away and stared straight ahead with jaw set. The color drained from his face—quite a feat in the swirling disco lights.

"What?" I'd never seen Pete creeped out by bugs.

I leaned down and managed to scoop up a handful of rotting debris. What I'd assumed to be leaves were rounded and colorful. Most crumbled at my touch, but one tattered yellow-red remnant felt silky as a butterfly wing. It snagged in the dirt, connected to a clod the size of my pinky—no, skinny limbs dangled from the dirt. Though filthy, the tiny humanoid shape had two arms, two legs, and a crushed head.

I gagged and looked away. Throwing the small creature back onto the ground felt disrespectful. But the path ahead shimmered like autumn after peak leaf-season, and my stomach lurched.

"There're thousands of them. What the hell happened?" I looked to the Ant leaders.

"Nashers," Muuyaw supplied. "Nasty creatures of little consequence."

"If something like this doesn't matter to you, what the hell does, you cold-hearted—"

"Ed, take it easy." Quinn reached back and squeezed my left knee, but she hadn't seen.

"They are not sentient," Dawa said as the cart surged past. "Much of the flora and fauna have died off. The nashers are a nuisance. They swarm at night to eat crops and unattended animals. Any disturbance to the natural order is a bad omen"—he gave his twin a withering look—"and injures the balance of the land. This particular plague is not missed, but neither are they gone." He pointed at a shining blue outcropping on our right as a cloud of bugs rose and vanished. "Nasher nymphs survive. They will be full grown in short order, but thankfully we won't have to contend with them."

He fell silent, apparently remembering the whole invade-the-Earth plan was sort of a sore spot with me. Thankfully the piles of dead nashers didn't extend far. We rolled out of the littered remains onto soft soil that would make good farm land if the rocks were cleared. Heck, I'd flattened the mother of all boulders back on the Easton's farm. Of course I'd used magic—Earth magic.

Even back then, the shield must have been redirecting spells to attack the world veil. That was probably the reason Ralph ended up out on the farm. But there were other ways to clear boulders. If the flea-bags could haul three people, they could certainly drag rocks to the edge of a field.

"Why not farming up here?" I asked Dawa.

"The painted plains are beyond our domain," he said with a shrug. "Use no more than necessary; take no more than you need. It is part of the path of balance we walk."

"Yet you plan to leave. That'll upset things more than cultivating new ground."

"Our gods have seen there is no other way and set the path before us."

Dawa spoke with quiet reverence, yet his words didn't ring sincere—as if he struggled internally to see the wisdom of abandoning their world. Muuyaw ignored our exchange, preferring to lash the fleas to an even choppier pace. Larmoth, their silent attending advisor, hugged the rail along the back of the cart as if trying not to throw up.

"Still, it's awfully pretty up here." Hopefully I'd planted a seed that would get Dawa thinking of alternatives to invading Earth.

We eventually made the ruins. They had looked to be closer, but that was an illusion of scale compounded by the flashing colors reflecting across the plains. Even now as our tires crunched onto broken blacktop, the rusting two-story building shimmered and swayed behind the curtain of heat rising off the pavement.

"Head for the shipping nexus," Pete called as he turned toward a line of raised loading docks. "These old warehouses will have foreman maps for directing drivers. Without that it'll take days to look through the place."

"I feel nauseous, and Ralph looks like crap," Quinn said as she turned to follow.

Our imp hugged the tank tight. Instead of leaning into the wind like some fantasy masthead, he pressed his cheek to the cool metal as drool dribbled from the corner of his mouth. Now that she mentioned it, my stomach was halfway between hungry cramps—which made sense given breakfast had been a fleeting affair—and that sick feeling of dropping in free-fall.

"Oh yuck!" Quinn jerked back, and her head cracked against my forehead.

Ralph gagged like a cat hacking up a fur-ball. Bits of wetness splashed my hand. He retched again and spewed sticky brown chunks across the tank.

"Those honey treats weren't such a good idea." I bit off a laugh because my stomach churned dangerously at the sight of the half-digested food.

"Watch it!" Manny's yell had me twisting around in time to see him veer off to avoid an impressive stream of vomit from Larmoth. Just when Dawa's aide looked to be done, he doubled over again.

"Flea steeds are a bad idea too. If we ever—" I grabbed on for dear life as the ATV swung left.

Pete stopped short, forcing Quinn to swerve again. He and Vance stumbled off, and both doubled over in syncopated sickness. The air turned stiflingly hot, and my head spun. Quinn stopped, but the world didn't. Breakfast clawed its way up, and acid burned my throat. The damned heat shimmers were everywhere. I squinted at the building, trying to anchor my reeling senses as the ground lurched.

A rug pulled out from under me. I tumbled along its length, managed to swing a leg off without hurling, and dropped to my knees on pavement. But the hard surface fuzzed, turning to loamy dirt. Another massive wave of nausea swept over me, the world lurched again, and all went still.

"What just happened?" Quinn was on hands and knees, spitting into the dirt.

Rainbows flashed off the rocks strewn across the open plain. With the engines off, all was quiet except snuffling clicks from the pair of fleas. I scanned the landscape. Grass sprouted in isolated clumps, slowly replacing the boulders stretching out along our path under oddly crimson clouds. Distant hills rose in a dark shadow where sky met ground.

"The buildings are gone." Pete wiped a sleeve across his mouth. "Did anyone else feel like they wanted to die?"

"You all spewed," Quinn said.

"Oh, and you're kneeling in the dirt for the fun of it?" I barked out a laugh at her scowl, relieved to find my stomach no longer rebelled. The others looked better too, even Larmoth. "So much for hunting up supplies." I turned to Dawa. "I don't suppose your people have ever brought anything out of a section of our world that's bled through."

"We don't enter them, but some of the other races are less discrete. They've pilfered mostly useless items, which they do not actually need. There's a gluttony loose in our realm. Why the gods would want to—" He bit off the sentence and narrowed his eyes. "You are entirely too easy to talk to, human."

"Please." I rolled my eyes in my best imitation of Piper when I ordered pizza at a fancy restaurant. "My name's Ed. Leave the whole unworthy human bit for your brother. He's better at it. So, the good news is that items we take out won't disappear."

"And we didn't get sucked off to wherever that little slice of abandoned heaven went when it phased out." Quinn patted herself down as if checking to ensure everything was still attached.

"An oasis pulls at its surroundings when it leaves, which accounts for the sudden illness." Muuyaw joining the discussion surprised me. "But nothing *living* departs with them. Even animals that wander into such areas get left behind when they move on."

So sneaky, evil twin had done a bit more exploring than his brother. The way he emphasized the word living conjured up disturbing images. I wouldn't put conducting a few unsavory experiments past the guy.

There wasn't much we could do about the missed opportunity, except continue to follow the staff. Trekking through the tall grass should have been simplicity itself on the four-wheelers, but deep ruts hid in the growth. The slow pace gave me time to reflect as we approached the brown hills. If a section of Earth couldn't pull people out of the third world, what happened if inhabitants of my world strayed out of such an area? Would they remain in the third world or be pulled away when their respective chunk of home moved on?

Home sounded good. Our two days on this side of the vortex had been wearying. Once this business was complete, there was a couch with my name on it—assuming the desert gave my house back. And there was a big round dog bed for Max.

Max hadn't shown his face since our jailbreak, but I could feel him out there watching. Normally, I wouldn't have been so sure, but something about this place had my senses on high alert. I sensed my loyal companion pacing along to our left—that and an odd vibration under the wide rutted depression we traveled. Ralph hissed and drew his dagger. Something rose beneath us.

"Get to high ground!" I slapped Quinn's shoulder and pointed to the steep bank.

She gunned us on an arrow path for the lip of the depression. I waved frantically for the others, and after a moment's hesitation they raced to follow. The Ant cart lagged behind. As the three ATVs drove up onto higher ground, the pony-sized fleas struggled in the soft soil. One hopped in place, while the other strained against its harness. That was when the lower half of the struggling animal tore off with a terrible ripping and spray of blood.

Hooked black tentacles snaked up from beneath to encircle the dying insect. Another set erupted alongside to grab the gory upper half that still had the feebly kicking front legs attached. The uninjured flea jerked and struggled until its harness snapped. It shot off using huge leaps to put distance between itself and the attack.

"Get up here while they're busy," I called to the three Ants.

"Busy butchering that poor bug," Pete said.

The crowned heads of two monsters swimming below the surface crested through the mud and grass. Flashing jaws joined the tentacles and ripped off hunks of meat. Muuyaw pushed Larmoth ahead of him as the three jumped off the cart. I thought it a rather magnanimous gesture until I realized he was using the timid advisor to ensure it was safe to venture on. The monsters fought each other for the last scraps.

Pete helped me hoist Larmoth over the edge, followed by the twins. We retreated to a safe distance and watched the half-seen monsters polish off the unfortunate flea. Those barbed tentacles swept over the cart wheels next, as if tasting each surface to ensure they hadn't missed anything good. Soon enough, the appendages withdrew and the creatures moved off along the rutted tract.

We stared down into the hunting ground for a good five minutes. I no longer sensed the hungry presence, but that didn't mean I was ready to go down there.

"We do not have enough seats for everyone to ride." Manny broke the silence.

"Simple math," I said, but none of us made a move.

"So…if we hit another patch of ground like that, we go around, right?" Vance's question had us all nodding, but we were really just stalling.

"The ground-dragons hunt quickly this time of year so their young do not go unattended." Muuyaw waved at the carnage below, inviting someone else to go first.

It took a long time and much arguing to jury-rig the cart with a tow mechanism that kept it from crashing into our ATV every time we slowed. Of course, Quinn and I got volunteered to do the towing because Manny wanted nothing to do with the Ants and Pete's ride didn't have enough torque to handle the extra weight.

Still, my buddy's farm-boy ingenuity came to the rescue. He cobbled together a length of tire irons to make a rigid connection from our hitch hook to the cart. The bulk of the pulling power came through the tow straps, but the bars helped stabilize and slow the cart when Quinn let off the gas. Applying the brakes at the end of a short test run was a whole new experience. The extra momentum drove us forward like a snow plow until the tires dug in deep. Sudden stops were out of the question.

By the time we got moving and had the mechanics of braking worked out, the sun was already making a beeline for the horizon. The rolling plains didn't offer much cover, so we chose to follow the staff and drive on. Navigating was simplicity itself. Except for circumventing the occasional gully and one other ground dragon hunting strip, I simply pointed Quinn in the right direction.

"If push comes to shove, you're still going to have to destroy the shield. They aren't going to like that." Quinn kept her voice low.

"I thought maybe we could ditch them along the way."

"That's going to be a little difficult at this point." Quinn glanced back at our tow vehicle.

Dawa and Muuyaw argued, while Larmoth split his time between playing middle man, scribbling notes, and trying not to get bounced off his feet. I imagined loosening the tow-bar at our next stop and hauling ass to get away from the pair. But I doubted we'd outrun their magic, plus we needed their cooperation.

"Help me get them to see reason. Dawa clearly doesn't want his people to leave. If Muuyaw sees it's in their best interest to stay, we'll have a fighting chance to stop this mess."

"The fact they'll be walking into desert on our side of the vortex doesn't faze them. They have too much faith in their gods making everything right once they cross." She patted Ralph's head then shook her own. "I can't see it. A more likely scenario is both worlds turn into wastelands and we're all screwed."

"There has to be a way to fix whatever's killing this world so they won't have to leave. Something must have changed recently."

We rode in silence for a time, while Ralph lounged between the handlebars and managed to nap without falling off. The impressive feat reminded me of Dwain's talent for sleeping in unusual places. Sure enough, I looked over at Pete and saw the sprite slumped against his back, snoring away.

I envied them. Last night had been a restless disaster as I worried about where Max had gone and whether we were doing the right thing bringing the Ant leaders along. Of course, we hadn't had much choice about the latter. If we only had to deal with Dawa things would be different, but Muuyaw was a hard sell.

The light faded as we rode along the edge of a long, narrow lake. This was still, deep water rather than the frenzied whitecap-filled great lakes we'd visited on tour. The air smelled of algae and moisture, and the temperature dropped to the point I dug out a light jacket.

Up ahead, the water spilled out into a stream that ran under a stone bridge off to our right. A massive dingy-gray spillway held the water down to a trickle. Rather than heading for the bridge, we detoured for a closer look because something about the structure's oddly rounded walls didn't look right. Fifty yards away, something definitely didn't smell right.

"That's wretched." Quinn pulled her shirt up over her nose.

A pungent dead-fish odor combined with ammonia and a few other chemicals covered up the natural waterfront aroma. The wall stood maybe twenty feet high and looked to be made of a single bulging gray stone. The surface was mottled with shades running from whitish to nearly black. The structure tapered toward each end and curved back into the lake proper.

"Weirdest dam I've ever seen," Pete said as we dismounted and walked to the shallow stream that ran out from around the wall.

The stream bed was four feet deep, but the water only a few inches. Rounded pebbles covered the bottom, just visible through murky red water. Wisps of green fluttered from the rocky surfaces, but the small fish and water bugs I would have expected were missing.

"You don't want to drink that." Pete called from the lake's edge near the end of the dam.

"We can always boil it." Vance looked from Pete to the canteen he'd pulled from his trunk.

Pete shook his head and waved us over. A large flat paddle swept down into the lake bottom just past the edge of the wall—no, not a paddle, a fin! Tendons stood out beneath the mottled skin where the appendage disappeared into deeper, darker water.

"It's a dinosaur!" Quinn said.

The massive creature was similar to—but different than—the aquatic animals detailed in scientific journals. It resembled the species people used to explain the Loch Ness monster, with a long tapered neck and those massive flippers. But ridges down its sides and a long translucent fin running the length of its back made it also look like some Godzilla of a seahorse—mutated by uncontrolled radiation and bent on tearing down high-tension wires.

"It's definitely dead." Manny strolled farther up the shoreline to get a look at the far side.

The creature lay on its side, blocking the outgoing stream. The crown of its head sat visible above the surface, one cloudy eye staring blindly into the setting sun. The water flowing around it ran redder than downstream.

We joined the road manager, and Pete let out a piercing whistle of appreciation. The water beyond the fleshy dam was deep, rising halfway up the monster's side to where a massive crescent of flesh had been torn away. Red still trickled from the ragged white meat.

"Crimson water mystery solved." Quinn looked through her raised finger and thumb as if measuring the wound. "That is one big chomp."

"More sand-dragons?" I asked.

"Too wide, unless they get a whole lot bigger."

"They do not," Dawa and his aide limped up to join us. Apparently traveling on the bucking wagon was taking its toll. Muuyaw stayed back with the vehicles, looking for all the world like he didn't trust us. "Ground-dragons also do not hunt in water. I am unfamiliar with what could have done this."

"It was a scavenger," Dwain said, making us all jump because he and Ralph had somehow managed to hop across the water and now stood on the thing's neck.

"Be careful, or you'll slip off," Quinn chided.

"Nah, the skin's grippy like shark's skin. We couldn't fall if we tried. See?" The sprite hopped and kicked his feet in a little jig, then knelt to finger the hide. "This poor gal died of infection. Something came along and took a nice bite after she washed up."

Dwain's magic tasted of saltwater and leaves as he probed the carcass. Helping us might have put him on the shit-list with the Ants, but they hadn't felt compelled to shackle his power. His magic was subtle, and I lost track as the power probed deeper.

"Yep, she got scraped up good on the underside," he said after a minute. "Wound went septic and led to organ failure. Hard way to go. Been dead…eh, I'd say about four hours."

"Wait, the chomp-master could still be around? That bite's a good six feet across." Pete studied the shoreline, then relaxed. "Must be aquatic. No tracks."

Ralph trotted along the length of the beast as we spoke. When he got back to Dwain, the imp tugged on his shirt.

"Hey, Ralph found them." Dwain's big grin was at odds with the news as he pointed to the far side of the stream. "Really big prints over there."

We coaxed the pair down and drove across the bridge to investigate. The tracks were five-foot-wide circles of compressed mud, then soil, then grass. Arcs along the leading edge of each print hinted at three stubby toes. The tree-trunk legs of an elephant came to mind, but this animal would be much bigger and we couldn't tell if it walked on two or four legs. As the prints progressed away from the shoreline they grew shallow, starting at a foot deep and shrinking to a few inches before getting lost in the tall wiry grass.

Even though something that big should be visible from a mile away, none of us wanted to linger. We moved on at a notably faster pace in spite of the jostling it inflicted on our passengers in tow. I wanted to make the foothills before dark.

"Wish I had sunglasses," Quinn muttered and shielded her eyes.

"Your wish is my command." I gave her a little squeeze and handed over the spare pair from my travel pouch.

"Well, aren't you the boy scout." She slipped them on, cursed, and gunned the engine.

We lurched forward at breakneck speed. Ralph slid down the tank, but sank his talons into my knee to keep from tumbling off. The cart creaked ominously under the strain of acceleration. I held tight and looked back to find the twins braced against the side rails as the cart bucked and swayed. Dawa's mouth dropped open and he pointed at something over my right shoulder.

A white and gray boulder the size of my little SUV lay off to the side of our path. Though encrusted with dirt and looking oddly damp, I couldn't understand what all the fuss was about until our passing disturbed a swarm of nymphs. They rose in a thick cloud, revealing ragged strips of dirty flesh hanging from the thousand-pound chunk of meat.

"Little faster?" I urged in a manly squeak.

Jim Stein

24. Mirage

WHEN WE were well past the rotting chunk of meat, Quinn
slowed to a less jarring pace and my kidneys sent up a little
cheer.

"Our monster-at-large must not have liked the taste of infected
meat." Quinn broke the tense silence.

"Wonderful, so it's still hungry." We'd fought things like that in the
past with what might generously be called limited success. "At least we
haven't run across any other nasties since leaving the village."

"They're too busy converging on the vortex. Looked like a damned
army when we first came across."

"Too much like one. I hope Piper and the gang are okay."

Silence again settled over us. We'd abandoned the others back at
Pete's farm, which meant they would take the brunt of those invading
forces. Among them, only Anna had magic. I'd seen that girl throw
back a mob of attackers, but self-doubt and emotions still undermined
her control.

Foothills loomed in the gloom ahead as rocky landscape gave way
to sparse trees that must have once been truly breathtaking. A braid of
delicate vines formed each trunk, with a spider's web of branches
fanning out at tight tiers that grew wider toward the top to form an
artistic vee. But as we'd seen in the forest, those wispy branches twisted

like arthritic hands and the purple-green leaves curled as though being sucked dry. Spikey shrubs replaced the tall grass and looked nasty enough to slice through clothes.

Sunshine still slanted from ahead, painting long caricatures across the ground behind us. The shadows trailed us, frolicking and overlapping as each vehicle dodged around vegetation. Movement drew my attention to a clump of trees about a half mile off on the left. Though a thin stand, their shadows merged under the setting sun, condensing and coalescing into a solid block.

Impossibly, the block stretched to three times the height and I found myself looking out at an elevated train track running atop a strip of stores with a majestic stone wall anchoring the far end. Incredibly, a couple emerged from the door of a red-brick shop, strolled across the sidewalk, and climbed the iron steps leading up to the train platform.

"Look at that!" I spun Quinn by her shoulders so she faced the scene.

It was definitely a mistake as far as driver safety was concerned. Our ATV slewed in the opposite direction as the handlebars pulled with her, the right-hand tires lifting off the ground. We both flew off and hit hard. The fall had barely registered when a barbed tail slapped me in the face, followed by an imp butt as Ralph slammed into me.

"What the hell—" Quinn didn't have time to finish her question because we had to scramble out of the way.

The Ant's cart barreled on, pushing the overturned ATV with the sound of grinding stone and metal. A fender ripped off, kicked up, and nearly took Larmoth's head off. The Ant leaders stood at the forward rail and rode the cart to a grinding stop, looking almost regal as the scene unfolded in slow motion. Muuyaw turned his head as they slid past, bestowing an imperious sneer that dressed me down more thoroughly than shouted obscenities.

"What the hell?" Quinn—on the other hand—had no qualms about screaming. "You could have gotten us killed."

I pointed out to where a commuter car sat loading passengers above the stores. Quinn gaped, as did the rest when they pulled up alongside our overturned vehicle. The vision shimmered, seeming less substantial than the warehouse we'd almost visited. The train itself wasn't fully in view. Yellow light poured from the long set of windows of the first silver car and about half of the second. The train pulled out, followed dutifully by the second and then a third car as each smoothly passed the platform and vanished.

"It's like a window into a movie set," Vance said.

"And it's fading." Quinn was right.

Streetlamps with heads bowed over the platform dimmed, as did the glass storefronts. The red-brick building the couple had left blurred into a dull red then brown blob. The scene shimmered, leaving only the copse of twisted trees sitting at the base of a shallow rise.

"That wasn't New Philly," Pete said into the silence.

"A running train? I didn't know they still existed." Quinn absently stroked Ralph's head.

"They don't." Vance said. "The precinct keeps records. The last train dropped out of service decades ago. The dwindling workforce just couldn't keep up with track maintenance and safety. It's why the National Highway Commission was formed to keep interstates open for trucking. Plus, commuter trains stopped early as the cities collapsed."

"So we looked back in time?" I didn't know what else to think.

"It's possible," Dwain said. "The world veil has separated the third and fourth worlds for thousands of years. With the magic failing, I think any moment along that timeline could bleed through."

"So that scene was pre-virus?" I thought of the massive sea creature and whatever had taken a bite out of it. "And we could have dinosaurs stumbling out as this thing deteriorates."

"Probably not." Dwain sucked air through his teeth as he chose his words. "These things aren't my specialty—you'd have to talk to Kokopelli for a better explanation. But you saw how flat and surreal the buildings and people looked, like watching one of your moving pictures. Most moments in time will be out of sync. Things and people wouldn't be able to move between there and here because a residual barrier exists. When the time on both sides is current day there is actually a hole through the veil that can be crossed."

"We'll have to take your word for it." What else could we do?

It took three of us to flip the ATV upright. Pete cursed and sweated as he tore away the broken fairing and rear fender so they didn't gouge the tires. Miraculously, the tow bar had only been twisted and was still usable. Dusk settled over our small caravan, and we moved out with headlights blazing.

As true night fell over the declining landscape, our artificial lights brought out a bit of its lost magic. Those once enchanting trees sparkled under the beams. Glittering spores left rainbow trails as they rose from the dying leaves and blew away on the gentle breeze.

It wasn't until we stopped for the night and shut off the engines that the subtle music of the place rose. The base of the hills offered a modicum of shelter, and we parked the ATVs in a semi-circle to cover our exposed side. As we unloaded, a quiet snapping like puffed cereal settling into milk rose from all around. It grew into a background static punctuated by melodic little croaks and airy calls from tiny throats.

By day we'd seen nothing alive except the occasional cloud of nymphs. But the night sang with a chorus of invisible life. I itched to grab a light and go explore—to see what creatures played in this symphony of nature. But more pressing matters needed attention.

Dawa and Larmoth joined us as everyone dug into the bit of food the Ants allowed for our trip. The advisor leaned heavily on the Ant leader, who wasn't walking so well himself. I assumed the bouncing ride had tired them, but Muuyaw moved effortlessly, which had me looking closer.

"You're hurt." A wet patch glistened along Larmoth's right hip.

Dawa half carried Larmoth using only his left arm because his right dangled at his side. Dwain and I converged on the pair from opposite sides and helped lower the advisor to the ground where we could get a better look.

The close-fitting smock he wore and the top of his trousers were sliced open. Blood welled out through a cloth pressed against the wound, looking black under the harsh camp lights. I called up just enough Fire to inspect the injury. In my Sight, red lines of infection already shone dull and angry as they radiated from the six-inch cut in his skin.

"Crap, that flying fender must have caught him when we flipped." My chest tightened—the accident had been my fault.

"No, this tear was made by a fang or claw. See here?" Dwain's power flowed over the area as he pulled back the temporary bandage. "Smaller slices along each side and punctures."

"It was the ground dragon." Larmoth spoke between panting breaths. "I didn't want to…there wasn't time."

"He hid the wound so we wouldn't worry," Dawa said. "With all the bouncing and jostling, I hadn't noticed the boy got hurt."

I could heal with the Fire element, but Dwain had been working with these people and knew their physiology. I watched him sooth the inflamed tissue and try to purge the infection. Fire would have burned the sickness out. The sprite had a subtle touch. His power infused and neutralized the rampant infection. Even with my rudimentary medical knowledge, I could tell something was wrong.

Dwain couldn't quite penetrate the layers of material building up over the area—over each of the tendrils of sickness as they continued to spread. The pockets and sheaths blocking him grew remarkably fast, like cancerous tumors on steroids. His power calmed the growths, but didn't stop them from encasing more and more of the area under a thick layer of tissue and bone. The build-up wasn't yet visible to the naked eye, but it was easy to see where the poor Ant would end up if the process remained unchecked. Out of the corner of my eye, Dawa winced and eased his right arm into his lap.

"Let me see that." I turned to the Ant leader, leaving Dwain to do his best.

"No need."

He turned away, but not before I caught a glimpse of the gash on his arm. My heart sank. I needed help from someone with his head screwed on straight. An injury put Dawa on the fast track to incapacitated. If Dwain or I couldn't heal him, Muuyaw would surely seize power and there would be no compromise.

In spite of his protests and attempts to pull away, I opened my Sight and reached for Dawa's injured arm. If Larmoth's condition was any indication, the faster we got to work, the better. Even so, Dwain fought a losing battle against the other Ant's immune system.

"Don't be a hero," I scolded. "I'll get a second opinion from Dwain before doing anything major."

Dawa looked as if he might argue, but sagged and presented his spindly arm. My music swelled, clean and pure after days of listening to the ear worm. Fire rose on the frantic lyrics of "Savior" by Rise Against. Though it was technically a love song, the words focused on saving while there was something left to save.

The lyrics didn't always need to suit the spell, but these did, as did the frenzied chorus. If Dwain's battle beside me was any indication, helping Dawa would take all of Fire's wild capabilities.

I sculpted music and magic into the glowing implement that was my spell, carefully probed the flesh of his bicep, and found...nothing. Oh, there was a gash very similar to the advisor's, but no sign of infection or out of control autoimmune response. In fact, the wound had closed over, forming a scab with perfect pink skin waiting under the crust. If I didn't know any better, I would say the injury was a week old. Even as I watched, blood and nutrients flooded the newly formed skin helping it thicken and push toward the surface.

"What the hell?" This ran counter to all I'd seen, all Dwain had learned of this place and its people.

"I told you I needed no help. Attend to our aide." Dawa pulled away with a heavy sigh and pleading look. "Please."

Over the next thirty minutes, Dwain work his subtle spells to cajole and coax Larmoth's body into stabilizing. The sprite had me help twice, once when he'd lost control of the infection in the hip socket and again when unexpected inflammation showed up at the lymph node under the left armpit. In both instances, I released Fire on a tight leash, and it hungrily consumed the toxic materials. But it couldn't destroy the underlying cause without consuming Larmoth from the inside out.

"That's it for now," Dwain announced. "Sleep will do him and us good."

"You look like hell." I smiled to take the sting out of the observation.

"As do you, my friend. Interesting technique with your elementals, like releasing a ravenous beast then jerking it back before it finishes eating. Powerful, but keeping that under control would wear me out. And we'll have more to do tomorrow."

"How bad is he?" I kept my voice low as we headed over to reclaim our abandoned meals.

"We can ease his condition. The others live a surprisingly long time as their deformities manifest. But it's painful and the rate of progress is different for each person. His body reacted faster than most, but we slowed things down. He should be able to function for another week, maybe two."

And that was a *good* prognosis compared to most. Wrapping up head-to-toe like a mummy made sense now. Their outfits were armor against life's little scrapes and cuts, which would be deadly for the fragile race. Just thinking of it made my head ache. Or that could be backlash from handling Fire.

Destructive spells sucked heat away, but healing magic used Fire on a micro-scale. I had to watchdog my own constitution, balancing the spell so it didn't drain me. Otherwise, I could end up in worse shape than the patient.

In spite of all my precautions, my head buzzed as I slumped down and tore into a cakey brownie supposedly full of fiber and protein. The soothing sounds of nature turned from mellow symphony to a cacophony. I felt about to scream, but the weight of an old familiar attention settled on me, stilling my angst.

The source was by the four-wheelers. *There!* Golden eyes gleamed from the shadows as Max pranced into our little camp and plopped down at my feet. He arched into a shuddering stretch, pushed his warm back against my thigh, and draped his heavy head over my left ankle. My fingers found thick fur and the headache vanished. I closed my eyes, content to forget about dinner. But the camp flew into chaos.

"Hey!" Pete yelped.

I cracked an eye open in time to see Ralph catapult off Pete's stomach and land squarely on Vance's groin. The deputy sat bolt upright, then slumped back in agony as the imp barreled toward me. Max raised his head and yipped out a greeting.

I sat in the middle of a whirlwind of black fur and gray skin. Ralph pounced on Max, who thundered away a pace only to lunge back with playful nips at the imp's tail. They darted right and left, both using me as a shield in their little game of war. Flashing teeth and swiping talons came perilously close to my vital parts.

"Come on, guys!"

They ignored me, and I crossed my legs out of sheer self-preservation, especially given poor Vance still lay curled on his sleeping mat groaning.

"What is this?" Muuyaw advanced on us, caught sight of Max, and recoiled with a hiss. "You bring a *manatoh* into our midst?"

The mock fighting stopped mid pounce, and something between a growl and groan vibrated in my dog's throat.

"Look closer, brother." As usual Dawa was the voice of reason. "See how the imp protects him? I feel it too, but this is no *manatoh*."

For once our surly captor took advice. He squinted at Max. Ralph had dropped the pretext of fighting to stand between the Ant and my dog, his hand gripping a fold of furry skin halfway up a foreleg and looking for all the world like a rider standing by his noble steed—an impression further reinforced when Ralph swung up to perch on Max's shoulders.

"I thought I saw…" Muuyaw being at a loss for words made me smile. "Perhaps you are right. Just a dog, a very big dog."

"His name's Max," I said, hoping to capitalize on the bit of respect that flitted across the Ant's face, but it was gone all too quickly.

"It is unusual for imps to associate with other species." Dawa looked over to Max and Ralph. "More so for your dog to find its way here."

"They've been through a lot together." I chose to stick with the truth and ignore his second statement. "I thought we'd see more imps in your world. Ralph got cut off early in ours, and we've only seen a couple roaming bands."

"They are migratory creatures with strange habits," Dawa said. "Even so, the twin gods use many races to prepare for our crossing. I do not know all involved, but imps have not been seen recently. As with the others, they have either been called to service or are in hiding."

"So, not everyone is on board with the divine plan."

"Most will not stay in the new world—only we Ants and a chosen few." The pleading look was back in his eyes, begging me not to press for more. I ignored it.

"What happens to everyone else?"

25. Helping Hands

A NNA BLINKED back tears as sheering wind swept them up into the vortex and sent her stomach to her knees. Roaring wind and flickering lights had her spinning, the seat under her butt and Charles' rigid back the sole reminders she still rode the ATV. The swirling disorientation lasted only a moment stretched across eternity.

They rolled out onto cracked earth under dim sunlight—still desert, but lacking the mounds of sand. It did not lack occupants. Thousands of the creatures they'd fought at the farm camped in tight knots across the desiccated plains. Though camping might have been too generous of a term. Most simply stood or sat on the shattered ground. A few tents with banners snapping in the wind did squat among the masses, but these were the exception.

"Here we go," Charles whispered, which was ridiculous because it wasn't like they could sneak past with their obnoxiously loud engine.

Yet that's exactly what they did. Charles drove slowly, threading between the disparate camps. Fifty yards was about the closest they came to any of the groups. Anna bit her lip and tried not to make eye contact as the stone trolls turned to watch them pass.

Either no one cared about new arrivals or these particular brutes lacked the intelligence to puzzle out who they were. Charles was magnificent. She'd have gunned the engine when the first troll noticed them, which probably would have triggered a feeding frenzy. But her companion remained remarkably calm and collected.

The road ahead dipped over a rise before vanishing in a gully. Once they were clear, she could try to contact Ed. The slow ride was nerve-wracking, but thrilling. Helping the cause made her feel alive—in almost the same way as getting lost in the music. Between Ed's quiet competence and Melissa taking care of the farm, Anna had been itching to contribute.

The high, silvery note of a horn sounded off to their left, and her smile slipped. A lone figure wrapped in tattered rags stood outside a tent in the distance. Three more sprang from the ground, spoke with the trumpeter, and zoomed toward them.

"Damn sand demons." Charles still didn't speed up.

The three came on fast, seeming to skate across the ground. The broken clay turned into fine sand as they passed, leaving three white trails stretching from the tent. Their magic felt similar to the Earth element Ed and the others used, except the power flowed loose and fluid beneath their skating feet.

"Just say the word." Anna hunched over Charles and readied her magic. "I can throw up a gust of wind to knock them on their asses."

"Just be still and let me handle this." Charles tensed, then relaxed. "Please."

The three demons surrounded them as Charles slowed to a stop. Red eyes and the hint of a flat wide nose showed from deep within each tattered shroud. They were proportioned like lanky athletes, tall and sinewy—although that last was simply an impression since they were covered from head to toe.

Power gathered in brown leathery hands she'd mistaken for gloved. Charles remained infuriatingly quiet. He propped a foot up on the front fender, looking relaxed and confident—wholly at odds with her own racing pulse.

The demon that had spotted them and sent the runners stepped up to confront Charles. She hadn't seen this one approach. All four looked identical, but the new arrival's bearing marked it as the leader.

"You should not stray from your lands." The dusty whisper poured forth like the sands of an hourglass, marking off time with metered patience. "What shall I do with you now?"

"We aren't here to interfere." Charles met its patience with his own. "Let us be on our way, and all will be well."

Anna blinked in surprise. Subtle power flowed from Charles. Similar to Spirit energy, but weak and diffuse—so much so that she doubted the man was aware of it. Perhaps it was simple charisma or force of will. But the lead demon wasn't quite buying it.

"Fourth world visitors are not welcome." The statement was met with more quiet resolve, and the demon teetered on the balls of its feet for a long moment. "Be certain you do not meddle in our affairs."

The demon gave a dismissive wave, and the others turned to leave. With a curt nod, Charles started the engine and drove on. The lead demon watched them putter off toward the ravine, cocked its head, and then melted into the ground.

"That was awesome," Anna said when they stopped at the bottom of the wide wash.

"Just an old service trick. Acting confident is half the battle." He pointed to tire tracks that cut onto the road from their right. "Looks like they came down the gully and hopped up to the road. They have a full day's head start."

"Let me try calling Ed."

Anna dug through the saddlebag, brought out her candle, and lit it. The smoke smelled of sage as she called up Fire. These small castings were fun. The tiny flicker of magic danced to the music in her spell and sipped eagerly at the candle's flame.

Ed, we need to talk.

No response.

Ed, it's Anna. I'm coming to find you. Don't destroy the shield until you are back at the vortex, or the portal will close and you all will be trapped. Can you hear me?

Something wasn't right. It felt as if she pushed through water, which was all kinds of bad for a fire spell. She tried again and was rewarded with a headache and similar results.

"Something weird's going on." She put the candle away. "Like this place doesn't allow firespeak."

"Onward then? If it hasn't rained, they should be easy to follow."

Anna nodded and waved to the road ahead. She tried firespeaking several more times throughout the morning. Something definitely blocked the spell. The desert in New Philly had a similar effect, but this wasn't shifting sand, just baked clay giving way to twisted forest as the road dwindled to a path. Back home the problem felt more like static, less...personal.

"Strange." Charles slowed, pulling her thoughts back to the present. "Tracks end here, and there's been a skirmish."

"A fight?"

Faint impressions next to the hard-packed trail showed where the other vehicles had pulled off. A couple of bushes were smashed and burnt and the ground looked scuffed up.

"No clear prints, but lots of feet moved around in a frenzy." He hopped off to run his hand over a furrow in the dirt. "These ruts could have been from moving supplies, but marks like this usually come from a makeshift drag for transporting wounded." He followed the track for a few yards. "Yep, standard two-pole arrangement. The ATVs pulled over, then angled off the trail, heading straight for that mound."

They walked over to an eight-foot tall gray gumdrop. Of course it wasn't really a candy, but the shape reminded her of the ones Ralph horded. This was smooth stone set into a hillside. Charles swept back leaves and debris to reveal tire tracks. The wall just beyond the tread marks was less weathered than the rest of the mound. She traced the arc of the lighter-colored material with her fingers.

"Recently sealed," Charles said. "They went underground. Maybe try your fire-talk again?"

"It's just not working!" Anna was pretty sure the problem wasn't with her magic. Something or someone didn't want her communicating...but she wasn't beat yet. "Let me try a seeking spell. It's a different element entirely."

Like all Brights, Anna carried basic spell components. She withdrew a fluffy brown feather from her supplies. For her to find something with Spirit, the music needed to be smooth. Ed taught them to look for songs that resonated on a personal level.

It was funny that Ed far outstripped her in magic, but used old pre-virus music. His songs were awesome, but Anna had spent months listening to, then following, the A-Chords on tour. Their songs touched her heart.

Billy opened with jazz-piano and synthesizer edging "Crystal Vibrations" into techno. She swayed to the haunting melody, called up an image of Ed perched handsome and proud on his ATV, and released the spell.

Spirit energy soared off to her right, paralleling the base of the hill. It connected, showing her an image of Ed hunched over a shallow stream that ran red. The feather slid from her palm to lead the way.

"Think you can follow that?" Anna grinned as she tied the spell off just below her sternum where a trickle of magic would keep the seeking active.

"I can until sunset." Charles nodded, but didn't seem at all surprised as he mounted their ride.

The engine let out a strange whine just as she was about to get on, echoing through the trees along their back trail.

"Hurry up. Hop on." Charles gunned the engine impatiently.

"Can't you hear that? Someone's coming."

"And we've got enough problems already. Your feather?"

A lone dirt bike careened up the path. Turf and leaves flew up behind the black-clad rider as they slammed a foot to the ground, pivoted into a tight turn, and raced straight at them. Stinging debris slapped Anna as the bike turned sideways and skidded to a stop less than ten feet away.

"You two are hard to track down." Curly dark hair cascaded out as the rider removed her helmet. "If I didn't know better, I'd say you didn't want to be found."

"Rhonda?" Anna wouldn't have thought Manny's elegant assistant rode a bike, especially a dirt bike.

"Why are *you* here?" Charles narrowed his eyes at the woman.

"Oh, Chucky, you know me—always want to be in on the excitement. The nice farmers managed to exhume this little gem." She patted her gas tank affectionately. "Imagine my surprise when I arrived at the barn to join up and found you'd left early."

"I didn't know you wanted to come," Anna said. "There was a lull in the bombardment, and Charles thought we should get a jump on things."

"No, *you* wouldn't have known, but I have a vested interest here too." She shot the drummer a glare that slid into a smile riding on silky words. "The Company would have my head if Manfred went missing, and the paperwork would be a nightmare."

"You're welcome to ride along. They're closer than we thought, only a half-day ahead." Her spell told her that much.

"Perhaps they had…engine trouble." Rhonda stared daggers at Charles.

Ed may have been right to worry about Manny's assistant. Charles had been wonderful in handling the three-wheeler, getting them past the demons, and tracking Ed. They were operating smoothly and didn't need anything getting in the way.

"Listen, Rhonda—" Anna screwed up her courage when those withering hazel eyes turned on her. "We're happy to have help, but Charles and I make a pretty good team. Just…let us get on with it. We don't have time for feuds."

That sounded rational while making it clear Anna wouldn't put up with bickering. Koko and Pina had given her this mission, and she wasn't about to let it spiral out of control. If she had to be the grown up, so be it.

"Well, our little groupie is all grown up." Rhonda held both hands palms out and cocked her head. "No offense. Just not what I expected. I will do my utmost to not interfere if that's what you want."

"Let's just get on with it." Charles sounded none too happy.

Anna rummaged in her bag. "Give me a minute to shoot off another tracer."

26. Double Dreaming

A NNA RUBBED sleep from her eyes as they bumped along following the feather. The night had been a disaster. Rhonda and Charles sniped at each other into the wee hours of the morning, making sleeping damned near impossible. The only plus side was the background song from the invisible creatures of the prairie. She'd listened hard, trying to drown out the "adults" and counting the stars blazing overhead as they twinkled up a storm. On a clear night back home, the brighter stars might flicker with a bit of color. Here, they all glittered like Christmas lights shifting through the colors of the rainbow. The chorus of sounds and lights helped her drift off, but all too soon, the night's concert ended and the too-large sun peeked over the hills ahead.

"I should take lead," Rhonda called over when the colorful boulders allowed her to ride up alongside the trike.

Charles shook his head and gunned them forward. Being on the move severely limited the woman's ability to pick fights. Holding a grudge wasn't in Anna's nature, but she found herself adopting Ed's distrust. Piper told her to watch Charles from the whole horny-man-at-night perspective, but her wary eye was now firmly locked on the slim powerful woman on the dirt bike.

They didn't know much about Rhonda, and everyone had been surprised to see Manny's assistant show up out of the blue in the company of Kokopelli—doubly so when one of the dark legion summoned her. The Dark Court might currently be helping, but none of them could be trusted. Anna had learned that the hard way.

"Slow down or we'll be eating dirt," Charles called over his shoulder.

"Oh sorry." Anna backed off on the spell, and the feather slowed. *Damn!* She unclenched her teeth and blew the tension out with a big breath. Emotions played havoc with her spells, and the power that unintentionally leaked into the seeking had poor Charles chasing her accelerating projectile. Anna wiggled in her seat, resolved to keep her feelings in check, and focused on the beautiful lights playing across the landscape.

She held up a hand to let reflections from the crystals dance across her skin. They'd quickly discovered the danger of looking directly at the rock outcroppings and their crystalline growths. Afterimages still plagued her, and stray flashes caught her unawares every few minutes. Still, it was beautiful.

More glitters ahead made her smile and want to dance through the silent rain of colors. But unlike the other reflections, these rose from a low outcropping and extended across their path in a shimmering wall.

"Shit!" Charles turned hard, and the right rear wheel came off the ground.

The wall shifted to intercept them. As it drew close, she saw it was made up of fist-sized creatures. Their translucent wings shifted through the colors of the surrounding gemstones. Charles whipped up the shotgun he kept strapped to the front fender and fired. The shots tore holes in the swarm that quickly filled back in.

Rhonda shot past, nearly clipping the front tire. A spray of glinting metal flew from a short gun with a fat round magazine that appeared in her left hand. The flechette darts cut a wide swath. But more bodies filled the gap, knitting the trap shut. Each small face had glinting orange eyes tucked in tight above a slit nose and mouth full of needle-sharp teeth. The humanoid figures were naked, but covered by fine white fur. Thorny horns sprouted from their cheeks, and a rudder tail—

segmented like a dragonfly's—twisted and spun as they jockeyed for position.

"Hang on!" Charles leaned low over the handlebars and kicked the engine into high gear.

"Wait—" Her breath caught as the trike leapt forward.

The world became cellophane wings and angry buzzing. Anna ducked behind Charles's shoulder to protect her face. Pain sliced at her knees and shins. They were through, but not clear. Furry bodies and shimmering wings covered the sides of the trike, her legs, and the saddle bags.

"Ow, they're biting!" Anna beat the vermin on her knee into paste, and kicked her other leg out trying to dislodge three more that clung to her calf.

They slewed wildly as Charles cursed and plucked off the little devils. Rhonda almost went down, but managed to skid to a stop. Unfortunately, stopping wasn't a good idea because the swarm came at them again.

Her companions were too preoccupied with biting vermin to bring their weapons to bear, and they hadn't done much good anyway. Pain sliced at her side. One of the little bastards had crawled up under her shirt and chomped down hard. She smashed it flat against her ribs then fanned her top to get the sticky remains to drop out. Several others abandoned the hard-sided saddlebag and flitted toward her.

"Get away!"

Anna batted at the three creatures. They hissed and lunged, catching her knuckles in the face, which only made them more determined. These little monsters were voracious, tenacious, and pissing...her...off!

A hot flush plunged her into a red haze—Milwaukee all over again. A small part of her tried to stay calm, to control the wild music that rose inside. But the torrent swirled out of control, dredging up Spirit energy. Music and magic fed off each other until the pressure was too much.

Magic burst forth with her scream, blasting the attackers off the trike and throwing them back into the oncoming swarm. The whirlwind she unleashed sucked up the shimmering mass like a vacuum, swirling them into a towering column before sweeping out across the crystal maze they'd come through.

Anna sucked in ragged breaths as the spell moved off. Her actions had been preternaturally clear, yet beyond her control—as if she watched from outside her body. The world returned to normal with a wash of shame and exhaustion. She sagged, but had the presence of mind to tie off the frayed ends of the spell. Residual energy flowed back, replacing a small fraction of what she'd expended.

"That was certainly impressive." Rhonda strolled to the trike, casually plucked the last little monster off her sleeve, and twisted it like a washcloth until it went still with a sickening crunch. "Now I understand all the fawning chatter on tour."

The woman stepped entirely too close. Anna smelled her musky fragrance, like rich loam mixed with night jasmine—overwhelming. She tried to scoot back on the seat, but the scent enveloped her and the world spun down into blackness.

Gray swirled as I drifted, the feathery touch of nothing caressing my skin. Or more precisely it was the lack of something touching me, for Tokpela was the absence of all. It filled the voids between realms. I hadn't landed between worlds since those early true dreams before my sleeping self knew the way to Koko's realm. Or maybe it was before the old god had fully latched onto me. Either way, to again slip silently through the gray was a shock—and boring.

I waited for magical lands to manifest, waited for some sign I was not alone. What was the point of true dreaming by yourself? The mists up ahead thinned, resolving into...nope, just more swirls.

I puffed my cheeks and blew out a stream of breath. Curiously, it didn't affect the smoky tendrils as it would fog or true smoke. But then, Tokpela was beyond the physical world. Did that mean I wasn't really here, that my "body" was just a mental projection? I raised a hand to my face. It looked solid and felt real when I touched myself.

After an eternity of waiting, running through what to do when we found the shield, and singing, I started in on poetry. Edgar Allan Poe was a favorite. I couldn't recall much, except his poem *The Raven*, which I'd insisted on reciting in eighth grade. Those dark days leant themselves well to Poe's morbid reflections.

I plowed through nearly the entire poem. Just as the speaker damned the bird back to Night's Plutonian shore and the raven uttered its final denial, the scent of wood-smoke drew me forward.

Flickering yellow lit the stubborn mists. A muffled male voice echoed from near the source of light. Words were impossible to make out, but the speaker paused between sentences as if waiting for a response. A second voice a good octave higher spoke a few words, waited, and then spoke again. It was all indistinct sound with only the modulation and pitch changes indicating a conversation.

The flickering grew brighter. The mists blazed as if on fire as the swirling fog reflected the light trying to burn its way through.

"Hello, is someone there?" The female voice was close and familiar.

Despite having no purchase, I managed to turn as Quinn drifted toward me. She wore only a white tee-shirt that complimented her bronze skin while barely covering her hips. My pulse raced. But then I realized I only wore underpants, and my ears burned—though they didn't feel hot when I ran a nervous hand through my hair. None of it mattered because Quinn still looked about blindly.

"Over here." I caught her hand before she sailed by. It was warm, solid, and clutched at mine.

"Ed? What the hell?" At my touch, her eyes came into focus.

"Can you hear them?"

Quinn was no slouch. Her look of confusion shifted to a disgusted scowl almost immediately.

"Yeah, but it's just mumbles." She snorted and raised an eyebrow. "Why are you in my dream, and where are your pants, sport?"

"Back at you." I was glad she didn't let go, but when she floated close and her bare thigh brushed my leg, whatever wittiness I'd been about to spout evaporated.

Deep, sonorous vibrations ripped through the mists, and we clutched at each other out of reflex. Dread washed over me, not because of the acoustic assault forcing its way through the Tokpela, but because my barely-dressed state would reveal an embarrassing physical reaction as Quinn's soft flesh pressed close. My thundering heartbeat certainly told me there was going to be an issue, but to my surprise nothing happened. My sigh of relief was buried under an avalanche of worry. Why hadn't—

"I will not be denied!" The words boomed through the Tokpela barrier like angry timpani, but dropped back to unintelligible rumblings with the feel and tempo of blistering curses.

"That was the horned serpent," Quinn pushed away from me, leaving an aching emptiness, but she kept hold of my hand.

Light flared from what could only be Koko's little fire, revealing three blurred silhouettes. As usual for the dream world Uktena wore his dragon body, its sinuous curves and folded wings unmistakable as they crammed in next to a bent figure with feathered headdress. That had to be Koko. The small person outlined to his right would be Pina, judging by the way an arm was cocked onto each hip. I could imagine her stubborn glare as the three tried to penetrate the fog.

I took all that in for a split second before having to throw a hand up to shield against the glare. The Tokpela blazed dazzling orange-yellow, absorbing and reflecting the fire's energy—bright enough to shine through my skin so the shadow of each finger bone stood as stark outlines before my face.

A high-pitched squawk from the other side would have been Pina's and the booming report an exclamation from Uktena, but there were no more words, just soft-edged muffles as the fog closed over the scene. The shadows revealed by the fire faded away as did their muted voices, until all was again gray silence.

"I don't want to go." Quinn's hand slipped out of mine, and she drifted away.

I clawed at the mists, trying to follow, but the mechanism that allowed me to move earlier was gone. I floated as if in space, helpless and alone. Time stretched as it had at the beginning of the dream, but I couldn't think, couldn't plan. Even my breath stilled. I simply was—floating in a frozen moment.

I woke with a gasp and sucked down a lungful of morning air as if surfacing from drowning. Although there wasn't much to remember, it was the strangest true dream I'd ever had—not just because Koko and company failed to make a real appearance, but because Quinn had been there.

Only the sprites had ever joined me in Koko's lands. But then, Quinn and I never made it to his realm, only floated between worlds clinging to each other. The memory of her body pressed against mine brought the stirrings that escaped me earlier. I could feel the weight of her thigh, her hand in mine—I *still* held her hand.

Of all the nights we'd spent on the road, Quinn rarely got to snuggle close. Something always managed to get in the way. It was a surprise to find her under my blue blanket, her fingers curled around mine, squeezing in warm welcome that had my mind racing.

"Sleep well?" she asked with a wicked grin, but took pity on me when I stuttered an unintelligible reply. "I've always wondered what those dreams of yours were like. Somehow I'd thought they would be more…informative."

With one last squeeze she released my hand and sat up. I lunged for the blanket as it dropped away, then blinked. Quinn was fully dressed in jeans and a graphic-tee. I looked down to find I too wore yesterday's clothes, though my sneakers sat off to the side with her boots. I'd donned everything from street clothes to ceremonial regalia in those dreams, but had never shown up half-dressed.

"Getting an eyeful?" More than laughter glinted in her big brown eyes.

"Um, sorry." I'd been staring at various parts of Quinn's anatomy during my mental clothing inventory and needed a safer topic. "Dream-wise that was a weird one. They were stuck on the other side of the mists."

"Or we were." Quinn pulled her boots on and shrugged into her jacket. "Do you usually have to swim through that mess to get to his place?"

"The Tokpela? Not since my early dreams. It's like we got caught in the transition phase that usually only lasts a moment. Don't know why you landed there."

"Maybe because I just happened to be lying next to you?"

"What's all the whispering about?" Pete boomed in an unnecessarily loud voice from just behind us.

I could have throttled him and his leering grin. To give my friend credit, he'd stopped trying to pry into my personal life when Quinn left on tour. Pete almost certainly had felt sorry for me at the time, but I'd gotten complacent when he hadn't resumed his lecherous push for details that were embarrassingly absent. His wagging eyebrows meant he'd simply been biding his time.

"Sorry to disappoint you," I said. "Quinn landed in my dream and we're trying to figure out what it means."

"Oh, I can tell you what *that* means." Again with the eyebrows.

"What's what mean?" Dwain hopped onto the rocks that had afforded us a bit of privacy.

"Don't you need to see to Larmoth?" The blanket to my right shuddered and groaned as Max stretched and let out a massive yawn filled with the stench of death—some things never changed.

"Nah, already checked him."

For such a flighty guy, Dwain did a great impersonation of a stolid boulder with no intention of moving anytime soon. I looked from humans to sprite and sighed.

"Okay, here's what happened."

By the time Quinn and I finished telling them about our encounter, Dawa and Vance had joined the circle of listeners. Manny made himself busy checking our rides, but was within easy earshot too.

"Sounds like they were locked out," Dwain said. "I've only seen that happen during court wars, although certain realms are known to be off limits and can have nasty surprises for uninvited visitors."

"Uktena made it through for a second," Quinn said.

"The third world is sealed to lesser gods," Dawa said with such authority that even Manny leaned in to listen.

"Sealed by who?" I didn't like the way he spoke of Koko and the others, and it must have shown on my face because he backpedaled.

"Perhaps lesser is too severe, but it is certainly sealed to newer gods. Sotuknang who oversees our twin gods has so decreed. When this world was to be destroyed, the veil was constructed to keep in all except those chosen to ascend to the fourth world and to keep all others out."

"But miraculously, this world survived." Manny stepped into the circle. "And since you set the vortex in motion, there's a gaping hole in those defenses. So why couldn't Ed's dear old dad get through to deliver a simple dream?"

"The Ants were there at what was to be the end. We helped the chosen people ascend and were ready to accept our fate." Dawa fell quiet with head bowed, then shook himself. "That is a story for another time. The vortex cannot counter Sotuknang's strictures on other deities. The twins may not leave and those without may not enter. Only emissaries may penetrate the veil, for they have not the power to trigger the protections."

Dawa fell silent, studying each of us in turn until his eyes settled on Max who chose that moment to let out a nice wet burp. I grimaced, but the Ant continued to study my dog with way too much interest. At least Dawa had been okay with Max showing up—unlike his brother.

"So where's Muuyaw this morning?" I saw Larmoth stretched out under a gnarled shrub, but there was no sign of the other leader in our small clearing.

"He has left to attend to some business of his god." Dawa didn't look terribly happy.

What business could the guy have a day's ride from their village? Especially when none of us had known where the staff would lead. When I'd taken a final bearing last night, the increased pull and blazing blue carvings told me we didn't have far left to travel. But we'd be climbing a lot of hills, starting with the ridge sheltering our camp.

"We can't wait long." Hell, even discussion of our dream ate into time we might not have.

"I can have Large Mouth up and moving in a half hour." Dwain spoke so casually that it took a moment for his words to register.

"The man's sick. Have a little respect!" Vance never got upset, but name calling was apparently a hot button.

"It's okay," Dwain waved away the deputy's outrage. "He likes the nickname on account of his outspoken nature as a kid. I don't think Ants use puns, so it really tickled him. We had a good laugh yesterday—and that's good for healing."

"Well, maybe the rest of us could just use his real name." My offered compromise mollified Vance, and Dwain certainly didn't care.

Good to his word, our sprite had the advisor ready by the time we'd eaten and stowed our gear. Though there was still no sign of his brother, Dawa recommended we continue and seemed confident Muuyaw would somehow catch up.

I was glad to see Max trotting alongside as Quinn and I led the procession. His disappearance after our escape had been like losing my best friend all over again, but the big doofus settled back in with our motley crew.

Dwain rode with his patient at the back of the cart. I didn't sense any magic. The two simply sat along the back bench and talked as we climbed hill after hill. The Ant laughed with a deep chuffing at odds with his wiry frame. Apparently, our friendly sprite was quite the comedian.

Dawa ignored the pair and stood with a firm grip on the forward rail. His own wound had fully healed, and he continued to pay way too much attention to Max as my dog bounded up the slope ahead. I worried he'd pieced together Max's role in disabling the guards. But maybe he thought my dog had something to do with his miraculous recovery—a thing the Ant leader seemed deeply ashamed of. That would explain why he treated Max like the second coming or something. Which wasn't too off the mark since I'd buried the big doofus once.

A simpler reason for Dawa's fascination could be he'd never seen a dog. Or maybe some residual power from the spell Pina used to bring him back still showed. That might have been what set his brother off too. I'd have to ask Dawa what the term *manatoh* meant.

"That's more like it," Quinn murmured in a voice that fuzzed my thoughts into a pleasant jumble.

I'd grabbed her tight around the waist when we cut across a steep hill. If I closed my eyes, I could imagine us floating in Tokpela, except my teeth rattled and our helmets cracked together with every bump. She pressed even closer than she had last night. Our layers of protective clothing didn't do much to diminish the enjoyable heat building between her back and my chest.

Unfortunately, the rear wheels picked that moment to lose traction and skid sideways. Quinn turned uphill, taking an even steeper path, but it kept the cart from rolling over. I fumbled for the staff. The fierce glow and pulsing told me we were close. Narrow pointed peaks showed above the rock-strewn ridgeline fifty yards ahead. The tires slipped and spat loose stone back at a cursing Dawa.

"Better slow up," I told her. "We're going to have problems with the cart."

"Can't, we'll never get going again." There was a note of devilish mirth in her voice that had me clutching her tight—and not for a fun reason.

"Holy fu—"

The front wheels leapt off the ground, putting us at a good thirty degree angle. I was certain we'd flip over backward, but the weight of our tow actually helped. Gravel and dirt spit out behind us as the four-wheeler revved and surged up the slope.

Other engines screamed from each side. Manny and Vance whooped and raced to the top. Pete looked like I felt as he held on for dear life. The wild ride ended abruptly as the front end slammed down onto hard stone. The cart spilled over the lip, and its momentum pushed us out into a wide crescent-shaped expanse carved from the side of the mountain towering before us.

My eyes swept up the gray cliff, up to towering peaks too narrow and uniform to be natural—closely packed spires rising above us, as if we were church mice perched on an old pipe organ. The towers on our far left were missing, replaced by a narrow waterfall that plunged down the sheer rock face into a crevasse.

"Are those doors?" Quinn whistled.

Rectangular openings dotted each tower at regular intervals. Spiral steps carved into the exterior connected many of the entrances, while others opened onto thin air or balconies with no railings. The massive place had the feel of Old Philadelphia, a deserted ruin.

"This place is old." I looked to the Ants.

The tall slender mass of dirt and grime standing at the front of the cart turned to face me. White-rimmed eyes glared from within a face brown with caked dust.

"It is one of the abandoned places from before the purge." The white rag Dawa pulled from his pouch turned muddy brown as he wiped the mess away.

"More like a city," Pete said as he walked over. "What's your stick say to do now?"

I slipped the staff from my belt. The pull and glow was strongest ahead, to the left, and…down? I swept the device around several times, but always with the same result. An archway stood at the base of the cliff city, but it outlined a rock wall instead of a door.

"Looks like there's going to be a basement or something under that arch."

"No time like the present." Pete moved to get on his ride when a whistling hum drew our attention skyward.

"Is that a bird?" Quinn shielded her eyes and tracked the dark object coming in from our right.

It flew high and straight, not very bird-like at all. Though distant, the object looked more like an elongated disk than an animal. It flew along the upper third of the towers and disappeared into the opening behind a balcony far above.

"You're sure about the abandoned part?" I asked Dawa.

"Strange things do occur." There was something odd about the Ant, as if he knew more than he was willing to say.

27. Writing on the Walls

W E RODE to the massive archway, trundling across the open stonework into the shadow of the cliffs like insects scurrying from the sunlight. Though more primitive, the towering city ringing the open ground rivaled those back home—mirroring the decades of neglect and decay.

Many lower balconies had crumbled or broken off, and spiral stairs ended abruptly between floors. All the glass and doors—if there had ever been any—were missing. Four more objects flew in and settled into entrances just fifty feet overhead. The flat, bold-colored boards ranged from nearly round to an elongated teardrop and definitely were not birds.

"That's impressive," Pete said as we stopped and dismounted.

The archway towered three stories high and was constructed of rough-hewn blocks that managed to fit tightly together. The keystone hanging high above was a smooth-sided exception with a round divot in its face where a crest or other decoration was missing. The wall it inscribed had a vertical seam running down the middle.

"Definitely a door," I said.

"No handles, no keyhole," Quinn said.

We spent way too much time prying at the door, looking for hidden levers, and even scouring the smooth tan stonework for secret entrances.

"I've got it!" Pete pointed off to the left and spoke with his finger jumping, twirling, and looping to follow the complicated route he'd worked out. "Take those stairs, spiral up to where they break off, jump to that ledge, shimmy across the top of the arch, pick up that next staircase, and take it up to that window."

"Just following those directions winded me," Quinn said. "Who the hell is in that good of shape? You'd need a bloody gymnast."

"I can do it, no problem." Dwain sounded more matter of fact than boastful. "But then what?"

"Well." Pete shrugged. "You work your way back down and open the door."

I eyed the massive doors and the three-foot sprite. "There might be a little leverage problem."

"Don't you have some...you know"–Pete made a few rapid explosions with his hands by throwing his fingers wide—"magic C-4 charges to blow 'em open?"

"Not my kind of spell," Dwain said.

"I could just throw him," Manny said.

"*Throw* Dwain?" Quinn looked incredulous. "What are you, twelve?"

"Seriously, like one of your footballs. I've got good aim. Hell, for that matter ant-man here could do it."

"Just stop with the name calling!" Vance's face turned beet-red.

"No one's throwing anyone." I knew Manny was strong, but I wouldn't have guessed that strong. "We'll stick with Pete's route. It's tricky, but if Dwain thinks he can handle it, that's our best shot."

It really didn't look possible. Some of those gaps had to be fifteen feet wide, and he'd be landing on crumbling stone. I'd seen Dwain take huge falls without getting hurt, but nothing so far indicated sprites could leap like lemurs.

"I can't let the sprite do this," Dawa said as Dwain sized up the route.

"He's got a name," Vance practically wailed.

"It'll be fun." Dwain's expression drooped at Dawa's stern look.

"It would be deadly. Traps will activate within if the door is not opened properly. It's an ancient line of defense. I will not risk Dwain. He still has much work to do with our injured."

"Pleeeeeaaaase let me try," Dwain begged, giving the impression he'd rather die in the attempt than slave away patching up sick Ants.

Dawa pulled a baseball-sized rock from his largest pouch and whispered to it. Power trickled into the ball. His magic was different from my elemental forces and didn't have the green edge of the sprites or the hard pulsing of Manny's power. His was a quiet, ancient energy.

"When the cities fell, our gods entrusted us with a key to the ruins. Let us hope what you seek indeed lies within. I do not use this power lightly."

Gentle warmth suffused the ball, like sunshine on a summer day, until it erupted into a blazing rainbow. The ball rose from Dawa's palm, drifted up to the keystone, and nestled into the empty recess. The keystone absorbed the energy, and a glowing line traced down the seam in the doors below. When the power reached bottom, the doors swung inward.

"I'll be damned." I was certain Muuyaw would never have allowed this.

At the Ant's nod, we walked into a round chamber under a domed roof. The room was a hundred feet across with no doors and smelled of dust and age. Max paced at the entry, unwilling to cross the line where stone floor gave way to tightly packed mosaic tile. A simple blue pattern swirled toward a black circle in the center of the room, and I found studying it too closely gave me vertigo. The soaring ceiling was painted sky-blue with the apex a good thirty feet overhead.

"Watch our rides, boy. We'll be back soon." Dogs understand way more than people give them credit for.

Six gleaming columns set around the perimeter were made of modern alloys, while the walls looked to be hewn rock. The pattern on the floor shifted as we approached the center—so not simple tile. There was no hint of magic; something like an LED display decorated the floor.

The blue swirl spiraled into the dark center, which left us standing on off-white flooring. Movement in the dark eye sent starburst lines shooting outward in a radial pattern. The design froze with twenty-one turquoise spokes radiating from the center to the outer wall.

"Which way?" Quinn asked.

The staff in my right hand burned bright no matter the direction. But when I lowered the rod to the floor, the designs took on a red hue and thrummed with eagerness.

"Straight down." I shrugged at her raised eyebrows. "Maybe there're stairs."

"Pictures!" Pete waved to the walls.

An image appeared on the wall at the end of each blue path. One path shone deeper blue than the rest.

"The starting point." Dawa waved us forward.

We must have been a funny sight, stepping up to the picture wall like tourists watching a movie—an image that was reinforced when I looked down to find Ralph quietly munched on a handful of the gooey honey treats.

The first panel showed an idyllic scene with people, Ants, and other beings scattered into the distance tending fields. Other small groups gathered around simple huts to smoke meat and mend clothes.

"Our world began with simple principles." Dawa stepped forward to explain the story behind the image. "All peoples were one with the land, followed the ways of respect, and took only what was needed. We were in balance with the world. These were hard lessons brought forth from the destruction of the second world. The people resolved not to let gluttony and greed infect the third."

We walked clockwise to the next section of wall. Here the scene showed perhaps a hundred people gathered at a simple wooden platform. Ants, humans, demons, and more formed the attentive crowd watching two men with hands raised skyward.

"Ah, this early ceremony praised the twin gods." Though unrehearsed, Dawa's narration flowed easily as he picked out aspects of the scene. "Notice how the workers bearing tribute come from all races. Cooperation led to shared prosperity as all honored the land and contributed what they could."

We continued around the perimeter, witnessing the rise of civilization on the decorative panels. Homes became grand multi-tiered structures, building materials were mined and smelted, and cities rose along the cliffs. The aerial view on one section showed the third world held many mountain regions.

On Earth, population centers and industry tended to crop up along rivers and other major arteries supporting trade and transportation. It was curious for the people of this land to isolate those centers of prosperity in hard to reach areas.

"All too soon, the need for 'more' outweighed respect for the land. Our world tipped out of balance." With a sad shake of his head, Dawa laid the pads of his right hand against a human woman who threshed grain alongside several Ants. The mountain in the distance belched smoke, and black dots—perhaps flocks of ravens—circled the upper parapets. "The people divided. Those of the way continued to tend to fields and streams, while greed spread like a cancer through the others.

"We thought the avarice would burn itself out and those others would regain balance. But it was not to be. Like snow gathers and clings to itself on a thin bough, the weight of their greed built. They collected more than any could possibly use. When nothing remained to increase their hoards, the bough broke—there was war.

"Men forged machines and weapons to take what others had. No longer did the races coexist. The Ants withdrew to our underground caves. Others retreated to their own domains to build walls and defenses. The first city fell without warning. No one understood how such a thing could happen. Soon enough the war shields were revealed."

We'd worked three-quarters of the way around the room. Rather than showing another action scene, the next panel held drawings similar to schematics. The top row of images showed hand-crafted artifacts. Tanned hide stretched between a frame of branches. Hand-painted designs or pictographs decorated the stretched material—a bird here, bovines similar in shape to the buffalo there, geometric designs, and a red hand print. All were in bright colors. Dangling feathers and ribbons trimmed most, although fur and a dried animal paw hung from a couple.

"The making of shields was a personal and sacred art. Shields for medicine and healing balanced with those of war. Not even war shields were crafted simply for destruction; both types offered spiritual protection aligned with their method of construction." He stabbed a hand at the lower half of the display where a row of uniform black shields with stark red designs stood on end like small surfboards—or soldiers. "These were produced for the sole purpose of making war and taking from others. They are aberrations of power, devoid of spiritual protection but combining magic and the so-called technology of these cities."

We moved on. Ralph and Dwain pushed to the front and stared with wide eyes as they shared a handful of chocolate candies and hung on the Ant leader's words. The battle depicted in stark, gruesome detail on the next section could have come out of our own history books. Explosions rocked the high walls of a citadel city, while projectiles and energy beams tore the defenders apart. They fought back valiantly, but couldn't match the maneuverability and firepower of the black and red shields that flew in from all directions. Some of the shields were empty teardrops, streaking in to decimate a heavily defended wall. Very human-looking people rode others. In addition to the destructive energies flowing from their war shields, the men and women riding them brandished spears and wide barreled guns that dealt death in equal measure.

It would be easy to feel sorry for the defenders. But hidden in the smoke behind the battle were row upon row of manufactured war shields burning in what must have been a surprise attack.

"They were out of control," Quinn said.

"Indeed." Dawa took us to the final series of images. "The great god Sotuknang saw how corruption and greed spread across the land. With a heavy heart he came to the Spider Woman. 'Take those still with songs in their heart to the river and seal them into hollow reeds. You will save them when the waters destroy this world.'

"He next went to the twin gods who watched over the poles and bade Pöqanghoya of the North Pole to work with his brother Palöngawhoya at the South Pole saying, 'When Spider Woman has done her work, you must again shake the world from its axis and destroy all that remain with a great flood.'

"We helped Spider Woman save those who still held balance and nature in their hearts. It was a pitifully small fraction of the population consisting mainly of the few humans who still tended fields and fished alongside my people."

Ants worked feverishly with a long line of dejected farmers. Some had bags and modest possessions tucked under their arms—a rake and shovel here, a bundle of clothes there. One little girl with a dirty blond ponytail carried a simple wood dollhouse, her doll dangling from one hand as she struggled to hold its home. But all these had to be cast aside.

The line split into four as the farmers approached the Ants. Not everyone got their own "reed." There were only four of the tall segmented stems sprouting from the ground along a river bank. If they were indeed plants, someone had been fertilizing the hell out of them because each was three feet wide. An Ant would open a seal along the front of the reed, help the next person in line step backward into the cylinder, then reseal the plant.

They had to be transport pods because successive pictures showed the Ants loading now empty reeds with the next person in line. Maybe the farmers shot up along the stems that disappeared overhead, or perhaps these were teleporters—a la *Star Trek*.

"At last, none remained who were fit to leave, and the reeds grew quiet."

"What about the Ants?" Vance asked. "Your people were farmers too. You helped the others. Surely your ancestors followed the way and deserved to live just like ours."

"Sadly, no." It was the first time Dawa gave the impression of being old. "We knew our place and returned to our tunnels."

"Not fair!" Vance was a bulldog despite the fact we were hearing ancient history. "They couldn't have been that much better than you. We can all see it, so why couldn't this bigwig god?"

Silly as it was, I found myself nodding along with the others. Something in the gesture made Dawa smile and he again seemed ageless.

"Our twin gods thought as you do. When the floods came, we'd sealed the tunnel entrances. Although my people were resigned to their fate, they had no interest in dying quickly. Ants had survived the prior worlds with such a technique, and it could do no harm to try."

We stepped up to the final two scenes. A pair of Ants in the first knelt at matching altars of alabaster stone. A moon had been carved in bas-relief on the face of one stone and a sun on the other. A sublime glow surrounded the Ants as they petitioned their gods.

"The twins saw what was good of my people and took pity on us. They ordained the first two leaders and stopped the waters short of our tunnels. Much of the third world and the greed were destroyed, but other races had been spared to keep the floods from reaching the Ants.

"Our twin gods charged my people with regaining balance. In our gratitude and relief, we promised to lead those who remained back to the way. Even after all we had witnessed, we were hopelessly naive."

All of us stepped to the final panel. The Ants again worked the fields, fished the river, and worshipped their gods. The cities stood abandoned and silent. But those other races squabbled and bickered. Trolls, sand demons, and the like huddled in clusters around the edges, demanding food from the farmers while refusing to contribute.

We'd arrived back at the bright blue path, the story complete. Everyone jumped when the pattern on the floor shifted. Even Dawa looked surprised as the path widened and split. A new walkway branched from that final scene to an alcove that somehow grew between the last panel and that original pastoral scene.

A new image materialized on the blank surface within. A swirling green tornado rose in the distance as Ant People gathered themselves. Brown fields of failed crops lined the road leading over the river and away from the Ant village where we'd been held prisoner. Dawa himself and his brother stood amidst their misshapen people, calling upon their gods.

"This is oddly recent." Dawa examined the walls as we stepped into the small room.

Unlike the other scenes, images surrounded us. Even the ceiling was decorated with clouds, a setting sun, and an early rising moon. The armies sent by the North Pole god were a constant stream through the vortex. Armies might be an exaggeration, but hundreds if not thousands of the creatures lined up to invade our world.

"What do you make of this one?" I asked with an edge of bitterness.

"With crops dying and the people unwell, the gods prepared a new land for us." He paused, unwilling to continue.

"More like stole ours," Pete said under his breath.

Dawa heard the comment and quivered with tension like an overtaut string. I thought he might fly into a rage. Instead, he clacked his jaw plates twice and regarded the scene surrounding us.

"The Ant People had lived in pain and subjugation too long. Their spirits were as broken as their bodies. The twin gods had always seen the good in this race and thought it time they too ascend to the fourth world. To do so would ease their suffering and bring healing.

"But the reeds that had saved the others were long gone, lost in the floods. My god Palöngawhoya of the south resolved to find a way through the world veil and allow his people entrance. But Sotuknang's will kept the worlds apart. It would take great magic to break through.

"So crafty Pöqanghoya of the north devised a plan. He and his brother would steal Lifebringer, Sotuknang's medicine shield. The great god had no need for it, but the power within would be enough to break through the worlds. The twins easily retrieved Lifebringer from its hiding place, for Sotuknang had all but forgotten the shield. But despite the spells they wrought upon it, the gods' magic could not turn such a tool into the destructive force needed to pierce the world veil.

"'It is over,' said the god of the north. 'Our people must stay in the third world, and we must tend it until the end of time.' But our southern god could not bear this answer, for his heart was soft and the Ants deserved to move on. He devised a way for the shield to seek magic of the Earth. Rather than trying to force through the veil, the healing power pulled at spells used in the fourth world. Every strand it found created a link between worlds and slowly began to draw them together despite the veil.

"Where the worlds crossed, a great turbulence arose, spinning the power of the shield and Earth magic into the vortex and creating a doorway. Alas, it is a doorway that is flawed, for the powers rage uncontrollably, feeding off one another, draining the shield's power, and raising havoc in all the realms. My god was heartbroken over what he had wrought. Always an agent of chaos, his brother delighted and sent the unworthy through to test the portal and prepare the lands beyond for the Ant People."

He finished and let out a huge sigh, as though relieved of a great burden.

"Well, you didn't read all that in the walls." Manny broke the stunned silence.

"No, but it is the way of things," Dawa replied.

"Well we're still no closer—" I broke off when the walls hummed and the floor lurched.

"We're dropping," Pete said.

I'd ridden the elevator in Mom's hospital and recognized the sensation. A glance back confirmed the main chamber was gone, replaced by a blank wall that slid upward as we descended. We stopped with a barely audible clank, and a low-roofed chamber replaced the domed one above.

I led our group out into the dimly lit room. The rock wall matched those above, and in the center of the room a ceremonial shield stood proudly on its stone pedestal. The staff vibrated, flared, and went dark.

"I thought it'd be bigger," Pete said.

The medicine shield measured a little over a foot across and was roughly round. Hide stretched like a drumhead across a white hoop fashioned of wood, or perhaps bone. The surface had been divided into quadrants, but rather than painted animals, the sun and moon occupied the upper sections and a mountain and lake the lower. Turquoise arrows set on wedges of color separated each quadrant and pointed to a blue-green circle in the middle.

The workmanship was beautiful, but hardly what I would consider godly. The artifact didn't glow, or speak to us, or do anything besides sit on its display.

"That's it?" Dwain popped the last of a handful of rainbow sweets into his mouth and danced forward to examine the shield. "Nothing special. I would think—yow!" His exclamation came as he raised a hand to touch the edge of the shield. "I take it all back. This thing is loaded!"

He touched the edge of the hoop again, smiled, frowned, and then smiled again. I cautiously reached my hand out and felt nothing—until my fingers brushed the surface. Dwain's reaction didn't do the overwhelming jolt of sensation justice.

Unbelievable power roiled within the confines of the artifact. I'd touched some potent magic since discovering my powers. Hell, I chilled with gods half the time, but those had been static shocks from scuffing my feet on the carpet of the supernatural as compared to grabbing the live electrical wire that was this little gem.

All beings and magic objects had a residual signature I could sense and see if I opened my Sight. The shield held its incredible energy close, sealing it away from casual observation. I never would have suspected it to be anything but an interesting piece of craftsmanship. The hole the shield left in my senses reminded me of the absence caused by Tokpela.

"We need Lifebringer to make things right." I shoved both hands in my pockets to keep from reaching for that power again.

"I suspected this was your goal." Dawa looked neither angry nor pleased. If anything, the Ant leader looked tired.

"Yet you helped us."

"I simply explained our history so that you might understand. I did not realize entrance to this chamber required understanding nor that the shield was here. What will you do with it?"

"Come on, you know your brother's plan is jacked right?" Quinn interjected. "Muuyaw and his god are so focused on getting out of here that they refuse to see it just won't work. They don't care how many people get hurt or killed. Worlds are dying, including the one you want. What good is following the chosen ones if it means destroying them, destroying us?"

"It is a question I have asked often of late."

I slipped off my jacket, wrapped it around the shield, and tucked the arrangement under my arm. Touching the thing didn't hurt, but I couldn't afford to be distracted until I knew how the Ant was going to play this. Dawa simply stepped aside, giving me access to the elevator.

"You won't try to stop us?" Quinn asked.

"He's tired of the bloodshed," I answered for the Ant leader. "This plan with the shield and vortex has strayed too far from the way."

"I am…we are no longer deserving." Dawa's voice was a quiet whisper.

"Ed, we need to talk about the shield." Dwain tugged on my shirt, but I couldn't spare time for him because Manny blocked my path.

"Why take it anywhere?" The road manager asked. "Light it up right here and be done with it."

"There might be a better way. We need to study the shield and piece together a plan."

"I distinctly recall you talking about how your god buddies said the vortex will cause total annihilation."

That was true, yet Koko had never specifically said to destroy the shield, only that it called out in pain for having been twisted from its purpose. How did you heal the healer? The secret hid in the swirling power. I'd wanted to recoil from the sheer magnitude of that energy. But the underlying pain and desire, that need to be whole again, rode beneath the surface, drawing me back to try and put things right.

"For the gods' sake, Ed." Manny's voice dropped to a harsh whisper. "They *killed* my people. We can't risk letting something this dangerous loose. I'd destroy it myself if I had my powers."

I was suddenly glad of the Ant's block on Manny, because the desperate ebony glint in his eyes said he'd do anything to crush the twin gods' plan. And I didn't think it had anything to do with saving more people—this was revenge, pure and simple. But he had no clue what we were dealing with.

"It's a moot point. I doubt we *can* destroy this thing." I unwrapped the edge of the shield and held it out. "Touch it."

He reached out, and a flash of panic had me worried he'd grab the shield and run. But Manny simply placed his hand on the exposed edge. His eyes grew wide, but I'd honestly thought there'd be a bigger reaction. After a long moment, he reluctantly pulled his hand away, and I rewrapped the shield.

"Damn it!" He went from pleading to pissed. "My fire wouldn't make a dent. Hell, it wouldn't even touch it. There's a void around the thing."

"Like Tokpela, right?"

Manny cocked his head. "Yeah, similar."

"Maybe something upstairs can help us figure this out. And we can pump Dawa for more information while he's in such a sharing mood."

For the moment we were in agreement, but it was a tenuous truce. Manny wanted swift, decisive payback. I couldn't comprehend what the man had lost, but did understand his need for justice. I shivered at the thought of what I might do if everything I loved were wiped out.

For now, we moved in the same direction—a direction that was suddenly blocked by an irate sprite with murder in his eyes. Dwain glared up at us with hands on hips and his lower lip pushed out, making me think fondly of Pina's tirades. My smile fled when he laid into us.

"If you two don't stop ignoring me, you'll only wish the shield could heal because I will whip your big dumb butts. The gods have ignored us sprites for eons, but I won't take it from a couple of overgrown..." He floundered trying to come up with a good word. "Well, I just won't take it. Got that?"

"Listen, we weren't—"

"I asked if you understood." That killer look was back in his eyes, but vanished when Manny and I both nodded. "Good, because I know what to do about the shield."

28. Reunited

"WHAT ARE you thinking?" I asked Dwain as the elevator rose.

The images on the walls changed to show the vortex from the other side. Trolls and demons camped on the surrounding plains. A shimmering river in the background would be the one skirting the Ant village and the jagged line of towers along the distant mountains the city ruins we now occupied. A lumbering shape strode along the foothills, leaving an impossibly long shadow under the setting sun. The moon had risen higher in the sky and waxed to nearly full.

"Would you stop admiring the picture for a minute?" Dwain's rebuke pulled my attention back. "The shield's power is contained behind a barrier."

"Yeah, like a layer of nothing. That's going to make it hard to manipulate."

"Nope, that's where you're wrong." Dwain's dark curls flopped as he shook his head. "The energy's in constant motion, but doesn't just churn in a circle. A thread of magic still quests out to your world. That's the line it uses to fish for Earth magic and feed the vortex."

The floor jerked as the elevator reached the main floor, and we all piled out. Depictions of third world history still ringed the room, and

Max sat obediently at the entrance, tail wagging in greeting—except he looked off to the far side of the domed chamber.

Three people studied the scene showing Ants stuffing people into transport reeds. I recognized the platinum blond hair cascading over the shoulders of the girl in the middle.

"Anna?" I tucked the shield under my arm and strode toward the trio.

"Oh for crying out loud." Dwain had every right to be frustrated, but what on earth would have brought the Bright into this world, and why in the hell were Charles and—my god, was that Rhonda?

"Ed!"

Anna ran over on tiptoes and wrapped me in a hug that had me clearing my throat. I didn't know where to put my free hand and ended up resting it on her shoulder. She trembled, and the protective instinct I'd harbored since meeting the young woman leapt forth like a snarling wolf looking for a target. Two readily presented themselves as I wrapped an arm around Anna and squared off against the adults.

"Are you two insane, bringing her through the portal? You know what she went through. If the creatures here got hold of her…" I let the implications sink in and gave them my best glare, which did little to impress either.

"Don't get your panties in a bunch," Charles said in that oh-so-superior tone he liked to use. "She got it in her head to come see you. I'm just along to help."

"Yeah right." I felt Anna stiffen, but swept my gaze from the drummer to Rhonda. "What's your story?"

"Trust me, you don't want to know." She looked over my shoulder to Manny as if hunting for support before focusing on me again. "Keep up the attitude and we're going to have a problem."

"Ed, it really was me," Anna said before I could press for better answers. "It's about the shield. You can't destroy it until you're back at the portal or you'll all be trapped." She glanced around at the others and sucked in a little gasp when she saw Dawa. "I know Koko told you it was okay, but now they think the vortex will collapse immediately."

"They're fricking gods. You'd think they could get a message through."

The thought of my all-powerful father risking Anna to deliver a message had me seething. Not to mention he'd never actually told me how to deal with the shield. I looked to Charles and Rhonda, feeling a bit sheepish as they nodded in unison, then scowled at each other.

"He did try to get through," Quinn said, reminding me of the failed true dream.

"Okay, but we aren't going to burn the shield anyway. It's too powerful to destroy." Anna's crestfallen look had me scrambling for something more. "But I appreciate the warning." *Lame!* "It hadn't occurred to me we wouldn't have time to get home. We'll have to make sure we don't mess with it too much before we're back at the portal. Any solution will have the same problem. Dwain has some ideas."

My stumbling back-assward words mollified her, and the smile that had fueled me though hard days on the road returned. At the mention of his name, Dwain straightened, puffed out his chest, and strode up with Ralph in tow.

"Sounds like you're all finally ready to hear—"

"Haahhh-roooff!"

"Maxie!" Anna exclaimed. "He's back!"

"Now, the dog?" Dwain huffed and crossed both arms over his chest.

Anna rushed to the doorway. Max must have wandered off for the three to enter without seeing him. He let out a happy growl with his front feet splayed and covered the girl with big sloppy kisses as soon as she stepped outside. You would have thought her face was smeared with peanut butter. The rest of us filtered out while the two finished their mutual lovefest.

"So what's your great idea, Dwain?" Anna sat against Max's side, stroked the long fur of his shoulders with one hand, and wiped at her eyes with the other.

Dwain glared around the group, daring one of us to interrupt. When no one did, he sat down to talk to the girl, pointedly ignoring the rest of us.

"We can leverage that flow of magic the shield needs. The gods mucked around, but couldn't change its basic nature. The magic flows strong through the shield, but now instead of taking in sickness and pain and sending out healing energy, it's sucking up those spells, ripping them through the veil and pumping the extra energy back into the vortex.

"I feel other energies being pulled in too. The shield no longer just seeks out Earth magic. It pulls at the life forces all around, like it's trying to drain everything."

"You got an awful lot of information with a brief touch." I wasn't jealous at all, even though I'd held the thing for a solid two minutes and didn't catch any of those nuances. But then again, I was no master healer. "So what can we do about it?"

"You cannot undo the works of a god," Dawa said.

"More like redo." Dwain held his right fist up to illustrate. "Here's the shield. It's sucking in all this energy from fourth world spells, the third world, you name it. Its normal function would be to push that back into something or someone that needs healing."

His left hand walked through the air a few steps, suffered some sort of massive stroke, and fell over. Dwain pumped healing energy from the shield with wiggling fingers and brought the other hand back from the brink of death so that it danced around kicking its pinky and thumb out with the sheer joy of being alive. We waited, but it just wouldn't stop dancing.

"Um, Dwain. The shield?" I prompted.

"Oh, sorry. So with a little nudging, I should be able to get the shield to send power away from the vortex and back into the land." The miraculously cured hand spread out to encompass the landscape around us, then pointed at Dawa. "Maybe even into your people."

"It can't be that simple." Though I wished it was.

"There's an enchantment on the original mechanism to fool the shield into thinking it's still doing good. But old artifacts gain awareness. It knows something's wrong. The tricky part will be shifting the incoming power to the new source. I'll have to be neck deep in there and really don't want to become its next meal. The third world is a big place. We need a few anchor points where the shield can start drawing off negative energy to purify. If that works it ought to naturally gravitate to the new source and finish the shift on its own."

"Brother!" Muuyaw stormed across the open rock to confront Dawa.

We'd been too focused on Dwain's puppet show to noticed Muuyaw come over the rise. The Ant looked disheveled and near delirium. If he'd been climbing the hills all day trying to catch up, he was probably at the end of his strength. But fervor gave him plenty of energy and righteous indignation.

"First you release these prisoners, now you bring them to the sacred ruins? Such treachery cannot be tolerated. You and your god have always been weak."

"There is hope in this." Dawa took a step back at his brother's intensity. "A chance to bring healing back to our people, to our land. Listen to—"

"I'll listen to nothing from interlopers who would defile our ways."

"But if we can return Lifebringer to its rightful function, there is no need to leave."

"I will not stay in this wretched place!" Muuyaw whirled on Dawa who shrank back. "Eons we have been trapped here, alone and cast out. I will not allow—"

He cut off mid-sentence, and it took me a moment to realize Muuyaw stared at my side. My jacket had slipped to expose the sun and moon painted on the shield under my arm. The Ant's face turned white, then purple-red. I honestly thought he might have a heart attack and drop over dead—I should be so lucky.

"They steal the key to our salvation!" he thundered.

Max growled and rose with head low and hackles up. My dog glowed with a dark aura. I'd never noticed such a thing on an animal, and the fact it was nearly black worried me. The ground shook as Max stepped forward.

Muuyaw stepped back and raised both hands, gathering power. Fire rose within me as I worried Max would get himself killed—again. Max stalked forward with deliberate steps. The ground lurched as his paw landed, making me stumble. Max continued forward, and the ground continued to heave—but not on every step.

My dog stopped with the Ant backed to the bitter edge of the steep drop-off. Yet the shaking continued in a slow deliberate cadence. A shadow fell over Muuyaw as a massive head rose above the ridgeline. Muuyaw laughed—not the jolly, boy-am-I-happy kind of chuckle, but the drunk-with-power maniacal howl of a man on the edge of sanity.

Several more shaking footsteps brought the titan into view. Its bone-white head was an oval that swept back over broad shoulders. The first impression was of a dinosaur skull, something like a stegosaurus or triceratops, but the white plating was scales, not bone. The barrel chest bore similar protection, except these were each the size of a dinner plate and flecked with navy-blue. We'd wondered if whatever chomped on the dead sea creature had walked on two or four legs.

Five tree-trunk legs supported the monster towering over my still growling dog. But the rearmost one was thinner, studded with spines, and more of a thick tail it used to push its hind end up off the slope. Although the head was the shape of a placid herbivore, the snout ended in a blocky square full of t-rex teeth and dangled down beneath its shoulders giving the impression of a massive spider. I recalled the car-sized chunk of rotting meat we'd passed. Calling up something like this was just over-the-top stupid. I mean, all of us could curl up in the thing's mouth if we didn't mind being a little friendly. It'd be like a carnivore clown car in there.

"Max, come! Now!" I used my best command voice.

Max slunk back to my side as the creature stepped out onto the plateau, passing right over top a still laughing Muuyaw.

"That guy's got some serious issues," Pete said. "Don't suppose you can whip up a little hotfoot for this thing?"

"Sure can." I hoped it would do some good.

This would take epic music, so I reached straight for ripping metal guitars and over-modulated power. Fire swirled around "The Vengeful One" by Disturbed. A fitting spell in this dying world.

I braced myself so I wouldn't fall as the monster came on, and targeted a forefoot. The thing was simply too massive to go after much else. My only heat sources were the cooling rock and my own body warmth, so there was no way to mount a sustained attack.

My first fireball splashed between black toenails the size of tortoise shells. The scales ended below the knee, and the lower legs and feet were a dusty brown of folds and creases that flexed as the foot ponderously pulled back from the blast.

A normal-sized opponent, say like a bull elephant, would have lost its leg to the flames. Even with my energy metered out, the Fire— always alive, always hungry—rolled across the foot and charred the skin.

An airy roar like the howl of wind whipping through a canyon thundered from its gaping jaws. I hit it again on the right foot, but instead of pulling away, the leg swept forward and past.

"Pete, get everyone back inside." I looked to where Dawa helped Larmoth toward the door. "Any chance of a little help?"

"I have nothing to fight such a creature. It is only vulnerable beneath the tail."

Of course it was. Handily, I already stood underneath, though I'd been hoping to rectify that. Instead, I pushed another blast out through my aching fingers. The fire splashed against the base of the tail high above. I didn't see any vulnerable spot or flashing outline like one of our video games would handily show. But the shot certainly got attention.

Creaking like trees in a hurricane sounded all around. This time the windy roar came from directly overhead as the monster's knees bent outward and that gaping mouth descended.

"Max, go!" I dove to the left, pulling him along.

The crack of a rifle sounded, followed by another and another. The Ants hadn't seen fit to return Pete's and Vance's guns. The shots came more rapid than my friend's lever-action rifle, and with the thumping impact of a high-powered weapon.

Crack…crack…crack!

I twisted away as the stone to my right shattered against yard-long teeth. Charles strode to me, an assault rifle cradled in both hands, pumping shot after shot. Flashes and sparks along its right eye ridge showed his grouping was tight, but the rounds weren't doing anything aside from really pissing it off.

"Under the tail!" I screamed as he paused to help me to my feet.

We stumbled toward the rear end, scanning for a weak spot. My arms ached with cold. The Earth element might be better suited to take on something this large. But the shield still fed off that magic, and using a spell in such close proximity could have disastrous results.

I readied another fireball, juggling the shield under my arm as I tried to line up a shot at what looked like a massive flying saucer, but was actually the creature's butt. The absurdity of trying to fight something that could kill me if it decided to take a crap had me giggling and cursing so hard I nearly dropped my bundle.

"Give that to Anna." Charles flipped his head behind us.

The girl stood close—too close. Spirit flowed from Anna in the tightly controlled pattern we'd practiced a hundred times. The tornado she sent out wasn't the fierce spell she'd unconsciously unleashed in the past. Inertia and mass remained our enemy. The titan snarled and snapped blindly at the dust and debris buffeting its head, which gave us a short respite. But Anna needed to get to safety.

"Take Max and this!" I shoved the jacket-wrapped shield at her as the spell faded. "Keep it safe." She looked about to argue, but I grabbed her shoulders and pushed her toward the entrance. "Go!"

"I'll distract the bastard. Go for the tail." Charles grinned as if we were actually making progress.

We stumbled off in opposite directions. The tail slammed down to my left, knocking me to the ground. Chunks of rock whizzed over my head as the spiked tip withdrew and poised for another strike.

The reports from Charles's weapon trailed off as he worked toward the front of the titan. I rolled to my feet, narrowly avoiding another tail strike and launched a fireball straight up the thing's butt. *Direct hit!* The hissing whumph of my fireball was followed by a ground-shaking roar that ended in a high-pitched wheeze.

My next shot tore power from an empty well, and I dropped to my knees. The attack earned me another wet explosion overhead and a shriek from the creature, but I'd hit the wall. The stone was frigid and slick with ice. Drawing on more Fire would send me into hypothermia. The assault rifle fell silent, so Charles was down or out of ammo.

An engine's whine cut through the fog clogging my thoughts. A faded red ATV cut around the titan's front leg and shot toward me. The slippery surface had the four-wheeler sliding sideways as the wheels locked up.

"Son of a bitch!" Pete cursed, skidded to a stop, and held out his hand. "Rest later, we've got us a monster to wrangle.

"What do you have in mind, hayseed?" I grinned around blue lips and scrambled up behind my friend.

Pete shot off none too soon. The deadly tail full of spikes punched a hole in the center of the icy patch I'd created. The battering ram actually skidded sideways as it hit, making me wish I could make the whole area a skating rink. But using Fire to form ice was about as inefficient as it got. I'd be frozen solid before I laid down enough to put the monster off balance.

We wove around the craters left by tail strikes and stomping feet. The titan turned to follow as Pete gunned the throttle. Our engine made tons of noise, but the winding path took too long.

"First we get his attention." Pete laughed at whatever expression crossed my face as I realized he was letting the monster catch up.

Terror if I had to guess, because he steered for a rear foot and zoomed underneath just as it lifted. I was sure it would stomp down and make a Pete-butter and Ed-jelly sandwich out of us, but the farm boy knew what he was doing. The titan roared and tried to snap at us, but momentum was on our side and the flashing teeth never got close.

"You're baiting it?"

"Get it mad enough and it'll follow you anywhere." Pete nodded over his shoulder and cocked a thumb at the far side of the plateau.

The slope we'd ridden in on was steep, maybe twenty degrees. Enough of an incline that I'd been worried about flipping over backward. But Pete pointed to the far end, where the last set of towers had broken off completely and plunged into the deep ravine running along the cliffs to the north. The river far below meandered out to feed the finger-lake where we'd first found the titan's footprints.

He made a beeline for the cliff, but a leg swept past on the left and smashed down ahead. I risked a glance back. The gaping maw lunged from above, a cavern of teeth surrounding a purple-pink tongue the size of a school bus. I pulled hard on Pete's right arm, forcing us to angle away, but knew we weren't going to outrun those jaws.

A second engine sputtered and revved. I thought I heard gunshots, but they were just the abused engine backfiring. Vance ran his silver and blue police ATV straight at us, swung wide, and shot off a few more deliberate backfires. The commotion confused our pursuer. The lunge turned into a half-hearted snap that missed Vance, but earned the titan a mouth full of stony pavement.

The next thirty seconds was a heart-pounding game of chicken as the four-wheelers darted together and apart, keeping the creature following, but confused enough that it never focused on one rider for long. A low wall of rubble marked the edge of the plateau. Despite Pete's skillful swerving, the mounting debris forced us to slow to a dangerous pace. Of course, we couldn't go much farther anyway unless the ATV had a winged mode I wasn't aware of. It was a long way to the bottom of that ravine.

"You dog!" I punched Pete on the shoulder. "The bigger they are…"

"The harder they fall," he finished. "Classic video game strategy. If you can't beat 'em, kick 'em off the screen."

Most games gave you a knockback move that didn't deal damage, but pushed your opponent away. If you'd maneuvered the unbeatable boss to the edge of the arena, using the attack brought an abrupt end to the fight. Unfortunately we didn't have a move like that. Anna's whirlwind at full strength might do the trick, but we'd been unable to get her focused and back up to that level. Plus, she was back in the pictograph room with the shield. I might be able to dredge up enough Fire to make a slippery patch, but the chances of the monster stepping right on that were slim, not to mention I'd be at the center of the ice.

"Hang on," Pete said. "Time to put the bull in the barn."

We shot through an opening in the wall of rubble and skirted the cliff edge. My stomach lurched into my throat, and I leaned away from the sheer drop. Pete—the maniac—stood on the floorboards as we danced along the precipice. Vance did the same on the other side of the line of broken rocks. Both men whooped and hollered, keeping the titan stomping in a tight circle to focus on one and then the other. I leant my voice to their efforts. Screaming at the top of my lungs gave the panic an outlet.

The plan worked fine, except the titan proved much more nimble than Pete had bargained for. It matched the ATV dance step for step, seeming to know by sheer instinct where its feet were in relation to the edge of the cliff.

We ran out of maneuvering room, our back tire caught a chunk of stone, and we flew over the wall. The machine smacked down hard just below that monstrous face, and the engine quit. If the rock had kicked up the other tire, we would have been thrown into thin air. But our current predicament seemed little better. Pete thumbed the starter, but the engine refused to catch.

I felt the magic before it hit, a tingling red energy streaming in from the entrance to the ruins. A blast of fire hit the titan square in the face, driving it back a step amid snarling and sheets of saliva. The flames didn't have the eager hunger of my elemental spells, but the monster certainly didn't like them. Manny strode forward, his right arm held high and fire steaming from his black knife.

"Someone has their mojo back," Pete said. "I still think he needs the knife."

"If you two hens are done gossiping, you might want to get the hell out of there. I can't keep this up forever."

The power ebbed and Manny's flames dimmed. The creature shook its head and took a step forward. The hind foot pivoted, slipped toward the drop off, but stopped just short of the edge—we'd failed.

Harassing it with the ATVs had been a good ploy, but we were out of options. Pete tried to pull me into a run. I shook him off, closed my eyes, and called up one of the new songs from the album Anna gave me. My tattoo flared into searing agony as I reached for Earth magic. I ignored the warning and pushed on. There was no other way.

Bass, guitar, and drums opened in synchronized solidarity. I let the music build, tasted the words I had so recently learned. The sentiment fit our situation perfectly and goosebumps rose along my arms. The titan might be huge, he might be more powerful than anything I'd faced before, but it was just one being—same as me. I held my ground as the flames died and the thing noticed me standing close enough to smell its fishy breath.

"Let's see who's going down." I honestly didn't know.

I also didn't know the consequences of unleashing the Earth element so close to the shield. But still I blasted out my forbidden magic with the Sick Puppies' song "You're Going Down."

Of course, I didn't target the beast. The element flowed smoothly into the ground. I'd missed using this kind of spell, missed feeling my way through stone, mineral, and metal as I did now. Dense deposits ran deep under the lip of stone supporting the edge. The last twenty yards of rock cantilevered out over the chasm, supported by a vein of gneiss with a fatal flaw. I slipped energy into the fractures, widening and encouraging the fault line to take the course of action that would occur naturally in the coming years.

A high, brittle snap rang out, followed by deep grinding. The titan's tail spikes and left hind foot sank out of sight. The ponderous beast canted backward as the stone shifted. With three feet still on solid ground it humped itself forward. Another snap like the crack of a gun sounded, and the entire ledge gave way.

The titan scrabbled with its front feet like a dog trying to get out of a pool, but had no claws to dig in. As its bulk tipped over the edge, the front legs lifted off the ground, overbalanced by the mass plunging over the side.

"Ahhhhyyyii." Muuyaw's cry sounded above the thunderous avalanche.

The Ant leader clawed the air, as if trying to stay upright himself. Power surged off him in great waves. His creature's roar of outrage turned to a mewl of despair. With only one shoulder and the head still visible the monster's fall abruptly halted, its momentum frozen for an impossible instant. Muuyaw's power flared like a cracked lightbulb, the spell winked out, and the titan plunged out of sight as the Ant collapsed.

"You okay?" Pete rushed to my side.

I didn't remember falling. Worse than that, I didn't recall grounding the spell. I braced for the backlash, even as I reached for the trace of power that had sheared the stone. But there was little to grab hold of—too little. The Earth element coiled back on itself, roiling and twisting like a basket of snakes and acting more like Fire than Earth. I made one more mental lunge, but it slipped away and surged through the rock beneath us.

"Come on!" I pushed to my feet and lurched forward on uncooperative legs. "The shield's drawing my magic back inside, back toward Anna and the others."

29. A Shell

"BUT WE'RE supposed to be back in the story chamber." Anna was going to trip if Charles kept racing downhill.

"Ed told me to keep you and that shield safe." Charles tugged her around a boulder dislodged by the fight above. "We can head back when things settle down."

He needed to stop pulling her along by the hand like a child. At this rate, she was bound to drop the medicine shield Ed entrusted to her. The drummer's protectiveness had been endearing as they hurried away from the monster. But he'd continued past the city entrance, taking them onto the far slope and away from the others.

Running to safety while her friends faced the evil Ant leader and his monster twisted a knife of guilt in her stomach. At first, the logic of getting the shield as far away from Muuyaw as possible made perfect sense, but now she wasn't so sure.

"Dwain can't fix the shield if we carry it away." Anna tried to stop, but huffed out a breath when Charles jerked her back into motion. "Doesn't it make more sense to have him with us?"

"We'll take the shield back when all's clear."

"It could already be safe." They had to be a mile down the steep slope by now, and hadn't heard much since those two sharp explosions that sounded like underground dynamite. "Listen, I'm serious. We need to head back."

Anna planted her feet and jerked her hand free. She hated to be mean, but the man was being stupid overprotective. He turned with a slow, heavy sigh that told her he was going to launch into a lecture. Charles had done a lot for her. He'd gotten them past the sand demons, tracked Ed's group, and even kept Rhonda from interfering when she'd made a grab for the shield in the confusion. But they had to get the magic straightened out, and there just wasn't time to hide out and play it safe.

But when Charles faced her, it wasn't to lecture. He leveled a wand charged with magic as dark and wild as its shiny black surface.

"We could have done this the easy way," he said as he held out his other hand. "The shield, if you please."

"That's what this is all about? Why drag me along if—"

The words froze in her throat as he flicked the wand. The spell hit like a cold wind, cutting through her from head to toe. She had no time to cry out or defend herself, and now couldn't move a muscle.

"He brought you along as insurance." Rhonda stepped into view behind Charles.

He whirled and snapped the wand up. "Not another step. You know what I can do to her."

"And now with the evil threats."

Rhonda didn't look worried, but Anna certainly was. The wand's power throbbed, wanting to do terrible things. Where on Earth had Charles gotten such a thing, and what did he want with the shield? The drummer had as much to lose as any of them if the portal unleashed its full power.

"Don't get cute with me. I know you Dark Court types. You might be fast as a cheetah, but I've trained with the best. You won't make it."

"And gasp." Rhonda covered her mouth, mocking surprise. "Your masters shall release the power of the shield, and chaos will rain down upon the world to remake all into your god's image, an everlasting entropy to worship."

"The likes of you won't stop it."

"Don't worry. I don't plan to do a thing."

The woman crossed her arms and examined nails that suddenly looked way too long to be manageable. Darkness moved behind her, just below the plane of Anna's vision because even her stupid eyes refused to budge. The shadow swelled, and a large black animal trotted around the rock.

Max! She wanted to run over, bury her face in his soft fur, and find this was all a dream. But Ed's dog kept his glowing eyes glued to Charles. Max swelled and shifted again. Not just his shadow. One minute the dog stood level with Rhonda's waist, and the next he came up to her shoulders. His hackles rose with a dark radiance shining every bit as brightly as those gold eyes. He pawed the ground twice and...Anna stumbled forward as the magic winked out.

"No!" Charles jabbed the wand at her, at Rhonda, and at a now normal-sized Max, but there was no power. "Fuck this."

He drew a heavy black pistol from under his combat vest and aimed at Max. Sullen red anger at being duped smoldered in her belly. But fear and white-hot rage burned it to ash when the gun appeared.

"Not Maxie!"

Power flooded her, sweeping away rational thought in the pounding chords of "The Immigrant Song" by Led Zeppelin—just like last time. Music and power took control, forcing her aside. She watched from outside her body as both hands raised a swirling mass of air. Jagged rock shards ripped from the surrounding boulders and joined the spell.

Max and Rhonda cowered back. Charles pivoted, dropped to a knee and fired. The first shot disappeared into her tornado, feeding the rage and the spell. He unloaded the entire clip, then turned to run as she swept a hand forward.

The spell caught him from behind, jagged debris tearing his clothes to ribbons. Blood welled from a hundred cuts. This wasn't like before. This was deadly. Anna shuddered at the thought of killing with Spirit, with the power of life.

No, not again! Not if she could help it.

She clawed back to her body, forcing herself to accept what she was—a child, a dangerous child throwing a tantrum. The thought wriggled and pulled, trying to escape, but she hugged it tight.

Wild and alive, happy to be unleashed, the spell fought her. It flayed her hands with shards of power. But she wasn't an animal, and her power wasn't evil. They were one. She held tight, promising herself never again to let go, never to lose control. They would get through this together.

She soothed the frantic music, letting the stones and dirt fall from the swirling energy surrounding the drummer. She drew Spirit and air together like a fine blanket, closing the seams and drawing Charles up to stand with arms pinned at his sides—every bit the prisoner she had just been.

Anna smiled, not at the spell, but at an inner wholeness that had been missing.

"She's not downstairs." Dwain stepped off the elevator for the third time.

I suspected he just liked riding down to the shield chamber and watching the scene on the walls change. The current art showed a great swelling of the vortex and frantic preparation among the Ants and other races strewn across the plains. The sky overhead ripped open, like a crack in the very fabric of the world.

Using Earth magic had been our only hope, but we needed to find Anna and the shield to put things right. The city entrance was half blocked with rubble, so she probably sought shelter elsewhere. Charles and Rhonda had gone missing too. Not finding the drummer smashed into paste was a relief. Hopefully he'd helped Anna get clear.

"You know the area." I turned to Dawa. "Is there another way in, some place they might be hiding?"

"This is the only ground-level entrance."

Keeping their heads down made sense, but the battle was over and they should have returned. With the titan gone, Muuyaw collapsed into a mumbling, incoherent heap. He lay curled around the carved wooden tablet that Dawa said served as his prayer book.

"We'll search from the four-wheelers." I waved Vance and Pete out the door. "Keep an eye on your brother."

"He prays to a god that has abandoned him," Dawa said with a sad shake of his head. "I fear Muuyaw may never recover."

"Don't worry, Ed." Dwain said as he stepped back onto the elevator and sank out of sight. "I've got my eye on that guy."

I sighed and turned to the last person in the room. Little Ralph looked up expectantly. I ruffled his ears, but still he waited.

"Your job's most important of all. Go find Max. Can you do that?"

I took his excited jitter at my dog's name for agreement. Finding Max *was* important. I refused to lose him again. Pete waved impatiently from the ATVs. I held up one finger and turned back to the imp, but Ralph had vanished.

We saddled up and headed for the edge farthest away from the sheer drop. They couldn't have gone far. As we approached the slope, Max trotted over the rise ahead. Ralph rode on his back, looking smug.

"One problem solved," I said.

"Look again." Pete waved us to a stop.

A blond head bobbed into view. Anna climbed up onto the plateau with a self-confident look mirroring Ralph's. If it hadn't been for that expression, I'd have rushed to help because power flowed from the girl in a narrow tether. The magic ended in a complex knot of energy tied tight around someone being dragged in her wake. Charles followed along looking distinctly pissed. I thought he walked, but as the pair came fully into view, I saw his feet floated a few inches above the ground. Anna spotted us right away.

"Where's Dwain? The shield's going haywire." She hurried over, which had Charles cursing as he bounced along the ground like a hot air balloon trying to land in a hurricane.

"He's inside." I raised an eyebrow at Charles.

"Charles is an ass." Anna gave the tether a tug, cutting him off when he tried to object. "He tried to steal the shield for some extremist cult. Rhonda calls them the Children of Chaos."

There was no sign of Manny's assistant. I didn't like the idea of leaving Charles tied up in Spirit flows like a Christmas present, but we didn't have time to unravel what was going on.

Anna handed over the shield, and I felt the wrongness as I flipped open my jacket. Power vibrated across the leather surface. Earth magic, my magic, filled the device to bursting and swirled down to disappear at its center.

A void of despair and misplaced hope sucked at the power, fueling the imbalance that had built to a breaking point. A great roaring filled my head. The far horizon out beyond the prostrate Muuyaw had turned the green-blue of angry ocean water. But the tide building in ferocity as it swept across the plains wasn't water.

"Gods, is that the vortex?" Quinn asked.

I nodded. The shield vibrated with anxious need. If it was one of the flying type, I think the artifact would have zoomed off to intercept the vortex. Dwain rushed out and threw himself on Lifebringer.

"Not good!" The sprite hugged the thrumming shield to his chest, then settled it across his knees and went to work.

His magic flowed, yellow sunshine soothing the tortured artifact. With my hand on the hoop, I followed some of his ministrations. A kind of roadmap was superimposed in my Sight, showing power flowing to and from the shield, the vortex, and the lands of the third world.

The frantic vibrations calmed under the sprite's power. He reached into the tangled workings of the device and gingerly lifted one strand of power away from the vortex. It immediately went unstable, convulsing and trying to reattach to others feeding the breach between worlds.

Dwain caressed the strand with his magic. It settled into a fitful twitching, and he carefully moved it away from the vortex. An image of the Ant village appeared beneath his work as he coaxed the strand to latch onto the edge of the field nearest the river. When it did, a trickle of energy—of my twisted Earth magic—flowed away to sink into the field.

Dwain plucked off another thread and then another, placing them at points we'd visited since entering the third world. The twisted forest got several threads, as did the painted plains, the village, and even the long lake with its dead sea monster.

The process took a toll on our sprite. His face grew haggard. Quinn knelt and held him upright when he tipped sideways and nearly dropped the shield. After he repositioned a dozen strands, Dwain sliced the incoming feed of Earth magic and sagged back against Quinn to catch his breath. His attention was still in his spell-work. I felt him there, watching—as was I.

"What the—" I gasped as Earth power flowed back to me with an electric jolt.

Another string feeding the vortex slipped away on its own and slid over to join one of the village strands. A second pulled off and reattached at the painted plains. The process accelerated. More and more of the power feeds detached until only three remained to push power at a suddenly sullen-feeling vortex.

The portal was already shrinking, having grown too large to support itself without the glut of power provided by the shield. That power now flowed into the land where the strands connected and a healing wave spread across the third world.

"I left a little feeding the portal so we have a way home," Dwain said.

"You fixed the third world!" I grinned like an idiot.

"All I did was make a loop." Dwain shook his head and blew out a breath. "The shield still sucks life from this world. It's a zero-sum game right now, so nothing's going to get better until I give it a new power source. That's the tricky part. We need it to siphon off disease, pain, and as much negative stuff as possible. But I'm not certain how to do that."

Dwain dove back in and removed one of the swollen gray power drains that leeched energy from an intricate web across the land. He tried to attach the squirming thing to the village, but it refused. Dwain's exasperation grew as he tested different locations only to be left holding the reluctant power input.

"Perhaps I can help." Dawa sat cross-legged beside the sprite and laid his hands on the hoop. "I am well versed in the suffering of this land."

A gentle hand wrapped around Dwain's spell and guided him to a chamber deep in the underground section of the village. Something in that particular spot called to the shield. The tendril latched on, and a kind of dark syrupy energy oozed toward the main workings of the shield.

"It is the place my people go when their infirmity grows too great," Dawa said.

They moved another power drain to the foot of the mountains and a third onto a distant shoreline. But growing unease prickled along the back of my neck. At Max's growl, I looked up to see Muuyaw push to his feet. The wooden tablet in his hand flared with power.

"No you don't." Vance strode toward him.

Ten steps from the Ant, crimson energy flashed across the deputy's chest and threw him back to land in an unconscious heap. Pete had been about to rush in, but instead hurled a couple of fist-sized rocks. A protective shield shimmered around Muuyaw and the first projectile bounced away. The second exploded into dust.

The tablet glowed bright magenta. Power poured into Muuyaw until his eyes blazed neon-purple and the wood smoked and crumbled to dust.

"I *will* leave this world." The Ant's words reverberated, his normal voice overlaid with a deep bass.

"Brother, there is no need," Dawa said. "We can fix Lifebringer."

"You are not my equal, not my brother!" the sonorous voice boomed. "None shall deny my escape from this wretched realm."

The flick of his hand released a bolt of energy that blasted the ground in front of the shield. Dwain flew backward still clutching Lifebringer, while Dawa and I rolled aside. The sizzling energy was pure and primal, altogether different and stronger than anything I'd felt before. Sprites were hardy. Dwain dusted himself off and bent to redo the last thread.

"Muuyaw's being a total dick," I said to Dawa. "You need to buy us time."

"I fear my brother is gone. Pöqanghoya now uses him as a vessel."

"The north pole god?" Pete frowned at the new and bigger rock he'd hoisted, before dropping it. "We're fighting a god-damned…well, god?"

"Calm down. There's no reason we have to fight." I said. "Dawa here will just call up his south pole counterpart to take care of this. Right?"

"Sadly, Palöngawhoya has dwindled to a mere echo of his former self and no longer answers."

"Well, crap." I turned to Muuyaw, or at least the shell that had been the man. "Dwain's left the portal open. Just go."

"It's always so simple for you humans." He glared at me, quite a feat with all that energy pouring from his eye sockets. "Time after time you have been saved, sent away to start anew." Anger built behind his words. "You are but insects to my power, and yet I am the one forever trapped—relegated to watch these lands, isolated from the cosmos. Only mortals may pass through the portal. I will see the world veil destroyed, shredded so it may no longer contain me. I...will...be...*free!*"

The rocks at my feet surged and stone spikes shot toward my chest. I threw out a shield of Spirit as I jumped back. The jolt of collision drove the next song I'd prepared out of my head.

"Help him finish." I pushed Dawa toward the sprite. "Dwain, tell me it's safe to use Earth now."

My arms and chest stung like I'd slammed an aluminum bat against a steel pole. My spell hadn't stopped Muuyaw's attack, but it did slow the stone spikes. When the power that drove them hit, my defensive shields shattered. At Dwain's nod, I forced myself to ignore the pain and scrambled to call up Earth with the easy power of Seether's "Country Song."

Shots rang out. Brilliant white flashes erupted in a tight grouping in front of the possessed Ant. Pete had Charles' assault rifle and took full advantage of the semi-auto mode. Muuyaw turned to my friend and raised a padded hand, but hot red flames splashed across the front of his shields.

Manny poured power into the attack, to the point the stone and sand melted in a ring before the ant-god. A jet of water slammed into Muuyaw's shields from behind as Quinn forged water from the little fall into a liquid drill. He swung from one attacker to another, unable to effectively counter, and his personal shields buckled under the onslaught.

"You are nothing!"

He could say anything he wanted, it bought us time. Time I used to find a good point of attack. I unleashed my spell with the galloping refrain, a simple tune to guide my element and shake the rock below Muuyaw. I grinned as the ant's eyes flew wide and he stumbled. His god-like shields might keep things out, but he still needed solid ground under his feet.

Dust rose from the contained quake, obscuring our view as much as the flaring bullets, fire, and water. With a mighty clap, Muuyaw's shields collapsed. He cursed as the spells converged on him, giving us the impression we were making progress.

"Enough!" A wave of his hand sent water and flames in an arc around him so they slammed together and the spells canceled out. Pete yelped and dropped his gun just before it melted to slag. My quake rumbled on, but some force of will stabilized the ground under Muuyaw.

Two dark forms flashed past. Max led the charge, looking to be twice his normal size. Perhaps it was a trick of the light or simply the fact his fur stood almost straight out. He lunged fast as lightning. His teeth should have sunk into Muuyaw's hip, but they slipped off, closed on a pouch, and tore the ornament from his belt. Muuyaw's arm shot out, unleashing crimson energy that parted around Max like fog.

Not to be outdone, Rhonda followed a heartbeat behind. She too grew larger as she ran. Her nimble steps turned into a long lope, and her arms lengthened to touch down between strides. Her wispy curls flounced then cascaded over her shoulders in a thick mane as her face and ears sharpened into a predatory mask. Rather than waste time on threats or feints, she simply slammed into Muuyaw. The impact drove the Ant to the ground under snapping jaws and hands tipped with sharp black talons.

The ant's padded fingers were a poor match for those deadly claws. Gashes opened on his face and arms. Rhonda's attack was more than physical. Dark energy flared with each strike. Max darted back in, still unable to get his jaws around the ant, but tearing his clothes and belongings to shreds.

But just as my dog and Manny's assistant had grown, so now did Muuyaw. Under the slashing attack, his features grew misshapen and knobby like those of the infected Ant People. But rather than clubbed hands and feet, those useless finger pads flattened into blades. He drove butcher knife fingers deep into Rhonda's sides and lifted her off.

His legs folded backward, and he pushed to his feet, still holding Rhonda in front of him. Her feline face twisted in agony as she slashed at his arms. Max managed to grab a particularly tough cord at his waist, which kept my poor mutt in range a moment too long. The double jointed leg swept forward and punted Max hard in the side. A sharp crack and yip exploded from him, but my stupid dog struggled to his feet and limped forward on wobbly hind legs.

I called up Fire, hoping for a clear shot, but someone grabbed my arm and pulled me back.

"Dwain's in trouble." Quinn's ashen face told me having her spell smashed had hit hard.

Sprite and Ant bent low over Lifebringer. They shivered as if freezing, and Dwain sucked in great lungfuls of air as he worked. I reached out to find oily power covered the surface, making it impossible for Dwain to place the next power drain. They'd moved perhaps half of the leeching strands, but the interfering energy flicked two of those free. Several of the healthy feeds they'd hooked to the land snapped, and a dull grayness darkened where they'd been anchored.

"We're not taking in enough to sustain the work." Dawa looked scared. "The land fails."

"They need more power." Quinn pulled at my sleeve.

Dwain strained, trying to hook the strand he held to a particularly dark portion of the twisted forest, but it just wouldn't reach.

"Try for this spot here." I pointed to a patch of dead nymphs on the painted plains, not far from another drain point, but closer to the strand Dwain wrestled.

As Dwain shifted his grip, the conduit pulled in on itself and shrank. The sprite pulled and tugged valiantly, trying to stretch it. Dawa lent his power to the effort, and I found I could wrap my will around the sprite's grip and push Spirit at him. The strand refused.

Dwain panted. "Maybe if we—"

291

"Will you assholes listen to what I'm saying!" Quinn cut off further speculation, and I was glad to see Dawa and Dwain wilt under her glare too. "Dwain, the land needs more power?"

He nodded. "If I can get three more connected we'll be—"

"More power to convert into healing energy, to stabilize the shield?"

"Yeah, or else this is all going to unravel."

"There's your power source." She pointed out at where a grinning Muuyaw now held Rhonda and Manny suspended in a glowing column of violet energy matching the beams shining from his fevered eyes.

Dawa scratched his chin and nodded. "Try this."

They used the leeching strand as a kind of vacuum. Initially, it didn't want anything to do with the thick oily power coating the shield. Dwain tweaked something, and Dawa muttered encouragement. A few more adjustments too subtle for me to follow had the suction cup mouth they held drinking in the dark energy—slowly at first, but with growing enthusiasm as it developed a taste for it.

Dwain unhooked half a dozen more power feeds from where they drained goodness off the land. These readily swept across the surface of the complex spell that was Lifebringer. Soon the artifact was clear of restricting power.

Behind us, Muuyaw let out a growl, flicked a hand, and sent a new wave of suppressing energy into the shield. The hungry drains drank deeply. More of the things detached from the land to take in this new power source.

Muuyaw tried to shut down his spell, but the leeches lengthened and stretched toward the ant-god. The shield swelled as it greedily gulped down power. Health and clean energy blossomed at the discharge points across the third world mini-map.

Muuyaw's growl turned to a scream. He shrank back to his former size as pulsing waves of magenta energy flowed into the shield. The strands glowed white hot, but the shield had been forged by the gods and made strong enough to handle the powers of creation.

The northern god's essence flowed into Lifebringer to be converted into healing energy. The vortex surged, gaining its fair share from the feeds Dwain had left in place. Muuyaw collapsed as the last dregs of energy left him.

The sated power drains fell slack. Under Dawa's expert direction, Dwain quickly attached them to points across the land where negative energy could best be pulled. In just a few minutes the shield lay whole and fully restored to its original purpose—a tool to help all of the third world, not destroy it.

30. The Journey Home

"WELL, THAT was a good idea." The compliment felt pretty lame, so I rubbed Quinn's back and gave her my best geeky smile.

"Dwain needed power." She shrugged and jerked a thumb at Muuyaw's body. "Might as well go for high-test."

Her sideways look and raised eyebrow were a silent rebuke for not taking her advice sooner. But she softened the blow by leaning in close. Her cheek and hands on my chest sent a warm thrill through me, and I drew her in tighter. She smelled of dirt and dust, but felt uniquely Quinn. I smiled at how she rubbed against me, until I realized she was wiping the grime onto my shirt.

"Hey!" I pushed her away amidst giggles.

That's when we noticed Dawa solemnly staring across at his fallen brother. Quinn sobered and stopped slapping at my hands.

"I'm so sorry, but we had no choice," she said.

"He made the choices for us." Dawa gave a weary nod. "I lost my brother long ago, but turned a blind eye to his departure from the way of the land, from caring for our people."

Manny staggered over to the corpse, checked for a pulse, and then kicked Muuyaw hard. Or maybe he kicked a dead god. The North Pole god had destroyed worlds in his attempt to flee this land. I couldn't blame Manny for his anger, but winced when he pulled the body up by its shirt and slammed it down hard. Rhonda, again just an athletic woman in embarrassingly scant undergarments—the only clothes that hadn't torn away in her transformation—limped over to put her arm around the road manager and walk him away.

"Dwain, I know you're exhausted, but could you…" I flipped my head at the injured woman.

"Yeah, yeah." He slipped Lifebringer into Dawa's hands before standing. "I want a raise, or better yet a vacation. Knife wounds are a bitch to close."

"We love you," Quinn called after the muttering sprite.

"Knights in shining armor don't get time off." For some reason my snide comment put a spring in his step.

Something cold and wet pushed into the palm of my right hand. I cupped Max's snout, gave it a shake, and bent to examine his wounds. Or at least that's what I started to do.

"Holy crap!" I looked my dog in the eye without having to crouch.

"There is old magic in him," Dawa said.

"Either that or someone's been hitting the gym."

Even with those glowing golden eyes, he managed the somber, hopeful look I'd come to love in my dog. I'd always been a sucker for that expression, and today was no different. I grabbed the big—really big—doofus by the ears and gave them a good rubbing. He smelled of bread, tuna, and a new hint of sulfur, but was still my best friend.

I ran my hands down his sides and prodded those hind legs that had been so unstable after he got clobbered. Nothing seemed to be broken. The few scrapes and cuts spotting his sides had already stopped bleeding.

Hot little pants blew into my ear as I knelt to check Max's pads. Ralph stood close, his eyes grew wide as they swept up the mountain that was now my dog. I thought the little guy might cry at the change in his friend, but instead he let out a sort of squeak, clambered up onto my shoulder, and jumped to Max's back. He straddled Max's shoulders with a huge toothy grin and tail lashing in pleasure.

"We've created a monster." Quinn smiled at the imp's oh-so-smug bearing.

I turned to Dawa, crossed my arms, and leaned against my dog—actually leaned against him, like you'd prop yourself against a frickin' wall!

"Will you pick someone to replace Muuyaw?"

"I…don't know." He looked lost and uncertain. "Twins are ordained by the gods. I am no longer a twin. Yet there may also no longer be a god."

"You said your god had grown weak and difficult to contact. Maybe he'll return stronger now that his brother is gone."

"Perhaps." Dawa again looked to his fallen brother. "What will be will be. In the meantime, we should return Lifebringer to its rightful place."

I felt I should argue. Koko had crafted the shield before the fourth world even existed. He certainly wanted the artifact back, and we still needed to talk to Anna and piece together what drove Charles to steal it. Yet I'd seen inside Lifebringer. The shield was intricately bound to the third world. It belonged here, not in the hands of some rival faction or even Kokopelli.

After sealing Lifebringer back in its underground chamber and using Earth magic to bury Muuyaw deep in the stone of his world, we started the long trek back.

* * *

"You're positive the portal will stay open for another week?" I asked Dwain when we stopped on a break.

"Yep. I never could have rigged it to work that way before, but now that the spells are nice and stable it was a breeze. As it draws in energy, the vortex will act like a closing wound. Those last three feeds will drop off like scabs."

"That gives us time to see how things fare back home and wrangle any critters back through."

Our little caravan had stopped just shy of the Painted Plains. The dazzling area was now truly breathtaking, an earthbound Aurora borealis lighting up the landscape ahead. New life whispered below the surface of all we passed, from rocks and trees to insects and animals.

Much of what we'd heard by night now ventured out under the setting sun. Even the stream and lake with its giant carcass teamed with life eager to recycle the unfortunate creature.

Things were by no means perfect. Dawa had to face down a pack of marauding trolls wanting a target for their frustration now that they were out of a job. Luckily, the brutes still held a great deal of respect for the Ant People and moved along quietly after much posturing.

"What about Ralph?" Dwain asked.

I shrugged. The alien little creature was family. Losing him would be as bad as losing Max had been. I couldn't bear the thought of it, but ultimately it would be Ralph's choice.

We got ourselves moving in spite of a kind of pleasant lethargy that settled over the group. Anna shot me worried glances as we approached the flashing lights ahead. She'd told us about their run-in with the nashers, but looked worried about the rest of us instead of herself. Something changed during the battle with Muuyaw. Even after Rhonda had spilled the beans about Charles, Anna insisted on being the one to keep him under wraps until we could turn him over to some sort of Dark Court justice department.

Rhonda herself proved to be from the Dark Court and was sent as an insurance policy against Charles. Although the Company—a useful euphemism for the court—assigned the man, he'd turned out to be a double agent. Her superiors discovered his ties to a rogue faction worshipping chaos and entropy. The group found destruction preferable to creation—not what you would call the live-and-let-live type. They'd even given Charles spells to help stop us. Letting the vortex grow to consume the Earth and wreak havoc on the realms was in their best interests. Who knew what else the jerks might have done with Lifebringer?

So Charles floated along like a parade balloon behind the three-wheeler carrying Pete and Anna. I gave her a reassuring thumbs up. A magnificent jeweled outcropping sat just inside the painted plains; large shapes poked around crevasses in the rock.

"Those are way bigger than nymphs," Quinn said as she slowed us to a crawl.

"And they don't have wings." I squinted through the dazzling display of crystals.

The gray-green bodies crawling over the rocks had slick bare backs. And their tails were pointed instead of segmented. One pulled its head from a fissure and jammed a handful of wriggling insects into its mouth, which sat below high, pointed ears.

"Imps eating nashers," I said.

About twenty imps scurried around, poking their heads into nooks and crannies to get at the flying vermin. We stopped to watch the feeding frenzy and see what Ralph would do. He tried to ignore them, but couldn't help an occasional sideways glance. There wasn't a great deal of variation between individuals, but with things like a rounded belly here and a slightly wider set of ears there, I felt I could easily pick our Ralph out of a crowd.

"So does this mean the killer dragonfly fairies are made of chocolate and sugar?" Pete asked.

Ralph did occasionally eat "real" food, but I'd assumed his overriding passion for sweets was a racial taste. As if in response to Pete's question, marshmallows appeared in Ralph's left hand. Instead of eating one at a time like normal, he brought the entire wad up to his mouth for a messy bite while contemplating the other imps.

"Do you want—" I cleared my throat, swallowed, and tried again. "Ralph, do you want to go meet them?"

Black eyes glistened in a face crammed full of worry, hope, and marshmallows. He slid slowly off the tank and took a cautious step, as if waiting for me to call him back. God, I wanted to. But I didn't. After one more look back, he walked over to the group.

An imp on the rock spotted him. Soon all those little faces turned on our little Ralphy. Imps paused with wads of nashers halfway to their mouth. Others gazed silently with wings and legs sticking between their fangs. Then a quiet riot erupted. Imps hopped down to crowd around Ralph.

We waited a good twenty minutes. As the sun set, Ralph joined his brethren in their hunt. He only cast one glance back, a silent farewell.

"Little guy's with his family now." Quinn sucked in a sniffle and wiped her eyes.

"Ain't gonna like the cuisine." Pete's voice was gruff.

I knew how they felt, and what he meant. Although Ralph dug around in the rocks like all the rest, he always came up with fluffy white cubes. It was a good thing Quinn still drove because I wouldn't have been able to make myself start the engine.

We made it to Dawa's village an hour after sunset. The accommodations were not luxurious, but the simple beds and spring water were a damned sight better than our last visit.

Larmoth still limped awkwardly, but Dwain gave him the once over and swore the Ant's body was no longer building up its protective layers. He said the problem now was breaking through what surrounded the infection in his hip and shoulder so his jump-started immune system could finish healing.

"It's gonna be the same with most of them," Dwain said after a long evening of house-calls. "I don't think the newly injured will have problems, but a lot of therapy is needed for the deformed people to regain some mobility."

"Can you train someone up before we go?"

"Best I can do is give pointers." Dwain sank down against the wall. "But they need healing magic too, and I haven't seen any evidence of *that*. Hell, they barely grasp first-aid. That shield really messed with these people."

Later, Quinn joined me out in the square. We sat on the edge of the town well and watched the stars. I couldn't pick out any familiar constellations.

"Do you think they're even the same stars as back home?" Quinn rested her head on my shoulder.

The night air grew cool, and we huddled under the big blue blanket from our room. Cleaning up had made us both feel human again. My hand slid up Quinn's side to the curve of her breast. She leaned in close, and my pulse raced despite our silly discussion.

"Seems like they'd have to be." I nuzzled her neck and jawline, apparently unable to get enough contact. "Otherwise we're like in a whole different universe."

"After all we've been through, *that's* what you think's impossible?"

"Well, you have to admit it's unlikely. That Sotuknang dude would have had to seal off a snapshot of the entire cosmos—black holes, flying saucers, and alien empires—just to isolate the people here who didn't respect the land. Then he or someone else creates it all again out in our world? Just seems like a stretch. I bet the stars are all the same, and we're just looking at the sky from a different angle here. Sort of like how you can't find your own constellations from the southern hemisphere. Doesn't matter anyway."

"Oh, why do you say that?" She raised an eyebrow.

"Because all that matters is that sparkle in your pretty eyes."

I winced at how corny that sounded out loud, but Quinn just laughed and tucked in closer. She pulled my hand up to cover her breast. I marveled at the feel, until her warm lips pressed against my ear of all places.

"That tickles." My head smacked her in the eyebrow as I squirmed away from the sensation.

"Ow, crap!" She rubbed her eye and looked down at my hand. "Really?"

"Sorry." Unwilling to give up the wonderfully soft and warm sensation, my hand managed to keep hold of her. It went about its business, ignoring the fact my face flushed red and I floundered trying to frame a better apology.

She reached up and cradled my hand, and I leaned in as a spark raced between us. But before my mouth found hers, Quinn stopped me with a finger against my lips. My chest ached as I tried to swallow my desire. I'd read the situation wrong again.

"One ground rule." Her finger made little circles on my lips as she whispered. "No apologies."

The next thing I knew, our mouths and bodies were pressed together. The lonely ache shifted to hot desire as our hands explored. What rose in me had the power of Earth, the abandon of Spirit, and the hunger of Fire—as if the best of my magic joined to forge a sensation beyond all others. There was music too, a throbbing, building, wordless melody rising toward a crescendo.

At some point we moved the blanket to the ground and took full advantage of the fact the village had shut down for the night. All sense of time fled, but when the horizon lightened, we gathered ourselves up and stumbled in a tangled heap to our ground-level room to get at least *some* sleep. I remember how she smiled at the goofy grin stretching my face, how we sat on the bed holding hands and kissing some more, but I don't recall getting any rest.

We dragged ourselves out for a farewell feast with Dawa's people. I didn't like the idea of taking food from the villagers because the crops weren't exactly spitting out wondrous bounty yet. But the meal turned out to be the same food we'd received in captivity. Toward the end, the honey cakes came out. My stomach threatened to rebel at how they were made and the poignant reminder of our missing imp.

"Don't you look like hell?" A true friend, Pete rarely exercised discretion. "Funny, Quinn has that same haunted look, like she was up all night doing something she now deeply regrets."

I punched him in the arm, just hard enough to hurt my wrist and get his attention. Stupid farmer barely flinched. We took the morning slow to give Dwain time with the villagers, but had to leave mid-afternoon to make the vortex before sundown. When the ATVs were rigged to go, Dawa rolled out on a one-person chariot behind another of his giant fleas.

"Where does he keep those things?" I asked Pete as we waited astride our rides.

"Underground, I bet. They're actually aphids. Back home, ants and aphids have a symbiotic relationship. Farmer ants even raise fungus for them."

Quinn gave my leg a squeeze and pointed to where Dwain trudged out of the commons area he used as an infirmary. I thumbed the horn and gave a friendly get-your-ass-in-gear wave. I drove with Quinn pressed close and comfortable behind me. At the sound of my horn, Dwain squared his shoulders and trotted over.

"Guest of honor seat." I pointed to the empty spot behind Pete. "You single-handedly fixed the whole vortex mess, so you get to ride out first to our adoring fans on the other side. Quinn and I will follow Anna to keep an eye on Charles. Manny and Vance are bringing up the rear."

Impatient as always, Rhonda had ridden out at first light and would meet us at the vortex. Dawa was our ace in the hole to avoid problems if any monsters lingered at the portal. Manny's assistant had no such protection, but after seeing her transform into something between a werewolf and demon-cat, maybe I should be more worried about the poor shamblers and trolls.

"I'll ride out with you"—Dwain swung up into the seat—"but I'm not leaving."

"Yeah right." Pete snorted, then sobered when Dwain didn't crack a smile.

"There's just too much to do here. I can't leave Larmoth and the others. Teaching even basic skills is going to take months, maybe years."

"Then we have to go back and change the timer on Lifebringer," Quinn said.

"Can't, and you don't want to leave the portal open. The folks here talk of more titans and worse wandering around. I need to do this."

It was a quiet procession as we worked our way to the tunnel entrance leading out to the forests. Max paced restlessly at every stop and ran ahead as soon as we started up again. The trees looked less ashen, and new buds had pushed most of the gnarled leaves off so the ground crunched.

Rolling out onto the grassy plains had my ears sighing in relief. It wasn't until we were halfway across the short thick grass that the much diminished vortex came into view on the horizon. What had been a threatening wall of green stretching across the entire horizon was now a funnel cloud with the footprint of a small cottage. Leaves and debris replaced the creatures that had been frozen in its swirling body and sky blue showed through, making the portal look distinctly bright and cheery.

In just three days, lush grass had overrun the shattered clay we'd ridden in on. No hordes camped on the open plains, and all too soon we were at the base of the vortex. Good to her word, Rhonda waited by her dirt bike.

"I swear it shrank as we rode up," Anna said.

"It's closing fast." Dwain slipped off the ATV, walked over, and stuck out his hand. "I guess this is it."

His grip was strong, but then sprites were always hardier than people expected. He worked his way around, getting hugs from the women and gruff goodbyes from the men. Max gave him a good snuffling too. I strode over with him to where Dawa stood by his mutant aphid.

"I'm glad we met." Shaking those ant pads was like grabbing a stiff oven mitt. "And thanks for the help."

"I would say the same. My people have a new chance. It's time all the races again try to work together."

"Wouldn't that be nice?" I turned away, but swung back with a sideways glance at Dwain. "Take care of…things. Okay?"

"If we're done with the sentimental crap?" Rhonda fired up her bike and crooked a finger at Anna and Charles. "Hop on, short stuff. I've got people on the other side just dying to meet this clown."

The bike shot into the portal doing twenty and dragging the bobbing drummer behind. Gods help anyone standing too close on the other side. Manny and Vance went next, but the deputy babied his much-abused silver four-wheeler, so the pair crossed at a more cautious pace. Pete shrugged, waved to Dwain, and swept his right arm forward in our video game clear-for-takeoff signal.

"Just us now," I said when Pete vanished. "You first, Max."

Max wagged his tail and gave a plaintive whine. I waved him on with more encouraging words. He finally slunk forward, sniffed at the ground in front of the tornado, then trotted back and sat down.

"Something's got him spooked." Quinn gave it a try, but the big doofus didn't budge.

"Okay, fine. We'll go first."

I kicked us into gear and rolled forward. Max stood, tail still slapping out a beat, but didn't follow. I hopped off, stomped over, and gave his snout a little shake with my fake growl. It was an old familiar move, more of a friendly talking-to than punishment. I scratched his nose and rubbed his ears, all the while telling him it was time to go and using lots of words like come, good boy, and of course his name.

Sometimes you had to play the game and do the ritual, but all it yielded was more tail slapping.

"He cannot leave." Dawa's hand fell lightly on my shoulder, but his words landed hard.

"Why?" I watched Max's eyebrows twitch left and right in worry.

"My brother was correct in one thing. He is *manatoh*."

"He's my dog." I preferred not to think of the interesting things Max had done in the past few days.

"He is a spirit animal, a powerful one." Dawa sighed and took Max's face in his hands. "The power in him sleeps, but it is still there. The veil will not allow his passage."

"Oh come on! Quinn's half witch, my dad's a god, and Rhonda is something crazy dangerous. So someone used a little magic on him. Big deal." *What exactly had Pina done to bring Max back?*

"Your friends wield great power, but your animal has been infused with ancient energy, with part of an immortal soul. I am sorry."

It wasn't a proclamation I was willing to take at face value. Quinn and I tried everything we could think of to get him through the portal. We walked him by leash to the base of the vortex, but his steps faltered and stopped ten feet away. I even wove my hiding spell around Max, but was again thwarted.

Stars pricked through the deep purple above. I sat with Max's heavy head on my knee, flat out of options.

"It's late," Quinn said softly as she laid a hand on my shoulder. "The others will be worried."

I blinked, surprised to see the sheen of moonlight reflecting off her dark curls. *How late is it?* My lower leg screamed when I pulled free, and blood rushed down to the numb stump that used to be my foot. Max perked up, looking all innocent as I stumbled around cursing.

"I'm not giving up on you!" I sighted down my finger at my dog, who gave a suffering sigh and trotted over to sit by Dwain. "Pina and Koko will help sort this out. How much time do we have, Dwain?"

The sprite jumped at his name and turned away from Dawa's unusual steed, which he'd clearly been petting.

"Day and a half, maybe two. But there's nothing I can do at this point to stop the portal from shrinking."

"Do what you need to, but make sure Max stays near." I let Quinn pull me to our ride and start the engine. "We'll be back."

I clutched Quinn tight and hid my face in her shoulder as we headed for the swirling wall, so thoroughly numb that I didn't feel us hit the vortex. The only sensation was of dropping into a dark pit as we headed home.

31. Home at Last

T HROUGH SOME trick of the portal, it was still morning back home. Clouds scuttled across a gray sky and threatened rain. Glorious weather considering all we'd had for months on end were clear skies and scorching sun.

"You took your sweet time." Pete walked across the grass with Melissa and Billy in tow.

People swarmed over the barn and farm house. Some were hammering loose boards back in place, but one crew framed out a wall to cover a giant hole where the back sunroom used to be. Vance and Manny spoke quietly with a pair of tall elf-like people by the fence that ran down the dirt drive.

"Hey, grass!" I saw sand dunes on the horizon, but with the exception of the vortex looming behind us, the farm looked perfectly normal.

"Yep, woke up the other day and...poof, no beach between the house and our tornado there." Melissa looked awfully perky. "Sand's been retreating steadily since then. It's clear to the highway and our outbuildings are back. Most of 'em slipped off their foundation, but at least they're not floating off in another dimension."

Pete offered Quinn a hand as we dismounted, then looked around. "Where's the pooch?"

"That's what held us up," I said. "Long story. Have you seen Pina?"

"She's been in and out"—he kicked a hole in the green fuzz at his feet—"and asking about Dwain. I haven't had the heart to tell her."

Melissa filled us in on everything they'd dealt with since we left. Anna hadn't done the story justice, nor mentioned her role in backing down some of the big bad uglies. The girl had gone off with Rhonda when the woman's brute squad showed up to "speak with" Charles. For all his flaws, I didn't envy the treatment he would receive.

We found Koko first. The old spirit wore his traditional clothing, complete with simple headpiece and feathers. I'd grown accustomed to seeing him in true dreams, but found the look suited him better than the fur coat and fedora he'd worn in those early days at the farmer's market. Pete had given him the rundown, but I filled in a few gaps as we sat and shared a simple lunch from Melissa's kitchen. Beans and weenies were so much better than dried veggies and questionable honey treats.

"You have done well in bringing balance to the third world," Koko said around a mouthful of buttered biscuit. "And Lifebringer?"

He leaned forward as if eager to hear. Koko looked much healthier than in our recent encounters. The deep stress lines around his eyes and mouth had smoothed back into those ageless crevices, and he no longer sagged under the weight of holding the veil together. I'd downplayed the fact that the shield had to stay put, knowing the old man wanted his creation back. Despite his posture, those sad eyes told me that he knew full well what we'd done, but just wanted to hear my take.

"Dwain made it right. Your shield's cleaning and revitalizing the land again instead of draining it. A small bit of the power will keep the portal open for another day or two."

"I suppose if the third world is to persist it must be so. And the sprite is not returning?"

"*Dwain* has to stay and help the Ant People heal." I was so tired of the gods refusing to acknowledge the lesser races, for sending me on a quest that had cost too much, for all of it. "They know nothing of medicine, and those mutilated by the shield stealing their healing energy need help to recover. And Max can't get back either. I don't know what

Pina did to him, but you can fix it, right? You can fix all of it." I cringed at the desperate hope in my voice.

"She had nothing to do with your friend's return. You can thank— or curse—Uktena for that. We were unaware that the great serpent also had a great heart. But it was not his place to do such a thing. With the Vortex shrinking, he has kept to the shadows."

"But the doorway is still open. He could bring Max back."

"The only way to do that is to revoke the power bestowed upon your dog. And that"—he gave a sad shake of his head—"is what keeps him alive."

Unwilling to accept his answer, I looked for Pina among the handful of defenders that stayed to keep an eye on the vortex. Given how the Neutral Council had forbade me to interfere, it was amazing to see a trio of gray-robed figures lending a hand. Even more striking were the black-clad men and women who took delight in poking and prodding two trolls toward the portal. The supernatural communities seemed perfectly capable of coexisting, which made me wonder if the whole light-dark battle was all that dire.

I finally found Pina in the house helping Melissa set out decorative flower boxes. She quickly dispelled my misconception.

"The courts come together in times of dire need, but the truce is always fleeting," Pina said after giving me a big hug that left dirty handprints on my jeans. "More leave each day. Only a few of us will stay to see that the vortex fully closes." She gave me an impish little smile. "I'm staying to give Dwain a big welcome home. Anna says he was quite the hero."

Ah, crap.

"Yeah, about that. He's still got some work to do."

As I gently explained, the light drained from her shining, expectant face and tears welled in those gorgeous green eyes. I felt like a bull in a china shop, trying to organize delicate teacups, but crushing them instead under my stupid, fat hooves.

Bringing up Max only made things worse. He and Pina had many sleep-overs in the hall closet she'd made into her bedroom, and she had no better idea than Koko of how to bring him home safely. I promised we would go visit them both before the vortex disappeared. Pina said she'd like that.

I left her sniffling and sipping herbal tea at the kitchen table and went to find Manny. The Dark Court never had a problem breaking the rules. I found the road manager skimming supplies off the pickup that rolled in from a trip to town.

"Sorry, slick, I don't see a way around this one." Manny took a big swig of his neon green energy drink. "Where has this stuff been all my life?"

The deranged clown on the can gazed at me with bulging eyes as Manny gulped down the last bit. I'd been addicted to the stuff most of my life, but more frantic energy was the last thing I needed.

"How about the Company?" I asked. "They've got to have more resources."

"This isn't a matter of more is better. These are fundamental laws set down by the most ancient deities. I'm sorry."

I'm sorry. I was so sick of hearing those words that I wanted to scream, to tear the can from his hand and mash it into the ground. Even worse was the pity in his eyes. *Manny, consort to dark forces, worried about how I felt. How crazy was that?* Guilt came swift on the heels of the bitter thought. The road manager had made his choice. Although not always a pleasure to work with, he'd been there when it mattered.

Manny and the band had even talked about forming their own promotion company to get everyone back on the road for album three. Now that the airways weren't jammed up by magic desert, communications flowed freely. The first tour had spurred other artists to push the envelope, and Billy didn't want the A-Chords to get left in the dust.

* * *

The following day, Pina and I gathered our courage and went back through the portal. This time we felt the wind tugging at our clothes and trying to push us back to our own side of the veil. The vortex stood only as tall as Pete's old tractor and about as wide. We pressed on through the thickening air until we popped out under sunny cobalt skies.

I raked fingers through hair that had become a bird's nest. Pina remained the never-changing picture of perfection, except for the shadow under her bloodshot eyes. Still, she put on a brave face, and we walked to where the Ants had built a new shelter. Three people stood next to the domed hut. Well, one person, Max, and a five foot tropical plant with broad leaves and commando boots.

The tree stumbled forward, heading straight for Pina.

"We brought this beauty up from troll lands." Dwain's face poked through the leaves where a pair of red and purple flowers the size of my fist hung upside-down like kissing sloths. "It's called a Royal Maiden and reminded me of you."

He hoisted the potted plant the last few steps, plopped it down next to Pina, and swept into a bow that would have been regal if not for the long serrated leaves sticking at odd angles from his curls. Pina looked up at the towering gift and rushed forward to sweep the surprised sprite into a fierce hug.

Dwain's face turned vivid crimson, but he wrapped his arms around her like he never planned to let go. Eventually they disengaged, and Pina bestowed a similar treatment on my dog, though I would say with not quite as much enthusiasm.

"Dwain has been quite a help," Dawa said when pleasantries had been exchanged. "We'd be lost without him."

"Yeah, about that…" Dwain turned to Pina, but she held up her hand.

"I know you have to stay. Let's just talk."

She slipped an arm into his and led him to the far side of the hut. I pulled a handful of dog treats from my pocket and held the peace offering out to Max. I felt horrible for treating him so roughly on the way out, but I'd been desperate to get him through the portal. One of the great things about animals is they seldom hold a grudge. Max gobbled down the treats. Then sniffed and pawed at my back pocket where the really good stuff hid.

The beef jerky came from Pete. I gave Max a big strip before bringing out the toy. Ralph still had Mr. Rabbit, but Melissa sewed eyes and a face on an old chunk of firehose to make an indestructible replacement. The foot-long toy was heftier and aerodynamic enough to throw. Dawa watched in amused silence while Max and I played.

My dog was never the best fetcher. In his version of the game he simply ran out and tagged Mr. Firehose as if to say, "I found it!" Then it was up to me to go get it for another throw. And of course farther was better. Every once in a while Max would forget the rules and actually pick the toy up, carry it back a few steps, and drop it before returning.

We collapsed into an exhausted, comfortable heap and shared the pound of jerky Pete had so generously provided. I didn't begrudge an ounce or a minute of sitting there next to Max and letting him wolf down as much as he wanted. This was a last meal of sorts—for both of us.

Though it took Pina a long time to say her goodbyes, the time to leave came all too soon. I ruffled that big, blocky head one last time, shook hands with Dwain and Dawa, and left the third world behind.

I woke late the next morning with legs aching from playing fetch. Sun streamed through the clouds overhead, cooking moisture off the siding and what was left of the porch. After months of desert climate, all of us had trouble coping with the humidity. Today promised to be oppressive.

When I saw it was nearly noon, I dressed and rushed out to the vortex. The normal entourage of watchers had dwindled to just a bored gray-robed woman and a painfully thin young man the height of an old-time basketball star. Pina and Koko stood watching what was left of the vortex.

"Won't be long now," Pina said.

The mighty vortex had shrunk to a dingy dust devil standing about waist-high. Light sparkled through the thin column showing the outline of the domed hut. I knelt and stuck my face into the swirling wind. The air was cold. Pushing into it was like pressing through a snow bank. The substance of the vortex gave way at first, but grew colder and denser the further I crawled.

"Careful," Pina warned. "It's been visibly shrinking. You don't want your head in there when it closes."

I gave her the thumbs up and started to back out. Two figures emerged from the hut on the other side. I blinked into the icy wind and strained to make out details as if looking through a grimy window. The small person was clearly Dwain. I could tell by that mop of hair. The broad form next to him had to be Max, but he had some sort of misshapen lump on his back.

Pressure from overhead pushed my face into the dirt and forced me to shimmy all the way out. The portal was an impossibly small toy tornado two-feet tall and nearly as wide. The winds slowed and dust curled out of the main body as it dissipated. As the energy dipped below what was needed to keep the sand and dirt spiraling up, the scene clarified for a moment.

Dwain paced back and forth waving. Max stood on his left, tail wagging, but with worried eyebrows darting left and right. His nervous expression calmed when a gray-green hand reached down to stroke his head. Ralph sat astride my dog's shoulders, grinning his sharp-toothed grin. He rubbed a long furry bundle against Max's cheek. My dog jerked his head left and turned back with Mr. Rabbit dangling from his mouth. I raised a hand, matching Dwain's wave, the vortex spit out one last gust, and the doorway to the third world vanished.

Epilogue

I FINISHED running the peeler over the carrot in my hand. The raw scent from the orange curls in the sink reminded me of how Max used to thump around in the kitchen while Piper and I cooked. He liked having a captive audience to admire his hunting prowess. He'd shake his toys, pounce on Mr. Rabbit, and generally show what a big badass he could be. Mr. Rabbit was wily himself and often flipped up onto the counter to escape. It's a wonder he never ended up on the menu.

"Not getting any younger here," Mom called from the kitchen table where she sliced the veggies I peeled for the stew.

"Sorry." I took the last of the carrots and potatoes over.

My kitchen happened to be north facing, so still had all the windows, which made it easier to work in than my parents' place with its open air east-facing first floor. Although the sand had retreated, it swept through town with enough force to blow out windows and doors. The township had people scouring old storage containers looking for suitable replacements now that magic no longer held back winter.

Fallout from our little catastrophe varied. Most residential neighborhoods like ours suffered damage from the avalanche of sand, but Bryn Mawr hospital and the larger structures had been whisked away before the desert flowed in to fill the void. Over the past three weeks, we'd confirmed that everything was back in its place—or at least within a few feet of its original location. Mom still hadn't said much about where she, the staff, and patients had gone during the weeks they'd been missing.

Now that the excitement was over and Mr. Conti's caravan of refugees had returned, New Philly's citizens worked on putting the pieces back together and coming to grips with the supernatural phenomena that rocked their lives. The number that simply accepted events at face value remained a pleasant surprise. Many more, like Mom, preferred to try to forget the whole affair. A few inevitable yahoos insisted we go to war and wipe out the nasties before they attacked again—ignoring the fact that they had absolutely no idea what they were talking about.

Mom chopped in machinegun bursts, dumped the carnage into her slow cooker, and grabbed the bottle of merlot—her secret ingredient for beef burgundy stew. She gave the dish a liberal pour, then surprised me by taking a big swig directly from the bottle. She swept dark hair shot with more gray than I remembered out of her face and repeated the ritual twice more.

"Drunken beef stew?" I asked with a none-too-subtle glance at the clock.

"Alcohol boils off." She used the half empty bottle to wave away my concern.

Yep, Mom didn't like talking about it, but the dark circles under her eyes said she wasn't sleeping well—nothing new for an on-call nurse, but the drinking certainly was.

"So, pretty crazy fall around here." I sensed she needed to talk because drinking at three in the afternoon certainly wasn't going to help.

She eyed me, eyed the bottle, and blew out a breath. When she closed her eyes, I figured the topic was off limits. Mom would talk about it when she was ready. I turned back to the kitchen sink to collect the peelings.

"We went…somewhere else." Mom shut down when I turned back, so I focused on cleaning up my mess, which for some reason let her continue. "The whole building, everyone in it. It got so dark outside that we thought there'd been an eclipse. But gray fog swirled all around the hospital. A few aides went outside to check and never returned."

"I've been in those mists. They're sort of a nothingness between worlds."

"Between—" She barked out a little laugh, reached for the bottle, but simply picked at the label. "That makes sense, because it felt like we moved around. The fog occasionally lifted to reveal different colored skies, or plunge us into deep winter, all kinds of madness. And, Ed,"— she swallowed hard and this time waited for me to turn and face her— "there were creatures out there."

We talked for a good twenty minutes, teasing out details of what the hospital staff had been through as they popped between realms. They'd touched down in the third world at least once, which begged the question of why everything didn't just get pushed through and stay there for the duration. Maybe some principle of physics prevented overcrowding or protected us from a Star-Trek-style anti-matter annihilation.

I'd be interested to hear if others had similar experiences. People had gone missing from all over the city. Most of Bryn Mawr's staff and patients were safe at home, but Mr. Conti and Deputy Vance still worked on a full accounting. Sherriff Connolly remained on the missing-in-action list along with about a hundred others. The list of confirmed dead grew slowly because Vance wouldn't add anyone unless an eye-witness came forward. With all the nasty insects and spiders running around, we'd yet to find an actual body.

"You and Quinn seem to be getting along quite well." Mom must have had enough supernatural talk because she didn't even use a clutch as she shifted the conversation and slammed it into high gear. "I hope you're taking precautions. Your father isn't ready for grandchildren."

"Mom! I—you—" I floundered for a response.

"Oh, *please*." Her confidence was back now that she was on the offensive, and damned if she wasn't enjoying herself. "You tested negative for the C-12 virus, and I've seen how you fawn over each other. I can't wait to get to know her better over dinner. You never bring the poor girl around."

"You're *not* going to talk that stuff with her. You can't."

She just gave me a noncommittal smile and recorked the wine. Sometimes having a nurse for a mom was a wonderful thing, other times…not so much. I like to think our little chat helped her work through the trauma. It would take more time to settle on the level of acceptance or denial that fit her best. Hell, that was true for all of us.

After dinner, I did my best to keep Mom from getting Quinn alone. I don't think she had any true intention of talking sex-ed with my girlfriend, but it didn't hurt to be cautious.

"Your dad's great and your mom's an absolute delight," Quinn said after our company left, Piper headed to bed, and we were alone on the couch. "And what a cook! We should have them over more often. She could give me lessons."

"That'd be great," I said, while my inner voice screamed and clawed toward our stack of overused excuses.

Falling asleep on the couch felt like old times, except our bodies were pressed intimately together and I didn't have to worry about the furry footstool snoring and letting out choking gas. It was a bittersweet reminder of how far we'd come together, and I resolved to do all I could to keep us moving forward.

* * *

"Ed?" Pina's high pure voice sang my name.

Her being in my house was hardly an oddity, but Pina always preferred to let me sleep, saying I looked too peaceful to wake. Since losing Max, she'd been absent more than not—to the point her little closet room had accumulated a thick layer of dust, a thing her presence magically keep at bay when in residence.

I cracked my eyes open to find I lay on a sandy floor in front of a cheery fire. Shadows danced on the white adobe walls. We were in a true dream.

"There's my sleepy head."

Pina stood over me and ruffled my hair the way I would have done to Max. Koko sat cross-legged on the other side of the flames, looking like his peaceful and enigmatic old self. Just as I vowed to practice looking that detached, the old man smiled and the merry sparkle in his eye had me flushing at my unkind thoughts.

"Everything okay?" I sat up and shooed Pina's hand away.

"Balance returns to the worlds." He shrugged as though there was more to the story.

"But?"

Undoubtedly he had some new mission or a dire warning to convey. Those were the only times he brought me into his realm.

"Don't look so wary. I simply felt we should talk. You have done well with little to work with. Brightness"—he waved Pina to his side and wrapped a fatherly arm around the beaming sprite queen— "pointed out how distracted I have been lately."

I thought he'd say more, but the pair simply stared for an uncomfortably long moment. It was good to see them bonding again, although I still worried about Pina's fawning adoration for the old god. But after losing Ralph, Max, and Dwain, I was happy she had an anchor. Time flowed differently for these spirits, but their silent regard lasted way too long.

"What is it you're trying to say?" I finally asked.

"The vortex threw many worlds out of balance, and things recover slowly. I thought you should know that the Dark Court is in turmoil and scrambling for new leaders. You and your half-brothers and half-sisters should be safe—or as safe as you can be from their attentions. Your friend Manfred is turning out to be quite the force behind the scenes in the new order. They seem more receptive to the notion that mankind's existence might be a good thing after all."

I thought of the worlds I'd seen wink out and the angst it caused Manny. But the hospital and other parts of New Philly had drifted around until they found their way home.

"Will their home world ever return, or was it actually destroyed?"

"Difficult to say, but I think the event would have been considerably messier if it had utterly destroyed those realms. Time will tell."

He smiled at the phrase and leaned on his glowing staff, which I hadn't realized was in his hand. I rummaged in the pouch at my hip. I'd lost the ability to be surprised at the change of clothing that so often accompanied entering the dream world, but was happy to see I wore a leather vest in addition to my breechcloth. My fingers closed around the wooden shaft that I knew would be there, and I held out the fragment of staff that had guided us to Lifebringer.

"Ah, very thoughtful of you." Koko took it from my hand, held it to the top of his staff, and the two fused together.

"I sort of borrowed a little bit to give Dwain." Pina said when she saw me trying to figure out why his staff still looked short. "He wanted it for an experiment with the shield, and I thought—after all he'd done for us—it would be okay."

She looked up at her mentor, lord, and quite literally god, with anxiety written across her porcelain features. Koko's smile was open and genuine. It struck me that he looked down at Pina in much the same way she looked up to him, and that their relationship might be more complex than I had always assumed.

"Our young hero is quite welcome to it," Koko said. "Unless I miss my guess, he yet has a surprise or two in store."

Again with the awkward silence. The fire cracked merrily, its heat a warm balm. I inhaled the clean scent of dusty sand and stone. It would be easy to simply zone out and "be" in the moment here. I gave it a try, but didn't last long.

"Okay, then." I clapped my hands. "Thanks for the updates and let's keep in touch."

"That we will." Koko turned away, but Pina cleared her throat and when he didn't respond elbowed the old god in the thigh. "What? Oh yes. Edan, I'm proud of you, son."

Pina smirked and gave a little nod. I don't know why the simple statement mattered so much, but it did.

~

About the author

Jim Stein's hunger for stories transporting the reader to extraordinary realms began under one meager bulb, a towel stuffed beneath his door to avoid parental censure. He huddled with Tolkien, Asimov, and all the greats and unknowns plucked from the drugstore shelves to spin tales of the imagination. After writing short stories in school, two degrees in computer science, and several decades as a Naval officer, Jim has returned to his first passion. He writes speculative fiction advocating the underdog and embracing protagonists with strong moral fiber, often overlaid with supernatural elements and a few dark twists. Jim lives in northwestern Pennsylvania with his wife, Claudia, and his muse, Marley the Great Dane.

I'd be eternally grateful if you'd share your opinion of *Strange Medicine* or any other books on my author page at Amazon https://amazon.com/author/steinjim. Just click on the book you want to review, click on reviews, and select "write a review." It need not be long, only takes a minute, and is so very helpful to new authors. – Jim

Made in the USA
Middletown, DE
08 November 2023

42197402R00198